MUSCLED SPLENDOR

Summoning her courage, the White Rose, Maggie Alston, peeked out from the wardrobe in which she hid. Nicholas strolled to the window, his brows furrowed in apparent concentration. The paisley silk robe, trimmed with black velvet, accentuated his broad shoulders. Even dressed casually, he exuded raw power and authority. He would be an adversary worthy of her.

Moonlight illuminated his face. Maggie stared in rapt fascination. Their previous encounters, fraught with tension and simmering emotions, had left no opportunity to study his bold beauty. His nose was too prominent to be called classical, but the full, finely carved lips softened the effect. A flash of heat sizzled along her nerves as she recalled the magical power of those lips.

Maggie's thoughts scattered as the silk robe slid from his shoulders and whispered to the floor. Her eyes widened. She could not look away, nor did she want to.

He was magnificent.

Firelight licked the firm muscles of his chest and taut stomach. A sprinkling of dark curly hair formed a tantalizing path downward, meeting with his male flesh. Her cheeks caught fire, but the sight was too irresistible to ignore.

A strange heaviness settled low in her stomach, while her breasts tingled with excitement. She closed her eyes against the forbidden sensations. There was no room in her life for wishful fancy. The simple act of survival consumed her days. The Rose consumed her nights.

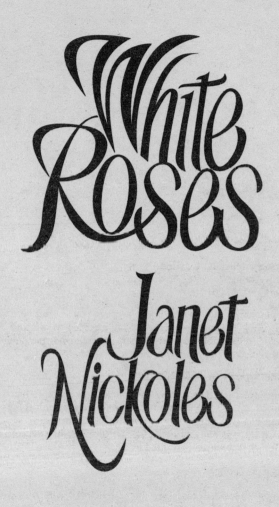

White Roses

Janet Nickoles

LEISURE BOOKS   NEW YORK CITY

For my mother

A LEISURE BOOK®

April 1998

Published by

Dorchester Publishing Co., Inc.
276 Fifth Avenue
New York, NY 10001

ISBN 0-8439-4374-2

Printed in the United States of America.

Prologue

Sussex, England, 1815

Darkness . . .

It had become an ally, a confidant, her only friend. Cloaked within its velvety folds, she could push the hellish visions from her mind, and focus on the only emotion driving her lungs to inhale, her heart to continue beating.

Hatred . . .

Pure and unfettered, it coursed through her veins, imbuing her with deadly purpose.

A shrill, keening cry from above pierced the veil of black surrounding her. The instinctual urge to glance upward had long since faded. Instead of fighting the painful, heartrending sound, she absorbed it into her soul.

The woman upstairs continued wailing her madness

until her strength apparently faded. Quiet settled over the tiny cellar once again.

Turning inward, she called forth the face of the man who had sentenced her to this purgatory.

I will break your spirit as easily as a dry twig snapped across my knee, young lady. When you are sufficiently punished for your defiant behavior, I will allow you to become my wife.

She would choose death before that day ever dawned.

He had taken her freedom, her future, and her dignity in one fell swoop. And she was only one of his many victims. The monster would pay for his crimes. In the end, when everything he owned was lost, she would reveal herself as the arbiter of justice.

A chuckle of amusement echoed through the room.

She froze in terror. The soft laughter abruptly ceased.

Fear coiled in her empty stomach. If she did not set her plan in motion soon, she would become as mad as the lost souls residing above her.

Footsteps thudded down the stairs outside. Her thoughts scattered into oblivion. She knew that the light, when it came, would be too bright.

The ominous creak of warped wood sent chills dancing across her naked flesh. Like a wolf caught in the steel jaws of a trap, she tore in vain at the iron manacles around her wrists.

A lantern swung into view, blinding her even with its muted glow. " 'Ello, missy. Time fer dinner.'' A cackle of anticipation filled the room. ''An' time fer yer bath. We don't want 'Is Lordship to think we don't take good care of you.''

His gaze swept her from head to toe as he licked his fleshy lips. ''It's a bloody shame 'e wants a virgin bride.''

Bile rose in her parched throat. *Tonight. It has to be tonight.*

"Wait!" Her voice sounded odd, deep and rusty.

"Decided to speak, did you?" He unlocked the manacles and pulled her up. "Me and the boys was beginnin' to worry."

"You—you must listen. I have jewels hidden away. They can all be yours if you let me go."

Squinting against the glaring light, she witnessed the unmistakable gleam of greed in his swollen, bloodshot eyes.

The expression vanished. "'Is Lordship would slice up me insides if I was to let you go."

Her voice dropped an octave, as she tried to purr with cunning persuasion. "What could he do if I . . . took my own life? Show him my grave, then vanish. Allow me to go free, and I will make you a wealthy man."

"I don't know. . . ." He snapped the iron around her wrists once again and backed away, his gray caterpillar brows furrowed in concentration. "I'll think on it."

The door closed and darkness returned.

The guard would eventually come back, spouting questions and more demands. Of course there were no jewels, but she would overcome that obstacle once she was free. In the end, he would relent. Her quest would begin.

"Justice."

The whispered word rolled from her tongue and disappeared into the inky stillness.

Chapter One

London, March 1817
Two years later

Silence descended by degrees.

Like a stone tossed into a placid pond, ripples of muted surprise passed through the gathering as the fourth Marquess of Rockingham, Lord Nicholas Lucien Stratford Grey, made his first appearance of the season.

He surveyed the brightly lit ballroom with cool disinterest. Each grand fete remained identical to the one before. The glittering chandeliers dripped costly beeswax at regular intervals. A quartet of musicians sat atop a platform in the back of the room, preparing to play. Little had changed since his retreat from society several years before.

After taking all of two steps inside, Nicholas felt suffocated. Each breath proved a struggle as cloying perfume mingled with the scent of warm bodies pressed into a small, close space. He only hoped his brief appearance would appease his persistent mother . . . and answer his own questions.

The crush of people parted as he approached, their shock transforming into speculation. He could read their expressions clearly. The men frowned, seeing him as yet another competitor, while the women saw him as the catch of the season. He smothered the urge to smile. Two years ago, he was the second son of a dissolute marquess, and could not have paid for their attention. Now, with both his father and older brother dead, he had become the hunted.

While ignoring the hopeful glances of every eligible—and not so eligible—woman in attendance, Nicholas searched the room for his mother. He intended to keep his freedom for many years to come. Now, if he could convince his determined mother of that fact . . .

"You will never find a suitable bride if you continue scowling at every young woman in attendance."

He groaned inwardly. "Mother. I was just thinking of you." Glancing to his side, he found her studying him with irritation.

The marchioness, Lady Eugenia Grey, was statuesque. The black bombazine gown molding her full figure made her appear even more imposing. Her hair, once as dark as his own, had slowly faded to a startling silver hue, but her eyes remained as sharp and clear as blue ice.

"May I say you look exceptionally lovely this evening." The blatant attempt to smooth her ruffled disposition met with failure, as he knew it would.

"If you could bestow such flattery on one of the young ladies here tonight, I would have a grandchild within the year." Her voice softened to a whisper. "It would not pain you to smile on occasion, Nicholas. You can be quite charming when you try.''

He sighed, weary of this particular argument. ''I am twenty-eight. There is ample time to fill the nursery with squalling babes.'' He brushed an invisible speck of lint from his immaculate sleeve, dismissing the conversation. ''If you will excuse me, I think I shall try my luck in the card room.''

She halted his escape with a sharp tap of her lace fan against his forearm. ''I have arranged an introduction with the Bolliver girl.'' Eugenia scanned the room and smiled. ''Ah, here she comes now.''

Nicholas followed her gaze, and then wished he had not. The anxious Lady Bolliver charged in his direction like a cavalry officer leading an advance. Her daughter, pale and near tears, was dragged behind, apparently ready to desert when the moment presented itself.

His scowl deepened, but he could not embarrass his mother by snubbing the women directly. Eugenia Grey had suffered enough of that at the hands of his perpetually drunken father.

Gritting his teeth through the introductions, he waited impatiently for an opportunity to free himself. His attention returned to them at the sound of his mother's distressed voice.

''It is quite frightening to realize a thief can enter your home as you sleep and take whatever he wishes.''

Lady Bolliver entered the gossip mill, her high-pitched, nasal voice setting Nicholas's nerves on edge. ''I have heard Lord Hampshire was relieved of a stunning pearl necklace that had been in his family for three generations.''

'' 'Tis most exciting,'' Lady Bolliver's daughter piped in, her voice as irritating as her mother's. ''The thief always leaves a perfect white rose on the pillow of his victim.''

''How . . . interesting,'' Nicholas remarked. ''There is a master jewel thief creating havoc among the ton. I take it no one has a clue to his identity.''

The daughter replied in a whisper. ''Well, there are rumors—''

''That's enough,'' her mother hissed, pinching the poor girl's arm. ''I am quite certain Lord Grey has no wish to listen to mean-spirited insinuations.''

Nicholas stifled the urge to laugh. The ton thrived on gossip like an alcoholic addicted to gin. It was a weakness he was counting upon.

His thoughts settled upon the elusive thief who had captured the imagination of society, along with many of their precious gems. He had heard the rumors alluded to by Lady Bolliver. Sly whispers named his cousin, Viscount Edward Turner, as the thief.

Nicholas had returned to London for one reason: to prove the allegations true.

''Mother, ladies,'' he said, bowing in apology, ''I must speak with someone on a most urgent matter.'' Nicholas made a swift escape, his mother's snort of disgust her only farewell.

Striding through the crowd, he surveyed the perimeter and found his prey. In the corner, a group of men lounged beside a lush potted fern, Edward Turner among them.

Hands tightening into fists, Nicholas regarded the older man. Like a chameleon, Turner changed his colors at will. Affable and charming one moment, cunning and ruthless the next. How easily his cold, reptilian eyes could put fear in the heart of a weaker adversary, but Nicholas remained immune.

Memories, buried for seven years, flooded to the surface.

Julia.

She had fallen prey to Turner's genial persuasion and paid the ultimate price. Even now, Nicholas's guilt could not be dampened.

He tore his gaze free.

With mild surprise, he realized he was not alone in his hatred. Standing a few feet away was an angel, staring at Turner with open loathing.

He wondered what the lovely young woman could have in common with a man like Turner. Perhaps she was a scorned lover. . . . Nicholas discounted the notion. She seemed too discerning, too composed, to fall under his cousin's hypnotic spell. And even Turner wouldn't be so willing to cast aside such a beauty.

As if sprinkled with diamond dust, her raven hair, piled high atop her head, sparkled under the bright candlelight. Her delicate features and petite frame were a sharp contrast to the unmistakable gleam of defiance reflected in her eyes.

As if sensing his stare, she turned and gazed directly into his face. A flash of recognition darkened her rich brown eyes to midnight.

He searched his memory. She remained a stranger.

The angelic beauty turned away, gliding through the sea of black evening coats and white gowns. Any young man foolish enough to approach her was coolly rebuffed with one frosty stare. She was obviously not hunting for a prospective suitor.

Hovering on the fringes of the gathering, she moved from one small group to another, offering only the briefest of greetings.

A group of twirling dancers swept by, obstructing his view, but his patience was soon rewarded. She reappeared, and promptly slipped through the doorway leading to the balcony.

Curiosity toyed with primal attraction.

Nicholas followed, pulling the French doors closed behind him. She glided along the flagstones and to the railing. She stared out into the night, her silk gown fluttering in a sudden cool breeze.

In unfettered appreciation, he followed the graceful curve of her body, his eyes drawn to the creamy swell of breasts peeking above the modest lace neckline.

Like a doe sensing imminent danger, she stilled. Turning slowly, the woman confronted his keen stare with one of her own. "I came here for a breath of fresh air and privacy, my lord."

Her husky, sensuous voice shot straight through him. He'd had numerous liaisons with beautiful women, but none had wrought such an immediate response.

"I, too, came to escape the crush," he offered quietly. Without asking permission, he joined her at the low stone wall enclosing the balcony. "I do not usually attend these functions, but I can say with utmost certainty that I have not had the pleasure of making your acquaintance."

She continued staring into the rose garden beyond the wall, her complexion bathed in bewitching moonlight. "I only arrived in London a few weeks ago, Lord Grey."

The fact that she knew his identity filled him with elemental pleasure, and explained the recognition he'd witnessed. "You have the advantage, for I do not know your name."

When she deigned to face him, her dark eyes revealed nothing. This was no young miss fresh from the schoolroom. Her dainty features and flawless skin bespoke youth, but deep, soulful eyes and full, pouty lips held a passionate promise.

"Are you here to make a match?" he queried, churning with both hope and dread.

"No, I have no interest in marriage."

"There, we have much in common already. You seem rather young to be a widow. . . ." He allowed the question, masked as a statement, to drift away.

Her brow rose, her tone dripping with cynicism. "And if I confessed to being a widow, would this then be the moment you make your proposition?"

Shrugging like a boy caught skipping his lessons, Nicholas grinned. "I am not known as a man who allows opportunity to slip from his grasp."

Her expression hardened to icy disdain. "I have no interest in anything you could offer. But perhaps one of the bored, wealthy widows inside would welcome your attentions."

"I do not recall offering you an arrangement."

A knowing smile parted her lips. "Lust is an easy expression to read, my lord."

Stunned by her frank speech, he watched as she wrapped the ivory silk shawl tight around her bare shoulders. "Now, if you will pardon me." Head held high, she marched away as Nicholas regained use of his voice.

"Stop!"

The authoritative command halted her. Placing a hand on her shoulder, he turned her toward him. Her eyes glittered with anger and a dash of challenge; she was not the least bit intimidated. If he had seen fear, or the coquettish flutter of her velvety lashes, he would have run for his life. Now, he could not.

"Tell me what you want," she said, shaking free of his touch.

"For now, I will settle for a name."

His request brought that elusive smile to her face once again. "I prefer to remain in anonymity. A woman must protect herself. And her reputation."

The whispered refusal crushed his tenuous control.

Her game of mysterious and winsome smiles only heightened his desire, and his curiosity. "Why the elaborate game? Perhaps," he added carefully, "Viscount Turner would answer my questions."

As cool as an iced sorbet, she shrugged. "That would be a waste of time. He and I have not been introduced." She arched her brow, as if daring him to put action to words. "But be my guest, Lord Grey."

"And if I did, I have the disturbing notion you would disappear like a ghost."

Tapping a slender finger against her chin, she studied him with mock consternation. "Quite the quandary. To stay or to go . . . I think I would choose the latter."

Nicholas's blood pounded like a native's drum. He took a deep breath. "I am not asking for the moon. A simple name will suffice."

"Very well." She smiled—a smile he was coming to hate. "You may call me Anne . . . or Evelyn . . . or Grace. . . ."

Realizing they could play the absurd game all night without a victor, Nicholas decided on a strategic assault. "If you will not give me your name, I shall take a boon in its place."

Enjoying her shocked expression, he found her lips with unerring precision. They were as soft and inviting as he'd suspected.

He tried to stop, but one kiss was not enough. Would never be enough.

Daring more—unable to do less—he tilted her face upward, smoothing his tongue along the seam of her mouth. As if taming a wild creature, he sought to subdue her with her tenderness. Instead of deepening the kiss, he brushed his lips across hers, once, twice. She felt as fragile as rose petals. He placed his fingertips against her neck and found her quickening pulse.

Her lips parted shyly, accepting the gentle exploration of his tongue. She tasted of lemonade, tart yet sweet. Passion and innocence.

With gentle, coaxing persuasion, he urged her toward a darkened corner. He wanted nothing to shatter this exquisite moment.

Hunger chased rational thought from his mind. "Come with me," he whispered against her kiss-swollen lips. "I know of a discreet inn. . . ."

She stiffened in his arms. Nicholas cursed his sudden lack of control, and his abysmal choice of words.

Before he could utter an apology, she slowly lifted the wispy hem of her gown. Slender ankles and shapely calves encased in white silk stockings came into view. "Why should we go anywhere? This *is* what you want, isn't it?"

The seductive purr and apparent disregard for propriety set him aflame. "You are a daring spitfire!"

A warning bell tolled in his fevered brain at her sudden capitulation, but Nicholas dismissed the danger. Passion wiped away reason.

He nibbled her lips, his appetite ravenous. "You are so lov—"

Blinding pain struck with the speed of a lightning bolt. Nicholas doubled over, agony centered in his groin. Speech proved impossible as he battled to remain upright.

"Next time, my arrogant Lord Grey, you will find a dagger between your legs instead of my knee."

"You—you tease!" he sputtered.

The tempting seductress stepped back, her face taut and pale. "Perhaps I am. But a gentleman would not accost a defenseless woman."

"Defenseless! If you had wanted me to stop, a slap across the cheek would have sufficed."

With trembling hands, she smoothed her gown into place. The tigress with sharp claws and bony knees had vanished, and she suddenly appeared vulnerable. And very young.

"I thought to teach you a lesson. I will admit, I may have been a tad too diligent."

He stared at her disbelievingly.

Regret colored her hesitant words. "I—I did not think. . . ."

Nicholas gulped air into his deprived lungs and waited for the nausea and pain to ease. "You damn well didn't think! You can damage a man for life with such dangerous stunts."

"I really must go," she whispered.

"Oh, no! You, my dear young woman, are staying here until I receive the answers I want. Beginning with your blasted name."

She backed away, her eyes fathomless. "You awakened memories I thought long dead; forgive me." In a swirl of sparkling sapphire, she fled down the stone steps leading into the garden, and disappeared into the night.

He lunged forward, preparing to give chase, yet the pain prevented him. He slumped to the ground and rested his head against the wall.

Any residual anger receded as a vision of her pale face whispered through his mind. He'd behaved like a lust-crazed animal. And with a complete stranger at that! Never had he allowed his body to run roughshod over his control.

Her sudden trepidation had been genuine. As genuine as her feminine response to his touch. Nicholas had felt the subtle signs of her arousal as clearly as his own. A chuckle erupted from his dry throat. *A dagger indeed!*

For the first time in nearly a year, he felt alive. Challenged. A new sense of purpose pumped through his veins. He would discover her identity and her secrets. Whether she realized it or not, this spitfire had thrown down the gauntlet.

The chase had begun.

Darkness disguised her journey through the silent town house.

Her nerves tingled with both exhilaration and fear.

As it had been each time before, entering the house proved easy. Too easy. Arrogance remained her only enemy now. One misstep, one miscalculation, and she might swing from the hangman's noose.

As she crept up the circular staircase, her bare feet were silent upon the rich carpeting. As she topped the second floor, a sound from below halted her progress.

Like a ghostly trespasser, she backed against the wall, holding her breath as the footman made his ritual pass around the first floor. She peeked down and watched him smother a hearty yawn with the back of his hand. Wax dripped on the beige marble tiles of the foyer. A curse slipped from his lips as he peeled up the wax and continued his tour.

As the footman and his candelabra disappeared, she moved down the hallway. All senses were attuned to her surroundings. In the dark, fingertips replaced eyes, gliding over smooth wallpaper and the hard ridge of each door frame.

Barely a whisper escaped her parted lips. Each breath was carefully measured. At the last bedchamber, she tried the knob.

Locked! So, they do take some precautions.

Without hesitation, she slipped two slender picks

from her pocket and set to work. In seconds, the mechanism clicked. Inch by patient inch, she nudged the door open. A shaft of pearly moonlight illuminated the canopy bed and its slumbering occupant.

Now, where did Lady Neville say she planned to hide her lovely diamond necklace and matching bracelet?

As she scanned the chamber, her gaze settled on the high rosewood wardrobe. *Ah, yes . . . a secret compartment in the back. Most ingenious, my lady, but perhaps at the next ball you attend you should limit conversation to needlepoint, or the weather.*

The thief glided over the oriental carpet, but froze as the sleeping woman snorted indelicately and rolled over.

After what seemed an eternity, she continued her journey, opened the wardrobe, and quickly located the compartment. The jewels felt like ice, cold and smooth against her palm. There was no time to admire their beauty now. With a smile, she slipped the necklace and bracelet into the pouch at her waist.

Now, to leave my calling card.

She slid the thornless rose from her dark woolen shirt and moved to the bed. Twirling the satiny petals against her cheek, she stared at her sleeping victim.

A sliver of guilt embedded itself in her heart. She plucked the useless emotion free. Her course had been set two years ago, when her life—and her sanity—were nearly snatched away. Now an insatiable thirst for justice guided her days and nights.

No one would stand in her way.

Let this be a valuable, though expensive, lesson, Lady Neville. Your admirers may not be what they seem. . . .

She placed the delicate white flower on the pillow, and departed the room as quietly as a wraith.

Chapter Two

"My lord, Viscount Turner has arrived, and is most anxious to speak with you."

Nicholas nearly dropped the cup of steaming tea he held to his lips.

The Grey family butler stood in the doorway, his face creased in apology. "I explained you were taking breakfast, but he was most adamant."

Hands trembling, Nicholas lowered the cup to the saucer. Turner was insane to believe he would be welcome. Or he was desperate.

Curiosity conquered Nicholas's hatred. "Did you show my *dear* cousin to the sitting room?"

Abbot cleared his throat, the only indication of his frustration. "Lord Turner insisted upon speaking with you in the library."

"Pushy devil," Nicholas murmured. Then a more disturbing notion took hold. "Has my mother come down for breakfast?"

"No, but I would expect madam at any moment."

Urgency drove Nicholas to his feet. If Eugenia Grey found her nephew in the house, there would be hell to pay.

Charging through the open library door, Nicholas closed it firmly and stared at his cousin. He was immaculately dressed in a black coat and burgundy-striped waistcoat, the crisp white cravat folded with artistic precision.

As Edward turned, Nicholas noted the barely concealed sneer on the older man's face—a face showing the subtle signs of dissipation.

"Still playing the role of a barbarian, I see." Turner's pale, brown-eyed gaze raked across Nicholas's white linen shirt, and then down to his fawn-colored breeches.

"Those who pay calls at this ungodly hour should think twice before attacking their host's attire." Nicholas slid into the chair behind the mahogany desk and strummed his fingers on the smooth, polished wood. "You have five minutes to discuss your business, Turner. Then I want you out."

Edward's thin lips curved into an icy smile. "Ah, the legendary Grey charm. I must say, I find it lacking a certain politeness."

"I don't have all day."

"As you wish," Edward said, perching his thin frame on the wing-back brocade chair. "Have you heard news of the latest robbery?"

"Are you speaking of the White Rose?"

"Yes, and it would seem Lady Neville is the latest victim."

Nicholas leaned back, his expression bland. "I am sure there is a point."

"Someone is trying to blacken my name and reputation. *That* is the point."

If Turner hoped to garner sympathy, Nicholas was happy to disappoint. "Why would someone attempt to carry out such a heinous scheme, when you are more than capable of blackening your own reputation?"

"Listen well, Grey. I have an enemy who is determined to see me ruined. Perhaps he is determined to see the entire family ruined."

Nicholas doubted that, but played along with the drama. "What is the connection between you and this thief?"

Eyes gleaming, Edward leaned closer. "I shall be blunt. Every victim attended the same ball as I. And each young woman I paid the slightest attention to was robbed the very same night. If I make a brief appearance, the hosts are robbed of their valuables. Three nights ago, Lady Neville's diamond necklace was stolen . . . the very necklace I so foolishly remarked upon earlier in the evening."

"Quite a damning set of coincidences," Nicholas remarked.

" 'Tis no coincidence. Someone wants the ton to believe I am a jewel thief." As if discussing the unseasonably chilly weather, Edward kept his voice calm. "Have you ever heard such a preposterous story?"

Edward had always been a difficult man to read, and now proved no exception. Either he was innocent, as he affirmed, or this visit was a clever ruse to throw suspicion away from himself and gain an ally. Nicholas preferred to believe the latter.

"I can understand why some would suspect you, Turner. Your love of gaming is well documented.

And let's be perfectly frank: you lose more often than you win. Much more.''

Edward's face flushed crimson at the jibe. "I always settle my debts. To suggest otherwise is a blatant lie.''

"I am merely pointing out what others must be considering,'' Nicholas said, watching a lone bead of sweat slide down his cousin's temple. It was indeed a rare occasion to witness the unflappable viscount so visibly upset. "This is all very interesting, Turner, but I fail to see why you wished to share this revelation with me.''

An apologetic smile graced Edward's face as he spoke with seeming humility. "I know we have not shared a friendly relationship in the past. . . .''

Leaning forward, jaw clenched, Nicholas waited. *Don't say it, Turner. Don't even whisper her name.*

''. . . but we are still family.'' Edward rose and walked to the window, peering through the maroon velvet drapes with apparent nonchalance. "I have Bow Street Runners searching for this thief, and they have found nothing. I know you have acquaintances who could look into this matter with the utmost discretion.''

Nicholas grinned. "You're not serious?''

Edward turned back, his deep-set eyes shining with outrage. "This is a dangerous situation.''

"Perhaps you should take yourself off to the country and allow the rumors to die down.''

"Be chased off by a felon? Absolutely not. Besides, I am determined to find a wife this season, and Lady Dewitt is the perfect choice. In fact, she will be attending the Tipton ball tonight, as will I.''

Head pounding, Nicholas remained still, keeping tight rein on his volatile emotions. "You had a wife. Or have you forgotten?''

Turner took a cautious step back, his suave smile slipping. "My God, man, that was seven years ago."

Rising to his feet, Nicholas leaned across the desk. The urge to strangle Turner with his carefully knotted cravat was nearly irresistible. "Some may call it an accident, but I know better."

"I had nothing to do with her death. That carriage overtipped in a blinding rainstorm."

His voice as soft as brushed velvet, and as dangerous as the blade of a dagger, Nicholas asked the question still haunting him. "Then explain why Julia felt compelled to flee your estate in the dead of night."

"I have no idea." Turner shrugged. "Who can understand a woman's mind?"

With the speed of a viper, Nicholas reached across the desk and grabbed Turner's cravat. Giving the neckcloth a vicious tug, he dragged his cousin closer. "You stole her innocence, you bastard!"

Edward sobered. "I've regretted my impetuous behavior, and I cannot change the past." His voice softened. "You may not believe me, but I did care for Julia."

Laughing bitterly, Nicholas shoved the man away. "You've never cared for anyone but yourself. You may fool the ton with your charade, but I know the truth. You wanted Julia only because *I* wanted her."

Edward sighed, trying in vain to mend his rumpled clothing. "If I'd known you were serious in your intentions, I never would have pursued her."

Nicholas didn't believe the contrite words for a moment. "Get out, Turner. This discussion is finished."

Edward's iron gray brows twitched at the sharp dismissal, though his cold smile remained constant. "One day, cousin, your arrogance will be your undoing."

A deep laugh bubbled from Nicholas's throat.

"Now there's a case of the pot calling the kettle black."

"Don't push me," Edward warned, his voice slick with undisguised venom.

Nicholas didn't move, hoping for any excuse to plant a fist in his cousin's face. "Is that a threat?"

As if sensing the danger of the situation, Edward stepped back and shrugged. "Not at all, Grey. But fear not; with or without your help, I will discover this thief's identity. And he will pay dearly."

He reached the middle of the room as the door swung violently open.

Nicholas stifled a groan. Eugenia Grey swept into the library with the haughty grandeur of a queen, her bombazine gown rustling like windswept autumn leaves. He'd always known she carried no fondness for her nephew, but for the first time he saw the true hatred in her frosty eyes.

Like a razor through flesh, her words sliced through the awkward silence. "You are not welcome in this house."

Seemingly unperturbed by the icy welcome, Edward smiled. "Madam, you are as lovely as ever. Seeing you now, I am reminded of my dear mother. Her loss is still keenly felt."

At the mention of her twin sister, Eugenia paled, her eyes misting in undeniable sadness.

The sight of his mother in distress lashed Nicholas's heart, and fanned his temper. "Turner, you know where the door is."

His cousin turned, and Nicholas glimpsed the flash of triumph in his cold amber eyes. The bastard had upset her on purpose!

"As you wish, Grey." He strolled from the room, the scent of his pungent cologne trailing behind.

Nicholas followed and slammed the door, the urge

to punch his fist through the dark wood subdued for the moment. "I'm sorry, Mother."

Turning back, he found her sitting stiffly on the chair Edward had vacated. A single tear slipped down her finely lined cheek.

Shock brought him to a standstill. In all his years, he had never seen his mother cry. Not even when her firstborn was brought home dead from the battle of Waterloo. Grief had always been a private matter, handled in solitude. Yet now, with a few carefully chosen words, Edward Turner had accomplished the impossible.

Kneeling in front of her, Nicholas pressed a crisp, snowy white handkerchief into her trembling hands. "I'm sorry. I should have tossed him out immediately." Smiling gently, he waited as she collected her tattered emotions.

"I was taken by surprise, Nicholas. Seeing him at a soiree or a ball is one thing, but it's quite another to find him standing in my home."

"I promise he will not be allowed entrance again."

She smiled, but the expression did not penetrate the sadness in her sky blue eyes. "You must think me a silly old woman."

"Never." Nicholas paused, craving answers, but unwilling to open old wounds.

"Why was he here?" she asked in agitation. "My nephew knows he is not welcome."

Nicholas sighed and came to his feet. "It is of no importance."

As always, Eugenia Grey would not be thwarted. "Tell me what he wanted."

"Very well." Nicholas sat at his desk and apprised his mother of the situation.

"And he actually came here for help. Wonderful," she exclaimed when he finished, clapping her hands like a young girl presented with a delightful gift. "My nephew must truly be frustrated."

"Yes, it would appear so. But I can't help but wonder if Edward *is* the White Rose. . . ."

Her glee ended. "I know that look well, Nicholas. You must promise to stay far clear of Edward Turner." She rose to her full six-foot height with casual grace. "Although I must admit I take great pleasure in my nephew's sudden distress."

"I cannot let this go." Nicholas replied, his voice rough.

Eugenia faced her son, her expression stern. "People close to Edward suffer untimely deaths. My dear sister, Ophelia, her husband, that poor Alston girl, and, of course, Julia."

Nicholas was shocked by the veiled accusation. "Mother, I know Turner is ruthless, but are you claiming he murdered his own parents?"

"If you are asking if I have proof, the answer is no. But that is what I have believed for nearly twenty-five years. First Ophelia tumbles down a flight of stairs in the middle of the night. Then her husband, George, shoots himself in a bizarre hunting accident less than three weeks later. It is a glaring set of coincidences."

The rumors still surfaced now and again. Nicholas had been a child when they died. And later he'd been too busy rebuilding the Grey family fortune—and learning to live under the yoke of his new title—to heed idle gossip. Now he hungered to know all.

He leaned forward, fingers interlocked beneath his chin. "Who is this Alston chit you mentioned?"

"Surely you remember Baron Alston. He owned a substantial tract of land near ours at Rockingham."

"Yes, I remember him vaguely . . . something of a recluse. And the girl was a shy little thing."

"The baron was not always so," Eugenia replied. "After his wife died of childbed fever, he was never the same. He lived for his daughter."

His mother cleared her throat. "As I was saying, somehow Edward was named the poor girl's guardian. If I had known sooner . . ."

"You would have snatched her away in the middle of the night," Nicholas finished.

"Yes, I would have done precisely that. Edward brought her to London for her mourning period. Then she vanished."

"Vanished! How could she simply disappear? And when the devil did all this happen?"

Eugenia wandered the room like a butterfly searching for a safe place to alight. "I believe you were on an expedition to invest in a shipbuilding enterprise when the baron died. My nephew assumed guardianship and brought her to London. He claimed she was not content, and sent her home with a companion."

Her voice softened to a whisper. "One month later, he was sporting a black armband. Evidently she died in a shipwreck off the coast of America. How she came to be there was never explained to my satisfaction."

Nicholas felt as if he'd unwittingly opened Pandora's box. He mulled over the conversation, knowing it would take time, and a shrewd investigator, to glean the truth.

"I'm sorry Turner has reminded us of this unpleasantness." Nicholas reached his mother and kissed her cheek. "Who knows? Perhaps the Rose will take care of Lord Turner. And if he is the thief, the law will see to his demise."

"Yes, perhaps . . ." Ignoring his devil-may-care smile, she watched him with somber intensity.

"Promise me you will stand clear of this wretched business. Edward may play the role of a gentleman, but he is a dangerous man."

"I understand my cousin."

She nodded as her chin rose to its usual imperious height. The crisis had passed. "Well then, I must be off. I have an appointment with Madame de-Fournier."

If Eugenia Grey had announced an appointment with old Bony himself, Nicholas would not be as shocked. "Madame deFournier . . . the couturiere?"

"Precisely. I find I am weary of black. And it has been over two years."

"Thank God! You are much too beautiful to wear that hideous bombazine a moment longer."

Her cheeks pinkened. "You, my dear son, are a rascal."

"And only you would find such a tame description."

"That is the prerogative only a mother can take." With that, she swept from the room.

His nerves still on edge, Nicholas took a deep breath. The time had come to uncover his cousin's sordid past. He tried to convince himself he was undertaking the task to prove his mother's allegations concerning her sister's untimely death.

The truth would not be denied.

He wanted revenge. For Julia. The years since her death had dimmed the pain, but not erased it. Now that the Grey family fortune was in the black, he had the time and resources to see his quest to fruition. Turner had claimed his last victim.

Banishing his dark thoughts, Nicholas returned to his desk and penned a letter.

A vision of deep brown eyes and shining raven-hued hair shattered his concentration.

She occupied his nights with increasing frequency, each dream more erotic and sensual than the last. She was a witch—a sorceress with full, pouty lips, alabaster skin, and high, firm breasts. . . .

He was startled by the fire in his blood that simple thoughts of the beauty aroused. Blast the woman! Now she was encroaching on his days as well.

Perhaps his mother would know the spitfire's identity. That night, he'd been in no condition to ask questions after his near emasculation. Nicholas quickly crushed the thought. If he mentioned his fascination, Eugenia would pounce like a starved tabby on a bowl of cream.

With his usual flourish, he scrawled his signature, affixed the Grey family seal, and tugged the bellpull hanging behind the desk.

Abbot appeared, his expression characteristically inscrutable. Nicholas began to rise from the chair, then thought better of the impulse. The aging retainer might begin to wonder exactly what his employer did when ensconced in the library for hours on end.

"Tell me, Abbot, did my mother accept the Tipton invitation?"

"Yes, my lord."

"Very good. I shall escort her myself." His quest to see Turner fall—and to find his spitfire—would begin tonight. Nicholas handed over the note. "And would you see that this is delivered directly into Connor Hennessy's hand?"

"Of course, my lord."

"By the way, Abbot, if Viscount Turner ever appears on our doorstep again, you have my permission to close the door in his face."

Abbot smiled. "With pleasure, my lord."

*   *   *

She was exhausted. Her body was drained.

Maggie never dreamed such weariness existed. Even the bent tin spoon she gripped seemed as heavy as iron. The grueling schedule of staying up till dawn, then searching for a dreamless sleep, was proving impossible.

The tiny one-room dwelling she shared with her adopted family seemed to shrink with each passing day. Two small wrought-iron beds, a table, three mismatched chairs, a sagging cupboard, and a battered stove comprised the entire contents of the room. Faded brown curtains covered the only window, and the warped door allowed wind and rain to enter at will.

It was little more than a hovel, but compared to the filthy, cramped lodging houses, it was a palace. Their home was plain, clean, and functional. And sadly, more than their neighbors would ever hope to have.

Maggie could have afforded a more stylish dwelling, but anonymity was more important than satin duvets or crystal chandeliers. People residing in the slums of London were too busy surviving to wonder about the three "brothers" living in quiet obscurity among them.

Thomas's hesitant question pierced her lethargy. "Maggie, are you feeling all right?"

Forcing a smile, she nodded to the boy and stared at the barely touched mutton pie. Her appetite, like her strength, seemed bent on desertion.

The raucous sounds of the street beyond the thin door receded as Maggie glanced across the table, and into Dare's intense eyes. "Somethin' 'appened. You ain't been yourself fer three days now."

"I told you, everything went as planned." She quickly lowered her gaze.

"Yer lyin'." His cold statement of fact did not

surprise her. From the moment she'd tracked him to a crowded dockside tavern over a year ago, Dare could see through her subterfuge as if she'd been spun from glass. The trait could be most irritating at times.

"Nothing happened," Maggie stated carefully, glancing at Thomas. Her veiled warning was unmistakable. Dare nodded in understanding.

She caught a glimpse of Thomas's worried expression and forced a feeble smile. Of the three, he remained the only innocent. The caretaker.

Abandoned by his gin-addicted mother, he had been destined for the workhouse, or worse yet, a prime candidate to be apprenticed to a chimney sweep. He would not have survived such a fate. Chimney boys died young.

Maggie and Dare had stumbled upon him, huddled in a dank alleyway, a threadbare coat his only shield against the cold. In his tiny hands he'd clutched a moldy piece of bread.

They had "adopted" him on the spot.

How could they not? His flaxen hair and clear indigo eyes would be the envy of the heavens. After all Thomas had been through in his six-odd years, he carried no bitterness. Their "angel" kept them from crossing the line into endless darkness. Thomas was the light—Dare and Maggie the shadows.

Suddenly the little boy laid his hand upon hers, his voice a whisper. "It's all right, Maggie. I know about the White Rose. Everyone in the market is talking about how the Rose is just like Robin Hood, stealing from the rich and giving to the poor."

Maggie held her breath. "Precisely what do you know?"

Thomas grinned. "I know you're the Rose, and Dare helps you."

Her stomach fluttered with dread, and not because

34

she feared Thomas would reveal the truth. He could be as silent as a mute when the need arose. But because she and Dare had wanted to protect his innocence. A difficult enough task in the slums, yet she thought that they'd managed.

His honest and caring nature was his greatest gift. And now Maggie had tarnished it.

She looked to Dare, searching for the right words to lessen the damage. He shrugged, his expression easy to read. "I told you we couldn't keep the truth hidden forever."

Forever had arrived.

"Thomas, I—"

"Don't worry, Maggie. I would never tell anyone. Never."

She smoothed his worried frown. "I know, angel. We didn't share our secret because ... well, you see ..."

Words failed her.

Thomas smiled. "I know stealing is wrong. But sometimes we have to do things we don't want to do."

Continually amazed by his keen intelligence, Maggie stared at the boy. Her constant tutoring had paid sterling premiums.

"Besides," he continued, "if it weren't for you, Mr. Lockwit, the baker, would have been thrown in debtor's jail. And then what would've happened to his babies? You're a hero! Everyone says so."

Maggie turned away from his blind adoration. She was no hero. She was thief. A criminal. Yes, the Rose helped the destitute whenever the need was great, but a Robin Hood she was not. Her motives were not noble and pure. They were born of darkness.

"Once we leave England," she stated firmly, "we

will never steal again. We won't even pick up a coin lying in the street. Understand?''

Thomas nodded, his expression somber. ''Yes, Maggie.''

''You never answered my question,'' Dare said quietly. ''What 'appened at the ball?''

Taking a deep swallow of ale, Maggie braced for the coming storm. When he wanted to know something, Dare was more persistent than anyone.

Lean, angular features and mercurial gray eyes lent him the look of a hawk. If the darkness in Maggie's soul was great, Dare's was boundless. Although two years younger than her own nineteen, he seemed older, wiser, and infinitely more suspicious.

''I may have made a determined enemy,'' Maggie whispered, heat flooding her face.

''What do you mean, an enemy?''

''The Marquess of Rockingham made an untoward advance, and I—I . . .''

''Bloody 'ell,'' Dare exclaimed in horror. ''You didn't shoot 'im, did you?''

Thomas, ever her defender, piped in with childish innocence. ''Don't be silly. Our Maggie would never hurt anyone.''

She winced, knowing it to be a lie.

Dare looked upward in exasperation. ''What did you do?''

''I—I kneed him in the . . . privates. Just as you taught me.''

The confession met with stunned silence.

Maggie watched in growing amazement as Dare's lips curved into a blinding smile, his whoops of delight filling the air. Never, in the entire time she'd known him, had he laughed with such abandon.

Soon she joined him, tears of mirth rolling down her cheeks.

Thomas giggled behind his hands.

"What did 'Is Lordship do when you banked 'is fire?"

Maggie sobered, remembering the blast of anger that hardened his icy blue eyes. "He was not pleased."

" 'E didn't touch you . . ." Dare's threat was implicit. Deadly.

"No, of course not." *Except for an unforgettable kiss* . . . "I escaped through the garden before he could recover. But," she added quickly, "I don't think he would have hurt me."

"Well, that tears it! No more robberies, Maggie. If the marquess lays eyes on you again, no tellin' what 'e'll do."

"Don't we have enough money set aside to travel to America?" Thomas asked hopefully, playing the role of peacemaker. A thankless task whenever she and Dare butted heads.

"Soon, angel. And then you can go to a real school." Maggie turned back to Dare. "And as for the Rose, *he* will continue his work."

"One of these days, our luck is goin' to run out. We'll end up in Newgate or—"

"No matter what happens, you and Thomas will be safe." She flashed a cocky smile she didn't feel. "No need to worry, the Rose will never be caught."

Or at least, not the real one.

Her friends remained ignorant of her ulterior motive for creating the brazen thief. As far as they were concerned, the stolen jewels, smuggled to a discreet buyer in Calais, were their ticket to a new life.

If an occasional pang of guilt was felt at what she had become, the emotion was always crushed when Maggie attended the next ball. Simply because of the circumstances of birth, the nobility had wealth to squander, and poor souls like Dare and Thomas had nothing.

She was ashamed of her own aristocratic background. She would see to it they never learned the truth behind her charade. Especially Dare.

When she looked up to gauge his reaction, he appeared to remain skeptical.

"I promise," Maggie said quietly, "two more robberies, and we leave England forever."

"You're sure?" Dare asked as he attacked the mutton pie once again.

"Two more." By then her thirst for justice would be quenched. Edward Turner would never harm anyone again.

Her weary thoughts drifted to the only man who might disrupt her carefully drawn plan. Lord Nicholas Grey.

She had tried to blot their meeting from her mind, with little success. Maggie winced at how easily she'd melted in his embrace. And with a stranger, no less! Although he was not completely unknown to her.

Even as a young man growing into adulthood, he'd possessed a mystical power over women, she remembered. One sizzling glance, and the fairer sex swooned at his feet like pagan sacrifices.

Now she'd learned that lesson in spades. With one kiss, she'd been reduced to a quivering puddle of need. Her skin tingled at the heated memory.

If he had been a portly, swaggering boor, he would have been easy to resist. Instead, Lord Grey possessed piercing azure eyes, hair as dark as a moonless winter night, and impossibly wide shoulders.

More than that, she had heard he was a man who hated losing. At anything.

Maggie hoped he would forget their impromptu,

and disastrous, first meeting. At the very least, she prayed he would not be attending the Tipton ball.

She'd held off his advances once, but twice could prove more difficult—and dangerous, for them all.

Chapter Three

Connor Hennessy strode into the library, his cheeks ruddy, and a gregarious smile stretched across his plump, boyish face. "Nicky, me boyo! It's been too long."

Nicholas grinned at the familiar greeting. Although the two men were the same age, Connor never failed to use the nickname whenever their paths crossed. It was a sign of their steadfast friendship, which began when Connor had stumbled upon a green young lord being attacked by a group of determined footpads. Connor had joined the fray, and together the two had made short work of the attackers. Since then, their relationship had become one of fraternal love. Brothers in every way but blood.

"You need a timepiece, Connor."

The Irishman laughed as he poured a snifter of expensive French brandy at the sideboard. "A man who lets a clock rule his life is only half a man, Nicky."

After settling his beefy frame on the black velvet sofa, Connor sipped the drink with sensual pleasure. "As I said, it's been too long."

"Too long since you've paid a visit, or are you referring to the brandy?"

Never one to equivocate, Connor pondered the question, then smiled. "Both. It's been too long on both counts."

Nicholas chuckled as he walked to the inlaid marble fireplace and stirred the glowing embers to life. "A lesser man might take offense at your honesty."

"There is no such thing between friends." Connor paused to drain the snifter, then sobered. "So what do you need done?"

"I wish it were as simple as that," Nicholas replied, uncertain where to begin.

"Why don't you be startin' with Edward Turner."

Nicholas blinked in surprise. "How the devil did you know?"

"He approached me and offered a hefty sum if I could find the Rose."

"And you turned down his generous offer?"

Connor nodded. "I'd bloody well live on the streets before I took a farthing from that man."

A quiver of apprehension vibrated through Nicholas's thoughts. "Why? Do you know something?"

"I've been hearin' things lately. Only rumors, Nicky. Word has it your cousin runs a string of exclusive brothels all over the city. But if he does, he covers his tracks well."

This information fueled Nicholas's determination. "It makes perfect sense. My cousin spends more time in gaming hells than tending his small estate. I've always wondered how he could lose so often and still keep his assets intact."

He crossed to the desk and removed a sheaf of

papers. "Connor, I want you to look these over."

The Irishman groaned in protest, but made no objection.

"It is a list of names and dates I've collected. In short, I want you to investigate the deaths of my aunt Ophelia, her husband, Lord George Turner, and Lady Julia Wentworth.

"Also, I want you to look into the death of a Miss Alston. Her father was the Baron of Chelsea. After her death, Turner petitioned the Crown, took the estate, and promptly sold it off. The particulars are all contained here," Nicholas added, handing the documents to a dumbfounded Hennessy.

Connor briefly scanned the papers as he spoke. "Your aunt and uncle died over twenty years ago. As for Lady Julia, her death was an accident." Connor's voice deepened with regret. "I know you cared for her, but why now?"

"I can accept that her death was an accident, but it should never have happened. I want to know why it did. I also want to prove my mother's allegations true concerning her sister's and brother-in-law's deaths."

"This will take time. . . ."

"I would not ask if it weren't important. Take all the time you need. And, of course, I will pay you handsomely."

Connor shook his head. "I won't be takin' your coin, and you know it."

The time had come for serious negotiations. "We both know this case will involve extensive travel. I will pay all expenses, and when you are finished, regardless of what you discover, I will see to it that you receive a case of this French brandy you love so much."

The Irishman hesitated only a moment, long

enough for Nicholas to see him glance with longing toward the glittering crystal decanter. "You drive a hard bargain, Nicky."

Grinning with satisfaction, Nicholas slipped his gold timepiece from his pocket. "Now that the matter is settled, I must go upstairs and prepare for—"

"I'm a wee bit confused," Connor said, coming to his feet. "What about the Rose? Don't you want me to try to track the thief down?"

"No, *I* will handle Edward, and the elusive thief."

An unholy smile split the Irishman's rounded features. "You believe Turner is the culprit."

"I've reached two conclusions. Either Edward is the thief, and is attempting to throw suspicion off himself, or he is being framed, as he so strongly asserts."

"So what will you be doin' about it?"

"I intend to catch the thief in the act. Tonight."

Connor whipped his weather-beaten hat against his knee and shook his head. "You've got too much bloody time on your hands, Nicky. What you need is a mistress to keep your mind *and* body occupied."

Laughing, Nicholas slapped his friend on the back and opened the door. "Perhaps you're right, Irish."

And tonight I intend to find her.

The air was stifling, the candlelight as bright as a midmorning sun. She hated the glare, and the crush of people that grew with each passing minute.

Through sheer endurance, Maggie buried her discomfort. With distracted impatience, she toyed with her white kidskin gloves. The dove gray muslin evening frock with matching tunic seemed more confining than ever. The stays of her corset pinched her ribs, and by morning she would have a multitude of small bruises for her trouble. Ringlets of hair brushed either side of her head, making her cheeks itch. Miserable, she was eager to be free of this glittering prison.

She surveyed the ballroom with a bored expression. Inside, her nerves stretched tighter than the strings of an ancient harp.

Sooner or later, the primped and preening members of the ton would begin to question her identity. It would be only a matter of time before they discovered that the aging Duchess of Blackthorne did not have a widowed niece named Mrs. Sanford, who'd returned from America to visit her only living relative.

Of course, the poor old woman *was* considered by all to be on the brink of senility. And more important, she had not ventured into London society for nearly three years. The duchess did indeed provide the perfect disguise.

Smiling softly, Maggie decided to send her ''aunt'' a token of appreciation—

The sight of Maggie's nemesis across the room erased her amused reflection. She glided easily through the throng, extending a polite greeting here and there as she moved closer to her quarry.

Viscount Edward Turner stood alone, his malevolent gaze raking the assemblage. Maggie crushed the urge to laugh aloud at his obvious predicament. The ton was one step short of giving him the dreaded *Cut*. But Maggie knew his supreme arrogance would eventually bubble to the surface. Like an aging wolf driven from the pack, he would try to reclaim his place.

As if on cue, he strode toward a demure young woman and her vigilant chaperon.

Ah, Lady Abigail Dewitt ... wonderful choice, Turner. Her father is the Earl of Montmouth, and very wealthy.

With avid interest, Maggie watched the tableau unfold. It was obvious to all that the poor woman was terrified, but Edward, oozing charm by the bucket, coaxed her onto the dance floor.

The sight sickened Maggie. Turner was old enough to be the girl's grandfather. *Enjoy your evening, Turner. By tomorrow, your name will be stricken from every guest list in London. . . .*

"Ah, the delightful Mrs. Sanford. We meet again."

Like a trapped animal, Maggie froze, unable to decide whether to flee or stand her ground.

The imperious Lord Grey had obviously not forgotten her. And he now knew her fictitious identity. He was a man who would not accept defeat.

"I don't believe we've been introduced," Maggie said through clenched teeth.

"Come now, surely you haven't forgotten our chance meeting at the Waverly crush. For me, the *memory* lingered for days."

She looked over her shoulder to find her tormentor grinning with perverse pleasure. "Lord Grey."

"So you do remember."

"Yes," Maggie offered with a strained smile. "Nightmares are often difficult to erase from one's mind."

His sudden burst of laughter drew more than one curious glance, and Maggie scowled at his good humor. "People are staring."

"Let them."

Maggie opened her mouth, ready to retort, but thought better of the notion. Lord Grey would like nothing better than to engage in a verbal duel of wits. If she remained quiet, he would grow bored and move on to the next possible conquest. . . .

"It won't work, you know." He seemed to know her strategy.

She answered with stubborn silence.

"A battle of wills, is it?"

She responded with an icy glare.

The amused twinkle in his sapphire eyes told Maggie the battle was just beginning. She tried to turn away, but his mesmerizing stare held her captive. His eyes were not a cold blue, but warm and tender, surrounded by a veil of thick, spiky lashes.

"Dance with me, spitfire."

Before the husky words could penetrate her hazy thoughts, he led her to the center of the ballroom. A quadrille formed, and they joined the other couples as the quartet began to play.

The din of conversation receded as Maggie realized all eyes were following them through the intricate figures. This was a drastic mistake. She had always managed to stay on the periphery of these gatherings. To flaunt her presence was an invitation to disaster.

She glanced into Lord Grey's eyes. They widened, and Maggie realized he had sensed her fear. He offered a gentle smile as they faced each other and stepped closer, their hands touching briefly as they circled, then retreated.

"I never apologized for our . . . misunderstanding the other evening," he said in a whisper, seemingly mindful of prying eyes and hungry ears.

"It has already been forgotten, my lord."

Their hands met again. She could feel his strength, his heat through their gloves.

"You are indeed fortunate, Mrs. Sanford. I am unable to forget our first meeting. It was most invigorating, up to a point."

"In the future, perhaps you should avoid overexertion, Lord Grey," she replied in dulcet tones. "One never knows when an affliction may recur."

"Your concern for my health is most appreciated.

But fear not, I shall guard against any future mishaps.''

She remained silent, content to watch his tall, lithe form move with languid grace and style. His black evening coat was molded to his body's masculine perfection. The satin waistcoat hugged his trim abdomen, accentuating the broadness of his shoulders. Dark hair, longer than fashion dictated, brushed his neckcloth in a sleek line. It was no wonder every woman's head turned when he appeared. Maggie was as guilty as any of them.

As the dance came to an end, she spun away, intent on fleeing before she fell victim to his potent charm.

He grasped her elbow and steered her toward the adjoining salon where the buffet was served. ''Allow me to get you some refreshment.''

''No, that—''

''But I insist. I *can* be a gentleman.'' His warm breath flowed gently across the nape of her neck. ''Allow me to prove it.''

Her stomach fluttered as he reached around her shoulder and handed her a glass of sparkling champagne from the buffet table. His clean, masculine scent, untempered by cologne, surrounded her—filling her with a strange lethargy.

Like a marionette, she allowed him to lead her into a quiet corner of the ballroom. She sipped the bubbly wine, careful to keep her gaze from straying into forbidden territory. With one smoldering glance, he could melt her resistance. And they both recognized it.

''I haven't yet told you how lovely you look this evening, Mrs. Sanford.''

Against her best efforts, heat flooded her cheeks. ''Thank you, Lord Grey.''

''And if I may be so bold, you seem far too young

to be a widow. When did your husband pass on?''

Her heart dropped to her stomach. Her flesh grew cold.

The inquisition had begun.

"My husband died a year ago," she said softly.

"Were you happy?"

Of all the possible questions she'd expected—prepared for—this one surprised her. "Why would you ask that?"

He downed the remainder of his champagne and handed the fluted glass to a passing footman before answering. "Curiosity, nothing more. Was it an arranged marriage?"

"Would that matter?" she asked, the subtle interrogation wearing upon her nerves.

"I'm beginning to understand. Your husband was old enough to be your father, and having such a young, beautiful wife was his undoing."

Maggie tugged at her gloves, ignoring his devilish grin. "You're being presumptuous. And quite rude, Lord Grey."

"You wouldn't be the first to make such an observation." His smile widened as he leaned closer. "So, did I paint an accurate picture of your past life?"

If you only knew, Lord Grey.

She smiled and edged back. "Not accurate in the least. Roger was young and quite prosperous."

"Forgive me for reviving such painful memories."

Maggie winced at the humble, sincere tone. She hated lying, especially to a man who seemed so honest. But lies were all she could give. "It is in the past, Lord Grey."

"Please call me Nicholas."

She looked up quickly. "I cannot possibly—"

"I insist. Only when we are alone, of course."

His arrogance awakened her dormant resistance.

48

"Well then, *Lord Grey,* I shall see to it we are never alone."

He laughed. "You're doing it again."

"Doing what?" she asked in strident tones.

"You are issuing a challenge."

Maggie fumed. "Then I will simply ignore you."

Answering with a secretive smile, he held her gaze with a sultry stare. She gasped as his hand slid up and down her spine in lazy strokes. An irresistible urge to arch like a contented cat caught Maggie unaware.

Step away . . . run!

But she could not. The heat and gentleness of his touch affected her like a drug. Powerful. Addicting.

"You were right to refuse my boorish offer," he whispered against her ear. "We should become better acquainted before we proceed to the next level."

"I—I told you once before, I am not interested in a tawdry liaison."

His hand drifted upward, grazing her bare shoulder before disappearing behind her back once again. "You say no, but your body quivers 'yes' beneath my touch. There is nothing tawdry about an arrangement between two unattached persons."

"You, Lord Grey, are an arrogant . . ." His hand skimmed the tiny buttons of her gown. ". . . conceited . . ." He pressed closer, his breath fanning a wisp of her hair. ". . . arrogant . . ."

"You're repeating yourself."

"Yes, well, some truths bear repeating," Maggie whispered, her voice husky and unfamiliar.

He chuckled and stepped back as a group of young men strolled by, casting overt glances in the couple's direction. Maggie took a deep breath and willed her traitorous body to cease trembling.

Like a message delivered straight from the bowels

of hell, *he* appeared in her sights. The blissful lethargy vanished. Turner's cold stare reached across the room like the web of a spider, trapping her in silky, lethal strands.

Instinctively, she edged closer to Nicholas.

He knows! Turner knows who I am. . . .

"It appears my cousin is a bit put out with me."

"You?" Maggie whispered with relief.

"Yes. Lord Turner asked for help in a certain matter, and I refused." Though the words were casually spoken, she sensed a simmering undercurrent beneath the civility.

Maggie could not resist the opportunity to plumb further. With a flick of her wrist, she snapped open the lace fan and cooled her heated cheeks. "I must admit, I have heard the rumors concerning your cousin. I'm surprised he was even invited this evening."

"An oversight, I'm sure," Grey answered smoothly.

When he added nothing further, Maggie looked upward and batted her eyelashes in what she hoped was a provocative manner. "Some are linking his name to this devilish Rose person. . . ."

One dark brow lifted in question. "I wouldn't think you were interested in idle gossip."

"Not usually, my lord. But if your cousin is involved, a woman must be careful."

"Don't worry. Viscount Turner will not bother you. Nor will the Rose."

A shiver raced across her flesh. "How can you be so certain? Do you know who the culprit is?"

"Not yet, but I hope to discover his identity very soon."

Terror settled as a lump in her throat. "But why would you concern yourself with this dreadful business? I'm sure you are a very busy man. . . ."

His expression became a mask of cold determination. "I have old scores to settle with my cousin."

Maggie touched his sleeve, drawing his attention. "So you believe the rumors are true."

"That is why I intend to track down the Rose. If Turner is the thief, it will be my duty, and pleasure, to see him exposed."

Maggie's curiosity was piqued. "You and your cousin are not close?"

Nicholas laughed bitterly. "I detest him. And he knows it."

"Yet he asked you for help."

This time, Nicholas's smile was genuine. "Yes, he's a very desperate man."

Dark pleasure coursed through her veins. "Wonderful," she murmured.

Nicholas's intense gaze pinned her like a butterfly under glass. "What is your connection to Lord Turner?"

Cursing her loose tongue, Maggie searched for a plausible evasion. "There is no connection. Your cousin is out to snare a titled heiress. I am neither titled nor an heiress."

"Which makes *us* ideally suited."

Maggie feigned innocence. "Suited for what?"

"You know precisely what I speak of. Passion, free of guilt. We will make a perfect match."

"Careful, my lord. Your arrogance is showing."

His laughter, soft and intimate, showered her with warmth. "I concede defeat. I am spoiled and arrogant. But perhaps," he added with an exaggerated leer, "all I need is the right woman to guide me back on the straight and narrow."

"You, sir, are a rogue."

"Yes, but a very nice rogue."

"There is no such animal."

He grinned with devilish amusement. "If you would allow me the opportunity, I could prove you wrong."

"Is that another veiled proposition?" Maggie queried, warming to the light banter. She laughed softly at his affronted expression.

"Never, Mrs. Sanford! I intend to see you home safely, as any good rogue worth his salt would do."

Before she could utter a protest, he escorted her through the mingling crowd, and into the foyer. "Please, this is not necessary."

"Of course it is. I have a tattered reputation to mend."

After a dour-faced butler helped them into their cloaks, the marquess took firm hold of her elbow and guided her through the door. "My carriage will be here in a moment."

"This is ridiculous! I can see myself home."

"But I insist."

Maggie knew he would not be dissuaded. Lord Grey was determined to prove a point. She shot a worried look down the street, praying Dare had seen her—praying he wouldn't do anything foolish. The rented hack, always nearby, rumbled slowly toward her.

"I take it you're staying at your aunt's home during your visit."

"Yes, she offered me the use of her home while she is visiting Bath."

A black gilded carriage appeared, the Rockingham crest emblazoned across the exterior. The door was quickly opened by a coachman, who nodded in deference as they climbed aboard.

"St. Albans," Nicholas told the driver before the door snapped closed with resounding finality.

Perched on the edge of the tufted leather seat, Maggie willed her body to relax. She knew Dare would follow her to Hell and back if necessary. With any luck, Lord Grey would deposit her on the doorstep as promised, and vanish. And hopefully he would not meet Horatio Jones or his wife Mabel.

The couple had been paid well for their temporary roles as butler and housekeeper. Their only duties were to collect invitations and make the town house look lived in. They did, however, have one distinct flaw. In the evenings, they tended to enjoy a healthy dose of spirits. She prayed they had already sought their bed for the night.

"Relax, Mrs. . . ." Nicholas leaned forward, his smile flashing in the dim light. "I refuse to call you Mrs. Sanford another moment."

"Then perhaps you should say nothing."

He moved closer, his voice deep and hypnotic. "You ask the impossible. Since you refuse to divulge your name, I think I shall call you . . . Athena."

She laughed. "The Greek goddess? Your choice is flattering, but a bit exaggerated."

With lightning swiftness, Nicholas moved to her side, his arm draped loosely around her shoulder. "I beg to differ. Your wisdom and wit are intoxicating, and as for your warfare skills, I have learned to watch your knees with a sharp eye."

"At times my temper overrules my judgment."

"I take full responsibility. The incident is forgotten," he replied.

She stiffened as his warm breath tickled the nape of her neck. He spoke in a lover's whisper. "Ever since I first saw you, I have become a man possessed."

The intoxicating words whittled away at her self-control. Like two halves of a whole, the daring alter ego she'd christened the Rose craved the exhilaration of his touch. The other half, Maggie, was terrified to let him closer.

On this night, the Rose claimed victory.

Unable—and unwilling—to let the moment pass, she turned to him.

As if sensing her capitulation, he pressed his lips to her cheek, her temple. "May I kiss you?"

Maggie smiled. "I think you already have."

Chuckling, he nipped at her neck. "I have learned my lesson."

"And if I say no?"

He paused, laving her flesh with his tongue. "I'm hoping you'll say yes."

"I think," Maggie whispered against his forehead, "I shall grant your request."

Tilting her face upward, he brushed his mouth across hers. "You've made a wise decision. I don't think I could have stopped."

Maggie shared his hunger. "I know. . . ."

The kiss, sweet and innocent, deepened. As if guided by an unseen force, her arms encircled his neck.

Seduction.

The word flitted through her mind as she melted into his embrace. He thought her a widow, free to indulge in mindless passion. With her future hanging by a single thread, she felt liberated.

Daring more, Maggie eased her tongue between his parted lips, reveling in the passion of the moment.

Staring into her eyes, he pulled back. "There is something between us that will not be denied. You feel it as well."

Regret intruded into the intimate darkness.

She was little more than a ghost, a phantom he'd named Athena. Soon Maggie would disappear, and he'd never know her true identity. Never whisper her real name in the darkness.

He leaned forward, his palm skimming the bodice of her gown. Desire, more potent than sadness, cleared her mind of residual doubt. Breathless, she waited for him to touch her, cup her aching breasts in his hands.

The carriage clattered to a halt.

Pushing his arms away, Maggie jerked backward.

"Damn!" Sliding to the opposite seat, he straightened his neckcloth. "We shall have to continue our exploration later."

"And if 'later' never arrives?" Maggie asked, her voice softened by regret.

He smiled with lazy intent. "It will."

The door opened. Maggie hurried outside, anxious to be free of his overwhelming confidence—released from her own insatiable need.

He followed, taking firm hold of her elbow as a light misting of rain began to fall. "If I didn't know better, I would say you have guests."

Maggie looked upward and gasped. Every window was ablaze with light. Her heart thudded to a stop, as did her feet.

Something was horribly wrong. . . .

Preferring to stay in the servants' quarters, Horace and Mabel rarely ventured farther than the kitchen.

No, it is too soon. . . .

Before she could voice a protest, Nicholas pushed the door open.

Chapter Four

Confusion reigned in the crowded foyer. Housemaids and groomsmen stood on one side of the room, talking amongst themselves as they watched the unfolding drama.

In the center of the melee, two aging men dressed in severe butler's attire stood toe to toe, glaring at each other.

Off in the corner, Nicholas noticed an old woman dressed in black silk, her body frail and stooped from the weight of her years. Hair as white as an angel's wing was braided into a coronet, and decorated with a multitude of drooping peacock feathers.

He soon realized she was the Duchess of Blackthorne. She watched the encounter with avid interest, a slight smile gracing her face.

He had met her many years earlier, and liked her proud spirit at once. It had been rumored she was in her dotage and retired from society. Looking into her keen, mischievous eyes, he doubted that supposition.

Becoming aware of the painful grip on his forearm, he turned to Athena. She had become an alarming shade of white, her body trembling. Her wide-eyed gaze darted from face to face, as if trying to discern friend from foe. She seemed lost. Terrified.

Before he could wonder about her strange behavior, his attention returned to the two combatants who appeared ready to come to blows.

The taller man stiffened, his tone tight with disdain. "I do not know who you are, or what you are doing in this house, but if you do not leave at once, I shall send for—"

"I work here!" the second man exclaimed in a quavering voice.

"*I* have been in service to the Blackthorne family for forty years, and I have never seen you before. You, sir, are an imposter!"

Nicholas grinned, feeling as though he'd walked into the third act of a badly written play. He stepped forward and cleared his throat. "Excuse me. . . ."

The bickering ceased.

"Perhaps we can be of assistance," he offered, tugging Athena along beside him. He approached the pivotal player of the strange production. "Duchess Blackthorne, you are as lovely as I remember."

The frail form inched forward, leaning heavily on a carved ebony cane. She gazed into Nicholas's eyes. "I know you, young man. You are a . . . Grey, are you not?"

"Yes, Nicholas Grey." Smiling, he nudged Athena forward. "And I'm sure you know your niece, Mrs. Sanford, from America."

The duchess eyed the young woman in seeming confusion. "My niece, you say?"

Athena hesitated, a worried smile quivering upon

her lips. Strange currents swirled through the room like an ocean undertow, leaving Nicholas to flounder in confusion. Then, like a candle sputtering to life, she rushed forward as if her fear had been nothing but an illusion. "My dearest aunt, forgive my inhospitable welcome." She embraced the older woman gently. "I was just so surprised to find you here. You should have sent word of your arrival."

The duchess seemed taken aback by the sudden show of affection. "Yes, well—"

"We have so much to talk about," Athena said, her words hurried. "But I'm sure you're exhausted from your long journey. Perhaps in the morning we can—"

"Oh, no. I think we will have much to discuss *tonight*." The duchess drew away and nodded toward the tall, red-faced butler. "Benning, please have some refreshments brought to the sitting room."

"Yes, Your Grace. But what should I do with this imposter?"

Athena laughed nervously. "He is not an imposter. I hired Mr. Talbot, temporarily."

With a dismissive wave, the duchess silenced the argument. "We shall settle that matter in the morning." She turned to Nicholas. "You will join us, Lord Grey."

Unwilling to see the curtain close on the unusual performance, he nodded. "I would—"

"I'm sure the marquess has other pressing engagements," Athena interrupted, her voice taut. "Thank you for escorting me home, my lord, but the hour is late. I don't wish to tire my aunt. I'm certain you understand."

Nicholas recognized a polite dismissal when he heard one. "Of course." He turned to the elderly woman and kissed her hand. "I would like to call on you, and your delightful niece, tomorrow.''

The duchess nodded. "I look forward to it. And please have your mother call on me, as well. I have not seen Eugenia in years.''

"It would be my pleasure,'' he replied before turning back to Athena. "May I speak with you a moment?''

With obvious reluctance, she followed him to the door. An array of emotions flickered across her delicate features, fear foremost. She was hiding something.

With each moment spent in her alluring presence, he discovered another layer of mystery. And sooner or later he would unveil them all—beginning with why the Duchess of Blackthorne seemed so surprised to see her niece.

"I will discover your secrets, Athena. Every last one.''

Her face drained of color. "I—I don't know what you mean.''

"Yes, you do,'' he replied in a whisper. "Until tomorrow.''

"I will be quite busy and ''

He pressed his fingers to her lips, wishing he could silence her with his mouth instead. "I will see you tomorrow afternoon. Even if I must scour the city to find you.''

Velvet eyes flashing with anger, she stepped away from reach. "You may try, but you will find me only if I wish to be found. Good night, Lord Grey.''

The door closed with a resounding crack.

Grinning, Nicholas strolled down the stone walkway to the awaiting carriage. She was definitely a handful—a mischievous, daring, beautiful handful. And she would be his.

The coachman swiftly opened the door as he approached. "Home now, my lord?"

"Not yet. I have an engagement at the Montmouths'."

As he settled into the leather seat, he was instantly reminded of their earlier, heated encounter. Athena, as he'd so aptly named her, had embraced him with gentle abandon, slowly succumbing to the irresistible attraction drawing them together.

An inherently passionate creature, she struggled to conceal that trait behind a cool facade. Yet beneath his touch—his lips—the mask shattered. Still she resisted his advances at every turn, making him all the hungrier.

His past liaisons with the fairer sex had been utterly predictable. After he assumed the title, all he'd had to do was crook his finger, and they flocked to him like lost sheep.

Nicholas smiled. Finally he had met his match. With time and persistence, he would wear down Athena's prickly resolve. He could be a very patient man.

The coach rumbled to a halt. He forced his thoughts back to the present, and quickly changed into a black silk shirt and woolen coat.

The roof panel snapped open and the driver peered inside. "No one seems to be at home, my lord. Are you sure—"

"Quite sure, Hoskins. Drive to the end of the street and wait for me there." Nicholas removed a silver flask of brandy from a concealed compartment and passed it upward. "Enjoy, my good man. It could be a very long night."

Without hesitation, he took a pistol from the compartment and slipped the weapon into his waistband.

If his assumptions proved correct, the Rose would be paying a visit to the Montmouth town house tonight.

And Nicholas would be waiting.

"Now that we are alone, why don't you tell me who you really are."

Maggie froze, gripping the dainty porcelain teapot so tightly she was astounded the handle didn't crumble in her hand. Her stomach quivered with dread as she continued to pour the steaming brew. She knew the Duchess of Blackthorne was watching, waiting for an answer. If Maggie had learned anything in the slums of London, it was to bluff if at all possible.

"It is understandable," she replied carefully, "that you don't know me, madam. This is my first visit to—"

"I am not senile, my dear, and the only family I have left are a few distant cousins in Cornwall. My younger brother did travel to America many years ago, but I have outlived all his children. So who are you?"

Staring into the older woman's curious face, Maggie knew the game was lost. The duchess's mind was as sharp as a gentleman's shaving razor.

"No, Your Grace, you are right. I am not your niece."

"Then perhaps it is time to tell me why you are intent on this amazing masquerade, and how you accomplished the feat. Without a sponsor to introduce you into society . . ."

Maggie met her probing gaze without flinching. "It was difficult, but a few impromptu meetings in Hyde Park made the task easier. I think the ton was curious. As for why, I'm afraid I cannot tell you that." Maggie gulped down her tea, prolonging the inevitable. "You needn't worry. The house is exactly as you left it, and I won't trouble you again. You may tell everyone I returned to America or,'' she finished in a whisper, ''you can call the magistrate.''

Silence thickened like a persistent London fog. Maggie tensed, ready to flee into the night if necessary.

''I don't believe this is a matter for the authorities,'' the duchess replied, her voice matter-of-fact. ''Shall we begin with your name?''

''I would rather not—''

''Any name will do. You may call me Dorothea.''

Hesitating only a moment, she answered with the truth. ''Maggie.''

Dorothea sipped her tea before speaking. ''You have obviously gone to a great deal of trouble to fool the ton. Are you hoping to snare a titled husband?''

If the situation had not been so precarious, Maggie would have laughed. ''No, I will never marry.''

''Never is a very long time, and I should know. I would hazard to say,'' Dorothea continued in a confidential tone, ''that Lord Grey is most interested.''

Nervous tension brought Maggie to her feet. She circled the room, examining the abundant bric-a-brac in the lavish surroundings.

''He is interested. But not in marriage.''

''Still a bit of a rakehell, is he?''

The urge to defend Nicholas spilled forth in a rush. ''Oh, no, he has been most kind. A gentleman.'' *Up to a point.*

Dorothea would not be dissuaded. ''Men are led by their loins. That is a fact.''

Maggie laughed. ''I didn't say he was a *perfect* gentleman.''

''My dear, the best ones never are.''

Feeling at ease for the first time, Maggie returned

to the velvet divan. It seemed perfectly normal to be in an elegant sitting room, sharing tea and sweetcakes. But like every facet of her life, it was nothing but an elaborate facade.

She was a fake. Yet the frail woman seated before her didn't care in the slightest.

"I have to go," Maggie said quietly. "I will bring trouble to your door if I do not."

"I can help you. Although the ton sees me as an aging eccentric, I am not without influence."

"I am involved in a . . . dangerous situation."

Dorothea's voice dropped to a whisper as she leaned forward, her eyes glittering with excitement. "Are you a spy?"

"Not precisely," Maggie murmured.

Pounding her cane in agitation, Dorothea's tone grew matronly. "Listen to me, young woman. You remind me of myself when I was your age. Young, daring, impetuous . . ." Her gentle hazel eyes clouded with memories for a brief moment, then cleared with determination. "Whether you wish it or not, I will help you!"

Fear, deep and endless, coiled in Maggie's heart. She couldn't allow this innocent woman to be drawn further into the web of deceit she had carefully spun. "I cannot—"

"Does Lord Grey know he is being duped?"

"No, he believes I am your niece." *At least for the moment.*

Dorothea rose, her gnarled hands gripping the cane for support. "He is not a man to be trifled with, as I am sure you are aware."

The subtle warning raised gooseflesh across Maggie's skin. "It doesn't matter. I will be traveling to America soon."

"Pray, don't tell me you are so foolish," Dorothea

said, her eyes twinkling in amusement. "If the Marquess of Rockingham wants you, as I believe he does, an ocean will not stop him."

Like a scorching desert sun, anger burned away her chills. Maggie stood and stiffened her spine. "Then it is time for Lord Grey to learn he cannot have everything he wants!"

Rusty laughter shattered the quiet. "If anyone can teach him that lesson, my girl, I would wager my coin on you."

Before Maggie could respond to that show of faith, the door swung violently open.

Dare burst inside, followed by an irate Benning. "Your Grace, this—this young man—"

"Maggie, are you all right?" Dare asked, his steely gaze sweeping the room.

"Yes, I'm fine. Why don't you wait for me in the carriage?"

Benning stepped forward. "Madam, I—"

"Leave us," Dorothea said quietly.

Years of ingrained service came to the forefront. Benning nodded and retreated, sweeping the door closed.

Standing as still as stone, Dare remained in the center of the room. To Dorothea, Maggie knew he appeared to be in complete control, but she knew better. She touched his arm and felt the faint trembling of his limbs.

He was afraid. Afraid of the elegant trappings, and the power wielded by those who lived in such opulence.

Maggie tugged at his frayed coatsleeve. "Dare, everything is fine."

His quicksilver eyes found hers. "I waited outside, but then I thought somethin' might 'ave 'appened. . . ."

"Maggie, aren't you going to introduce your friend?" Dorothea asked quietly.

"Yes, of course. Your Grace, this is Dare. Dare, this is the Duchess of Blackthorne."

He stepped back as Dorothea approached. "Don't worry, young man. I won't bite."

Ignoring her, he turned to Maggie. "It's gettin' late. Thomas will be worried."

"And who would Thomas be?" Dorothea asked, directing the question to Maggie.

Floundering for an understandable answer, she opened her mouth, only to be interrupted by Dare's harsh voice.

" 'E's family."

Maggie winced as his hostility seemed to grow with each passing minute.

Dorothea seemed oblivious. "It is quite late. Why don't you collect Thomas and return. There is more than enough room—"

"We won't stay in this 'ouse," Dare ground out with barely concealed contempt.

Understanding his deep-seated fears was one thing, but Maggie wouldn't allow him to hurt Dorothea. "Dare, apologize to the duchess at once." Although Maggie spoke quietly, the thread of steel in her voice captured his attention.

"But Maggie—"

"Dorothea has been nothing but kind and gracious. And she knows I am not her niece."

This news shattered his tenuous composure. "Bloody 'ell!" He backed away, bumping into the edge of the serving cart. Teacups and saucers clinked and skittered across the smooth wood of the cart.

"Fear not, young man. I intend no harm. In fact," Dorothea continued in hushed excitement, "I have not felt so young in a very long time."

65

As if jolted awake during a nightmare, his breathing calmed, his gaze locking with Dorothea's. "I'm . . . sorry about bargin' into your 'ouse."

"It's quite all right. I admire your desire to protect your friend."

Maggie knew how much the grudging apology cost him. She smiled into his stoic face, offering her gratitude.

She turned to Dorothea, knowing this would be a farewell. "I thank you for—"

"For not summoning the magistrate?"

"No. For being so kind to us."

Dorothea sighed. "I cannot fathom what kind of trouble you are in, my dear, but if you ever need me, please send word at once." A playful smile parted her lips. "And as for my *niece,* I hope to see her at the next rout."

Her meaning was clear. Maggie's identity would remain secure. For now. "Promise me, Dorothea. If word should come out that I am an imposter, you must play the role of an outraged victim. For your own safety."

Dorothea lifted her rounded shoulders a fraction. "I do not desert my friends." Then with surprising strength, she tugged the bellpull.

Benning appeared, his worried expression relaxing when he realized all was well. "Yes, Your Grace?"

"Show my niece and her . . . coachman out."

He blinked in confusion as his gaze settled on Maggie. "Your niece, madam? But you have no—"

"Of course I do, Benning." Dorothea moved forward, the peacock feathers in her hair dancing back and forth with each step. "Has the trip addled your wits?"

"Most certainly not!" Though he said nothing

more, his expression remained skeptical as he escorted Dare into the foyer.

Maggie paused, unable to conceal her naked longing. A strange bond had been formed this night, and she felt the sting of loss.

Unable to say more, she rushed through the door, colliding with *her* butler, Mr. Talbot.

"Miss, I think it's time me and the wife went home. The young man paid us already, but I wanted to thank—"

"There's no need. I should be thanking you."

He nodded and slapped a weathered hat on his balding head. "Well then, good luck, miss."

Luck. Maggie wanted to laugh. Luck had never been particularly kind to her, or her family. And she had the unnerving sensation her good fortune would soon run out.

Though Dorothea had promised to keep Maggie's secret safe, gossip flourished like wild ivy among the servants. Soon they would all begin to wonder about the mysterious niece who appeared from nowhere.

Maggie couldn't waste time dwelling on possible failure. Too much time and effort had been invested to cry defeat.

She shivered as a plan coalesced in her mind. Tonight the White Rose would strike twice. And by morning, Nicholas Grey would forget about his promised visit to the Blackthorne home.

He was about to become the latest victim of the Rose.

Chapter Five

Fear pumped through Maggie's veins, turning her flesh to ice. Her scheme had gone horribly awry.

Now she was trapped—in the Marquess of Rockingham's bedchamber.

She crouched inside the massive oak wardrobe, unable to move a single muscle in her cramped position. Her black woolen shirt clung to her damp skin, chafing and itching until she thought she'd go mad.

Nicholas Grey had not lied. He was determined to catch the thief.

At the Montmouth town house, Maggie had spotted Grey crouched behind a hedge. She'd followed him as he crept around the building, obviously waiting for the Rose. She grinned at the irony of the situation. The prey he searched for was now hidden right beneath his nose.

She had been certain pure stubbornness would keep him at the town house for most of the night. Instead, he'd returned home earlier than planned. The realization of how close she'd come to disaster formed a hard lump in her parched throat.

Summoning her courage, she peeked through the doors of the wardrobe. He strolled to the window, his brows furrowed in apparent concentration. The paisley silk robe, trimmed with black velvet, accentuated his broad shoulders. Even dressed casually, he exuded raw power and authority. Nicholas Grey would be a worthy adversary for the Rose. But he would never win.

Moonlight illuminated his face. Maggie stared in rapt fascination. Their previous encounters, fraught with tension and simmering emotions, had left no opportunity to study his bold beauty. His nose was too prominent to be called classical, but the full, finely carved lips softened the effect. A flash of heat sizzled along her nerves as she recalled the magical power of those lips.

Maggie's thoughts scattered as the silk robe slid from his shoulders and whispered to the floor. Her eyes widened. She could not look away, nor did she want to.

He was magnificent.

Firelight licked the firm muscles of his chest and taut stomach. A sprinkling of dark, curly hair formed a tantalizing path downward, meeting with his male flesh. Her cheeks caught fire, but the sight was too irresistible to ignore.

As he walked toward the bed, Maggie reveled in the suppleness of his corded thighs and high, tight buttocks. She'd seen drawings of ancient Greek statues in her father's extensive library. None compared to the flesh-and-blood man standing before her.

A strange heaviness settled low in her stomach, while her breasts tingled with excitement. She could imagine his hands touching her, stroking. . . .

She closed her eyes against the forbidden sensations. There was no room in her life for wishful fancy. The simple act of survival consumed her days. The Rose consumed her nights. To continue even the most innocent of liaisons was a call to disaster. Never again would she place her trust in a man. She'd learned her lessons well.

Opening her eyes, she realized Nicholas had finally sought his bed. She eased the wardrobe door open.

Minutes had become hours as she'd hidden between the folds of his fine woolen coats. Her thighs screamed in protest as she stretched her legs to the floor. Maggie waited for the tingling to pass as she watched the form sprawled across the high platform bed. The satin coverlet rose and fell in deep, constant rhythm.

She edged toward the bureau, anxious to take a bauble and make her escape. She still had to pay a visit to the Montmouths' before dawn.

A diamond cuff link winked in the amber light. With regret, she swept it and its mate into the cloth pouch at her waist.

She stifled a small smile. Nicholas wanted "Athena." He also wanted the Rose. God help her if he ever discovered they were the same person.

She concentrated on the task at hand. Once the cuff links were discovered in Turner's home, Nicholas would have the proof he needed. His cousin would be arrested, and the mysterious thefts would cease.

Maggie smiled. Although Nicholas didn't realize it, they were allies, both anxious to see Viscount Turner fall from grace.

As silent as the air surrounding her, she crept to the bed and slipped the calling card from her shirt. A lock of dark hair caressed his temple and, without thinking, she swept it back with one finger. Soft as silken threads; she could not resist one more touch. She stroked the glossy strands. Once. Twice.

Her breath lodged in her throat when a small smile curled his lips. He appeared no older than a boy, his face relaxed and utterly handsome.

Fatigue weighed down her limbs. She hated using him—hated stealing from him.

Tell him . . . tell him about Turner's evil. Nicholas can protect you and the boys.

Impossible.

If Edward Turner discovered she was alive . . . Maggie shuddered at the thought.

Regardless of her past, she was now the Rose. A wanted criminal. Even the Marquess of Rockingham could not protect her if she were captured.

With bitter regret, Maggie kissed the fragile petals and placed the flower on the pillow.

Forgive me.

Roses.

The scent enveloped him, tantalizing his senses. Nicholas inhaled deeply as he swept the lingering remnants of sleep from his mind. He stretched.

The dark-haired beauty still controlled his dreams. All through the night, she had teased him into unbearable hunger. Gliding forward as if to touch him, then retreating. And always with that wistful, shy smile upon her lips. Every time he'd reached out, aching for her satin skin, she would vanish like swirls of smoke.

Gritting his teeth until his jaw ached, Nicholas willed himself to relax. The urge to assuage his stubborn flesh nearly overwhelmed his control. He hadn't had to resort to that remedy since being a stripling lad.

Rolling to his side, he opened his eyes to slits against the glaring morning sun.

He blinked in surprise.

A flower lay on the other pillow next to his head.

Like a man mesmerized by the glowing eyes of a cobra, he held his breath in horrified amazement.

The wilted rose seemed to mock his stunned reaction.

Nicholas leaned over and gingerly picked up the flower. Several limp petals fluttered down to rest on the pillow.

It cannot be. . . .

Leaping to his feet, he slipped on a robe and yanked the bell-pull with vicious force.

He paced the room, the thornless stem clenched in his fist as he tried to convince himself it was a prank, a mistake. But he knew what the damned flower meant.

Abbot appeared in the doorway, his arms laden with plush, snow white towels. "Good morning, my lord. I trust you slept well."

Behind him, two heavily muscled footmen maneuvered buckets of steaming water inside. With practiced ease, they filled the massive porcelain bathtub tucked away in the corner of the room.

Once they were gone, Nicholas closed the door and confronted his butler with a scowl. "What is this?" he asked, holding the hated object at arm's length.

Lifting one brow, Abbot perused the object. "That, my lord, appears to be a rose. A rather sad specimen, to be sure. Would you like a vase?"

Though not the slightest hint of a smile graced the elderly man's face, Nicholas knew from experience that Abbot was enjoying the exchange.

"No, I do not want a vase. I want to know how this flower came to be in my bed."

Abbot sobered instantly. "My lord, you do not believe . . ."

Nicholas marched to the dark mahogany bureau. The truth would be denied no longer. "My diamond studs are missing."

Rage, as cold and black as a winter's night, coiled through his insides. The cuff links had been a birthday present from his brother, Terrence. The last gift Nicholas had received from him.

"Are you quite certain?" Abbot asked softly as he carefully lowered his tall, thin body to one knee and searched the carpet. "Perhaps they rolled over the edge and—"

"No, they're gone." Nicholas grasped the butler's elbow, helping him to his feet.

"I take it this is the work of the White Rose."

Nicholas nodded, his thoughts distracted by anger. While he'd dreamed of that elusive beauty, Athena, the thief had entered his home and stolen one of his most precious possessions.

The game had risen to a new, more dangerous level.

"Abbot, I want you to say nothing of this to my mother. Unless . . ." Nicholas's heart plummeted to his stomach.

As always, Abbot read his mind with uncanny precision. "Madam awoke an hour ago. She received no rose."

"So it would appear I was the intended victim."

"Yes, my lord. The question is why."

"That is what I intend to find out," Nicholas growled.

"Would you like to send word to Mr. Hennessy?"

"He is out of the city attending to other matters. I will retrieve my property, and the Rose will wish he had never chosen me as a target."

Abbot turned away, his expression clearly troubled.

"This thief is obviously quite daring. And, need I say, dangerous."

"Don't worry, Abbot. I will be careful."

"And if you should need assistance . . ."

"You shall be my first choice."

Athena's delicate features darted into Nicholas's mind. Their meeting would have to wait.

Another reason to curse the Rose to hell.

"Abbot, I had promised to call on the Duchess of Blackthorne this afternoon. Please send my regrets."

"Of course, my lord."

As the door closed, Nicholas glanced down at the flower still clutched in his hand.

Nothing remained but a fistful of crushed petals.

Edward Turner stared into the dancing flames, and cursed the Rose.

The reputation he'd nurtured and protected like a beloved child was being stolen bit by bit. Each day his invitations dwindled. Each outing in Hyde Park brought one more snub or whispered innuendo of guilt.

Hotter than the red-orange fire in the hearth, rage inflamed him. "I will find you. And then I will cut out your heart with a butter knife—"

"*If* you can find him."

The high-pitched, melodious voice subdued the violent thought.

Leaning back in the threadbare wing-back chair, Edward scowled at the interruption. "I am still lord and master in this house. As such, if I desire your company, I shall ring."

Seemingly unperturbed by the cold welcome, Drager placed a tea tray on the table.

Edward watched his butler, valet, and trusted confidant pour the steaming brew into one chipped porcelain cup. He was a man of towering six-foot-five height, and as thin as a will-o'-the-wisp. Truth be told, he resembled a walking cadaver, his skin and flowing mane of hair as white as bleached bones.

Although Drager's appearance was startling to most, the servant was loyal to a fault. If asked to walk naked through fire, Drager would do as commanded with calm acceptance.

Edward's thin lips twitched in amusement. Knowing he could control life—or death—always made him feel like a god. Omnipotent. No one could hurt him . . . except the Rose.

Gripping the arms of the chair, he cursed the thief once again. "Drager, have we had any callers?"

"One. You've been invited to Lord Wellingham's ball. The event is tomorrow night. It would seem he waited until the last possible moment to issue the invitation."

"He is probably hoping I have already made plans for the evening."

Terror gripped Edward's fluttering heart. Lord Harry Wellingham owed him a sizable sum from the gaming tables. Thus, the only reason the earl had invited him was fear Edward would demand payment in full. Numerous others had somehow managed to pay their markers, leaving them free of potential blackmail. He had to find the true thief, before it was too late to mend his tattered reputation.

"Whoever the Rose is," Edward mused aloud, "he obviously has a personal score to settle with me."

" 'Twould appear so," Drager said. "That being the case, the culprit could be anyone in the ton."

"I doubt that. There are very few who have the temerity to attempt such a plot."

"How will you discover the correct one?"

Edward rose and walked to his desk. "I have compiled a list of those who would have the most reason to see me ruined."

Taking the paper, Drager perused the lengthy roster of names, his snow white brows lifting in surprise. "The Marquess of Rockingham . . . and his mother?"

Edward nodded. "She has always hated me. I would have taken care of her long ago, if not for Grey."

"Perhaps they are working together."

"I have considered the notion. My cousin is still frothing at the bit about Julia."

As if fearing a blow, Drager stepped back. "That was seven years ago."

Smiling coldly, Edward returned to his chair. "You should have watched her more carefully, my friend."

"Y—yes, my lord."

"At any rate, I don't believe Grey is orchestrating this plot. If my cousin wanted revenge, he would simply call me out and be done with it."

Drager's expression remained puzzled. "Then why are their names on this list?"

"Merely a precaution. The mastermind of this scheme is someone in the peerage. My dear aunt may know something that could be of use."

"Shall we watch her house then?"

"That would be a prudent first step. Find out who pays calls—who her acquaintances are. Question the staff. They are a closemouthed lot, but should you offer a monetary inducement . . ."

"And if that doesn't work?"

"Choose another approach," Edward replied with a dismissive wave. "I'm sure they have families. Young children . . ."

As small and black as his soul, Drager's dark eyes lit with anticipation. "I'll see to it myself."

"Don't be ridiculous. Your features and size are much too recognizable. Find some riffraff at the docks. If it should come to that, be certain they meet an untimely end. There must be no connection to me.''

"As you wish." Drager started for the door.

"One moment, I have another task. I want Grey followed as well. He is particularly chummy with Mr. Hennessy. They could unwittingly provide the information I need."

"I will see to it at once."

"And Drager, I would like some companionship this evening before I attend the ball. See to it."

Drager's lips curled into a knowing smile. "The usual, my lord?"

"No. Perhaps a blonde tonight."

Nodding, the manservant disappeared as silently as he'd entered.

Lust, hot and sweet, coarsed through Edward's veins. It had been too long. . . .

As if summoned by a vengeful ghost, *her* delicate face drifted into his thoughts. He'd had such glorious plans for his future bride.

Regret, an almost foreign emotion, crept into his heart. Crushing her will had been his goal in sending her to the asylum. Instead, she'd accidentally managed to end her own life.

Edward lifted his cup of tea in mocking salute. She was one of a select few who had managed to escape.

His past accomplishments dimmed as expectation of the coming evening filled him with keen pleasure. He would have a warm, malleable body in his bed. Later, with any measure of luck, he would persuade Lady Dewitt to stroll with him in the garden. And should her doting father discover them in an intimate embrace . . .

With a languid hand, Edward reached down and massaged the growing bulge in his tailored trousers.

Yes, it had definitely been too long.

Chapter Six

Dare fingered the blade of his dagger. "Maggie, I've got a bad feelin' about this one."

"Don't worry," she said for what seemed the hundredth time. His anxiety was becoming contagious.

"I don't like it. Things are too quiet."

"Lady Dewitt and her parents are still at the ball." *And still being charmed by that devil Turner.*

Maggie had made a brief appearance, stunned to find him in attendance. She'd firmly believed his name would have been stricken from every hostess's guest list. Once again, she had underestimated his cunning.

Young and delicate, Lady Dewitt seemed completely infatuated with the older man. Maggie had made the same mistake years before. Edward could be as gentle and caring as a devoted father or friend. Until his dark side slithered to the surface. Then he showed no mercy.

Just as she would do. No mercy.

As for Nicholas, he'd been in intimate conversation with a dark-haired beauty. The sight had cut Maggie to the quick. Her jealousy transformed to bitter sadness. He deserved a real woman, not a ghost. And that was all Maggie had become. A ghost, masquerading among the living.

Dragging her thoughts to the present, she turned to Dare. "Did you remember the gold watch?"

He nodded, digging into the pocket of his frayed coat. "The old man didn't even feel me pinch it from 'is waistcoat."

"You were lucky, nothing more."

Dare smiled. "I bet 'e was fair screamin' when 'e found it gone." He slipped the watch into her palm as the moon peeked across the night sky.

Releasing the tiny latch, she stared at the detailed engraving opposite the clock face. Her stomach churned. A dragon stared back, two small rubies set into the beast's eyes. It was a distinctive design, and one that would put Edward Turner in prison.

"You never did say why you wanted that particular trinket," Dare said as he scanned the dark exterior of the town house. "And I don't understand why you wanted me to pinch it. You're better at pickin' pockets than anyone I know."

Because I cannot bear to be within two feet of Edward Turner, she thought, ashamed of her cowardice.

Sensing his unease, Maggie looked at her closest friend. "I have unfinished business with the gentleman."

His shadowed eyes found hers. "You're settin' 'im up. You want everyone to think 'e's the Rose."

She offered no rebuttal. Dare had finally stumbled upon the truth. The burden of secrets seemed heavier than ever, but she could not tell him everything. She had sworn an oath to avenge herself . . . and Dare.

"My business is personal," Maggie whispered, praying he would let the subject die.

His voice became a feral growl. "Did that man 'urt you? If 'e did, I'll—"

"Someday I will explain, but now I have work to do."

He opened his mouth to protest, until she pressed her palm to his lips. "I want you to go home now. If something happens, take Thomas and leave England."

Dare jerked away. "We are leavin' this bloody country together. So just be sure you pull this off."

Maggie grinned at his fit of temper. "Has the Rose ever failed you?"

"Not yet, but I got a queer feelin'. . . . I should go in—"

"Absolutely not."

"What if you need 'elp?"

"Someone has to stay with Thomas."

Grudgingly, Dare nodded. Maggie breathed a sigh of relief. She hadn't told him about her visit to Nicholas Grey's home. Dare would become even more protective. And time was running out.

"Remember, if anything happens, you must take Thomas and run."

"Maggie, I can't—"

"Promise me."

Running a hand through his heavy, tangled hair, he spoke wearily. "Damn, but you're a stubborn wench. I swear I'll take care of Thomas."

"And?"

"We'll leave England. All three of us."

"And you have the nerve to call me stubborn?"

He ignored her sarcasm. "Be careful. If it feels bad, just get out."

Flashing a confident smile, Maggie ducked around the hedgerow at the side of the house. She paused, watching as Dare melted into the shadows. He was safe.

She reached the servants' entrance and tugged the black woolen hood, improvised into a mask, over her face. Usually she didn't bother to conceal her features, but tonight felt different. Dangerous.

Removing the lock picks from her pocket, she brushed against the door. It breezed open with a gentle creak.

Cold perspiration beaded her brow, but she crushed the nervous impulse to flee. The final nail had to be driven into Turner's coffin. Tonight.

When the watch was discovered, along with the rose, the ton would not be so forgiving. From there, they would discover the small cache of jewels, including Nicholas's cuff links, hidden in the viscount's home. Jewels she would secrete away in his residence later tonight.

One more time, and the nightmare will finally end.

This would be the last visitation of the Rose, and the legend would fade into oblivion.

Crouching low to the ground, she slipped inside.

The tinkling chimes of a distant clock and the rapid thump of her own heart were the only sounds to be heard.

She crept upstairs.

As a precaution, she slid a knife from the leather sheath at her waist. The weapon, a show of force she could never use, offered a dose of courage she desperately needed.

With meticulous patience, she located the bedchamber and eased the door open. The heavy velvet drapes were closed, allowing only a sliver of dim light to penetrate the hushed darkness.

Like a formless shadow, Maggie moved toward the bureau and the ornate gilded jewel box. The delicate lock on the small doors gave way with little resistance.

She opened the velvet-lined drawers one by one. *It isn't possible. . . .*

Maggie had attended a soiree two days before and the box had been filled to brimming with jewels.

Now they were empty. All empty.

The hair at the nape of her neck rose.

Sensing a sudden movement behind her, she spun around. Her hand struck a solid object.

A deep male voice bellowed in pain. Only then did she realize she still clutched the dagger. Moonlight illuminated the razor-sharp blade, and the unmistakable glint of blood.

Panic shot through her veins. She dropped the weapon and raced toward the door. A heavy, muscular arm coiled around her neck. She clawed and kicked, unable to pierce his iron hold. The arm tightened. Dots of bright light danced before her eyes.

''Hold still, damn you!''

The harsh whisper barely penetrated her terror. Defeat sapped her last ounce of strength. She lowered her arms.

''That's better,'' the man said against her ear. He released his hold on her neck, only to grab her wrist with ruthless intent, twisting it behind her.

Biting her lip, Maggie refused to show him her fear, or her pain.

''Now, shall we uncover the truth?'' He steered her toward the window and yanked the drapes aside. Faint silvery light cut a narrow path through the darkness.

Maggie blinked and turned away, her stomach churning. She was helpless. Just as she had been two years ago when Turner had consigned her to hell.

"You're pathetically small for a thief with such a legendary reputation."

That voice . . .

Her blood ran cold, then heated to a simmering boil.

Nicholas Grey had captured the Rose.

"I believe it's time for an unmasking," he whispered.

With painstaking slowness, he pulled the hood from her head. He grabbed her chin, jerking her face toward what light there was.

A gasp of disbelief echoed through the darkness. "My God, you're nothing but a child! You haven't even sprouted your first whisker."

Her legs became as limp as willow branches. The boyish disguise of a ragged coat and torn breeches had fooled him in this light. And the dark soot she'd smudged on her cheeks continued the deception. At least for the moment.

"Nothing to say . . . Rose?"

Deepening her voice, and using the thickest Cockney accent she could muster, Maggie feigned astonishment. "You think I'm the bleedin' Rose? You've got it all wrong, guv'nor. I'm a simple dubber, and I—"

"Pardon my ignorance, but what is a 'dubber' precisely?"

"Why, 'tis a lowly lock picker. Nothin' of importance."

"So," Nicholas said softly, "you decided to ply your trade. Here. Tonight."

"That be the 'onest truth. I thought to lift a few pieces of silver, a trinket 'ere and there. Then I'd be on m' way."

After a deep, nervous breath, she continued, forcing

sincerity into her quavering voice. "I've learned m' lesson, I 'ave. I'll get meself an 'onest job." She sniffled, wishing she could produce a tear to further the deception. "If you let me go, I'll turn over a new leaf. Make a go o' things, I will."

He released the bruising hold on her chin. "You spin an interesting tale, boy. And I can almost believe you. . . ."

He smiled. Maggie relaxed.

". . . except for the fact that you smell like a freshly cut rose. Now why would a simple dubber carry such a flower on his person?"

In her fear and bone-numbing shock, she had forgotten the rose lying snugly against her bound breasts.

His casual smile vanished. He jerked her arm, arching her back like a bowstring. "Now, where would a clever lad like you hide your calling card?"

"Bugger off," she said in a hiss, almost hating him at that moment.

He ignored the comment and reached inside her woolen shirt.

Although rough and impersonal, his touch sent a flash of searing heat through the core of her being. His scent, pure male, unadorned by cologne, teased her nostrils. She cursed her weakness and closed her eyes, willing her body to remain still.

Nicholas tugged the rose free. "Now, boy, do you have any other far-fetched tales?"

She said nothing. Silence would be her next defense. The only weapon she still called her own.

"What's this? No more declarations of innocence?" His mocking laughter lacerated her already frayed nerves. "You, my young felon, have a choice to make. You may tell *me* who you are working for, or you can tell the magistrate."

Maggie bit the side of her cheek to keep from grinning. The arrogant marquess would never believe the "boy" he had caught was intelligent enough to plot the robberies. And now was not the time to enlighten him.

"Shall I choose your fate for you?" Nicholas asked, giving her a firm shake.

Laughter bubbled in her throat. Her fate was already sealed. Hanging, rotting in Newgate, or, if she were particularly fortunate, deportation.

"Speak, damn it! I don't have time——" The sudden clatter of wheels and the steady clip-clop of horses's hooves stifled the remainder of his demands.

Following his intent gaze, she watched the carriage rumble to a stop. The lord and ladies of the house had returned.

"Bloody hell," he murmured, dragging her away from the window. "We must leave. And very quietly."

His predicament became clear to Maggie. "It looks like I'm not the only one trespassin' tonight."

He spun her around, his expression concealed by darkness. "You are coming with me. Now."

Indecision held her immobile. Her disguise, helped by the muted light, had fooled him. But for how long? She trembled at the thought of his anger. If he discovered the woman he'd kissed was the Rose, she was sure he would make certain she paid dearly for her ruse.

As if he'd sensed her fear, his voice softened. "Don't go weak-kneed now."

His sudden gentleness calmed her tattered nerves, and doubled her guilt. "All right, Yer Lordship. Lead the way."

Her ready capitulation seemed to surprise him. "One sound, one misstep, and I will tie you to the nearest stick of furniture and wash my hands of you."

She shrugged.

"I would ask for your word, but that may be too much to ask of a common criminal."

She smiled inwardly. Nicholas would soon discover the Rose was no common thief. The game was not over. It was just beginning.

Rushing to the door, she pressed her ear to the dark wood, then cracked it open. "No one's about."

Muted voices drifted upward from the foyer.

"We'll 'ave to go down the servants' stairs," she whispered.

"Lead the way, boy. I wouldn't want a dagger shoved in my back."

The knife! In all the confusion, she'd forgotten her inadvertent attack. "Did—did I 'urt you?"

"We will discuss my health later," he replied, pushing her into the hall.

With cautious, slow steps, they traveled down the stairs. The kitchen and pantry were deserted, and they wasted no time.

Together they dashed through the door and into the waiting night. The cool breeze washed over her heated flesh, penetrating her shabby clothes like icy needles.

Nicholas stood a few feet away, his triumphant smile revealing straight, white teeth. Like an ebony banner, his hair whipped across his face. Her heart fluttered in rapt fascination. *So handsome* . . .

And there in lay the trap. She'd been fooled by charming words and noble faces before. Never again.

"What the devil are you staring at?" he asked, his brows drawn in a suspicious line.

There was no time to think or plan. She spun around and raced toward the hedge. Sensing Nicholas at her heels, she made her legs churn faster.

A hand clamped over her shoulder with brutal strength.

Twirled around like a rag doll, she felt his hands clench her forearms in a viselike grip. She kicked at his shins and clawed at the arms holding her. He remained as immovable as stone.

"Hold still, you bloody fool!"

She ignored the harsh command. Aiming for his weakest point, Maggie jerked her knee upward. She missed, striking the solid muscle of his thigh.

With a grunt, he tossed her to the ground. Before she could leap to her feet, a pistol appeared, aimed squarely at her head.

"Stand up."

Stunned by the violence of his actions, Maggie stood on wobbly legs.

Nicholas gave a shrill, curt whistle, and the Rockingham carriage rumbled toward them. "Listen well, boy. I am tired and my arm hurts. We are going to climb into that carriage with no further displays of stupidity."

His familiar arrogance fired her temper. "And if I don't? Will you put a 'ole in me 'ead?"

"Don't tempt me."

Fear blossomed into full-blown anger. "So, go on! You'd be famous, you would. The great Marquess of Rockingham captured the Rose. You'll be a bloody 'ero."

His cerulean eyes glittered with a frightening light. "I see we have much to discuss. Beginning with how a grubby street urchin—and a thief—would know who I am."

Her heart beat a sickening rhythm in her chest. She cursed her loose tongue, and Nicholas's intelligence. Given enough time, he would uncover all her secrets—her deceptions. She could not allow that to happen.

Filling her lungs with cool air, she opened her mouth, prepared to shout her presence to all of London, prepared to take the consequences. She managed one shaky scream as his fist flew toward her face.

The world slipped into comforting darkness.

Chapter Seven

The infamous Rose was little more than a child.

Even now, Nicholas found the discovery unnerving. The mastermind behind the thefts had chosen his accomplice well. If a tattered boy from the streets was captured, the magistrate, even the ton, would be hard-pressed to believe the tale.

Staring at the dirt-streaked face, he waited for the boy to awaken. Already the slender line of his jaw had begun to darken. Nicholas regretted the blow, although he'd had no choice. His search for the Rose had to remain a private matter until he discovered the truth.

The lad had been prepared to shout at the top of his lungs. Why he'd apparently chosen to go to jail, rather than speak to Nicholas, was a mystery begging to be unraveled.

As the coach rumbled down the quiet streets, amber

rays of sunlight spilled inside and illuminated the sprawled figure.

Nicholas's intense gaze drifted to the smudged face. Fragile features belied the boy's gender. Not even the smudges of dirt and soot could hide the pale luminescence of his complexion. Blond hair, streaked with muddy brown, grazed his bony shoulders. He needed a long, hot bath, with an abundance of strong soap.

The little urchin was far too pretty for his own good. With the passage of time, his face would assuredly fill out, and a sprouting of whiskers would save his fragile neck. How he'd managed to survive was readily apparent. What he lacked in physical strength, he more than made up for with sheer bluster and bravado. For that reason alone, Nicholas admired him.

The lad's thick, dusky lashes quivered, then rose. His eyes scanned the interior of the coach with obvious confusion.

Nicholas smiled to himself, anticipating the moment the boy would recall what had occurred. And where he was.

His gaze finally found Nicholas. "Bloody 'ell."

"And a good morning to you," Nicholas said. "How's your jaw?"

Silence greeted the question.

"Come now, surely you can do better than playing the mute. Why don't we begin with your name?"

Lifting his chin to an imperious angle, the boy turned away. Then, like a ball fired from a cannon, he lunged for the door handle.

He was halfway through the opening before Nicholas grabbed his ragged coat collar and yanked him back inside. "I'm beginning to think you need a sound thrashing!" Cradling his throbbing arm, Nicholas leaned forward, his patience at an end. "Now, either you sit still, or I will truss you like a Christmas goose. Do you understand?"

The boy squirmed on the seat as he nodded with obvious reluctance.

"Now, I suggest you find your tongue and give me your name," Nicholas demanded.

This time the boy flashed a crooked grin. "Just call me Dubber."

"That is your occupation, not your name."

"Maybe, but it'll do fer now."

Nicholas accepted the defeat. At least the boy was finally talking. "Well, Dubber, now that the introductions are complete, perhaps you could explain this." He slipped the gold watch from his pocket and dangled it in the air.

The boy's eyes widened as he reached for the pouch at his waist—the pouch Nicholas now held in his other hand. "Looking for this?"

"How did *that* get in me bag?"

Nicholas tried not to smile at the pathetic charade, but lost the battle. "Come now, you can do better than that."

Dubber slapped a hand over his heart in a parody of indignation. "You don't believe me?"

"Not in the least." With supreme effort, Nicholas hardened his expression. "This is my cousin's watch. He is never without it. I want to know how it came to be in your possession."

A myriad of emotions flitted across the young face: fear, confusion, and what Nicholas discerned as cunning deliberation.

"I want the truth. Where did you get the watch? And how do you know who I am?"

Brushing a lock of limp brown hair from his forehead, Dubber grinned. "I make it my business to know."

Nicholas ignored the youthful arrogance. "Who tells you which houses to rob?"

"Who would you *like* it to be?"

The strangely intuitive response warned Nicholas to be wary. "I would be willing to help you, *if* you give me the name of the man who hired you."

"I work alone, Yer Lordship. Always 'ave."

The boy's seemingly endless supply of cockiness wore on Nicholas's patience. "Don't play me for a fool! Someone in the ton is feeding you information. You know exactly who to rob, and when."

"I'm not sayin' nothin' more." Dubber turned away, staring out the window.

Exhausted, hungry, and with the slash in his forearm burning like a hot poker pressed to his skin, Nicholas was finished playing the game.

"So," he remarked softly, "you think to use silence as a shield. Well, I believe I can give you all the quiet you need. Perhaps a day of complete solitude will jar your memory."

The carriage slowed to a stop, and Nicholas rapped against the roof panel.

The coachman's confused face appeared. "Yes, my lord?"

"Take us around back. I don't want our *guest* to be seen." Especially by his inquisitive mother. If she discovered he'd been hunting down the Rose, there would be no placating her temper.

"You should be quite familiar with my home, and my bedchamber," Nicholas remarked, noticing a tide of pink wash over the boy's cheeks. Perhaps the lad was not without a conscience after all.

Nicholas reached into the woolen pouch and removed his cuff links. "If I had not retrieved my property, your trouble would have increased tenfold.'' The door swung open, but Nicholas held the boy back. ''Tell me what I need to know. I can protect you.''

An expression of almost utter despair clouded Dubber's brown eyes. ''But then, who would protect you?''

''Who would I need protection from?''

Dubber added nothing, his face set in stubborn lines.

Grudging admiration pinched Nicholas's heart, but he remained firm. ''Very well. Perhaps by tomorrow you will feel like speaking the truth.'' He climbed down and grabbed the gangly lad by the arm. ''Time to see your new home, Dubber. How long you stay depends on your cooperation.''

With that prophetic statement, he led the boy through the kitchen, ignoring the astonished gasps of the cook and scullery maids.

Abbot appeared, his expression as bland as dry toast. ''May I be of assistance, my lord?''

''Yes, I need the key to the cellar door.''

At the request, Abbot's brow rose slightly. ''I see.''

It was obvious he didn't. And Nicholas was in no mood to enlighten him yet.

''Why, my lord, you are bleeding.''

Abbot's concerned tone reawakened the pain in his forearm. Nicholas glanced down at the boy. His head was bowed, shoulders drooping in abject defeat.

''It was an accident, nothing more,'' he said, strangely unwilling to name Dubber as his attacker.

Dubber glanced up, his eyes rounded in apparent surprise.

Nicholas quelled the urge to recant his decision. He had given the stubborn lad a chance to tell his story, and he'd refused. There was too much at stake to soften now.

He held out his hand, and Abbot placed the key in his palm. After opening the thick oak door, Nicholas paused. "This will be your room until you decide to tell me the truth." He nudged his young charge down the short flight of stairs.

"It's not a room," Dubber said beneath his breath. "It's a bloody prison."

"Prison or not, you have chosen it. Unless . . ."

"Do yer worst. I've been in filthier places than this."

Guilt threatened Nicholas's resolve. For just a moment, he saw terror flicker within Dubber's dark eyes.

"Tell me what you know," Nicholas said quietly.

Shaking his head, Dubber stared at the floor.

"Very well, you will stay. At least I can look after you here . . . keep you safe for the time being."

"I don't need—"

Nicholas grinned. "Yes, I know. You don't need help." His smile slipped. "I could place you in a room upstairs, if you swear you will not try to escape."

"And you'd believe me?" Dubber asked in obvious amazement.

"Yes. If you give me your word."

Say it, lad. Give me your—

"I—I . . . can't do it, Yer Lordship."

Nicholas's estimation of the boy rose to new heights. *A thief with honor.*

"I'll have blankets and a hot breakfast sent down later," he said.

And with a gentle push, he closed the door.

Darkness . . .

This time it offered no comfort. No sanctuary.

Maggie squeezed her eyes closed, afraid to confront the oppressive wall of black. She tried to breathe, but the weight of fear pressed down, sapping her strength.

Time ceased to exist.

Her mind flashed from the present to the past. Months of her life had been stolen. Two months of endless darkness, punctuated by desperate screams. Her cries for help had echoed through her prison, absorbed by the damp earthen walls.

You escaped once . . . you can do it again. . . .

"I can't! I don't have the strength." Maggie whispered the refusal aloud, her voice breathy and harsh.

Open your eyes. . . .

Repeating the words like a desperate prayer, she did as the inner voice commanded.

Darkness retreated.

The cellar pantry was not pitch-black as she'd feared. A barely perceptible shaft of light emanated from the far wall. Dust motes danced, sparkling like diamond chips as they passed through the muted sunlight.

She ignored the pungent aroma of onions and garlic resting in wooden bins. Her focus remained on the small, boarded window.

Like a sleepwalker, she inched forward. The thrill of freedom coursed through her, making her almost giddy with anticipation.

She stared at the tiny opening. Her optimism waned. She was slender in frame, but the size and location of the window proved daunting. Even on tiptoe, Maggie could not reach the sill.

Searching the murky room, she found a rickety step stool and placed it beneath the window. The aging wood groaned beneath her weight, but held firm. She reached up and tugged at the rotting boards covering the glass.

She worked quietly, wincing at the noise as, one

by one, the boards popped free. The room was now flooded with light.

Now to break the glass.

Pulling a tattered handkerchief from her pocket, Maggie wrapped her hand and tied the ends of the cloth. She paused, listening for the sound of footsteps. Sure that no one approached, she held her breath and punched through the first pane of glass. The jagged shards tinkled like bells as they dropped.

Fear overran patience. Without pause, she jabbed her hand through the last three panes. The slim strips of wood separating the glass splintered and crumbled.

Maggie smiled in jubilation, until pain asserted itself. The cloth had protected her knuckles, but the top of her hand was striped with bloody cuts.

"This is all your fault, Nicholas Grey!"

The charge was irrational, but she felt better nonetheless. When he discovered his prize prisoner had escaped, he would be livid. She grinned, wishing she could witness the event.

Her grim humor faded.

She didn't want to be embroiled in a battle with Nicholas. He'd saved her. He could have easily taken her straight to the magistrate. Instead he'd given her safety, at least for the moment.

Yet to allow intimacy would lead to disaster. She no longer belonged in his world, and she was certainly tired of living in the slums.

Maggie sighed as she brushed away fragments of glass from the windowsill. *I don't know where I belong anymore.*

And poor Dare. He would be worried sick at her sudden disappearance.

The sound of muffled voices and soft footsteps shattered her thoughts.

Without a moment to lose, she squirmed through

the window, ignoring the pieces of razor-sharp glass that penetrated her clothes and flesh as she wiggled her waist through the tiny opening.

Her hips followed, then her thighs.

Almost . . . there.

The cellar door slammed open.

"I've changed my mind. . . ." She heard Nicholas swallow the rest of his words.

"Oh, no you don't!" she heard as she felt Nicholas grab her ankles and pull.

She flailed her feet and shrieked. "Let me go!"

She felt Nicholas lose his grip. "Damn it! Get back in here."

"Go to 'ell!" With that succinct command, she kicked backward, her heel striking something solid.

She slithered the rest of the way through, and escaped.

The little thief was gone.

Ignoring the trickle of blood from his nose—where that wretched boy had kicked him—Nicholas rushed upstairs. It was no use. The boy was gone. Cursing, he returned to the cellar, aware Abbot had fallen in step behind him.

"I take full responsibility, my lord. I should have mentioned the window, but I never thought . . ."

"It's all right. I doubt Newgate could have held the boy."

Now Nicholas was back to the beginning, no closer to having the answers he needed. The lad had outwitted him once again, and taken his secrets with him.

Staring at the jagged shards of glass and the drops of glistening blood, Nicholas knew he was not the sole cause for the boy's flight. Like a fox trapped in a snare, Dubber had fought for freedom, heedless of his injuries. Yes, Nicholas had been harsh, but it wasn't as if he'd flogged the child. . . .

Abbot's calm voice broke his reverie. "I shall have the window repaired at once. As for the boy, I fear we will never see him again."

Nicholas refused to believe that. As Dubber's fragile features darted through his mind, a strange sense of recognition remained.

Perhaps it was merely the fact that the boy reminded Nicholas of himself as a child: cocky, defiant, and always in one scrape or another. He felt a kinship with the elusive child.

He had to discover if there was a connection between Edward Turner and the boy. If he handled the situation carefully, he might be able to save Dubber.

And see Turner receive his just reward.

Nicholas followed the pungent aroma, certain it would lead directly to his cousin. How the man could stand the stench of his own cologne was a mystery. But anything was preferable to the crowded ballroom from which he'd narrowly escaped.

Slipping inside the darkened study of Lord Wellingham's town house, Nicholas paused before closing the door. The glowing tip of a cigar wavered in the darkness, revealing Edward's location.

"Hiding, Turner?"

"Yes, you have found me out, Grey. My welcome this evening was less than enthusiastic."

"Did you expect the ton to welcome you with open arms?"

Edward shrugged lightly. "I expected at least a modicum of civility. But no, I was not completely surprised."

The silence deepened as Nicholas searched for a way to shatter Turner's tight control. Perhaps the truth would loosen his cousin's tongue.

"It may interest you to know," Nicholas began, "that the White Rose paid me a visit."

Edward turned toward him, his shocked expression unguarded. "What? Why would he choose you?"

Nicholas proceeded with care. "I have wondered that myself. I do have suspicions. . . ."

"You have a clue to the thief's identity?"

"I thought perhaps you, or one of your lackey, could be the culprit."

Edward scoffed. "Why the devil would I wish to rob you?"

"You asked me for help, and I refused. What better method to draw me into the fray?"

"You weave an entertaining tale, Grey, but I must assure you, I am not the Rose." Edward eased onto the maroon divan, rolling the cigar lightly between his thin fingers. "I, too, could create a plausible story. Someone is trying to implicate me in these robberies. Someone who hates me. I can think of one person who carries such feelings. My dear, misguided aunt."

Nicholas moved closer, hatred pumping through his veins like molten lava. "I could call you out for such an implication."

"Yes, you could. I used your charming mother only as an example. She detests me, and she moves freely among the ton. And you, of course, have never hidden your animosity."

"I doubt my mother and I are the only ones who wish you to Hell."

Edward blew a smoke ring, his expression strangely detached. "Were I intent on relieving young ladies of their jewels, I certainly would not lay a trail to my own door."

Much against his will, Nicholas realized the truth in his cousin's words. Anyone could be the culprit . . . except Edward Turner. He'd known from the beginning. But his need to seek revenge for Julia had blinded him to the obvious.

The boy . . . I have to find the boy.

"You believe in my innocence," Edward said with cool confidence.

The urge to smash the smugness from Turner's pallid face was overwhelming. Nicholas moved closer. "You may not be the thief, but you are not innocent either."

Flicking the remainder of his cigar into the hungry flames, Edward stood. "I have neither the time nor the inclination to listen to groundless accusations."

Edging closer, Nicholas pinned him in place through sheer force of will. "Trust me, *cuz*. They will not be groundless for long."

"I do not take kindly to threats, Grey. So be careful. Why, if anything untoward happened to you, my dear aunt would be all alone in the world—"

Nicholas swung his fist, striking Edward square in the jaw.

Tumbling backward onto the divan, Turner's eyes widened in disbelief. He wiped a trickle of blood from his cut lip, staring at the crimson drops with pathetic amazement.

Anger still simmering, Nicholas leaned over his cousin. "Don't ever threaten what's mine. I made the mistake of letting you live after you seduced Julia. Never again. If my mother should so much as trip on the hem of her gown, a bloody lip will be the least of your concerns."

Fear flashed in Edward's usually unreadable eyes. Then, as if realizing what he'd revealed, he looked away and removed a handkerchief from his jacket.

He dabbed the blood away, his voice as cool as an autumn rain. "I've always known you were a barbarian. Your actions have proven it." Edward tucked the bloody cloth into his pocket and came to his feet. "This night will not be forgotten. And, as for your veiled accusations, there is nothing in my past you can use as a weapon. Nothing."

"Perhaps not. But there are always persistent rumors. Those who remember your mother still whisper about her strange, untimely death."

"That was an accident."

Nicholas smiled. "Of course it was."

Strolling to the door, Edward turned back, his face once again an impenetrable mask. "Someone should have taught you that curiosity can be a dangerous thing."

"Dangerous, yes," Nicholas replied softly, "but also very enlightening."

Edward said nothing more as he disappeared through the doorway.

Easing into the nearest chair, Nicholas rubbed his stinging knuckles and took a deep breath. On this night, he had made a dangerous enemy.

Chapter Eight

She shouldn't have come.

Maggie stepped back into an alcove above the ballroom, knowing she couldn't stay, yet unable to muster the will to walk away.

Like a smitten schoolgirl, she needed to see Nicholas one more time . . . and whisper a final farewell. Tomorrow she, Dare, and Thomas would be on a ship bound for America. If she remained in England, Nicholas—or Lord Turner—would eventually discover her identity. The risk was too great.

Sadness, sharp and piercing, penetrated her heart. For the first time in her life, she felt the stirrings of love.

Perhaps she had loved Nicholas since that long-ago afternoon at the pond adjoining their estates. Even then, he'd been dashing and bold. Beautiful. Unattainable. She'd peered around the trunk of a gnarled oak tree, and spied him wooing her own lovely young governess. Maggie had been at first shocked, then intrigued by the mystery of man and woman. With whispered words and tender caresses he'd eased Miss Templeton down onto the soft grass. Maggie had run then, envy and embarrassment driving her home.

Her innocence had remained unsullied until she met Edward Turner. He'd stolen her naivete, along with her freedom, and shown her the ugly and cruel side of man. It was a lesson she could not forget.

The dark thoughts receded as Nicholas appeared. Drawn by the irresistible force of his presence, she stepped from the shadows.

He was shouldering his way through the crowded ballroom with single-minded determination, his expression fierce and unapproachable. Suddenly he stopped in midstride.

She inhaled sharply as he scanned the room intently. As if they were connected by an invisible wire, his gaze drifted upward.

Sapphire eyes found hers.

A fluid warmth seeped into her body, draining her will like a sieve. Nicholas smiled. She was lost.

He mouthed the word *stay,* then strode toward the winding staircase. He disappeared from view, and the spell was broken.

Maggie fled from the alcove and raced toward the servants' stairs. She was not a coward, she told herself forcefully, just practical. Tonight the Rose had one more task to complete before slipping into legend.

Fleeing down the stairs, her peach-colored gown swirling about her legs, Maggie prayed to escape.

A shadow appeared before her.

She skidded to an abrupt halt to avoid a collision.

"You're becoming quite predictable." Nicholas stood before her, leaning casually against the doorjamb. His playful smile stole her breath—and her heart.

"Predictable. What a dreadful word," Maggie whispered, losing herself in his sultry eyes.

He moved closer until only inches separated them. "You can run for only so long, *Athena*. Sooner or later you must face what is between us."

The husky tremor of his voice ignited her blood. She was tired of running. Tired of living one charade after the next. Perhaps, for this one night, she could forget the past and exist only in the moment. . . .

"I think it would be prudent to return to the ball," Nicholas said, glancing over his shoulder.

Maggie peeked around his broad chest. A group of chambermaids in mobcaps and starched white aprons stared at the couple with amused interest.

Smiling, Maggie curled her arm through his. "Perhaps you're right. But I think I would like to see the garden instead."

The invitation was blatant.

His eyes gleamed with understanding. "It would be my pleasure."

The servants stepped aside, smiling behind their workworn hands. As Nicholas led her through the processional, he bowed his head in respect. "Ladies . . ."

Titters of surprise and sighs of wonderment followed them as they slipped through the doorway and into the hushed silence of the night. Nicholas led the way to a deserted gazebo in the center of the overgrown rose garden.

"It would seem the gardener is somewhat lax in his duties," Maggie commented, trying to ease her nervous tension.

"Lord Wellingham spends his blunt at the gaming tables and horse races." Nicholas tugged her gently into his arms. "But it should serve our purpose well enough."

His relaxed manner and charming smile calmed her nerves. "And what purpose would that be?"

"*You* asked to come here. I am but your humble servant."

Maggie laughed. "Humble? Never."

"Perhaps not," he whispered, "but I have been enslaved since I first saw you."

The confession captured her soul.

Maggie brushed the wayward lock of dark hair from his brow. "You know nothing of me, Nicholas. Just as you are a stranger to me as well. Yet I feel . . ."

"As if somehow, we are connected."

Her breath lodged in her throat as he lowered his head and pressed his lips to hers. The kiss was gentle, offering her the choice to break free. For Maggie, the decision had been made when their gazes clashed in the ballroom.

She parted her mouth, running her tongue along the velvety seam of his lips.

He stopped her. "I must warn you. If this is another game of tease and run, I—"

She silenced him with another slow, lingering kiss. Dragging her hands down his chest, she spoke with quiet determination. "Tonight there will be no running. I want to feel everything."

His breath, spiced with brandy, warmed her cheek. "And so you shall, but perhaps we should retire to more comfortable surroundings. . . ."

Maggie resisted the invitation. Her courage would be lost if she had time to ponder her impulsive decision. Now was the time to feel—the time to say good-bye. "No, I want to be here. Beneath the stars."

Nicholas grinned. "It could be dangerous to stay in the garden. Others may intrude."

With a daring flourish, Maggie whipped the cravat from his neck. "I thought you relished danger, Lord Grey."

"I was only thinking of your reputation," he said, releasing the buttons at the back of her frock. "I must admit, the chance of being discovered does add a certain . . . peril."

A moan slipped from her lips as he lowered the gown past her shoulders. The cool air danced across her breasts, covered only by a thin silk chemise. A shiver of anticipation cascaded down her spine and pooled in the secret places of her womanhood.

His eyes glowed with unrestrained desire. "You are perfection." As if opening a gift wrapped in fragile tissue paper, he slid the silk downward, revealing her completely.

She clutched his coat and pulled him closer, aching for his touch. He obliged the unspoken command, and kissed each nipple with holy reverence.

Arching her back, she offered herself to his need, and her own.

Nicholas shuddered in awe. If he died at this moment, he would leave the earth a contented man. The woman he'd dreamed of for nights on end was finally in his arms.

The breasts he worshipped with his mouth were perfectly shaped and voluptuous, her nipples a luscious shade of pink.

Like a stranger in a foreign land, he continued his exploration of her lavender-scented skin. He reached lower, dragging the hem of her gown upward as he stroked her taut, silken thighs. Higher still, he slipped under the cotton drawers, squeezing and shaping her rounded bottom. With an ease he'd learned at an early age, he found her pulsating center. She was damp and swollen, her slick flesh quivering beneath his fingertips.

Her hands clasped his head tighter to her breast. "Nicholas, please . . ."

"Please what?" he countered, blowing a puff of air against her beaded nipples.

"Love me. . . ."

The urgent request shattered what little control Nicholas still called his own. As if pleading for freedom, his shaft strained against his tailored trousers. The need to possess her consumed him like a firestorm, with no rain in sight.

"Touch me," he commanded in a gruff whisper.

Her delicate hands, encased in white kidskin, skimmed his heaving chest and released the tiny ivory buttons of his shirt.

"Not with the gloves," he said.

She removed them with languorous care. Her eyes, as dark and mysterious as the surrounding night, held his gaze.

He captured her wrist, pressing his mouth to the fluttering pulse point, then to the palm of her hand, then the top—

Nicholas paused as his lips brushed across several strange ridges marring the velvety plane of her skin. "What the devil—"

She jerked her hand free. Glancing into her rounded eyes, he saw fear register within their depths.

"What happened to your hands?" Nicholas asked. "Are those cuts?"

"Yes, I—I broke a teacup."

He grabbed her wrist again. "How did you manage to cut the top of your hand, and not your palm?"

Shaking her head, she tried to pull free. He gripped

her slender wrist more tightly and tugged it beneath a shaft of brilliant moonlight. His astonished gaze skimmed her trembling form. What he'd thought were shadows were actually angry red welts striping her shoulders and ribs.

"How did this happen?"

She didn't answer, her expression a terrible mixture of horror and sadness.

Deep brown eyes . . . long, velvety lashes . . . delicate feminine features . . . No! Impossible!

The truth struck him like a fist to the belly.

He reached out and grasped her chin. With a sweep of his thumb, he brushed away the fine dusting of powder on her jaw. A bruise of pale yellow confirmed his unthinkable suspicions.

Nicholas managed only one word. "You!"

Jerking her gown into place, she stepped out of his reach. "I—I don't know what you mean."

Rage and disbelief swelled in Nicholas's chest. He looked at the lustrous raven hair, hating the lies. Without warning, he snatched the wig from her head. Tied back in a queue, her dark blond hair marked him a fool.

"You lying, scheming—"

"Please understand," she whispered, backing away. "I never meant to deceive you."

Fighting the urge to strangle the truth from her devious lips, Nicholas followed. "You have played me for the fool from the moment we met!"

"I didn't want to involve you, but—"

"It's a bit late for that," Nicholas said angrily. "I am up to my knees in your perfidy." He seized her shoulders, giving her a firm shake. "Tell me why!"

Her terrified gaze darted away, centering on something beyond his shoulder.

Nicholas spun around.

Pain exploded in his temple. Fighting to remain conscious, he crumpled to the ground.

"That's fer touchin' her, you bloody bastard!"

Athena's voice rang out, penetrating the fog in his mind. "Dare, how could you!"

" 'E had it comin'. *And* 'e knows who you are."

Nicholas forced his eyes open. She was kneeling beside him, her expression bleak, and brimming with profound sadness. "Forgive me, Nicholas. I wish I had met you sooner. Before—"

"We've got to go. Now!"

His gaze following the gruff voice, Nicholas expected to see a hulking behemoth. Instead, his attacker was a slender young man, holding a stout stick in one hand—a deadly dagger in the other.

"I don't know who you are," Nicholas ground out, pain battering his skull with every word, "but you will pay for that."

The boy replied with a sly grin as he twirled the lethal blade in his fingers.

Nicholas turned his attention to Athena, hating yet desiring her at the same time. "This is not finished."

"Yes, I'm afraid it is," she replied. "There can be no other ending. Good-bye." As if spun from air, she and her protector vanished into the darkness.

Staggering to his feet, Nicholas clutched the dark-haired wig so tightly his hand ached. "I will find you," he shouted into the night.

His voice softened. "You will not escape again."

"What the 'ell was that all about?"

Maggie ignored Dare's question as she tossed garments into a battered trunk. She wasn't prepared to face the barrage of questions. Not yet.

"Thomas, are you packed and ready to go?" she

asked the boy who was seated on the bed, his thin, bony legs dangling over the side.

"Yes, Maggie. Are we riding in the boat tonight?"

Tweaking his nose, she smiled. "Not tonight, tomorrow. And it's a ship, not a boat."

With the carefree exuberance of youth, he launched himself into her arms. "Soon we'll have a pretty house, Maggie, with cows and sheep and ponies—"

"All those?" she asked in playful sincerity. "Where on earth will *we* sleep?"

Thomas giggled, coming over and wrapping his slender arms around her neck. "Don't be silly. They'll be in the barn, of course."

"Of course," she echoed.

Hugging him tightly, Maggie reveled in his innocence. For this little boy, she would do anything. His safety took precedence over everything else.

She glanced over Thomas's head, and straight into Dare's angry gaze. Words were unnecessary. He wanted answers, and he wanted them now.

Lowering Thomas to the ground, she removed a pouch of coins from her pocket. "Angel, would you take this next door?"

The boy's excited expression saddened. "I'll miss Mrs. Pippins and the babies . . ."

Maggie dropped to one knee and smoothed his soft flaxen hair into place. "I know, but perhaps someday we'll come back to England and pay them a visit."

His smile returned, beautiful and glorious. "Oh, yes, that would be grand!" He skipped through the doorway, swinging the pouch in his tiny hand.

Taking a deep breath, Maggie closed the door.

Dare wasted no time. "I want the truth. What the 'ell was 'appenin' between you and the marquess?"

Resentment bubbled inside her. Dare was like a brother, a true friend, but he was not her father. Although, she realized sadly, her own father would have been equally outraged by her loose actions.

"You were there," she answered shortly. "He stumbled upon the truth. There's nothing more to tell."

Dare's accusing eyes pinned her in place. "You told me 'e wouldn't be at the ball. But 'e was, and you knew it."

"I wasn't sure Nicholas would—"

"There! That's what I'm talkin' about! You call 'im by name."

Maggie stepped forward, uncertain how to calm him. She'd never seen him so agitated, his brilliant gray eyes flashing with volatile emotion.

"Dare, you're upset for naught. Nicholas is—was my friend. . . ."

"Don't lie to me. I saw you."

Uttered in tones of condemnation, the simple statement shattered Maggie's tenuous control. He'd seen more than her confrontation with Nicholas. Dare had also witnessed the passionate prelude.

Embarrassed and enraged by the violation, she lashed out. "How could you, Dare? You should have shown yourself at once!"

"And spoil your little tryst?"

Stunned into silence, Maggie stared at her friend, trying to understand his outrage. He seemed so distant, a stranger.

"How can you speak to me like this, Dare? I thought we were friends.. . . ."

Like a sail deprived of wind, he sagged into the closest chair. He leaned forward and rested his elbows on his knees, unable to meet her eyes. "I just don't want to see you get 'urt. 'E's a gentleman, a marquess, and 'e'll never marry you, girl. Never."

Maggie knelt before him, aching to comfort him,

but knowing he wouldn't accept her touch. An occasional hug, or the tousling of hair, was the extent of Dare's propensity for closeness.

"I'm not a child," Maggie began softly. "If I wish to spend time with Lord Grey, I am free to do that."

"I know, but—"

"Please listen. I knew from the beginning there would be no future for Nicholas and me. I wanted a little piece of the present. A moment that was only mine."

"And I ruined it fer you," Dare admitted, looking away.

"No, I ruined it with lies. Nicholas has every right to be angry." She sighed, weariness weighing upon her heart like a millstone. "It doesn't matter now. Tomorrow we'll begin a new life."

She smiled as Dare nodded. Her heart lighter, she resumed her packing, humming.

"Maggie, what's this?" Dare held a sealed letter in his hands.

Heavier than ever, the millstone returned.

"I need you to deliver that message to the magistrate."

His eyes widened. "You want what?"

"Slip the note into someone's hand, then leave. They won't detain you. They will be too curious about the contents."

"And where will you be?" Dare queried, his expression hard and suspicious.

"I have an errand."

"Not as the Rose . . ."

Maggie sighed, wishing Dare were not quite so clever. "I have to do this."

"You've lost your wits! The marquess caught you once, and if I 'adn't been there tonight, 'e would've 'ad you again."

112

"I'm not going anywhere near Lord Grey. I have unfinished business I must take care of tonight."

Grudgingly, Dare relented. "I 'ope you know what you're doin'."

"I do." The forceful declaration was a lie. Fear touched icy fingers to her heart as she smiled and went to the door. If Dare sensed her misgivings, he would tie her to the nearest chair. "Now go deliver that message. I'll have Mrs. Pippins watch Thomas tonight."

"When will you be back?"

"Two hours, at most."

Dare paused in the doorway, his face a mask of determination. "If you're not back, I'll come lookin'."

Tension seeped from her tight muscles. "You're very sweet to worry about me," Maggie said, anticipating his reaction with a grin.

"Sweet! I'm not a bleedin' 'eart—"

She closed the door on the remainder of his outraged denial. Her smile slipped. Their entire future, or lack of it, rested on her success tonight.

She would not fail.

Chapter Nine

The room, dark and forbidding, raised chills across her flesh. Even the pale glow of a reluctant moon did little to ease her mounting anxiety.

Maggie pressed her back to the wall and swept her shoe-blacked hair from her forehead. Breathing deeply, she calmed her fluttering heart. Her nose wrinkled at the moldering smell of decay hanging in the air. The ceiling, the dark-paneled wood, even the frayed furnishings seemed to emanate evil. It was as if the owner's wickedness had been absorbed by the objects surrounding him.

She shivered at the notion, realizing it was her own fear—her memories—fueling her apprehension. Closing her eyes, she listened. All she heard were screams, the cries of unending pain she couldn't ease.

Perspiration beaded across her icy flesh. *I can't remember. Not now.*

Through sheer will, she banished the sounds echoing through her mind. Inching along the wall, she reached the desk and sighed in relief. Before her last reserve of courage could fade, Maggie opened the lower-right drawer. Careful not to rustle the old newspapers and business ledgers, she lifted them free.

Now was the most difficult part. She slid her fingers along the outer edge of the drawer box, searching for the spring release. Edward Turner had underestimated her intelligence once too often. She'd seen him use the secret compartment years ago and stored the knowledge for future use.

It has to be here. . . .

A click reverberated through the study.

Smiling in victory, she pushed on the false bottom of the drawer. It swung open, revealing more ledger books. Maggie wished she could light a lamp and scan the contents, but there was no time.

With all speed, she finished the last task of her dubious career. Edward Turner could return in hours or minutes, depending on his luck at the gambling tables. She took heart in knowing that any success he enjoyed would vanish within hours.

The Rose would be captured tonight.

Maggie replaced the contents, closed the drawer, and hurried to the door. The barely discernible sound of footsteps reached her.

She stepped back as the sound moved closer. Terror rooted her feet to the worn carpeting.

Run!

The terrified inner voice snapped her paralysis. She raced to the windows. They were nailed closed, not to keep intruders out, but to keep people locked in. She pushed anyway, panic guiding her hands. The window refused to budge.

Slowly the knob turned.

Without coherent thought, Maggie snatched a pewter candlestick from the mantel. She reached the door as it creaked open. Bracing herself on the other side, she waited, the weapon lifted high over her head.

A towering figure entered the room.

Maggie's hope of escape died. Only one vile creature of such immense height walked the earth.

Drager! Turner's henchman. And he was as merciless as his employer.

The muffled clatter of carriage wheels and horses' hooves approached the house, shattering the grim silence.

Edward had returned.

Drager hesitated, then departed the room. *Like an obedient dog seeking its master.*

Her hope was reborn. With a bit of luck, she could slip out the back as Edward entered through the front.

She counted to ten, then cracked open the door. The dimly lit foyer was deserted. She darted down the hallway.

Time slowed. The darkened hall seemed to stretch farther with each hurried step.

Freedom lay just beyond the next door.

As if conjured from a nightmare, a bony hand clamped down on her shoulder.

Maggie whirled, swinging the candlestick like a club.

A grunt echoed as she struck flesh, but the hand refused to release its punishing grip. ''You're a spunky one, I'll give you that.''

Lifting her into the air like a rag doll, Drager tossed her to the wall with bone-jarring force. She slid to the floor, her ears ringing. A dogged sense of failure drained her resistance. Drager would never allow her to leave the house. At least not in one piece.

''Well, now, what do we have here?'' Turner's cold, purring voice was hauntingly familiar.

Bile rose in her dry throat.

"I caught this little whipper trying to make off with a candlestick."

"Let's have a look at the daring lad. In the study."

Drager grasped her tattered collar and thrust her forward. Knowing it was useless to struggle, she remained limp. She needed time to clear her muddled thoughts and conserve her strength. At least the two men had assumed she was nothing more than a common housebreaker. That assumption would work to her advantage.

Drager tossed her into the middle of the room. Maggie stood slowly, keeping her blurry gaze focused on the faded carpet. If she looked into Turner's face, he would see her fear and loathing. He was a master at deciphering emotions, and twisting them to his advantage.

The manservant lit the fire and the oil lamps, flooding the room with eerie golden light.

"Now, young man, do tell how you managed to break into my home," Edward said, easing into a chair. "You have my full attention."

Terror held her voice hostage.

"Speak up, boy. Lord Turner does not like to be kept waiting." To emphasize his words, Drager grabbed the back of her neck. His fingers dug into her flesh like talons.

"I—I'm sorry, Yer Lordship," Maggie whispered. "My family . . ."

"Yes, yes," Edward interrupted in a dismissive tone. "I'm sure they're hungry and living in a cold, damp cellar. So you thought to steal my silver and help them. How wonderfully noble."

As comfortable and well worn as her own skin, bitter hatred infused her with strength. Slowly she looked upward into the pale eyes of the man she'd sworn to ruin. For the first time in two years, she faced him, not across a crowded ballroom, but toe to toe.

He smiled. "My, what hostility I see. Is that fierce expression directed at me, or merely my class?"

Be careful; he's testing you.

"You bleedin' toffs are all the same," she said in a hiss.

"Ah, so it is my class." Edward paused, his gray brows wrinkling in apparent confusion. "You seem familiar to me."

The urge to flee nearly overwhelmed Maggie's control. She held her ground, certain that if she ran, Edward's suspicions would soar.

"I've never seen you before," she replied in a cocky tone.

Edward appeared unconvinced. "Drager, what do you think?"

The cadaverous giant eyed her from head to toe. "I don't believe I know him."

The probing interrogation wore on her lacerated nerves. Even a cold, rat-infested jail cell was preferable to this. "Go on and call the magistrate. I ain't afraid."

Edward's smile sweetened—so sweet it raised gooseflesh across her skin. "I don't believe that will be necessary." He glided toward her.

She flinched as he raised his hand toward her cheek. He ignored the reaction and wiped away a smudge of soot Maggie had carefully brushed on herself.

"I think once we clean you up, you'll be passable."

She jerked away, fresh terror constricting her chest. "No, I—"

"Don't be too quick to reject my offer," Edward

chided. "I may have a job for you. One of my establishments could use a strong, industrious lad."

"I—I don't need a bleedin' job. I work fer m'self."

"I'm sure a life of crime is much more exciting than fetching coal or emptying chamber pots. However I think you should reconsider my offer."

Shaking her head, she stepped back and bumped into Drager's unyielding form.

"I was hoping to avoid an unpleasant scene," Edward whispered sadly. "Drager, perhaps you should convince the boy it would be to his advantage to say yes."

Maggie's composure snapped at the subtle threat. Like a cornered animal facing death, she lunged forward. She clawed at Edward's surprised face before Drager seized her arms and dragged her backward.

Two ribbons of blood creased Turner's cheek.

His stunned expression transformed into a mask of rage. "You filthy guttersnipe! You will pay for that blow." He turned to Drager. "Show our little friend what happens to those who attack their betters. After the lesson, take him to the House. A few days there should break his spirit. If he refuses to cooperate, kill him." His anger apparently spent, Edward strolled from the room.

Maggie looked into Drager's dark, glittering eyes. Her blood ran cold.

The first blow of Drager's fist caught her off guard, and squarely in the ribs. Air whooshed from her lungs as splintering pain radiated through her body. Gasping, she doubled over, praying he would finish with her quickly.

Images of Thomas's grinning face and Darc's sober expression danced through her mind like shadows. She'd failed.

The second blow struck her in the stomach, clearing her mind of every thought except the lancing pain. A third clipped her jaw.

The floor rushed forward to meet her face. Nicholas's arrogant smile flashed in her mind's eye.

As darkness enfolded her, she wondered if he would miss her. Or ever forgive her.

Edward paced the study, his rage diminishing with each controlled step. He touched the slender welts on his cheek, unable to believe the boy had actually attacked him.

It was too bad the little thief had such hatred, or Edward might have considered keeping the boy here. He needed an interesting diversion, and once the lad healed, perhaps he would be more amenable to the employment offer. And if not, he would scrape the bottom of the Thames.

Imagining the boy's terror as death approached, Edward smiled. His enjoyment ended as a persistent pounding sounded at the front door. He waited, wondering who would have the temerity to pay a call at such a late hour. The knocking ended, followed by the unmistakable sound of raised voices coming from the foyer.

Pasting a congenial smile on his face, he opened the study door. Foreboding tightened his muscles. He stared at one of his obviously terrified groomsmen, and two men he recognized instantly—the magistrate of the district, Christopher Woodson, and Connor Hennessy.

Edward's flesh crawled with repugnance. The grinning Irishman was above coercion and supremely arrogant. Woodson was no better. He, unlike numerous others, refused protection money or bribes. He followed the dictates of the law as if they were holy tenets.

Accusation shone from their eyes. Deep in his bones, Edward knew the impromptu visit was somehow connected to the Rose.

Refusing to cower like a guilty man, he stepped into the foyer. "Gentlemen, it is rather late for visitors. May I ask—"

"We have a warrant to search the premises," Woodson interrupted as he handed a document over.

Edward's heart pumped faster, not with fear, but with exhilaration. If these holier-than-thou men wanted to play games, Edward would oblige their pursuit with pleasure. Although, as opponents went, he doubted they would provide a sufficient challenge.

"If this is concerning the nasty rumors that I am a jewel thief," Edward said, "I can assure you, they are absurd."

Grinning, Connor strolled forward. "Well, then, you'll have nothin' to worry about. Let's start in the study."

The magistrate nodded his agreement, and they brushed past Edward as if he were little more than a piece of furniture.

A kernel of uneasiness lodged in his stomach as the two men charted an unwavering course to the desk.

Somehow, they know. . . .

Moments later his suspicions were confirmed.

Connor jerked the lower-right drawer open, then produced a slender dagger from his weathered boot. Edward watched in growing agitation as Connor pried open the secret panel. They would find nothing except ledger books. Books they could never tie to his illicit collection of brothels and gaming hells.

Smiling in anticipation, he waited. They would pay

dearly for barging into his home with unfounded accusations.

"Well, now, I've discovered the pot of gold," Connor exclaimed. "Or should I be sayin' a pot of rubies, pearls, and emeralds." His look of triumph was undeniable. "You've got some explainin' to do, Lord Turner."

Speechless, Edward watched as a handful of jewels appeared in Connor's chubby palms.

"I'm fairly certain these lovely pearls belong to Lord Hampshire, and the emerald choker . . ." Connor's amused voice droned on, cataloging each gem and smiling.

Edward clasped his trembling hands behind his back. Shock coalesced into deep, black rage—and grudging respect.

The Rose had accomplished the impossible. He'd spun an intricate web of rumor and innuendo, laying the groundwork for this astounding discovery.

The only question was how. No one was allowed entry into this room except himself and Drager . . . the boy! The grubby brat had placed the jewels in the drawer.

The realization only brought more questions. There was no possible way the cocky lad could have discovered the secret panel by chance. He'd known exactly where to find it. Edward stroked the marks on his cheek as the truth appeared with crystal clarity. A traitor lived in his midst.

"Lord Turner, this evidence is overwhelming, to say the least," Woodson offered, eyes gleaming with victory.

"I must disagree. Someone is painting me the villain, and I know who the culprit is."

Connor chuckled in obvious disbelief. "And who might that be? Wee fairies, perhaps?"

As if he were a volcano on the verge of eruption, hatred simmered inside of Edward. If Woodson had not been present, Edward would have carved the smirk from Hennessy's plump face. But there would be time for that later.

"No, not a fairy. A housebreaker." Edward paused, pleased by their sudden attention. "When I arrived home this evening, my manservant discovered a filthy boy in the house. He attempted to steal a candlestick from this very room."

Connor remained skeptical. "So you're sayin' a boy broke in, left these jewels worth a fortune, and then stole *one* candlestick."

"It may seem ridiculous, but I know where the thief is."

"And where is that?" Woodson asked, frowning.

Edward hesitated. He had no wish to reveal that he'd ordered Drager to take the boy to one of his brothels. The news of his special enterprises would blacken his reputation beyond redemption. "If you'll be patient, my man will be here any moment. He can verify all I've told you." Edward strolled to the sideboard and lifted a crystal decanter of brandy. "May I offer you some refreshment while we wait?"

The magistrate shook his head, eyeing the amber liquid with clear distaste. "No, thank you. Liquor clouds the mind and destroys the spirit."

Edward smiled coldly. *Sanctimonious prig.*

Ignoring Hennessy's avid gaze at the bottle, he poured himself a generous drink and settled into a chair. "I should warn you both. When my innocence is proven, I'll expect an apology printed in the London newspapers."

Connor grinned. "And if you're guilty, I'll be seein' *that* announcement printed in the London newspapers."

My dear Mr. Hennessy, you have no idea with whom you're dealing. But one day . . .

The door burst open, ending Edward's silent vow.

Drager appeared, his eyes widening when he noticed the visitors. "My lord, I—"

"Your timing is impeccable." Edward stood and waved a dismissive hand toward his unwanted guests. "Please tell these gentlemen what occurred here earlier this evening."

"Well . . ."

"Don't dawdle, man. Tell them."

Drager nodded, his worried gaze flitting from the magistrate to his employer. "I discovered a boy robbing the house. I grabbed him, and Lord Turner told me to take him away."

"And where exactly did you take him?" Woodson asked.

"Go and fetch the boy," Edward said to Drager, hoping to divert the magistrate from that bit of information. "I'm sure that with the right persuasion, he will tell his story truthfully."

A lone bead of perspiration glided down Drager's temple. The manservant, usually as unemotional as a stone, was more than agitated. He seemed terrified.

"Drager, is there something you wish to tell me?" Edward asked, his voice a cold warning.

"I was taking him to—to the . . ."

"Magistrate," Edward provided, his expression purposely bland.

"Yes, that's right. But the little hellion, he . . ." Drager stepped back as if expecting a blow. "He escaped."

Smiling, Edward advanced toward his servant. "You allowed a stripling lad half your size to escape? I find that difficult to fathom."

"He—he was pretending to be asleep, and then

124

like a flash he jumped from the carriage. I gave chase, but he knew every alley like it was his own backyard.''

Connor's grin returned. "How very convenient. Why, my own dear father, God rest his soul, would have a hard time swallowin' that bit of tripe.''

Raising his hand, Woodson signaled for silence. "I believe, in this matter, he's telling the truth.''

Edward lifted the snifter of brandy in a mock salute. Perhaps the noble magistrate was not a complete idiot after all.

"But," Woodson continued, "our investigation will move forward. And you, Lord Turner, are still a suspect.''

"Surely you're jesting.''

Connor appeared equally displeased. "We found the evidence, just as the informant said we would.''

"Yes," Woodson said calmly, "but I have no doubt there was a boy here, and he has the remaining answers. Drager told the same story as Lord Turner without prompting. It is conceivable the lad knows something.''

He knows everything, Edward mused. "Of course it's conceivable. The boy planted those jewels. And on the very same night someone tells you to search my house. Am I the only one who finds the situation a bit too convenient?''

Silence settled over the room as Edward watched the play of emotions flit across Woodson's usually bland features. "Though I am not completely convinced of your innocence, Lord Turner, you may remain a free man. At least until we find this boy. But I warn you, if you leave the city, I shall issue a warrant for your arrest.''

Edward swallowed his retort. "I would not dream of leaving. I intend to prove my innocence.''

Connor tipped his hat, his smile mocking. "You should pray we find the mysterious lad. Or you could be spending the rest of your years in a jail cell. I don't think the ton will hurry to your aid."

"One day, Hennessy, someone might take offense at your presumptuous speech." *And slice your impertinent tongue to ribbons.*

Connor laughed. "Aye, I've been told that, but it all depends on who I'm addressin'."

"Perhaps," Edward purred, "you both should leave now. I have had a most trying evening."

Woodson tugged at Connor's arm. "Come on, then, we've got work to do."

Playing the role of consummate host, Edward escorted them to the door. "Be careful, gentlemen. London can be a most violent place. Especially at night."

With keen pleasure, he watched Connor's chubby-cheeked grin disintegrate into a flat, menacing line. "Are you threatenin' us, Lord Turner?"

Edward slapped a hand over his heart. "I'm saddened you would even think such a thing, Mr. Hennessy."

"Believe me, *Yer Lordship,* I've thought much worse."

"Good evening, gentlemen," Edward said softly.

He returned to the study and eased into a chair, sorting through all he'd learned. The night had not been a disaster, but a complete success. And once he had the boy, Edward would have the key to the puzzle.

Turning to a subdued and trembling Drager, he spoke with calm detachment—though inside he seethed with impotent rage. "You have disappointed me. I will give you the opportunity to redeem yourself."

"Y—yes, my lord."

126

"I find it quite distressing that Woodson and Hennessy knew of the secret panel in my desk. I want you to question the staff. Use whatever method you choose, but I want the traitor found."

Drager shook his head. "No one here would—"

Edward slammed his fist against the chair. "Someone did! I will have loyalty in my own house. Do you understand?"

"I—I shall see to it in the morning, my lord."

"And beginning tonight, I want you to find the little bastard you misplaced and bring him to me."

"Do you wish me to keep after Lord Grey?"

"Naturally. My cousin and Hennessy are good friends. Don't let either of them out of your sight. Hire whomever you need to see it done." Edward stared at his manservant. "Well? What are you waiting for?"

With the speed of a man half his age and size, Drager fled the room.

Closing his eyes, Edward envisioned the numerous forms of persuasion he would inflict on the guttersnipe. Slowly, methodically, and, if need be, painfully, the truth would be revealed.

Once Edward obtained the information he needed, the poor, misguided lad would suffer a tragic accident—before the esteemed Mr. Woodson could question him.

Edward retrieved his glass of brandy and downed the liquor in one swift swallow. As always, the thrill of the hunt—and the certainty of success—roused his dormant lust. Yet he quelled the impulse. There would be time enough to enjoy the pleasures of the flesh after he captured the boy and coaxed the story from his lips.

Soon the mysterious mastermind who called himself the Rose would be unveiled.

Chapter Ten

Jostling back and forth, Nicholas braced himself, telling Connor to do the same. Their carriage sped down narrow cobblestone streets and swerved around corners. Curses of anger and raised fists followed in their wake as passersby scrambled out of the way.

The Irishman wiped his brow, his round face unusually pale. "You're goin' to be the death of me yet, Nicky. Can't you slow this bloody thing down?"

For the first time in twelve long hours, Nicholas smiled. "Hoskins is an expert driver. He'll get us to the wharf in one piece."

Connor scowled. "I hope you're right about this."

Nicholas knew his friend was not speaking of their hurried trip. "Don't worry. The boy and his friends will be there."

"If you hadn't heard the name, Dare, we would still be searchin' East End. His reputation with a blade is enough to curl your toes."

"He's proficient with clubs, as well," Nicholas murmured, rubbing the small lump on the side of his head. "What else do you know of him?"

"Very little. People give the young man a wide berth. Word has it he's always been a loner. No one even knows if that's his true name. As for the other two lads, they're a mystery."

Not for very long . . .

Closing his eyes, Nicholas signaled an end to the conversation. The previous night flashed through his mind, rekindling his anger.

Connor remained ignorant of Athena's role in the fiasco. Nicholas had blamed footpads, Dare among them, for the blow to his head—and his pride.

Although Nicholas trusted his friend implicitly, something held him back. He needed his multitude of questions answered before he performed the unveiling. But who would be revealed? Good God, he still didn't know who the culprit was!

The beautiful woman he'd named Athena knew the stringent rules of society as if born to them. The boy, Dubber, obviously knew how to survive on the harsh London streets. And they were both the infamous Rose.

Even now, Nicholas could not reconcile the two diverse images. The only certainty—Edward Turner remained at the heart of the puzzle.

The Rose was more than a mere jewel thief. She had appointed herself the sword of justice, with Turner's downfall her goal. The woman, who'd entranced him at first sight, had manipulated him like a marionette. She'd stolen from him. Used him.

And on this morning, the mystery would be solved.

Connor's strident voice punctured the silence. "We're probably on a wild-goose chase, Nicky. The boy's neighbor, Mrs. Poppins—"

"Pippins."

"Mrs. Pippins wasn't very friendly. Why, she looked ready to tear us apart."

"She didn't have to say anything," Nicholas replied. "It was obvious the boys had no intention of returning."

"How can you be sure they've booked passage? They could travel overland to Portsmouth or—"

"No, they wouldn't risk being recognized." Athena's farewell had been laced with certainty, but Nicholas kept that thought to himself.

When Connor had told him about Turner's near arrest and the mysterious boy, he knew real fear. If his cousin captured her again, Nicholas would never discover the truth. It was more than eager curiosity or fear for her safety driving Nicholas.

He still wanted her. And he almost hated her for that.

As the carriage clattered to a halt, the raucous sounds of the docks and the tang of sea air penetrated its interior. Hoskins snapped the door open, and Nicholas stepped down.

Connor followed, obviously relieved that the ride was at an end. "So, Nicky, where do we begin?"

"The *Ophelia*."

"How can you be so bloody certain?"

"Early this morning I sent for the passenger manifests. There are only three ships docked that will carry passengers. One is headed for Calais, one for the Indies, and the *Ophelia*—my flagship—is sailing to America."

"I don't believe it!" Connor laughed. "You think the boy and his friends are tryin' to escape on your own ship."

"We shall soon see," Nicholas murmured. The Rose's thorns were about to be snipped.

*   *   *

Each breath was a struggle. Each step excruciating.

How she'd managed to make it home last night still amazed Maggie. The daring jump from the carriage had been painful, but easily accomplished. For all Drager's physical strength, his mental faculties were something of a joke.

Clinging to Dare's arm, Maggie shuffled forward. A wave of pain immobilized her aching body. "Wait a moment."

Dare held her upright, his expression grim as he surveyed her obvious agony. "We're not takin' another step until you give me the bastard's name. You wouldn't tell me last night, but you'll damned well tell me now."

She shook her head, instantly regretting the action. Her vision blurred as she struggled to remain standing.

As if afraid he might cause her more pain, Thomas touched her hand gently. Maggie looked into his eyes, red and swollen from the fountain of tears he'd cried at her bruises.

The sight tore at her heart. "I'm fine, angel. Please don't cry anymore."

"Maggie, I'm scared." He sniffled, wiping his nose on his coatsleeve. "Promise you won't leave us. We're a family. . . ."

"She's goin' to be fine," Dare offered, patting the boy's head. He turned to Maggie. "You need a doctor."

"There's one on board the ship," Maggie argued, determined to win the battle of wills.

"You need rest, and I need to find the man who—"

"Dare, if we don't leave England today, I will end up in prison, and the authorities will not stop with me. They will take you, as well."

131

Thomas cried in earnest now, his slender frame jerking with each sob. She cursed herself for carelessly exposing him to the harsh reality of their situation, but Dare had to be convinced of the truth.

Hugging the boy, she looked into Dare's unrelenting stare. "We have to board that ship. Please," she begged, "come with us."

Seconds ticked as Maggie watched the war raging inside him. Finally he nodded. "Fine. Let's go then. They won't 'old the ship for three ragamuffins like us."

Pulling the threadbare cap down over her forehead, Maggie moved as quickly as her trembling legs allowed.

Within minutes, they reached the ship. It was smaller than she'd expected, but immaculate. The snow white sails were tied down, every piece of brass polished to a blinding sheen.

Still gripping her arm for support, Dare led her and Thomas up the gangplank.

Euphoria flooded her, easing her discomfort: justice had finally been served. Even if Edward Turner managed to elude arrest, his reputation would not be as fortunate. For Maggie, that would have to be enough.

Her happiness dimmed as Nicholas's grinning face darted to mind. Her brief time with him had not been enough, would never be enough.

With each step taking her toward an escape from English soil, her sadness sharpened to a physical ache. It's for the best, she told herself forcefully. Nicholas would never forgive her for the lengthy list of sins she'd committed. She deserved his condemnation and nothing more.

Squeezing her eyes closed, she battled the impending tears and pushed his visage from her mind. The years ahead would provide more than enough time for bitter regrets. Now she had to focus on their escape.

Suddenly Dare stopped, his body vibrating with tension. Maggie followed his steely gaze. A short, portly man in a captain's uniform blocked their path at the end of the gangplank. With arms crossed over his chest, and a scowl darkening his weather-beaten features, it was apparent he had no intention of letting them pass.

"Stay 'ere," Dare murmured. "I'll see what 'e wants."

Maggie held him back, unable to quell her sudden apprehension. "No, something's wrong. . . ."

The overwhelming sensation of being watched prickled her flesh. Turning slowly, she gazed down the plank.

Nicholas Grey's cold, forbidding eyes met hers. His smile chilled her blood.

She looked back toward the captain, now flanked by three burly sailors.

Trapped.

A veil of darkness obscured her vision. Panic bubbled to the surface. Trembling, Maggie clasped Thomas to her waist. *My God, what have I done?*

As if their situation were not precarious enough, Dare whipped his dagger from its sheath. His gaze flitted from Nicholas to the captain. "Everyone stay back," he shouted, his voice shaking with rage.

His smile long since gone, Nicholas strolled up the wooden plank, hands raised. "There's nowhere to go, boy. Put the knife down and—"

"I said stay back!"

Knowing Dare could throw the weapon straight into Nicholas's heart, she seized her friend's wrist.

"No, not like this. We need a distraction."

The plank shifted beneath her feet. She glanced over her shoulder to see Nicholas inching closer.

There was no time to consider the merits of her swiftly drawn plan. She would provide the diversion, and Dare and Thomas would escape. "Dare, take him," she whispered, passing the boy over. "When the time is right, run."

"What the devil are you talkin' about?"

She smiled sadly and touched his cheek. "I have to do this. Promise me you'll take care of Thomas."

Without hesitation, Maggie moved back down the gangway. Ignoring Dare's harsh shout to stop, she looked into Nicholas's blazing eyes.

Like a silken thread, his soft voice spanned the distance between them. "Did you truly believe you could escape?"

Holding his gaze, she smiled. "Did you truly believe you could catch me?"

With a jaunty salute, Maggie leaped into the water.

Shock, mingled with profound disbelief, held Nicholas immobile.

Even as he watched her disappear beneath the murky depths, he couldn't believe she'd had the courage to do it.

Admiration of her spirit transformed to dread.

Could she swim?

Almost immediately he overcame his bone-numbing fear. Without pause, he shed his coat and dove into the chilly water. Swimming straight down, he searched the darkness for a glimpse of pale skin or a flash of clothing.

His lungs burned with the relentless need for air. He returned to the surface, gasping. Glancing in every direction, he expected to see her swimming away, wearing a cocky smile.

He saw nothing except a tattered woolen cap bobbing in the water.

He dove again.

Deeper.

Not a single shaft of light penetrated the darkness. Like a blind man, he swept his arms back and forth, reaching for a sleeve, a shoe. . . .

Where are you, damn it!

Grief and defeat filtered through his limbs, sapping his strength. His strokes slowed. His legs cramped. Nicholas traveled downward, ignoring the pain and his need for air.

When even hope seemed impossible, something brushed his hand. Clutching at the foreign substance, he soon realized it was cloth . . . a coat! Dots of bright light danced through his blindness.

Time had run out.

Racing to the surface, he dragged the precious cargo behind him. He prayed it was the woman, and not some other unfortunate soul who'd met his end in a watery grave.

Just when it seemed his lungs would explode from the strain, he burst into the light. He inhaled sharply and stared at the slender form in his arms. Her face was as white as fine porcelain, her lips tinged blue.

As cold as her flesh, fear chilled his soul.

With long, fluid strokes, he reached the pier where Connor stood waiting. No words were necessary as Nicholas passed her limp body to his friend.

Ignoring the small crowd gathering to watch the drama, Nicholas climbed from the frigid water.

Instinct guided his actions. He rolled her on her stomach and straddled her thighs. Pushing on her back, he forced the water from her lungs. Sliding his hand beneath her chest, he felt a faint but steady beat.

Nicholas turned her over gently. Frustration and terror invaded his voice. "Breathe, damn you! Breathe."

Seconds ticked like a drumbeat pounding through his mind. As if a mere touch could restore her, he stroked her cheek.

Suddenly she gasped, coughing up more water.

"Thank God," Nicholas murmured as her face regained a faint pinkish hue. She'd never looked more beautiful.

Her eyes fluttered open. "Dare . . . Thomas?"

Certain her friends had slipped away during the rescue, Nicholas glanced at Connor. "I'm sure they're gone."

The Irishman smiled. "Well, they could've, that's for certain."

Nicholas followed his friend's pointed stare. There they stood, the young man, Dare, and the boy, Thomas.

"You could have escaped," Nicholas said quietly, overwhelmed with grudging respect.

Dare stared at him, his expression painted with rage. "If Mag—"

Nicholas tucked away the near blunder for future reference.

"If she had died," Dare continued, "I would've cut out yer 'eart."

"Then it's lucky, for both of us, that *he* will recover."

The boy, Thomas, stepped forward, tears glazing his eyes. "Th-thank you, sir." Suddenly he launched himself into Nicholas's arms.

Stunned by the spontaneous display of emotion— the inherent trust—he patted the child's back with awkwardness.

Unnerved by the strange sense of fulfillment the contact brought, he released the boy.

Connor's voice shattered the tense silence. "Nicky, I think we should be goin'."

Turning his attention back to the woman, Nicholas found that she was lucid and watching him with quiet intensity. Fear and regret dulled her delicate features. She shivered, her recovery far from complete.

He swept her into his arms and followed as Connor plowed a path through the crowd of onlookers.

Glancing over his shoulder, Nicholas wondered if the boys' loyalty would continue. They remained tight on his heels, Dare brimming with open contempt.

Nicholas would deal with the young man's hatred later.

First he had to discover the truth.

Chapter Eleven

A dull throbbing drove the lingering whispers of sleep from her mind. Slowly, Maggie became aware of a strange tightness surrounding her midsection. Reaching beneath the coverlet, she felt tight bindings wrapped around her ribs.

Like a candle sputtering to life, memories burst into her mind.

Dark, endless water . . . burning pain . . . and Nicholas.

She remembered him clearly, dashing and confident, as he'd walked up the gangway. Then, when she'd leaped into the river, his surprise had filled her with pleasure. Until she'd collided with the water.

The impact had driven the air from her lungs, and brought agony to her bruised ribs.

She had sunk like a stone.

Nicholas had saved her.

The thought irritated her beyond comprehension.

The man was worse than a shadow—unshakable, and always one step ahead of her carefully drawn plans.

Knowing she had to face her situation, Maggie opened her eyes. The room was lavish and unfamiliar. The canopy bed she rested upon was draped in forest green velvet. Ivy-patterned wallpaper adorned the walls, while a dainty rosewood escritoire sat in the corner near the window.

It was a beautiful room, but still a prison. Maggie had no doubt the door was securely locked. After all, she was a wanted criminal—a desperate, dangerous jewel thief. *If they only knew . . .*

The murmur of approaching voices silenced her musings. Nicholas's deep, rumbling tone was all too familiar.

Feigning sleep, Maggie squeezed her eyes closed. She had no desire to see his victorious expression. She'd failed. It was a bitter truth to accept.

The gentle squeak of door hinges signaled a presence. Surrounding her like gentle hands, Nicholas's elusive masculine scent drifted across the room.

Her heart quickened with dread, and with another, more powerful emotion. She tried to deny it was desire, but the lie would not be borne.

Laughter bubbled in her throat at the irony of the situation. She still wanted him. Wanted the very man who could destroy her.

"You can stop pretending. I know you're awake."

Maggie had expected cold triumph, perhaps even hatred to color his voice. Instead he sounded resigned and weary.

Detesting her cowardice, she took a deep breath and looked at him. He stood at the foot of her bed, his face scored with lines of exhaustion.

"How are you feeling?" he asked, as if speaking to a stranger.

She couldn't blame him for that. They *were* strangers, separated by a chasm of lies. "I've felt better," she finally replied. "How long have I been here?"

"Two days."

Her mind whirled in disbelief. "That's impossible!"

"The physician gave you laudanum to ease your pain. You have slept the entire time."

As she absorbed that fact, the incident at the wharf filtered through her thoughts. An elusive memory niggled at her for recognition.

She remembered lying on the pier, seeing Nicholas, and . . . Dare!

Maggie was unaware she'd spoken the name aloud, until Nicholas answered, "Your friends are fine. For now."

Her nerves tingled with urgency. "What do you mean, 'for now'?"

Nicholas strolled to the window and gazed through the cream-colored draperies. His continued silence unnerved her more than words.

Finally he faced her. "We will discuss Dare and Thomas later. I want to know who hurt you."

The sudden change of topic threw her off balance. "I don't know what—"

"The physician said the bruises on your jaw and arms, and your cracked rib, probably occurred before you tried to board the ship."

Maggie held her breath, wondering how much he knew—how much he wasn't saying. Caution guided her reply. "I had an accident."

His expression remained impassive. "And where did this *accident* occur?"

"That is none of your concern."

Like a storm unleashed, he charged toward her, planting his fists on either side of her head. "You have made it my concern. Now tell me the bloody truth. I know my cousin hurt you. Why? Why do you want Viscount Turner named a jewel thief? What the devil did he do to you?''

Maggie grinned with false bravado. "If you're so certain I'm the Rose, why am I not in prison?"

His cold smile transformed her fear to terror. "I have other plans for you," he whispered, his warm breath fanning her cheek. "You and I have unfinished business."

His icy blue eyes thawed, revealing the inner fire she knew so intimately. Her heartbeat quickened in anticipation. Parting her lips, she waited, knowing he was within a hairbreadth of kissing her. She would offer no resistance. Desire remained the only truth she could give him.

He moved closer, his heavy-lidded gaze focused on her lips. Then, as if awakening from a dream, he blinked, the fire extinguished.

"Now, where were we?" he asked, backstepping several feet.

Maggie smiled inwardly. He could pretend uninterest, but his body betrayed the effort. The faint trembling of his hands and the flush of color on his cheeks were all the evidence she needed.

"I believe we were discussing the Rose and my cousin," Nicholas continued.

"I would rather discuss Dare and Thomas. I want to see them."

His expression hardened. "That's not possible."

For a brief moment, her hope soared. "You let them go?"

"No, they are still here. For how long is up to you."

"They had nothing to do with this! I acted alone."

Nicholas leaned closer until only inches separated

them. "I think we should allow the magistrate to make that decision."

She stared into his face, horrified by the implication. "That is blackmail."

"I will do whatever it takes."

His abounding arrogance shattered her control. "How dare you threaten my friends. My family!"

Nicholas smiled. "You, my little imposter, have no idea how much I would dare."

Suddenly his lips were upon hers, fierce and probing. Ribbons of warmth unfurled in her stomach, erasing every thought. She returned the kiss with blind hunger, threading her fingers through his silky, raven hair.

As if starving for air, he gasped, breaking the sensual contact.

Reality struck her then.

Maggie twisted away, hating the strange power he had over her, but hating more her own body's betrayal. She pushed at his chest, awakening the pain in her ribs.

Grabbing her hands, he quieted her frantic movements. "Lie still. I didn't mean to hurt you." His voice, gentle with remorse, gave her hope.

"Please, Nicholas, if you don't want to hurt me, then let me go. Let my friends go."

He sighed and released her. "It's too late for that."

"No, it isn't. We will walk out the door and simply disappear."

An unfamiliar emotion darkened his eyes. He seemed frustrated and almost saddened by her words. "Is that what you truly want?"

No, I want you. . . .

Aloud, she said, "Yes, I want my freedom."

"I don't believe you." He stated the fact so calmly, she remained speechless in the face of his certainty.

"Even if I let you go, you would never be free."

"Perhaps not," she admitted, "but at least I would be alive."

"No, you wouldn't."

Her heart thudded painfully in her chest. "What do you mean?"

"My cousin already suspects you're here."

Maggie's throat turned dry. "How—"

"He had us followed. I saw his man, Drager, at the wharf. I'm sure he is convinced I'm harboring the Rose."

As Drager's pallid face swam through her mind, her voice weakened to a whisper. "What did you tell him?"

Running a hand through his tousled hair, Nicholas paced the room. "I told Turner you were a servant's son who tried to run away from home."

Even to Maggie's ears, the story was thin, at best. "Surely he didn't—"

"—believe me? Of course not. But he would not challenge me directly. My cousin is probably hounding the magistrate as we speak."

Easing to a sitting position, she pleaded her case further. "Don't you understand, if I remain here, you'll be caught in the middle. I cannot involve you in this."

"I have been tangled in this damned web since you nearly turned me into a eunuch at our first meeting."

Offering no defense, Maggie blushed at the memory.

"If you give me your name," he said softly, "tell me what happened, I can help you and your friends. I can't do that without the truth."

Indecision stole her voice. If she revealed even a kernel of the truth, Nicholas would peel away the layers like an onion. Her soul would be laid bare. If Lord

Turner discovered her true identity, he would seek his revenge through those she loved. The risk was too great.

"At least tell me your name," he said, weariness deepening his voice.

Maggie shook her head and waited for his angry explosion.

He replied with icy calm. "I had hoped you would be reasonable, but I should have known better." He strode to the door. "When I return, you will tell me everything."

She opened her mouth, whether to rail at his arrogance or beg him to stay, she would never be certain.

The door slammed closed with resounding finality and the lock clicked.

Once again, she was a prisoner.

Easing from the plump mattress, she walked the length of the room. Each breath pulled at her tender ribs. The walls seemed to press in, suffocating her with their closeness.

She ignored her surroundings and her fear, focusing on her bare feet as she paced the floor.

Weary to the marrow of her bones, Maggie knew she had to regain her strength as quickly as possible.

All their lives depended on it.

Nicholas charged down the hallway until he reached the last door. He paused, trying in vain to quell his raging temper.

The blasted woman wouldn't give an inch! Why couldn't she see he was trying to save her?

Because you threaten and bully her at every turn.

The truth of the inner voice would not be silenced. Instead of coaxing the story from her with gentleness, he'd attacked her with the safety of her friends.

He'd had no choice.

Time was a precious commodity. Turner could arrive at any moment, with Magistrate Woodson in tow. His cousin would not rest until the Rose had paid dearly for his . . . *her* crimes. The bruises ravaging her too-slender body provided undeniable proof. Even now, Nicholas's blood ran cold at the pain she'd endured.

Forcing a semblance of a smile, he tapped at the door as he removed the key from his pocket. His smile vanished when the door breezed open.

Surely they didn't . . .

Fear coiled in his belly. If Dare and Thomas escaped, his only bargaining chip would be lost, the game finished.

A housemaid appeared in the hallway, her mobcap askew and her arms laden with fresh linens.

She stopped abruptly when confronted with his towering form. "Oh, my lord, what—"

"Where are the boys?"

Her plump cheeks colored under his unwavering stare. "In—in the kitchen, my lord."

Nodding a curt thank-you, Nicholas rushed down the stairs. He'd given explicit instructions that the lads were to be locked in the guest room at all times.

What the devil was Abbot thinking?

Passing through the kitchen doorway, Nicholas ground to a halt. He blinked, unable to believe his eyes. One of his unwilling guests had been transformed into royalty.

There in the center of the room, young Thomas appeared to be holding court. Seated at the head of the heavy oak table, he smiled at the cook, scullery maids, and groomsmen flocking around him. As if he presided over a royal banquet, an assortment of sweetcakes and biscuits adorned the table.

Thomas grinned happily as he downed a cup of

milk in one continuous swallow. "That was quite delicious," he exclaimed, dabbing at his lips with a napkin. "Thank you very much."

Nicholas stared at the boy in profound wonder. He spoke like a young prince, no hint of street Cockney lacing his words.

A smile twitched at Nicholas's lips. The angelic-faced lad could tempt Saint Peter himself from the heavenly gates. Judging by the enamored expressions of his staff, Nicholas would have to tread carefully with the boy, or confront the mutiny of his employees.

Seemingly invisible to the rest of the room, a lone form lounged in the shadows.

Dare.

Impenetrable and unyielding, he wore his isolation like a tarnished coat of armor. He reached out to no one, and no one reached out to him. The thought imbued Nicholas with sadness. He, too, had lived a solitary life, but surrounded by well-meaning servants, and little else.

His brother, Terrence, had buried himself in the Grey family library, preferring dusty tomes to human company. Their father had only two loves, port and gaming. The alcohol had killed him, and his incessant gambling had nearly bankrupted the family.

If not for his mother's love and strength, and Abbot's caring tutelage, Nicholas could have become a mirror image of the young man. Alone . . . hiding behind a shield of detachment.

He crushed the empathic feelings. In order to save them all, he would have to play the role of a heartless bastard to perfection.

Clearing his throat, Nicholas waited for his presence to be acknowledged.

Abbot noticed him first, his back stiffening as an

uncharacteristic blush graced his cheeks.

Silence rippled through the room.

One by one, each pair of eyes discovered Nicholas standing before them.

"Abbot, my instructions were quite clear on the matter of our guests."

"Yes, my lord, but young Thomas was curious about the house. And he was quite famished. . . ."

Dare appeared from the shadows. Like heat from a roaring fire, hostility emanated from the young man. By the time Nicholas finished his performance, Dare would hate him even more.

Thomas clambered from his chair, a wide grin dimpling his cheeks, and his eyes shining with unwavering trust. "Hullo, sir."

Disgusted by what he must do, Nicholas looked away.

Standing behind his young charge, Dare placed one hand on Thomas's shoulder. The gesture said more than words. It was a clear and definitive warning.

Nicholas knelt before the boy. "Thomas, would you like to visit . . ." He flashed his warmest smile. "It would help if I knew your friend's name."

As if seeking permission, Thomas looked up into Dare's stony expression.

Dare replied for him. "You don't need 'er name. We won't be stayin'."

Frustration burned to a flashpoint. "Very well," Nicholas said sharply. "Come with me if you wish to visit your nameless partner in crime." Ignoring the reproachful looks of his staff, he strode from the kitchen.

Temper rising with each forceful step, he reached her room and unlocked the door. Before he could step aside, Thomas barreled past him and dove onto the bed. Dare followed more sedately, studying the room as if searching for the quickest escape route.

The woman's eyes moistened as she hugged the boy to her chest. Nicholas knew the embrace must be painful, but she betrayed no discomfort, only pleasure.

"My angel," she whispered. "I've missed you so. Are they taking good care of you?"

"Oh, yes! The cook made me the sweetest strawberry tarts, and our room is grand. Why, our bed is so large, Mrs. Pippins and all the little ones could sleep on it. . . ."

Nicholas lounged in the doorway, content to allow the reunion to unfold for now. He didn't have the heart to do otherwise.

With her wan complexion and bruised jaw, she appeared fragile. Defenseless. The ivory silk nightgown, buttoned to her slender neck, painted a picture of virginal innocence. Her honey gold hair—the true color—had been washed and brushed to a shimmering glow, fitting her delicate features to perfection.

She was exquisite.

He almost wavered.

Once Thomas finished his effusive praise, the woman turned to Dare. "You should have done as I asked."

"Would you 'ave left us?" Dare replied, his tone a mild rebuke.

Proving his point, she said nothing.

Slowly, she faced Nicholas. "May we have a moment of privacy?"

Her warm, cocoa-colored eyes pleaded for permission.

Nicholas could not give it.

"I will give you one more chance," he said quietly. "Tell me who you are."

148

With her gaze focused on the satin coverlet, she shook her head. "It would serve no purpose. I confess. I am the White Rose, and I acted alone." She took a deep breath. "If you would notify the magistrate, I will make a written confession. I don't think a trial will be necessary."

Lunging forward, Dare's eyes were wild with fear. "I'm the Rose, not her! I did it all."

"Lord Grey knows the truth," she said, her voice steady. "Don't lie for me, Dare."

Though humbled by their unwavering loyalty, Nicholas had no choice. Casting his expression in stone, he went to the bed and lifted Thomas down. "Say your farewells now."

Rage darkened her eyes to midnight black. "You won't do this."

"I can, and I will. Dare has confessed. That is all the proof the magistrate will need."

If she had been capable of the feat, he sensed she would have lunged for his throat at that moment.

"As for Thomas," Nicholas continued, "he seems to be a quick-witted lad. I'm certain he will make a fine tradesman's apprentice."

As if on cue, Abbot appeared in the doorway. "Pardon the intrusion, my lord, but Mr. Hennessy has arrived."

"Show him to the study," Nicholas replied, closing the door. He turned to the trio of angry faces. "You may remember my friend from the docks. Did I also mention he is a Bow Street Runner?"

Like a wild bird suddenly caged, her anxious gaze flitted about the room. Nicholas fought the urge to hold her and ease her fear.

Placing a hand on Thomas's shoulder, he steered him toward the door. "Come along, then."

Suddenly, the child with the winsome smile and

trusting nature became a whirlwind of thrashing fists and feet. "No! I won't go . . . I won't."

"Don't make this difficult." Nicholas gasped as Thomas kicked him squarely on the shin.

Murder blazing in his eyes, Dare rushed forward. "Let 'im go, you bastard!"

Lurching backward, Nicholas wondered how he would live down the disgrace of being bested by two scrappy boys. He'd counted on the fact that she would die before allowing her friends to be hurt. He couldn't be wrong.

"Stop it! All of you!" Like a thunder-clap, the terrified scream finished the struggle.

Nicholas stared at the huddled form on the bed, a single tear gliding down her pale cheek. If not for the faint glimmer of defiance shining from her face, his shame would have been his undoing and he would have relented.

He battled the desire to confess and cleanse his soul. Once he'd solved the mystery of her past, and Turner's role in it, Nicholas would seek forgiveness.

If she didn't slide a dagger in his back first.

As if embarrassed by her show of weakness, she rubbed the telltale moisture from her face. "I would speak to you, Lord Grey. Privately."

Dare shot a scathing glance at Nicholas. "I won't leave you alone with 'im."

"I'll be fine," she answered wearily. "Take Thomas to your room, and I will explain everything later."

"Surely you don't trust—"

"You must trust me," she whispered. "Please."

After a grudging nod, Dare grasped the little boy's hand and led him from the room.

Now, with the moment of discovery at hand, Nicholas felt a strange sense of impending disaster. He ignored the troubling emotion. Sitting at the foot of the bed, he fulfilled the desperate need to be close to her. It wasn't close enough.

Hundreds of questions circled his mind. He settled upon the simplest. "I would like to begin with your name."

Her smile, twisted and sardonic, raised gooseflesh across his skin. "I was christened Margaret Elizabeth Rose Alston."

The name skirted the edge of his thoughts, strangely familiar, yet elusive.

"You don't remember her," she chided, her velvet eyes dull with fatigue. "Sometimes I barely remember her myself."

The incongruity of the statement sent a chill down his spine. "What do you mean?"

"Margaret Alston is dead."

Chapter Twelve

Maggie whispered her name again. It rolled from her tongue with an awkward strangeness. "Margaret Elizabeth Rose Alston."

Anguish assaulted her as she remembered the naive, trusting girl she'd been two years ago. It seemed more than two. It seemed a lifetime.

She pushed the remembrances into the darkness. To recall the girl she'd once been, would then mean being confronted with what had happened later.

Those demons were too powerful to face.

She stared into Nicholas's stunned expression. "Alston . . ." he murmured. "My God, you are the Baron of Chelsea's daughter!"

Nodding slowly, she awaited the next question with open dread.

His eyes widened. "Everyone believes you died in a shipwreck. How did you survive? And why the devil are you living on the streets?"

152

The rapid-fire queries drained her meager reserve of strength. Resting her head in her hands, she replied with weariness. "I was never in a shipwreck. Turner needed a plausible excuse to explain my disappearance. My death."

"But you're obviously not dead," Nicholas said in exasperation. He sighed, and gently lifted her chin. "I know you're tired, but I must have the entire story. It's the only way I can help you."

She gazed into his tender eyes, unable to speak, unable to form a single coherent thought.

"Let's start at the beginning," he offered, as if sensing her confusion. "How did Lord Turner become your guardian? Did you not have other family who—"

"There was no one." Maggie looked away as her father's smiling countenance filled her mind. His untimely death had shattered her idyllic world.

Her chest ached. Grief and sadness pressed down upon her like a stone. She was saved from tears by Nicholas's next question.

"Why did your father choose Turner?"

Hatred consumed her grief. "We met the viscount in the village one afternoon. He played his role well," Maggie said with derision. "He charmed my father into an invitation, and for the next few months he was a constant visitor."

Nicholas gripped her hands, his voice suddenly tense. "He didn't touch you or—"

"He treated me like a beloved daughter. Never an untoward glance or romantic gesture." She smiled bitterly. "He played his part so well, even I was duped."

"Along with your father."

Affronted by the faint undercurrent of scorn in Nicholas's voice, Maggie turned to him. "You don't understand. My father was not a worldly man. He hated London, and he hated parties. He was a man who loved nothing more than to putter in the gardens or fish in the pond."

Maggie sighed, her sorrow as keen as a nightingale's cry. "My father trusted everyone. It was his greatest strength."

"And his greatest weakness," Nicholas added softly.

She offered no rebuttal. Her father had put his faith in the wrong man.

"What did you say when your father told you of his decision to make Turner your guardian?"

"He never had the chance to tell me." She brushed away an unbidden tear. "He was ill for weeks, but he never told me." Guilt crept into her voice. "I didn't see it."

Nicholas touched her cheek, then pulled her into his arms. "I'm sure he didn't want you to worry."

"He went to sleep and never awoke. The physician said his heart failed."

Maggie sighed, welcoming Nicholas's tender embrace. She'd had no one then, and had faced her sadness and confusion alone. A strange sense of rightness flowed through her as she rested her head on his shoulder. His arms tightened around her, as if he sensed her need for contact.

"Tell me what happened next," he whispered against her ear.

The moment shattered.

Rubbing the sudden gooseflesh on her arms, she pulled away. "Three days later, the solicitor read my father's will. We lived a simple life, so naturally there were no great bequests." Bile rose in her throat. "Turner strolled in like the lord of the manor and told me to pack my things for an extended stay in London.''

"He certainly wasted no time."

"No, when we arrived a paid companion was waiting.''

Nicholas smiled coldly. "Of course. My cousin is a stickler for the proprieties. Whom did he hire?"

"A Miss Montclaire."

"Montclaire . . ." Nicholas's eyes widened with recognition. "She was listed on the passenger manifest alongside your name."

Maggie stilled in confusion. "How did you happen to see that document?"

"I've been digging into Turner's past. My mother mentioned your name, and since you're a part of that past . . ."

She bristled. "So why are you asking me these questions? You must know—"

"I know nothing. You have proven to be as elusive as Turner." Nicholas paused, his brows drawing together in perplexed thought. "If you're still alive, then your chaperon—"

"—is most assuredly dead," Maggie whispered. "Your cousin doesn't leave loose ends."

"Do you have proof?"

"If I had, do you think I would have gone to such extremes to see justice done?"

Leaping to his feet, Nicholas paced the room, head bowed as if in deep thought. He stopped in midstride. "I'm beginning to believe you are the only one who has survived being in Turner's clutches."

Maggie started to speak, then stifled the thought. *No, not the only one.*

"What happened after he brought you to London?" Nicholas asked.

She froze. *I don't want to remember that! I cannot!*

"Margaret, you must—"

"My name is Maggie," she said sharply, unable to bear the sound of the name.

As if treading across shards of glass, he approached her carefully. "Maggie suits you much better." He perched on the edge of the bed, making no move to touch her.

For that small blessing, she was grateful.

"Tell me."

The command, cloaked in gentleness, urged her to speak. "Turner began looking at me strangely. He would touch my cheek or my arm. . . ."

Rage colored Nicholas's voice. "By God, if he—"

"No, he did nothing further. It seemed very innocent at the time. I was so blind. So naive."

"You were a girl who'd just lost her father."

Maggie closed her eyes against the visions of the old Margaret cowering in her room. She had vowed then not to play the role of a timid mouse. If only she'd found her courage sooner.

"Was Turner pressuring you somehow?"

She nodded. "He told me that after the mourning period was finished, I would have one season, and then he would announce our engagement."

Nicholas's eyes blazed with undiluted hatred. She shrank back. He seemed on the verge of a deafening explosion.

Taking a deep breath, he spoke with deceptive softness. "My cousin planned to marry you, whether you were agreeable or not?"

"I knew I would rather die than marry such a vile man. So I decided to run away."

"Blast it, woman! Why didn't you come to me or my mother? We would have helped you."

"I wasn't sure where to go, but the point is moot.

He caught me before I could sneak from the house.''

The pitiful cries from that night reverberated through her mind. That night was the beginning of her hellish journey.

Afraid to face the visions, Maggie shook her head. She preferred blindness.

Nicholas clutched her shoulders. ''What did he do to you?''

No escape ... trapped.

Her throat was as dry as bonemeal. ''He said I needed to be taught a lesson. And he knew just the place that would teach me to become more 'biddable.' ''

Silence stretched like an abyss neither wanted to cross.

Finally Nicholas spoke. ''Where, Maggie? Where did he take you?''

Dreams, shattered and irretrievable, filled her thoughts. Battling the spectres of the past, she squeezed her eyes shut. ''He took me to a—a private asylum. I—I was kept in the cellar for two—two months. I finally convinced a guard to help me escape.''

''My God! I cannot believe the bloody bastard would do such a thing. I will see him in hell. . . .''

Nicholas's venomous litany became little more than a distant droning in her ears.

The degradation and heart-rending screams crept through her carefully constructed walls of defense.

Chained. Cold, damp walls. Whispers of scurrying paws. The musty scent ... like an ancient tomb. A tomb ... Buried ... What if they forget me!

A scream of terror burst from her lips.

Warm hands gripped her shoulders. ''Maggie, stop it! You're safe now. No one will hurt you again.''

The voice, rough with fear and concern, punctured

the veil of dark memories. "Nicholas?" Maggie opened her eyes.

He sat before her, so close his ragged breaths caressed her cheek. Remnants of fear drove her to touch him—to reassure herself the nightmare was over.

With an icy, trembling hand, she stroked his cheek and reveled in the roughness of his dark shadow of beard. The rasping sound echoed through the lingering stillness, bringing an almost absurd sense of normalcy—a normalcy she desperately needed to wipe the darkness from her tortured thoughts.

"Your valet should be shot."

Nicholas stared in confusion. "My valet?"

She stroked his cheek again. "No proper gentleman would be seen without a clean-shaven face."

His smile was a glorious thing of beauty. "Now, there is something I haven't been called in quite some time."

Maggie feigned innocence. "Clean-shaven?"

"No, a proper gentleman."

Nicholas watched her full, trembling lips form the faintest of smiles. He grinned back, unwilling to show her the rage battering his senses. Nausea roiled in his belly as he pictured what she'd endured. The fear. The hopelessness. And he knew with certainty that she had not shared the more horrific memories. He didn't have the heart to push further.

"Now you understand why I became the Rose. I know my methods seem wrong, but Turner must be destroyed. If you tell the magistrate you suspect your cousin is the thief, he will—"

"No, Maggie." He said it with finality.

Bitterness deepened the lines of weariness on her face. "Why? Because your reputation may be tarnished along with your cousin's?"

Nicholas laughed at the outrageous charge. "I

don't give a whit for my reputation. People can think what they bloody well like.''

"Even if your mother is drawn into the fray?"

"While my father lived, my mother withstood more innuendo and mean-spirited gossip than you could imagine.''

Maggie stared at him with no sign of penitence. Her eyes shone with dark certainty. "Your cousin will not stop until everyone he deems a threat is dead and buried. Lady Grey is no exception.''

Chills swept unencumbered across his flesh at the thought. "I would see Edward Turner dead before—''

"Then we are in agreement. He must be stopped.''

"Turner will pay, but not for crimes he did not commit.''

She scoffed openly. "Don't tell me the rogue wishes to do the *honorable* thing.''

Nicholas understood her deep-rooted bitterness. She had lost her father much too soon, nearly been forced into a hideous marriage, and been locked in an asylum. If anyone had a right to mistrust motives, it was Maggie.

And although in the past he'd been known as the consummate rakehell, he did have a deep sense of honor. He'd never touched innocents, had paid his debts in a timely fashion, and had tried to bring honor to the title he'd never wanted. Turning his back on those tenets would serve no purpose now.

"I know you're upset, Maggie. But I will not stoop to Turner's level. Besides, being labeled a thief is much too compassionate a punishment for my dear cousin.''

Maggie worried the satin duvet with her fingers. "You do not know him as I do. He is the cruelest human being I have ever known.''

Like razors, her whispered words sliced at his soul. "I swear, Maggie. Edward Turner will pay for what he has done to you." *And to my family.*

Questions of how Maggie survived such hell thundered through Nicholas's mind. But one look at the dark circles beneath her eyes and the lines of fatigue marking her pale complexion silenced them. She needed rest. She needed to heal.

He brushed an errant strand of honey gold hair from her cheek. "I prefer this color much more."

A girlish blush tinted her skin. "I detested that wig. It was unbearably warm and scratchy."

"But the disguise was perfect. I would never have suspected Dubber and Athena were one and the same."

"I'm sorry I lied to you, but I could trust no one. I took no pleasure in the pretense."

"I know." Nicholas chuckled, grazing a fingertip down her cheek. "And had I been in your place, I wouldn't have trusted me either."

She smiled. "You were quite persistent."

"It's one of my more irritating traits."

Her eyelids drooped with weariness.

"Lie down and rest," he said softly. "Once you've made a complete recovery, we will decide what course to take."

Offering no argument, she eased under the coverlet. Nicholas tucked her in like a child, placing a chaste kiss on her forehead. "Sleep well, Maggie."

He waited until her breaths became deep and even, then stood, rubbing the stiffened muscles of his neck. Utterly exhausted, he wanted nothing more than to stretch out beside her and hold her. But sleep was a luxury he could ill afford.

A chill skittered down his spine as he pictured what Turner would do if he discovered that Margaret Alston was not only very much alive, but also the in-famous White Rose.

Nicholas had to protect her. He had failed Julia. He would not fail Maggie.

Nicholas walked into the study to find Connor pacing the room like an expectant papa. With all the revelations he'd just heard, Nicholas had forgotten his friend was waiting.

"Now who needs a bloody timepiece," Connor quipped, his impatience concealed by humor.

Ignoring the early hour, Nicholas strolled to the mahogany sideboard and poured a whiskey. He downed the fiery liquor in one swallow.

After a deep, cleansing breath, he turned to his friend. "Tell me you have good news."

Connor settled into a wing-back chair. "It's not good, but not hopeless either."

"I'm in no mood for riddles," Nicholas said sharply, his patience at an end. "I need to know what you've discovered, before Turner decides to darken my doorstep again."

"So that's the way the wind blows."

"What the devil is that supposed to mean?"

Studying his chipped fingernails like a bored aristocrat, Connor responded in a light tone. "Why, it's as clear as rain, Nicky. You're already attached to those three street urchins upstairs. Especially the girl."

Dumbfounded, Nicholas stared at the grinning Irishman. Once again, he'd underestimated Connor's keen attention to detail. "How did you realize the truth so quickly?"

"Well now, there are some differences between men and women, you know."

"I don't need a bloody anatomy lesson," Nicholas

bit out, his temper rising in proportion to the absurdity of the conversation.

"Ah, you'd be right about that. Why, you're a legend when it comes to affairs of the heart."

Nicholas's voice growled in warning. "Irish . . ."

"Well, now," Connor said, puffing out his chest, "women have been endowed with lovely breasts and shapely hips, but no Adam's apple."

"Your eyes are as keen as your taste for my brandy."

"Aye, that they are," Connor remarked proudly.

Nicholas leaned against the mantel, curling his hands into fists in frustration. He glanced over his shoulder and into his friend's concerned expression. "We are running out of time."

"You're right in that." Connor sighed in exasperation. "I've located almost all the staff that worked for your uncle at the time of his death. Those still alive, at any rate."

"And?"

"There's only one I haven't found yet. A scullery maid who would've been about fifteen years old at the time."

A sense of urgency vibrated through Nicholas's taut nerves. "You believe she may know something?"

"Perhaps. With the uproar your aunt's death caused, none of the staff noticed until days later that the maid had vanished."

Nicholas's excitement ebbed. "If Turner had known she'd witnessed something, he would have most assuredly murdered her, as well."

"I don't think so, Nicky. Her belongings were gone, and an innkeeper in the neighboring village said he remembered her leaving on the morning mail coach."

"He is certain of this?" Nicholas queried, afraid to hope.

Connor nodded. "The innkeeper knew the girl's family. She never returned."

Nicholas slammed his hand against the mantel. "How the devil are we supposed to locate her? It's been over twenty years. For all we know, she could have died."

"Her trail led to Dorchester, then nothing. I've got two men combing the area. If she's there, they'll find her."

Like a caged lion, Nicholas paced. "It's like searching for a bloody ghost!" There was a moment of silence before either spoke.

"So who is she?" Connor asked quietly.

Nicholas knew his friend was not referring to the mysterious scullery maid, but to the guest upstairs. He was strangely reluctant to share her true identity. A primitive need to possess all of her—including her name—held his tongue.

"She seems a mite young. . . ."

Nicholas didn't care for Connor's cloaked insinuation. Even if the charge was true. "Make no mistake, my friend. She is a woman. And she is under my protection."

Connor rose and moved closer, apparently not intimidated by the veiled warning. "She's not your usual choice in women, Nicky."

Turning away from his friend's insightful gaze, Nicholas wanted to deny the charge, even as a fantasy of her soft, pale body, writhing beneath his, flashed through his mind. The quandary he now faced crystallized into stunning clarity. Maggie was well born, a baron's daughter, yet she'd lived in East End, surviving with only her wits and her body?

The idea was suddenly inescapable. Horrifying.

And yet he still wanted her with such voracious need that it terrified him.

"You are overstepping your bounds, Hennessy."

"That, my dear son, is a charge usually leveled at you." A new voice.

Nicholas groaned aloud. *Not now . . .*

Pasting a halfhearted smile on his face, he turned, his voice mild. "Mother, you're home much earlier than expected. Did you enjoy the Kensingtons' house party?"

"Yes, it was most enjoyable."

Like a courtier, Connor stepped forward and bowed. "Lady Grey, 'tis a pleasure. And as always, your beauty leaves me breathless."

Eugenia laughed with girlish delight. "Mr. Hennessy, you become more charming, and more outrageous, each time our paths cross."

"Which never happens enough," he quipped, plopping his weathered hat on his head. "But now I must be goin'."

"Come by in the morning," Nicholas said softly. "I will explain the situation then."

Eugenia stepped between the two men, her eyes illuminated with mischief. "Would this *situation* concern our three guests?"

Gazing into her determined face, Nicholas sank into the nearest chair with a heavy sigh of defeat. "You may as well stay, Connor. I don't think I can do justice to the story twice. Mother, have a seat. This could take a great deal of time."

Chapter Thirteen

Gripping the railing with damp palms, Maggie paused at the head of the stairs. She closed her eyes and took a deep, shaky breath.

After a week of quiet recuperation, her body was stronger. Her emotions remained ragged. For two years she had buried Margaret Alston beneath layers of secrets and deception. The White Rose . . . the widow Sanford . . . Margaret . . . Maggie.

She was none of them.

She was all of them.

Maggie opened her eyes. Nicholas stood at the bottom of the staircase.

For a moment, the ability to breathe proved impossible. Nicholas was resplendent in formal black attire, his dark hair gleaming beneath the muted glow of oil lamps. His full, sensuous lips curved into a soft smile—a smile she hadn't witnessed for the past week. He had been noticeably restrained during her

165

convalescence. One perfunctory visit each afternoon had been the extent of their contact.

Now Maggie wanted more. And the thought was terrifying.

Her need for him grew and blossomed with each moment spent in his commanding presence. Powerless to resist, she had decided the risk was worth the reward. With the future beyond her control, the present was all she could claim. And Nicholas was the prize—the sliver of light in her fractured soul.

Stomach fluttering, head spinning, she descended the stairs.

"You look lovely," he said, brushing a chaste kiss across the top of her gloved hand.

She toyed with the wispy lavender silk of her gown as heat crept across her cheeks. "You should not have gone to such expense. A few day gowns would have sufficed."

His lazy gaze swept her from head to toe. "I was not speaking of the gown." With a gentle caress, he touched her jaw. "The bruises are nearly gone."

Warmth curled within her, leaving her breathless. Speechless.

"I am sorry I struck you. If I had known . . ."

"But you didn't," Maggie replied softly.

His expression turned deadly. "No one will touch you again."

Craving the feel of his skin, she nestled her cheek against his palm. "No one but you."

As the fire in his eyes diminished, he slid his hand free. "Shall we join the others in the drawing room?"

Stung by the subtle rejection, she stepped back. "Has something happened?"

Nicholas's smile, too smooth, too polished, heightened her confusion. "No, nothing has happened."

"Your cousin has not returned?"

"He has not left his house. He's probably busy licking his wounded pride."

"But he was not arrested," she said, struggling to understand the change in Nicholas's demeanor.

"No, but gossip abounds. The ton is convinced he is the Rose."

"Lord Turner will not give up. As long as I remain, you and your family will be in danger."

Brushing the back of his hand along her temple, Nicholas's suave smile vanished. "My cousin will never harm you, or my family, again."

Maggie pressed his hand tight against her cheek. "Don't underestimate him. He is a violent man."

"I know exactly what kind of man Edward Turner is." With those words, Nicholas led her toward the drawing room. "Now, no more doom and gloom tonight. My mother will be down shortly, and she has been chomping at the bit all week to renew your acquaintance."

Maggie stopped in midstride. She'd known Lady Grey would be told of her unexpected guests. Yet the thought did nothing to allay Maggie's trepidation. "Exactly what have you told her?"

"I told her the truth."

"Everything?" she asked, her voice little more than a croak.

Nicholas chuckled. "Except for the particulars of our first meeting—every man has his pride. And of course the exhilarating carriage ride we shared . . ."

Ignoring his perverse humor, she paced the foyer. "But I am a thief. Surely she—"

"—admires your strength and courage. She has become your greatest champion. As for Thomas, my mother is completely enamored with the lad."

Tucking Maggie's arm in his, he led her forward. She considered fleeing back to her room, but thought better of the ridiculous notion. She had decided to stay and confront Lord Turner. Surely Lady Grey would prove easier to face than her nephew.

Nicholas patted her hand. "Where is the daring young woman who picks locks as easily as she fools the ton?"

"She is about to face your mother."

"Don't worry. I've told her to be gentle in her inquisition."

"If you're trying to calm my nerves, you have failed miserably."

"I think I have the perfect tonic to ease your misgivings." With a secretive smile, he pushed the door open and ushered her to the center of the salon. "May I present the honorable Miss Alston."

Maggie's gaze swept the room. Standing beside the fireplace, Dare and Thomas stared at her in wide-eyed astonishment. She understood Thomas's surprise. He had never seen her dressed in her lavish costumes. But Dare had witnessed her numerous transformations. He'd even teased her about the fancy attire. Now his obvious surprise frightened Maggie beyond words. An invisible wall seemed to rise between them.

Thomas shattered the awkward silence. "Maggie, you look like a fairy princess."

She bent down, opening her arms wide in invitation.

He barreled into her waiting embrace. "Are you all better now?"

"I feel wonderful," she murmured, ignoring the twinge in her ribs. Holding him at arm's length, she perused his freshly pressed breeches and starched white shirt. "And look at you! Like a young prince yourself."

Tugging at the stiff cravat, Thomas frowned. "I

don't think I'd like to be a prince if I had to wear *this* every day."

Maggie laughed and pulled him close. "I understand completely," she whispered against his ear. "I miss my patched breeches."

Nicholas knelt beside them, tapping Thomas on the shoulder. "Now, young man, off to the kitchen for your dinner."

With regret, Maggie released her hold. Supping with Thomas and Dare had always proven to be her favorite part of the day. Now, within a week's time, their simple lives had been transformed. And she couldn't be certain if it was necessarily for the better.

A discreet cough signaled Abbot's presence. His usual solemn expression was softened by a gleam of undeniable enjoyment. "Come along, Master Thomas. The cook has prepared a very special surprise for you."

The boy followed Abbot to the door. "Maggie, will you read me a story before bed?"

"Of course, angel. I will tuck you in myself."

She sighed as the door closed.

Like a winter wind, Dare's cold voice cut through the room. "Why'd you let 'im do that, Maggie?"

Confused, she stared at her friend. "What do you mean?"

"Why did you let 'im send Thomas away. 'E belongs with us." Dare turned his accusing gaze to Nicholas. "Isn't 'e good enough to sit at your fancy table?"

"You are overstepping your bounds," Nicholas said. "I sent him to the kitchen because he will be more comfortable there."

"Maybe more comfortable for you."

Praying she could defuse his temper, Maggie moved slowly toward her friend. For whatever reason,

Dare had chosen Nicholas as an outlet for seventeen years of rage. And when Dare was well and truly riled, no one was safe.

"Don't do this," she said in a soothing tone. "We are guests here."

"We're not guests," Dare said angrily. "We're prisoners!"

"That's enough," Nicholas said softly.

Too softly for Maggie's comfort. She stepped in his path, hands raised. "This is all very new to him. He doesn't understand—"

"Maggie, stay out of this," Dare said. "I don't bloody well need you to make excuses for me."

"What you need," Nicholas growled, "is a lesson in manners."

Hands clenched into bony fists, Dare's icy gaze never strayed from the man looming above him. "And you think you're the man to do it?"

"Stop this at once!" Maggie stomped her foot in utter frustration. "Both of you are behaving like children."

Dare's face reddened at the chastisement. "We don't belong 'ere. We're not like them."

"And where do you belong?" Nicholas asked, his voice harsh and unrelenting. "In a hovel made of thatch and moss? Is that the kind of life you wish to give Thomas? As for Maggie, do you truly believe the Baron of Chelsea's daughter belongs in East End?"

Unable to meet Dare's shocked expression, she closed her eyes. Another deception laid bare.

"What's 'e talkin' about, Maggie? Your mum was an actress, and your father ran off."

After a deep breath, she faced his obvious confusion. "I lied to you about my past. I knew if I told you the truth, you would never trust me."

" 'Ow could you tell *'im*," Dare asked, waving a dismissive hand in Nicholas's direction, "and lie to me?"

Through his outrage, Maggie sensed his hurt. She had betrayed him. "I wanted to tell you everything. . . ."

Standing behind her, Nicholas placed his hand on her shoulder. "Miss Alston had no choice in the matter. I forced her to tell me what happened."

"No, Dare is right to be upset. I should have told him long ago." Reaching out, Maggie tried to offer comfort to her dearest friend.

He jerked away. "I want the truth. Every bit of it."

"I don't believe now is the right time," Nicholas said, gripping her shoulder more tightly. "Miss Alston is still recovering."

"I can speak for myself!" Resenting the high-handed intrusion, she shrugged off his touch. "And you had no such compunction a week ago."

Dare smiled slightly, but remained silent.

With a stony expression, Nicholas offered a stiff bow and strolled to the door. "I will leave you alone to sort out the misunderstanding."

Once he was gone, Maggie sank into the cream-colored divan, willing the tension from her body. Playing the role of mediator had taken its toll.

"I'm waitin'."

His curt statement forced a heavy sigh from her lips. For his safety, she would have to tread carefully. "Very well. My father *was* the Baron of Chelsea. He died, and I came to London with my guardian. He wanted to marry me, but I refused and ran away." Her imprisonment at the asylum would remain her secret. That information would send Dare over the edge. "Then," she finished with a quivering smile, "I met you and Thomas."

171

"And yer mum?"

"She died a few weeks after I was born." Maggie held her breath, praying Dare would accept the meager details without question.

Set in stubborn lines, his lean, angular face diminished her hope. "Who is 'e?"

The icy tone of his voice tolled a warning bell. "What do you mean?"

"I know you, Maggie. You wouldn't 'ave run unless the bastard 'urt you. What's 'is name?"

Her heart thudded a painful beat against her chest. "It doesn't matter. I am free of him."

Dare's eyes widened in sudden understanding. "The man with the gold watch . . . 'e's the one!" Seemingly lost in thought, he paced the room. "That's why you decided to play the Rose. It was never about makin' a new life in America, or 'elpin' people in East End."

He ground to a halt, his eyes flashing with cold accusation. "This was about revenge!"

Maggie flinched under the barrage. Each charge, accurate and painfully true, lashed her heart to ribbons. "I'm sorry."

"Sorry! Didn't you ever think about Thomas?" With each word, Dare drew fresh blood. "What if somethin' 'ad 'appened to 'im?"

"I made provisions," she replied in hushed tones. "You and Thomas would have been well taken care of."

Dare's mouth fell open, his eyes wide with amazement. "Bloody 'ell! You don't understand at all."

"I would have died if my actions had somehow hurt you."

"What about you, Maggie? Did you think we'd be satisfied with a few pound notes while you swung from the gallows?"

"It consumed me—my anger," she whispered, unashamed of the tears pricking her eyes. "In the beginning, revenge was all that kept me alive. I breathed it like air. But when I saw the suffering, the hunger in East End, I thought I could help."

Dare glanced away, running a hand through his long hair. "Don't go turnin' into a water spout," he muttered. "I'm as guilty as you are. Sometimes I dream of revenge. I dream of slittin' his skinny throat. . . ." His jaw snapped closed, his face blanching white as muslin sheets.

Staring at her clenched hands, Maggie allowed him privacy while he gathered his emotions. Weakness, to Dare, was more abhorrent than any other thing.

In a matter of seconds, his fear dimmed, his expression weary. "I admit, I liked the idea of stealin' their jewels right from under their pointy noses." His lips twitched upward. "I bloody well enjoyed it."

Maggie inhaled as the tension flowed from her body. "Am I forgiven then?"

Settling beside her, he nodded. "I know why you didn't tell me who you were. I can be a bit touchy when it comes to you upper-crusters."

Risking rejection, she placed her hand on his. Instead of pulling away, he slowly laced his fingers through hers.

"Maggie, I want us to go to America like we planned. Tonight, when everyone is sleepin', we can take Thomas and sneak out."

She wanted to say yes. She wanted to scream the word to the heavens.

Yet she could not.

Like a festering wound, the horrible darkness of the cellar would not leave her soul. Visions of Edward Turner's evil haunted her without end.

Even for Dare and Thomas, she could not stop. "I

promise we will go. But now is not the time.''

Dare's calm demeanor vanished. ''It's the marquess, isn't it? 'E's the reason you don't want to leave.''

They had come full circle.

She wanted to deny his charge, but the lie lodged in her throat. She'd never dreamed of allowing a man possession of her body. The very thought had chilled her blood. Now, instead of fear, she felt the awakening of desire. But sharing her revelations with Dare was out of the question. His temper, barely in check, would flash to a melting point.

Battle-weary, she sighed. ''Lord Grey is a good man. If you would give him the chance to prove it . . .''

The soft click of a door latch silenced the room like a thunderclap.

Nicholas could not have returned at a worse time.

Shock held him immobile.

Nicholas stared at their clasped hands, trying to make sense of the unfolding tableau. In the past week, he'd never seen Dare touch Maggie in even the most cursory manner. And now they were huddled together, hands intertwined, thighs pressed close.

Holding his breath, Nicholas remembered the cramped one-room hovel Dare, Maggie, and Thomas had shared.

Two beds. Only two beds.

Dragging his gaze upward, Nicholas met Dare's insolent stare. A crimson mist settled over his vision. His hands trembled with the need to wrench Maggie from Dare's side.

With ruthless intent, Nicholas reined in his temper, even managing a dim smile. ''Am I interrupting?''

He watched as Maggie tried to pull her hand free.

Dare's grip tightened. "We're not finished talkin' yet."

If the lad wanted a fight, Nicholas was happy to grant his wish. "I believe you are."

Maggie jerked free. "I will not stand by and watch you bait each other."

Leaping to his feet, Dare stared at Nicholas with absolute hatred. " 'E's the one causin' all the trouble. We can't trust 'im!"

"I will not spar with you," Nicholas ground out. He turned to Maggie. "Dinner will be served in moments."

As if claiming ownership, Dare grabbed her arm. "Don't go with 'im."

Nicholas stepped closer. "Release her."

"Please," Maggie said, her eyes pleading, "let me speak to Dare. You don't understand what—"

"I understand more than you, apparently. Your young friend is rude, impertinent, and *jealous.*"

Her stunned expression surprised Nicholas. And laid his doubts to rest. If Maggie and Dare had shared an intimate relationship, she would not appear so dumbstruck by his announcement.

Nicholas's pleasure vanished quickly.

Like a wild beast, Dare lunged forward, his teeth bared in a feral grimace. A flash of silver appeared in his hand.

Cold fear squeezed Nicholas's heart. He swept Maggie from Dare's path—away from the knife.

Instinct guided his movements. Feinting left, Nicholas grabbed Dare's wrist from the right. He exerted steady, deliberate pressure until the dinner knife fell to the floor with a gentle thud.

Seizing Dare by the collar, he shoved him into the divan. His weight pinned the boy in place.

Calm restraint was no longer an option.

Through his rage, Nicholas felt Maggie yanking on his arm. "Let him go!"

He looked over his shoulder, amazed she could continue to defend Dare. Her eyes, wide with terror, seared his soul. Nicholas glanced away, hating the intangible bond between Maggie and the boy.

"Stay clear of this. It is past time Dare and I came to an understanding."

A shower of blows rained upon his shoulders. Nicholas ignored the ineffectual attack. "Listen well, boy. As long as you remain in my home, you will treat me, my mother, and my staff with respect. If you cannot, you will leave. Do you understand?"

He waited, praying Dare would heed the ultimatum. Instead, Nicholas realized the boy had heard none of the warning. The color had drained from Dare's face. Sweat beaded across his brow. His eyes, glazed and unseeing, were chilling to behold. He could almost smell the boy's anger—and fear.

Ragged breaths echoed the room as Dare finally spoke. "Please, don't . . . 'urt me. . . ."

Unnerved by the frightened capitulation, Nicholas released his bruising hold and stepped back.

Rushing to Dare's side, Maggie squeezed his shoulder. "All is well. Nicholas would never hurt you."

Like a drunkard, Dare lurched to his feet and stumbled backward. "Don't touch me! Don't ever touch me again." He charged from the room, tears gleaming wetly on his pale face.

Nicholas slammed his fist against the divan. He'd handled the situation badly. But what else could he have done?

Maggie appeared before him, her shoulders shaking with belated emotion. "How could you!" With the swiftness of an adder's strike, she slapped him smartly across the cheek.

176

"What the hell . . ." Stunned by her actions, he stroked his stinging face.

"Don't ever touch Dare again."

"I believe he made that point quite clear. And I did not strike him. Though he deserved it."

"Perhaps you should have." She paused, and he saw her shoulders slump.

Nicholas raked a hand through his hair, his voice raised in confusion. "What the devil does that mean?"

Maggie sighed. "For an intelligent man, you can be as dense as wood."

He'd been called many things, most of them justified, but *dense* could not be counted on the list. Before he could refute her words, she continued in a scathing tone. "In one fell swoop, you stole the only thing he can call his own. His pride."

"Damn it, Maggie! The boy was threatening me with a knife. One of us could have been injured."

Her voice rang out with certainty. "Dare would never harm me."

Nicholas chose not to argue that point. He'd been painted the villain, and that was that. "All I am asking for is civil behavior. The boy is altogether too stubborn and arrogant."

"Traits *you* carry like a badge of honor," she retorted.

Deep brown eyes flashing with angry fire held Nicholas captive. Seeing the passion with which she spoke, he felt his anger melt, a grudging smile of admiration forming on his lips. "Touché, Miss Alston. Your barb has struck home."

As if sensing victory, she softened her tone. "I hope that means you will offer an apology to Dare."

"If he reciprocates, I will be happy to."

His reply renewed her anger. "You know perfectly

well he will not apologize.'' She worried her bottom lip as she paced before him. ''There must be a way to bring two thickheaded men into agreement. Perhaps if . . .''

Focusing on her words proved impossible for Nicholas. Tendrils of hair caressed her temple and brushed her shoulders. He sucked in his breath, imagining those silky strands of burnished gold fanned across his pillow . . . her body opening beneath his as he claimed her.

''What—what are you staring at?'' she asked, the color of her cheeks deepening.

Without conscious thought, his voice dropped to an intimate whisper. ''A gentleman would never reveal his libertine thoughts. Suffice to say, your passion and beauty leave me speechless.''

Her sable lashes fluttered downward like a curtain, concealing her thoughts.

Nicholas turned his attention to her lips. Soft and luscious; he ached for one taste.

Hunger drove him forward.

Her tentative voice stopped him cold.

''Those are lovely words. Yet for the past week you have treated me like a sister.'' After a trembling breath, she faced him. ''I don't know what you want of me.''

In an ageless battle, lust clashed with honor. His body, heated and aroused, urged him closer. His mind screamed a warning to run.

Margaret Alston needed more than he could give, he realized suddenly. She deserved a man who loved her unconditionally. After abandoning Julia when she'd needed him most, Nicholas couldn't bring himself to consider the notion of love. Even for Maggie.

He turned away, loosening his cravat. ''Forgive me. I have overstepped my bounds.''

"Where is the daring marquess who kissed me at our first meeting, and then again in his carriage?"

Her poignant question filled him with self-loathing. "Trust me. You're better off without him."

Her bitter laughter raked across his nerves, opening fresh wounds. "How novel. The rogue has sprouted a conscience. You had no such scruples in your carriage."

"That was a completely different situation, Maggie."

"Why, because my name was 'Athena'? Because I was playing the role of a widow?"

"Yes! That has everything to do with it. Once I take care of Turner, you will be free to marry."

She stared at him, her expression seemingly amused, and at the same time horrified. "You think to pack me off to some—some man once this matter is settled?"

"You will have to marry eventually."

Her lips curled into a soft, beguiling half smile. "I think not."

Nicholas shuddered. He could feel himself losing control. He could almost envision her, hand extended, offering him a plump, red apple.

Poor, misguided Adam. He never stood a chance.

Her arms coiled around his waist, her breasts grazing his chest. "Oh, Nicholas, you have worried for naught. I have no desire to wed anyone."

Of their own volition, his hands spanned her slender hips and dragged her closer. "You say that now, but someday . . ."

"Trust me, Lord Grey. I will never change my mind."

Soft hands slid under his shirt.

Nicholas groaned. Like smoke rings, all his honorable intentions vanished.

Cupping her taut buttocks, he pulled her tight against his rock-hard arousal. There was no time for gentle wooing. He found her lips, plundered her mouth with his tongue. Risking more, he palmed one breast, savoring the firm flesh. He brushed his thumb across her nipple, teasing it to attention.

Soft purrs echoed from her throat as she slid her hands to his chest. "Please, Nicholas, don't deny me this."

He gasped at her bold request, and even bolder actions. She was no innocent. Her skillful hands and tempting mouth would put a king's courtesan to shame.

But Maggie is not a whore . . . she is the daughter of a man your mother called friend. She's practically a child. . . .

The inner voice droned on, berating him for each transgression—each unholy thought.

Nicholas pushed her away gently. "Maggie, this isn't right. You are a guest in my home. I cannot abuse that privilege."

Gazing into her eyes, he saw a single flash of pain. She blinked once, and it was gone.

His stomach churned in self-disgust. "I am sorry."

As still and serene as ivory marble, her face betrayed nothing. "If you don't mind, I think I will go to my room. I am not . . . feeling well." Without a backward glance, she swept from the room, head held high.

Nicholas let her go, wishing she would have slapped him again.

Chapter Fourteen

Maggie cursed the lavender silk gown for its impossible hooks. She cursed the stubborn French corset, the laces twisted into tiny knots. Above all, she cursed Nicholas Grey. *Damn his streak of misplaced honor!*

She'd nearly begged him to make love to her, and he had refused. Not that he hadn't wanted to accept her blatant invitation. The evidence, pressed snugly against her stomach, could not be denied.

Tears scalded her eyes. Behaving like a prostitute at Covent Garden, she had made an utter fool of herself.

Maggie refused the luxury of tears. Why did men believe women could not find happiness unless shackled by the bonds of marriage? The very idea was ludicrous. Then again, what choice did her sex have? Power was tied to wealth, and few women had the financial resources to maintain their freedom.

Pacing the room in nothing more than a cotton

shift, Maggie fumed at the injustice. Why should women be denied the power of passion? Men certainly had no moral dictates ruling their primal urges. Mistresses were as common as gin-makers.

Maggie yanked the satin ribbon from her hair. And how many husbands leaped into their marriage beds as virginal as their brides were expected to be? "Ha!" she crowed aloud. "Nary a one!"

A soft tap at the door ended her diatribe against the masculine sex.

Jerking her arms into a soft satin dressing robe, she marched to the door. If one more concerned housemaid offered her hot tea, warm milk, or a cold compress, Maggie would scream.

With barely concealed frustration, she swept the door open. "I do not need—" Her mouth snapped closed.

No overworked servant stood on the threshold. Adorned in an iridescent peacock blue, tunic gown, the towering form loomed above her. The piercing azure eyes and amazing height could only belong to one woman. The Marchioness of Rockingham.

Maggie groaned inwardly. Clutching the lace collar tight against her neck, she offered a stilted curtsy. "Lady Grey, I—"

"There is no need for such formality."

Suddenly Maggie found herself enfolded in a welcoming embrace. As elusive as a childhood memory, the faint scent of lilac wafted from the plump bosom pressed to Maggie's cheek.

"Oh, my darling girl," Lady Grey murmured. "To think you have been alive all this time. Had I only known . . . I failed you miserably. But never again."

Maggie shook her head before stepping away from the sheltering arms. "No, Lady Grey, you did not fail me. Viscount Turner did."

The older woman's expression became a stony mask.

Like mother, like son.

"We will not speak his name. At least not on this night. And I insist you address me as Eugenia."

"Very well. If you will return the courtesy and call me Maggie."

"I would be delighted." Eugenia's misty-eyed gaze swept Maggie from head to toe. "I always knew you would grow into an incomparable beauty. But you have surpassed even my expectations."

Embarrassment, and a tinge of anger, heated Maggie's cheeks. "I daresay that if I'd had the face of a withered crone, Edward Turner would have ignored my existence." Too late, she realized she'd steered the conversation back to a topic they'd agreed to put to rest.

Eugenia scowled, her eyes flashing with open hatred. "You are certainly correct on that score. My nephew does not have a decent bone in his miserable body. But," she added carefully, "not all men are reprobates and scoundrels."

Remembering Nicholas's iron control, Maggie offered no denial. Instead, a change of topic seemed in order. "I am sorry I was unable to greet you earlier. "I was not . . . feeling well."

With liquid grace, Eugenia eased onto the hunter green chaise longue near the window. "Yes, my son said you were indisposed. He himself looked a bit green about the gills."

"Good!" Mortified she'd spoken the thought aloud, Maggie slapped her hand over her mouth.

Girlish laughter filled the silence.

Maggie stared at the imposing woman who laughed with the delight of a toddling child. "You will lead my son a merry chase."

"I have no intention of leading Nich—Lord Grey anywhere."

Silver-tinged brows rose in patent disbelief. "Don't try my patience. Every time you utter his name, you become as red as a pomegranate."

"Annoyance, nothing more," Maggie replied with a dismissive wave. "Your son is arrogant, stubborn . . . why, he even locked me in his cellar!"

Eugenia frowned. "Yes, he told me about that debacle. And I, in turn, gave him a firm set-down. Although, had he known your true identity, I'm sure he would have offered more suitable lodgings." Her voice softened. "Nicholas can be quite determined when it comes to those he cares for. And I believe he has come to care for you."

"Lord Grey has made it quite clear that once my safety is assured, he will busy himself with finding me a husband."

Rising slowly, the first overt betrayal of her age, Eugenia moved to Maggie's side and sat. "The past is sometimes difficult to escape. You must understand that more than most."

The words, haunting and true, stripped Maggie of all her well-worn defenses. Weary to the marrow of her bones, she offered a shaky rebuttal. "I have no wish to marry anyone. And I told him that."

"My son has said those very words to me many times." Eugenia's lips curved into an almost sad smile of acceptance. "After Lady Wentworth's death, he was a changed man."

Maggie's attention was piqued. "Wentworth?"

A rosy blush crept across the older woman's cheeks. "I should have said nothing."

"I won't tell him you mentioned her name," Maggie assured her.

"No, my dear. That is Nicholas's past, and his to share if he chooses."

A flutter of apprehension alighted in Maggie's stomach. "Did he . . . love her?"

As if taking her measure, Eugenia stared hard into Maggie's face. After a moment, she nodded. "I believe he did. Although he never told me directly. Nicholas is a very private man."

The sharp sting of jealousy pricked her heart. Maggie had thought honor stood between them. Instead, the ghost of another woman lurked in the shadows.

The truth snatched her breath away. She was selfish. She wanted Nicholas to love her, and she wanted her freedom. At this moment, the two seemed as incompatible as the sun and moon.

"My intent was not to upset you," Eugenia said, patting Maggie's hand.

She shook her head in weak denial. "Nicholas's past is of no concern to me. I'm sure he will find a lovely bride one day."

Although Eugenia remained silent, Maggie saw the gleam of hope in her eyes. "I cannot be that woman," Maggie said. "I will never wed."

"That is an all too familiar refrain." Chuckling, Eugenia stroked Maggie's cheek. "I shall leave you to rest now. I expect to see you at breakfast. We have much to discuss." She paused at the door, and glanced over her shoulder. "I am so happy you're here, Maggie. Your father would be proud of the woman you've become. As proud as I am."

"I've done little to warrant such an emotion," Maggie replied.

Eugenia smiled, her clear eyes bright with conviction. "You have survived, my dear. Survived when others would have given up hope. Remember that."

The door closed, leaving Maggie alone to ponder Lady Grey's parting words.

Yes, she'd survived, and the White Rose had saved a few less fortunate souls along the way. Perhaps her father would understand the choices she'd made.

She glanced upward, as if expecting a mystical affirmation from the heavens. None came, but her spirits remained effervescent. She had never cried defeat. And now it was time to teach Nicholas Grey that particular lesson.

The carefully tended fire in the hearth had long since become glowing orange embers. The cognac slid down his throat with delicious heat, numbing his body into relaxation.

Slumped in a wing-back chair, Nicholas considered pouring another—his fourth of the night. Forgetfulness was his goal, not unconsciousness. Sighing, he placed the snifter on the floor at his feet. The deep amber color only reminded him of Maggie's eyes. Warm . . . mysterious . . .

"Damn her!"

Tension filtered through the flimsy barrier of alcohol. His hands curled into bloodless fists as he imagined her in his arms. Imagined her soft breasts nestled in his palms.

Shaking his head, he forced the erotic thoughts from his mind. He was trapped. Trapped between lust and honor. He'd vowed to protect her, and to do that he had to keep her close. Yet living under the same roof was proving too great a temptation.

And Maggie was not aiding matters. Her provocative and sensual assault threatened to pound his resolutions to dust. If he took her into his bed, he would be no better than his cousin.

Why couldn't she understand he was acting in her

best interest? Maggie could shout her abhorrence to marriage from the spires of St. Abby's cathedral, and it wouldn't matter. After the turmoil in her life, surely she craved stability. A family. Children.

Babes, with honey gold hair and brown, mischievous eyes.

Nicholas slammed his fists against the chair. Pain raced up his arms, banishing the seductive picture.

There was only one course to take and still maintain his sanity. He would stay close enough to watch over Maggie, but he could never be alone with her.

Like an archbishop reciting a prayer, Nicholas repeated the words.

He could almost believe them.

Until the achingly familiar scent of lavender and rose reached him.

No sound marked her presence. Yet he knew that if he turned, she would be there. Enchanting and beautiful as an angel—as passionate and fiery as a gypsy. Both untouchable.

He sighed, weariness stealing the bite from his tone. "Go away, Maggie. There's nothing for you here."

Husky and sensuous, her voice whittled away another layer of his control. "I couldn't sleep. I thought perhaps a book . . ."

"You've been painfully honest. Don't lie to me now."

Soft footfalls signaled her approach. He tensed, half afraid she would touch him. Equally afraid she would not.

"Very well, I knew you were here. And I wish only to speak to you. Nothing more."

She appeared before him dressed in a shimmering aqua silk robe, her bare feet peeking beneath the hem. Shadows concealed her features, while sun-kissed hair tumbled about her shoulders in sensuous disarray.

Against his better judgment, he watched her bend down and toss a log on the dying embers in the hearth. Sparks flew as fire consumed dry wood.

Light flared into the room, and Nicholas closed his eyes. "Go to bed, Maggie. I'm in no mood for idle conversation."

"Your mother paid me a visit this evening."

Nicholas remained silent. Perhaps she would give up her campaign if he ignored her long enough. But how could he? Her elusive fragrance hovered above him like a mist on foggy moors. The delicate whisper of silk proved an irresistible temptation.

Opening his eyes, he found her seated across from him, perched on a small brocade footstool. A slight frown marred the seamless perfection of her face.

"Have you been drinking?" she asked, eyeing the empty brandy snifter.

He smiled for the first time, his voice laced with sarcasm. "Don't worry. I haven't imbibed enough to allow a romantic seduction."

Lips, full and inviting, curved into a knowing smile. "How dreadfully boring, my lord."

"Boring, yes, but infinitely safer."

"Safer for whom?

Nicholas had asked her for the truth. He could offer nothing less. "For me, Maggie."

Taking a deep breath, she faced him, her gaze strangely intense. "Is that because of . . . Lady Wentworth?"

He froze, his hands clutching the fabric of the chair in a death grip. "Who told you about her?" The conversational tone of his voice surprised him. Inside, his belly tightened with rage.

Evidently Maggie sensed his anger. She paled, her fingers toying with the folds of her dressing gown.

"All I know is her name. Lady Grey said nothing else."

"My mother," he said with a growl, "should have honored my privacy."

"Don't be angry. She did not tell me anything."

He rose from the chair, intent on escape. Knowing he could never run fast enough, or far enough, mattered little at the moment. "I believe I'll seek my bed."

"Please, Nicholas, tell me about her."

Maggie's quiet entreaty splintered his control. "I will not discuss Julia with you or anyone else!" He took a step, only to be halted by Maggie's hand clasped around his wrist.

"You cannot run forever," she whispered. "You taught me that."

Her expression, sadness mingled with hope, compelled him more than words. She had bared her soul and revealed the scars. Nicholas could do no less.

He sighed and slumped back into the chair. "What do you wish to know?"

Now that the moment had arrived, Maggie felt the stirrings of fear. Perhaps resurrecting a ghost was not the wisest decision. Yet she couldn't resist.

"How did you meet her?"

"Almack's."

"Was this recently?"

"Seven years ago."

Maggie smiled at the curt responses and his unyielding expression. Evidently Nicholas was intent on offering crumbs. She wanted the whole loaf.

"The ladies at Almack's actually admitted *you*, a renowned rogue?"

His lips lifted in a sardonic smile. "I have been told I can be quite charming."

"Did you charm Lady Wentworth?" Maggie asked, striving for a lighthearted tone.

"Why do you want to know this?" His eyes betrayed not a flicker of emotion. "Julia has nothing to do with our situation."

"Then why won't you tell me?"

"It is none of your concern."

"I think it is," she replied, placing a hand on his knee.

As if her touch burned his flesh, he leaped to his feet and went to the sideboard. He returned with a crystal decanter. "You're amazingly perceptive," he said, pouring another drink. "How much do you want to know?"

The faint thread of warning in his voice gave Maggie pause. Yet she sensed that if she turned away now, he would keep his secrets buried. Buried with the mysterious Julia.

"I want to know everything."

"As you wish." Nicholas downed the brandy in one smooth motion. "Lady Wentworth had her coming-out ball at Almack's. She was . . ."

Somehow, Maggie swallowed the hard lump in her throat. "Beautiful?"

Staring into the fire, he nodded. "Exquisite. As fragile and delicate as a porcelain doll. Pale blond hair, deep green eyes . . . the ton was enchanted."

As you were, Maggie thought with growing unease. Not only was she battling a ghost, but a veritable goddess, as well. "So you courted her."

"Eventually," he replied.

"And did she return your affections?"

As if recalling a pleasant memory, he smiled. "Eventually."

Maggie turned away, unable to bear his wistful expression. She had more questions, but the strength to hear the answers became as elusive as shadows. She started to rise.

Nicholas seized her wrist. "What's wrong? Is my story not to your liking?"

She wanted to plead fatigue, a raging headache, but the lies refused to make an appearance. "I didn't realize it would be so difficult."

"Trust me, Maggie. You've yet to hear the worst of my tale." His grip tightened on her wrist.

She flinched, knowing he was unaware of his strength. He loosened his hold and soothed her skin with his thumb.

His dark brows crinkled in apparent confusion. "Where was I?"

Oh, Nicholas, you are about to break my heart.

"Ah, yes, the courtship." He leaned back into the chair, his mouth set in grim lines. "Things progressed rapidly. I was prepared to ask the earl for Julia's hand, and I knew he had no objection. Then I made an unforgivable mistake."

Maggie tensed. "What happened?"

"In my jubilation, I shared my happy news with the wrong man."

Holding her breath, she waited for him to say the name aloud—a name she had cursed to hell for the past two years.

Nicholas's gaze held hers, refusing to let her look away. "I can see by your expression you know the man."

Numbness settled into Maggie's limbs. "Your cousin."

"Exactly," he said in a cold, barren voice. "Two days before I was to meet Julia's father, I bumped into Turner at White's. Evidently he'd seen a wager in the book concerning who would claim Julia's hand. The odds were two to one I would take the prize."

Nicholas leaped to his feet, rage scoring his face into harsh, relentless lines. "I told Turner about my plans . . . how certain I was Julia would make the perfect wife." He laughed bitterly. "The bastard wished me well."

Maggie could envision Turner, his smile warm, his eyes as cold as a Scottish winter. She'd seen the expression many times.

"What did he do?" she finally asked, uncertain what twisted path Turner might have chosen.

"For whatever reason, my cousin decided he wanted Julia, and he knew her father would never give his approval." Nicholas slammed his fists against the marble fireplace mantel. "The following evening at a ball, he lured Julia into a deserted room."

"He—he forced himself on her?" Maggie asked in a horrified whisper.

"Julia was very sheltered . . . innocent. She probably didn't understand what was happening until it was too late. They were discovered together."

"What did you do?"

"I was not in attendance that night. If I had been, it never would have happened."

"Nicholas, you had no way of knowing what he would do."

His fists banged against the marble again. "What do you think I've been telling myself for all these years! It doesn't make a damned bit of difference. She is dead."

Unable to bear his suffering, Maggie jumped to her feet and wound her arms around his waist. "It wasn't your fault," she murmured, pressing her cheek against his back.

Spinning around, he pushed her away. "It was, Maggie. As soon as I heard what had happened, I rushed to her side. The gossip was already horrific. Her reputation would have never recovered from the blow. I told her I didn't care what Turner had done to her.''

''And did you care?''

Nicholas turned back to the fire, his body vibrating with tension. ''Of course. Yes, it mattered. I was enraged. Turner stole what belonged to me.''

Maggie ached to smooth the harsh lines in his face, but sensed he would reject her comfort. ''What did Julia say?''

''I told her to pack her things. We would go to Gretna Green and be married at once. She flatly refused.''

Maggie understood. ''She didn't want your reputation to suffer along with hers.''

''Yes,'' Nicholas replied, his voice harsh. ''She then proceeded to tell me she was accepting Turner's marriage proposal. They would be married by the end of the week. I told Julia I would call Turner out and kill him. She begged me, on her knees, not to do it.''

Tears burned Maggie's eyes—not only for Nicholas, but for Julia, as well. ''And you relented.''

Nicholas faced her, his expression forbidding. ''I hated her at that moment. Hated her weakness. I walked away and never saw her again.

''They married, and he took her to the country to escape the gossip. A few weeks later, she died in a carriage accident.''

''Was it an accident?'' Maggie whispered, knowing how dastardly Turner could be.

''The magistrate ruled it as such. There was no evidence of outright murder. But I know she was running away. Something happened that sent her into a blinding rainstorm. The coach overturned, breaking her neck.''

Shivers danced across Maggie's skin as she clutched the robe tight against her chest. Julia's life paralleled hers to an eerie degree. Young and sheltered, they had both been deceived by a monster. Julia had not survived. Maggie had.

She shook her head. "I never realized there could be another."

"It seems," Nicholas said, "my cousin and I share the same taste in women."

Though she couldn't deny his assessment, the thought left a bitter flavor on her tongue. "Are you saying you're attracted to me because I remind you of her?"

Standing over her, he studied her as though she were a work of art, his gaze journeying across her face. "There is a resemblance . . . blond hair, delicate features . . ."

Maggie didn't move as his finger traced the path his eyes had just followed.

"Yet you're nothing like Julia."

Like a double-edged sword, his words sliced through her heart. She batted his hand away. "No, we are nothing alike. If Julia and I were cut from the same cloth, I would be dead."

"You're right. Although just as lovely, she never possessed your strength and courage." He snagged a lock of her hair, caressing it between his fingers. "I cannot love you, Maggie. I cannot risk losing you."

Dazed by his somber pronouncement, she shook her head.

He bent lower, until his brandy-spiced breath fanned her mouth. "If I had truly loved Julia, I would have fought for her. She was my weakness, and Turner took advantage of that to play his insane games. And in the end, he took her from me."

Maggie gasped as his lips brushed across hers, then retreated. "I—I don't understand. . . ."

"Trust me in this," he whispered against her cheek. "Lust and even companionship are possible, but not love. The price is too high."

Her confusion became sad understanding. Nicholas was trying to drive her away with words meant to wound. "Perhaps I'm not interested in love."

His bitter laughter raked across her nerves. "Yes, you are. Another similarity between you and the fair Julia. She looked at me just as you're doing now."

"And how is that?"

"As if I were the daring knight, ready to slay dragons."

Maggie blinked in astonishment as a giggle burst from her throat. "A knight slaying dragons?"

His face darkened as his jaw clenched tighter.

She soon realized he was blushing, and furious. "I'm so—so sorry," she stammered, wiping tears from her eyes, "but I certainly don't need a knight in shining armor to rescue me. I've managed on my own quite nicely, thank you."

"Then what do you need, Maggie?"

She sobered instantly. "I've already told you." She framed his face with her palms. "I want my freedom, and I want you."

A grudging smile formed on his lips. "In that order?"

"I'm afraid so."

"You're too damned stubborn for your own good."

"So I've been told." Sensing his capitulation, Maggie leaned closer, daring him to pull away. "I'm going to kiss you, Lord Grey."

Love . . . the past . . . the future, none of it mattered. With all the tenderness blossoming in her heart, she kissed him. Daring more, she explored his lips with her tongue, absorbing his gasp of surprise. He clutched her shoulders.

A fierce expression hardened the lines in his face. "I swore I would not touch you. I swore that I was a better man than my cousin."

Maggie felt the shifting momentum. In desperation, she glided her hands down his chest. "You're nothing like Turner. He never offered me a choice. But I know if I asked you to stop, you would."

Nicholas shook her gently. "Then tell me! Tell me to stop."

"I cannot," she whispered, the words torn from the very center of her soul.

Her reply seemed to unleash whatever control he still possessed. His lips crushed hers, plundering her mouth. Grabbing fistfuls of his hair, she returned his passion with a hunger of her own.

As if time were an enemy, he swept her to the floor, the soft Persian carpet cushioning her body. Tearing the sash from her robe, his hands parted the silk material with a jerk. The plain cotton shift had ridden up her hips, leaving her dark, feminine curls exposed to his hungry gaze.

"So damned beautiful," he murmured, straddling her thighs.

The heat from his eyes scorched her trembling flesh. She reached up, aching to pull him down and cover her with his powerful form.

He seized her wrists, stretching her arms above her head. "You have bewitched me from the moment I first saw you. And if we go further, nothing will change." His voice softened. "I thought . . . no, I believed I loved Julia, but in the end I couldn't save her, even with the promise of marriage. I cannot make that mistake again.''

Relief, and a strange sense of loss, filtered through Maggie's limbs. She would have her freedom. She would have Nicholas. She wondered if it would be enough.

''Do you understand?'' he asked, his face inches from her own.

Maggie smiled. ''I understand perfectly.''

Chapter Fifteen

"God help us both," Nicholas murmured as physical need battled his weary conscience.

He cursed his weakness, and reveled in it. He wanted to run from the room with his soul intact. He wanted to plunge into Maggie's willing body until they were both limp and sated.

Right or wrong mattered little as he stared at the gift before him. Firelight cast her skin in warm golden hues. Her hair, thick and lush, flowed across the carpeting like spilled honey.

Rich brown eyes darkened to the color of night as she met his gaze without a hint of shyness. "Shall we continue upstairs?"

"It's too late," he said softly. *Too late for both of us.*

With impatient hands, he tore the flimsy cotton shift from her body—the last barrier shielding her from view. "Perfection," he whispered, gliding his fingers down the slender column of her throat, her delicate collarbone, and her breasts. As luscious as plump fruit, they quivered beneath his palms.

A sigh slipped from her lips as she arched her back, nudging her flesh more firmly into his hands. Obeying the tacit command, he licked and teased one shell pink nipple to a taut peak.

Soft mews of arousal echoed through the room. Her hands pulled him to her body. "Nicholas, please . . ."

He blew against the moistened bud before moving to its mate. "Patience, my rose. All in due time."

Nicholas only hoped he could follow his words with action. His hardened flesh strained against his breeches. Nestled against the soft fur of her womanhood, his hips moved of their own accord, mimicking the act to come.

Torturous pleasure consumed him. He couldn't wait. Another weakness he was unable to conquer.

Gasping for air, he wrenched his shirt open and tossed the garment aside. He stretched across her languid form, her breasts cushioning his chest.

"Am I hurting you?" Smoothing his tongue across her kiss-swollen lips, he absorbed her puffs of excitement.

Her hands fluttered across his spine. "No, I've wanted to touch you since . . ."

"The ballroom?" he murmured.

"No, your bedchamber."

Nicholas stilled. "What do you mean?"

Her cheeks flamed crimson. "When I took the diamond cuff links, I was hiding in the bureau. I—I watched you."

Instead of being angered by his loss of privacy, the provocative confession fanned his desire. "Did you enjoy watching me?" he whispered against her mouth.

199

"Yes . . ."

"And you wanted to touch me, as you are now?"

"I wanted to touch you . . . everywhere."

Rearing upward, he rolled to his side and stripped the breeches from his body. A groan slipped through his clenched teeth as his swollen shaft sprang free. Driven by a primal urge, terrifying in its intensity, he covered her again.

He stared into her flushed face, then followed her wide-eyed gaze to his loins. Ripe with agonizing need, his sex nudged the velvety softness of her stomach.

"You're different than I remember," she said, her complexion suddenly white.

The truth struck like a meaty fist. For all her sensuous bravado, she was afraid.

"My God, Maggie, did someone hurt you?"

Her eyes closed. Seconds later, they fluttered open, free of fear. "I was merely surprised by your obvious attributes."

The flip response only angered him more. "Don't lie to me now. You told me Turner never touched you."

"I swear he did not."

"Then who?"

She caressed his jaw, her smile utterly beguiling. "The past has no place here. Only the present matters."

By the stubborn angle of her chin, he knew he would receive no answers tonight. "I promise you, I will erase every bitter memory you still hold."

Her eyes clouded with a sadness so piercing and hopeless, he wanted to shout his outrage to the heavens.

"Tonight, Nicholas. Make me forget for this one night."

The simple request shattered something inside him. An emotion, too foreign and elusive to grasp, flitted through his soul. Her arms curled around his neck and drew him closer, easing his troubled thoughts. She rained kisses on his lips, his chin, his throat, any patch of skin she seemed able to reach.

"Maggie," he gasped as her teeth nipped his shoulder, "you are making this difficult."

Husky laughter vibrated against his chest. "I'm not trying to be difficult," she murmured. "I am simply impatient."

"Then let us see how impatient you truly are."

With gentle persuasion, he eased her thighs apart and settled between them. "Open wider," he whispered, before taking a reddened nipple deep in his mouth.

She moaned, spreading her legs further. Slowly he inched down her body, anointing her porcelain skin with his lips.

When he reached the soft, feminine curls, she jumped. "Nicholas! What—"

"Hush, just relax . . . bend your knees, sweeting. . . ."

Slowly she did as he'd asked, her eyes wide with wonder. Carefully, gently, he probed the delicate folds of her flesh with his thumb.

She bucked beneath his hands, her head thrashing from side to side.

Nicholas shared her desperation. The earthy scent of woman tantalized his senses. Unable to temper his need, he tasted her, stroking her to the precipice of climax. With one flick of his tongue, he pushed her over the edge.

Her keening cry of fulfillment shattered the remnants of his control. He sheltered her writhing body with his own. Muffling her hoarse whimpers with his mouth, he eased into her sleek passage. As snug as wet leather, her honeyed walls squeezed his manhood to the point of bursting.

Gritting his teeth, he tried to forestall his own culmination. Then her nails raked across his back and shredded his resolve.

He stared into her luminous eyes and kissed her. "Hang on to me, Maggie. I cannot wait."

She smiled, curling her slender legs around his hips. "I have waited forever."

With a growl of primitive satisfaction, he slid farther into her.

Impossible!

Even as he butted against the fragile membrane, Nicholas refused to believe the staggering implication. Sweat dripped from his brow like rain as he forced his body to remain still.

He gazed into her pallid face and searched for the truth. "You lied to me, damn you!"

"It doesn't matter."

"It bloody well does." He ached to smash through the barrier, yet knew he had to stop.

Like the daring thief she was, she stole the choice from him. She lifted her hips, impaling herself on his shaft.

Too late . . .

Aware of her clenched teeth and tense muscles, he tried to move slowly. His body refused the virtue of patience.

"I'm sorry," he murmured as he pumped into her, driving her hips forward with each thrust.

Imminent release boiled through his blood. He plunged into her one last time, crying her name as he spilled his seed. Shaking and utterly spent, he lowered his head to her shoulder.

Never had he felt such a powerful, all-consuming

climax. Never had he taken a maidenhead. The very idea terrified him.

As if sensing his fear, she stroked his hair, his back offering wordless comfort—comfort Nicholas did not want or deserve. And to complete his dark thoughts, he knew that soon he would swell with need once more.

With potent self-disgust, he slid free of her body. Streaks of blood marred her inner thighs. Irrefutable proof.

He should have been furious at her charade. Instead he felt helpless, and unable to repel his sense of impending doom.

The nightmare with Julia flashed through his mind in blinding clarity. In order to save Maggie, he would have to recant the declaration he'd uttered only minutes ago. And this time he would not fail.

"We have no choice now, Maggie. As soon as possible, we will be married."

Shock held her tongue hostage.

The aftermath of exquisite pleasure, mingled with her lost innocence, vanished. Of all the possible scenarios she had devised, none had included his sudden proposal. She'd expected anger and condemnation, not marriage.

Feeling exposed, vulnerable, she leaped to her feet and clutched the silk robe around her body like a coat of armor. Perhaps she had simply misunderstood his words. "I'm not certain what you mean. Although quite ridiculous, it almost sounded as if you were proposing."

"There is nothing ridiculous about our current situation. And I am deadly serious in my intentions."

She blinked, staring into his granite hard features. Her passionate, tender lover had transformed into the arrogant blueblood she recognized only too well. "Why the sudden change of heart, Nicholas?"

He turned away and shrugged into his wrinkled breeches and shirt. "If you had been honest about your state of virginity—"

"—you never would have made love to me," she added bitterly.

"Precisely."

"So you wish to marry me in order to atone for your mistake."

He faced her, his expression suddenly weary. "We cannot escape the fact that you were an innocent until this night. I should have realized—"

"I lost my *innocence* long ago. A few drops of blood cannot change that."

"Don't trade words with me," he growled. "Whether you wished it or not, you were a virgin."

She marched toward him and poked a finger against his chest with each determined word. "I will not marry you."

Seizing her wrist, he pulled her against his body. "Why? Suddenly you cannot bear my touch?"

She shivered in awareness. The scent of lovemaking permeated their skin like an exotic perfume. Maggie tried to pull free. His grip tightened.

"Answer me," he purred against her ear. "Tell me the truth."

Like an ocean wave drawn to the shore, she swayed closer to him. "No, your touch is wonderful."

"Imagine sleeping in the same bed. Taking our fill of each other, night after night." His words wove a hypnotic spell. "What difference would a legal union make between us?"

As if slapped across the cheek, she tore free of his hold. "It would make all the difference in the world! Marriage only empowers the man, never the woman."

He threw up his hands in frustration. "What the devil are you talking about? You would have all that I have, a title, a home, and funds to spend as you wish."

"I have no wish for an exalted title, and as for money, if I invest wisely, I shall live a very comfortable existence."

His complexion reddened. "And children? I planted my seed in your womb, Maggie."

Without conscious thought, she let her hand drift to her stomach. The idea of bearing his child suffused her with warmth. Fear snuffed out the glow. If their union bore fruit, Nicholas would drag her to the altar, willing or not.

"I know there are ways to prevent conception. . . ."

"None of which we used tonight," he snapped.

Heat flooded her cheeks. "It is very close to my time. I am certain there is nothing to worry about."

He edged toward her, his overly sweet smile setting her nerves on alert. "Maggie, you're being foolish. Marriage is not a death sentence."

She backed away, her hands raised to fend off his advance. "You cannot seduce me into changing my mind."

"You had no such qualms earlier."

"And you swore you would never marry me."

At a stalemate, they stared at each other.

Nicholas broke the tense silence first. "I did not say I would never marry. I have always known I would have to take a wife, albeit not for many years."

Conviction steadied her voice. "I cannot be that woman."

"I will not be thwarted by Edward's mistakes!"

"And I will not pay for Julia's weakness, or her betrayal."

Trembling, he advanced with hands clenched into fists. "What the devil does that mean?"

Maggie stared into the dying fire. "I am not blind." She faced his thunderous expression, the truth etched across his features. "I will be your confidante, your lover, but never your wife, Nicholas."

As if all his strength had been spent, he slumped into the chair. A chuckle rumbled from his throat. Soon harsh laughter filled the room.

"Maggie, your outlook on life is very unique. You will play the role of courtesan, but not the more esteemed role of wife." With insolent leisure, he let his gaze journey down her body. "And what will you do if I should tire of your services?"

As if he'd struck her, she staggered backward. "How dare—"

"Come now, surely you are not so naive. The life of a mistress can be very unforgiving."

Cruel and cutting, his words sliced through her heart. Instinctively, she realized he was trying to wound her as she had wounded him with her rejection. The thought offered little solace.

She drew the tattered remnants of her pride together and marched to the door. "I will forgive your heartless words, because I know how angry you are."

"Anger does not begin to describe my present emotion."

Ignoring his sarcastic tone, she continued as if he'd never spoken. "As for your detailed description of a courtesan's life—which I must assume you gathered from firsthand knowledge—I will never find myself in such a predicament."

"How can you be so certain?" he asked, the dark humor gone from his voice.

"Because you are the only man I have ever wanted. The only man I will ever want."

His fists slammed against the chair. "Then marry me!"

Irrational fear gripped her soul. "Ask anything of me, Nicholas. Anything but that."

His calm voice halted her on the threshold. "This is not over, Maggie."

Tears welled in her eyes. "I know."

Sighing in profound relief, Maggie slipped undetected into her room. Sagging against the door, she closed her eyes. How could such a wonderful night have become such a nightmare? Nicholas had awakened her body to the delights of passion; then he'd spoiled the magic with his proposal.

Marriage . . . to be at the mercy of a man . . . even one as wonderful as Nicholas.

The very thought left her mouth as dry as Roman parchment. Margaret Alston, the sheltered baron's daughter, would have said yes, and delicately swooned in his arms. Now it was too late.

In her soul, she knew he was an honorable, caring man. Yet her memories of darkness refused to disappear. She was trapped by her own unrelenting fear.

Even more terrifying, Nicholas would never give up his quest. She'd learned from experience how persistent and dauntless he could be. A union between them would prove disastrous. Somehow she had to convince him of that fact.

Suddenly, light illuminated the pitch-black room.

Her breath lodged in her throat as Dare appeared from the adjoining dressing room, a taper of candles in his hand. After the violent altercation with Nicholas earlier, he had stayed in his room, refusing to see her. He'd chosen the worst possible moment to break his self-imposed exile.

"Dare, what are you doing out of bed at this time of night?"

His cold gaze raked her body. "I could ask you the same bleedin' thing. But we both know the answer, don't we?"

Trembling beneath his condemning stare, she forced a smile to her suddenly parched lips. "I have no idea what you're talking about."

He slammed the candelabra to the nightstand, his eyes blazing with fury. "You've been with *'im!*"

"You—you're being ridiculous," she said, her voice little more than a croak of denial.

"Don't lie to me, Maggie." He moved closer and flipped the tousled hair from her shoulder. "What the 'ell are these marks on your neck, then?"

Nerves stretched to the point of snapping, she hurried to the washstand and splashed her fiery cheeks with cool water. "I don't believe now is the time to discuss this."

"I warned you about 'im, and you wouldn't listen."

"No, you are the one who refuses to listen." She turned and faced her accuser. "Lord Grey is an honorable man. In fact, he has asked me to marry him."

Ashen faced, Dare slumped to the bed. "I don't believe it."

"Trust me, I was as shocked as you."

He swallowed hard, running his hands through his disheveled hair. "What did you tell 'im?" he finally asked, his gaze directed toward the far wall.

Maggie owed him nothing less than the truth. And yet she could not give it. If she told him she'd rejected Nicholas's proposal, Dare would flaunt the fact in his host's face. For the sake of a calm household, she offered a compromise.

"I told Lord Grey I would consider his offer."

Dare leaped to his feet. "You're not really goin' to do it, are you?"

"Whether I choose to or not, it is my decision to make."

"I'm warnin' you, Maggie. If we stay 'ere, there'll be trouble."

Like a well-worn blanket, familiar sadness settled upon her shoulders. Drooping beneath his hard-eyed stare, she sank to the bed. "Lord Grey is not like other titled gentlemen."

" 'E's blinded you, 'e 'as. But 'e'll show his true colors one day." Dare went to the door, his hand poised above the knob. "And when 'e does, I'll be 'ere to protect you. I won't let 'im 'urt you."

"Dare, please . . ."

The door glided closed.

". . . wait."

She sighed, hugging a plump pillow to her chest. She knew her friend had likely spoken with complete accuracy. There indeed would be trouble, for all of them.

Chapter Sixteen

The aroma of eggs, honeyed ham, and freshly baked sweet breads wafted from the breakfast room. Maggie's stomach churned, but not in hunger. The steaming bath she'd taken earlier in the morning had soothed her body, but not her restless thoughts.

Even her dreams had conspired against her. Images of tangled sheets . . . his sleek, muscled body . . . his mouth, tasting her . . .

She shook her head, banishing the erotic tableau. Facing Nicholas in the harsh light of day seemed a daunting task. Yet she had to remain firm in her resolve to keep her freedom. If he caught a glimmer of weakness, she was sure he would pounce like a starved lion finding prey.

"Don't dawdle there, Maggie. Come in and join me."

Maggie paused in the doorway, her gaze sweeping the room. Lady Grey was seated at the head of the oval cherry wood dining table. Nicholas was nowhere in sight. For that boon, Maggie murmured a prayer of heartfelt thanks. She was in no mood for another clash of wills.

"I'm quite alone," Eugenia continued with a knowing smile. "Young Thomas and Dare have eaten."

Nodding, Maggie moved to the sideboard and filled a plate.

"And my son had an early meeting with the solicitor."

"Where are the boys now?" she asked, taking a seat across from Eugenia.

"Thomas was most anxious to visit the new litter of pups in the carriage house. And naturally Dare followed. He is very protective of his young charge."

Curiosity lurked behind the innocent observation. Maggie merely nodded. "Dare thinks of Thomas as a brother, just as I do."

Eugenia dabbed her lips with a crisp linen napkin, settling her gaze on Maggie. "I am glad you were not alone during the past two years. When I think of what might have happened . . ."

"I'm fine. None the worse for my travels, I assure you."

The words, meant to comfort, brought a frown to Lady Grey's face. "Don't lie to spare my feelings. When my son brought you here, you were deathly ill."

"And I've made a complete recovery."

"I would not say complete," Eugenia said before taking a sip of tea. "You are still quite pale, and your appetite . . ."

Maggie followed her stern gaze to the plate of untouched food.

"And," she continued, "you have circles beneath your eyes."

"I didn't sleep well." Maggie focused on her breakfast, taking a few bites to mollify her hostess.

"Are you in pain? Perhaps the physician should—"

"I have no wish to be poked and prodded again," Maggie said. "I suppose it is the uncertainty of my situation. I need a home for myself, and Thomas and Dare."

Eugenia's silver-tipped brows rose in confusion. "Your home is here, until you wed, of course."

Groaning, Maggie tossed her napkin to the table. "Not you, as well."

"I take it you have had a similar conversation with my son?"

Maggie shrugged lightly, realizing how close she'd come to disaster. She had no wish to discuss Nicholas's marriage proposal with Eugenia. Clashing with *two* determined Greys would be a skirmish she could never win.

"When is Lord Grey expected to return?" Maggie asked, her hands knotted into fists.

"Soon, I suspect." Eugenia leaned closer, her voice lowered to a conspiratorial tone. "I had hoped to discuss your reintroduction into society, without my son present."

A lump formed in Maggie's bone-dry throat. "My what?"

Eugenia smiled gently. "You have seen the very worst of men, but once you begin attending social functions, you will see that not all men are as cold-hearted as my nephew."

Maggie took a deep breath and reined in her rising temper. "I have attended social functions, and I have no desire to meet prospective suitors."

212

Soft, girlish laughter echoed through the room. "I never would have dreamed the quiet, docile child I knew would become such a strong-willed woman."

"Children grow up, some more quickly than others."

Sighing in apparent defeat, Eugenia nodded. "Perhaps you are right. Now may not be the most opportune moment to announce your miraculous rebirth. You are still recovering your health. But," she added in a warning tone, "the ton will begin to wonder about my mysterious houseguest."

"I agree," Maggie said softly.

Since arriving in Nicholas's home, she'd had two choices—run, or stay and face Edward Turner. She'd chosen to remain, knowing she would have to reveal her true identity eventually. If even one passing acquaintance noticed a similarity between Margaret Alston and the widow Sanford . . .

"My dear, you've become quite pale," Eugenia murmured. "I have upset you."

Maggie waved away the older woman's concern. "Not at all. I am merely wondering what kind of plausible story we can create to explain my appearance."

"Yes, it will be quite the challenge. The tale should be simple, but believable."

"Whatever we decide," Maggie said, "the ton will soon witness the resurrection of Miss Margaret Alston."

"No, they will not."

Wincing at the harsh tone, Maggie forced her gaze toward the door. "Good morning, Lord Grey."

He ignored her salutation.

Like gathering storm clouds, he swept into the room. Dressed in severe dark attire, he whipped the black cloak from his shoulders and tossed it into a chair. His expression, cut in unyielding lines, set her nerves on a razor's edge. This was the man who'd pointed a pistol at her head. A man who showed no mercy.

He focused a steely eyed gaze on his mother. "Whose beef-witted plan did I happen to overhear?"

Instead of being intimidated by his fierce scowl, Eugenia laughed. "Oh, Nicholas, that blustering look may strike terror in the hearts of most, but I know you too well."

Content to remain silent for the moment, Maggie watched the exchange with growing amusement.

A muscle twitched in his jaw. "I asked a question."

"Very well," Eugenia said. "I—"

"It was all my idea," Maggie interrupted, lifting her chin for the battle to come. "I cannot stay cloistered in this house indefinitely."

"You will stay until I deem it safe."

"I will do as I please, Lord Grey."

His hands clenched into fists. "I have never met a more stubborn chit in my life."

Maggie turned to the matriarch of the Grey family. She was watching them, her sapphire eyes twinkling in apparent enjoyment.

Nicholas glared at his mother. "I cannot believe you would sanction such a dangerous scheme."

Her smile faded. "*You* did not see through Maggie's disguise for quite some time. As for the ton, they are a fairly mindless lot. If we find a way to explain her long absence —"

"Viscount Turner is not mindless," Nicholas said. "He will know the truth."

Eugenia paled, her delicate hand fluttering to her throat. "I did not consider that."

"Stop frightening your mother," Maggie said, rising to Eugenia's defense. "Lord Turner will say nothing."

Nicholas rounded the table and leaned over her. "You cannot be certain."

"Yes, I can. And I will not hide any longer."

"Maggie, dear, perhaps my son is right," Eugenia said. "Once Turner is arrested, we can be more assured of your safety."

Glancing from mother to son, Maggie tried to quell her burgeoning excitement. "Is he going to be tried?"

Tugging his cravat free, Nicholas slid into a chair, weariness scoring his features. "If Turner had not discovered a *boy* in his study, the magistrate might have acted, but not now."

"Then why do you believe he will be arrested?"

"Nicholas, you didn't tell her about your investigation?" Eugenia asked.

Hope swelled anew in Maggie's mind. "Tell me. What do you think Turner has done?"

Smiling for the first time since his arrival, Nicholas patted his mother's hand. "Would you allow us a moment of privacy?"

Maggie's heart began a staccato beat at the thought of being alone with him— in fear or anticipation, she could not decide.

Eugenia leveled a steady gaze at her son. "And leave the two of you without a chaperon?"

"I promise to behave myself."

A sound, very close to a chuckle of disbelief, erupted from Lady Grey's lips. "See that you do." She swept from the room, leaving the door noticeably ajar.

Tensing, Maggie watched as Nicholas pushed it closed. "Now, where were we?"

"You were about to tell me about your cousin," Maggie said.

"Very well." He took his seat, meeting her gaze without apology. "I did not wish to share my investigation with you until I had proof."

"Proof of what?"

"I believe Viscount Turner had a hand in his mother's death, perhaps even in his father's hunting accident. Connor Hennessy is searching for a maid who may have witnessed my aunt's death."

Excitement pounded through Maggie's blood, leaving her light-headed. "When? When will you have what you need to arrest him?"

"I don't know. It could be days, or months."

Maggie closed her eyes, resting her head on the back of the chair. "I cannot stay hidden here for months."

"Would that be such a terrible fate?"

"Not terrible, but dangerous for your family."

Footsteps sounded behind her. Opening her eyes, she looked up to see Nicholas's face above hers. "You are the one I am concerned about." He stroked her cheek. "By the way, good morning."

She gasped as his lips brushed across hers with featherlike softness. "Did you sleep well?" he murmured.

"No."

"Neither did I."

The kiss deepened, wringing a mew of pleasure from her throat. She reached upward, dragging her hands through his silky hair.

"Let me taste you," he whispered, coaxing her lips to part.

Drowning in heat, she did as he asked, their tongues colliding in a feverish dance of need.

Breathless and craving more, Maggie pulled away, trying to stand. She wanted to hold him, explore his body with her trembling hands.

He held her gently in place. "No, stay as you are."

She bit back a moan as he cupped both her breasts. Like a sculptor with fresh clay, he molded her flesh. Through the pale ivory silk of her gown, he thumbed her nipples into taut beads.

"So lovely," he murmured against her ear. "I wish I could take you now . . . on the table."

The image burned in her thoughts. And in that moment she could refuse him nothing. "Yes, Nicholas. Please—"

"Damn, Maggie!" As if struck, he released her quickly, his chest heaving. "I did not mean to let this go so far."

Bereft and abandoned, she reached out. "But I want you."

He stepped back, his glittering eyes pinning her in place. "Anyone could walk in and discover us."

The idea of Lady Grey gliding into the room unannounced dampened the fire in Maggie's blood. "I suppose you're right."

"Unless you've changed your mind."

"About what?"

"Marriage."

Painfully aware of his dubious plan, she shot to her feet. "You did that on purpose! You were trying to— to seduce me into accepting your proposal."

"Listen well, Maggie. Had I planned a grand seduction scene, it wouldn't be in the breakfast room, in the middle of the day."

Arms crossed over her chest, she studied him, searching for signs of deceit. "Then why did you kiss me?"

"Because I can't keep my bloody hands off you!" he roared.

Her outrage crumbled at the confession. "What a marvelously sweet thing to say."

"Sweet? My God, Maggie, most women would have slapped my face for such a blatant statement."

"But then," she said, moving closer, "I am not like most women."

"Yes, I've discovered that." Nicholas stepped farther out of reach. "You never answered my question."

"What question?"

"Have you reconsidered my proposal?"

Silence, as deep and unforgiving as the night, settled upon the room. She shivered in the face of his stoic expression.

Coward . . . coward. The inner voice taunted her with its undeniable truth.

Taking a deep breath, she tried to say yes—tried to banish the panic gnawing at her soul. "I . . ."

The words lodged in her throat as the scent of musty earth and the clink of iron chains shattered her composure. *It's not real. It's a memory . . . only a memory.*

Turning away, she gripped the back of a chair for support as her legs threatened to buckle beneath her. "I cannot marry you, Nicholas."

"Cannot, or will not?"

"Both."

"Very well," he said with calm determination. "I will not broach the subject again."

She faced him, uncertain if this was merely a change of tactics. "What are you saying?"

"I'm bowing to your wishes. I will never ask you again."

She should have been elated by his surrender. Instead, bitter sadness pinched her heart. "I wish I—"

Raising his hand, he silenced her overture. "You have made your decision." With cold gallantry, he

218

pulled back a chair. "Have a seat. We have other matters to attend."

Maggie sagged onto the chair. "Are you referring to our . . . arrangement?"

"What a delicate way of phrasing it," Nicholas said with a chilly smile.

"Perhaps I should stay elsewhere until Turner is out of our lives."

"I don't believe that will be necessary. As for my damned cousin, he would not dare harm you here. If you're content to leave things as they stand, so be it."

Staring into his somber face, she searched for the man she loved, but could not completely trust. Beneath the frosty blue of his eyes, she saw his confusion.

"I am sorry, Nicholas."

"Sorry?"

"For hurting you."

His impenetrable mask slipped. "Perhaps in time . . ."

She ached to give him the small concession he sought. Fear held her tongue silent.

His expression grew fierce and primitive. "I hate the fact that I still want you."

As if peering through crystal-clear Venetian glass, Maggie envisioned the truth. Sooner or later he would begin to hate her. But until that day, she would snatch what little happiness was offered, without complaint.

"Will you come to me tonight?" she asked quietly.

"I am beginning to fear I can refuse you nothing." His anger apparently forgotten, Nicholas curled his lips into a wicked smile of promise. "I am at my lady's beck and call."

"So you will do anything I ask?"

"Within reason, of course."

Feigning deep concentration, she tapped a finger against her chin. "And who will decide what is reasonable?"

He leaned across the table, his heavy-lidded gaze focused on her mouth. "I leave that to your discretion."

With her fingertip, Maggie traced the masculine planes of his face. She wanted to commit every beloved feature to memory. "You're very beautiful."

His rich laughter turned her insides to pudding. "I've been called many things, but never beautiful."

"I'm sure I am not the first to comment on your handsome appearance."

"Probably not. But most women are too timid to voice such honest thoughts to me."

"How dreadfully sad," Maggie whispered, lost in the sweetness of the moment.

Nicholas inched closer. She parted her lips in anticipation.

A discreet cough froze them in place.

Abbot stood in the doorway, his unerring gaze focused on a far wall, his complexion noticeably pink. "My lord, please forgive the interruption—"

"Yes," Nicholas replied shortly, "what is it?"

"Mr. Hennessy has arrived. He says it is most urgent he speak with you immediately."

"Damn right it's urgent," a thick Irish brogue called from beyond the door.

Before she could protest, the man burst into the room.

"We've got trouble, Nicky. Serious trouble."

Chapter Seventeen

Nicholas pushed away from the table —away from Maggie's flushed face and tempting lips. If not for Abbot's timely interruption, he had no doubt he would have accepted the open invitation in her eyes.

Last night he'd sworn he would not touch her unless she accepted his proposal. He'd thought to seduce her into changing her mind. Instead, she had turned his own strategy against him.

Connor's strident tone pierced his thoughts. "Didn't you hear me, Nicky?"

"Yes," he murmured, tearing his hungry gaze from Maggie. "You mentioned trouble."

"Aye, that it is." Connor's eyes brightened when he noticed Maggie. "Why, Nicky, would this be the drowned waif you pulled from the water?"

Much against his will, Nicholas performed the introductions.

Then he gritted his teeth as Connor oozed his Irish

charm. "Miss Alston, what a pleasure it is to finally be makin' your acquaintance. I can see why Nicky has kept you hidden away." He kissed the top of her hand, lingering a bit too long for Nicholas's liking.

Nicholas had never considered himself a jealous man. Yet now he had the irresistible urge to toss his closest friend from the house.

Maggie blushed prettily, her smile geniune. "Lord Grey has mentioned you often, Mr. Hennessy." She batted her eyelashes in a decidely coquettish fashion, irritating Nicholas even further. "Are you here to arrest me?"

Slapping a hand over his heart, Connor gasped. "And deprive the world of such a beautiful flower? Never, Miss Alston. I must follow my conscience in some matters, you see."

Nicholas had had enough of their innocent flirtation. "If you two are finished, perhaps you could share your urgent news."

Connor's lighthearted expression vanished. "Urgent, it is. Magistrate Woodson is on his way. With your cousin."

"Damn him," Nicholas said, turning to Maggie.

As if the slightest draft could sweep her over, she swayed.

He rushed to her and gripped her shoulders. "I want you to go upstairs and rest. I'll speak with Turner."

She shrugged off his touch. "I will not hide like a terrified child." She raised her chin and crossed her arms over her chest. "I intend to stay."

"You will go," Nicholas said through clenched teeth, "or I will carry you to your room myself."

Laughing, Connor stepped between them. "You're both too stubborn and hotheaded fer your own good."

"Hennessy, stay out of this."

Maggie grinned. "I'm pleased to know I'm not the only one Nicholas bullies at will."

"Oh, no," Connor said with mock seriousness. "He does it to everyone. That's why he has so few friends."

Nicholas slapped his palm against the table. "Have you two lost your wits? The magistrate will be here any moment, and you're discussing my lack of friends."

Duly chastised, they looked away.

"Now," Nicholas continued, "did you find the scullery maid?"

Connor plopped into a chair, his face creased with fatigue. "No, and I'm beginnin' to worry. She left Dorchester and came to London five years ago."

A dispirited silence settled over the room.

Maggie spoke first. "We will never find her."

Hating her defeated tone, Nicholas touched her hand, stroking the velvety skin. "It will be more difficult, but not impossible."

"Nicky's right. I've placed an advertisement in the London papers, asking her to come forward."

Unimpressed, Maggie shrugged. "If this woman knows Lord Turner, she could fear a trap and run even farther out of reach."

Nicholas squeezed her hand. "You stopped running. Perhaps she will do the same."

A soft tap at the door ended the discussion.

Abbot entered, his voice lowered to a whisper. "My lord, Magistrate Woodson and Viscount Turner have arrived."

"Where are they?" Nicholas asked, keeping his gaze locked on Maggie.

"In the blue drawing room, my lord."

Suddenly Maggie clutched Nicholas's arm. "Where are Dare and Thomas?"

"I believe they are still in the carriage house, miss."

Her concern for the boys' whereabouts piqued Nicholas's curiosity. Perhaps there was more than one thread binding her to Dare and Thomas. And it appeared Turner was once again the key.

Connor's keen-eyed stare focused on Nicholas. "I can see the cogs turnin' in your head. What are you plannin'?"

"Just mulling over my options," Nicholas repied easily. Once he escorted his unwanted visitors out, he would coax the answers from Maggie. He turned toward her. "I want you in your room."

"But the boys—"

"Connor will keep them occupied and out of sight."

Nodding, the Irishman headed toward the door. "I'll keep the mites out of trouble, along with myself. I'm thinkin' the magistrate wouldn't care to know I'd warned you ahead of time."

Once he was gone, Nicholas gripped Maggie's elbow and propelled her to the door. "You are leaving. Now."

She jerked free of his hand and stepped back. "I have to face him, Nicholas. He will discover I'm alive sooner or later."

"It will be later."

"You're being unreasonable."

Nicholas watched as her eyes sparkled with outrage, her cheeks blooming with color. And her lips, set in a delightful pout, awakened his lustful thoughts. He leaned closer, catching a whiff of delicate lavender-rose fragrance.

"You try my patience," he whispered against her ear.

Abbot's cough dampened the mood. "My lord, I would remind you of your waiting guests."

"Always the voice of reason, aren't you?"

"Yes, my lord. It is one of my more esteemed traits."

A nervous giggle slipped from Maggie's lips, the only betrayal of her fear.

Nicholas knew she was correct. It was only a matter of time before Turner learned she was alive. But it would not be on this day. "Abbot, please escort Miss Alston to her room."

"You cannot order me about like chattel!" she exclaimed.

The aging retainer stepped closer, a tender smile easing the stiffness of his face. Content to let the butler work his magic, Nicholas waited. When it came to subduing bursts of temper, Abbot was a master.

"Miss, I believe it would be prudent to allow Lord Grey to handle this matter. Think of him as the calm in the eye of the storm."

As if mesmerized by the soothing tone, Maggie allowed him to lead her toward the door. "I know how strongly you feel on this subject," Abbot continued, "but as I have learned in my many years of distinguished service, it is imperative we search for the correct time and place to make our wishes known. . . ."

The door breezed closed, and Nicholas breathed a sigh of relief. Abbot would see a substantial increase in his Christmas bonus this year.

Grinning to himself, Nicholas went to the sideboard and poured a cup of tea.

Nothing delighted him more than making Edward Turner wait.

*   *   *

Nicholas paused in the doorway, taking stock of his visitors.

Magistrate Woodson paced the room, fidgeting with his coat collar. Turner stood at the window, hands clasped coolly behind his back.

Smiling to himself, Nicholas strode inside, anxious to begin the day's entertainment.

"Christopher, what a pleasure to see you again." Nicholas enjoyed the shocked expression on his cousin's face. He obviously didn't know the magistrate was an old family friend. "How can I help you?"

With a last tug at his neckcloth, Woodson stepped forward. "Lord Grey, please forgive our unexpected visit. I know how busy you—"

"He is here to search this house," Turner said with a cold smile.

Nicholas laughed with genuine amusement. "Why the devil would—"

"I know the boy is here. My man saw you bring him here, and the lad has never left."

"So," Nicholas purred, concealing his rage, "you've been watching my home."

"Only as a precaution," Edward replied smoothly.

As if sensing an imminent explosion, Woodson moved between them. "Lord Turner believes the boy you pulled from the river is the same young man who robbed his home."

"Then I'm afraid Lord Turner has misled you."

"I have done nothing of the sort. Lord Grey is merely trying to hide his own role in this attempt to blacken my reputation."

Casting a skeptical glance at Turner, Woodson said, "So now you're claiming Lord Grey is behind the jewel thefts?"

Perspiration beaded Turner's forehead. "Not directly, no . . ."

If not for the fact that Maggie was upstairs, Nicholas would have continued toying with his cousin. But now was not the time to take undue risks. "Christopher, I'm sorry Lord Turner has led you on this goose chase."

"It is no goose chase," Edward said, his voice rising. "I have proof."

Woodson glared at the interruption. "I would like to hear Lord Grey speak."

"It's all right, Christopher, I can understand my cousin's distress. Unfortunately, the boy I rescued is not a thief. He is the son of one of my parlor maids."

"Then produce him now," Edward demanded.

"I'm afraid that's not possible."

"I knew it." Triumph curled Edward's lips into a victorious smile as he turned to the magistrate. "We must search the house immediately."

"Where is the lad?" Woodson asked.

"In Rockingham," Nicholas replied. "He was running with a wild group of boys, and his mother decided to send him home to stay with grandparents."

Edward snarled in disbelief. "How bloody convenient."

"You are more than welcome to discuss this with the boy's mother."

Praying his bluff—his lie—would stand, Nicholas strode to the door. Heaven help him, he didn't even know if he had a maid old enough to have a child. *Don't disappoint me, Mr. Woodson.*

He grasped the gleaming brass handle.

"Lord Grey, that won't be necessary," Woodson said.

Nicholas fought his widening grin and turned to the magistrate. "If you're certain . . ."

Woodson nodded. "A mistake has been made." He glared at a seemingly speechless Turner. "It will not happen again. Forgive the intrusion, Lord Grey."

"Think nothing of it. And if you have further questions, please send word at once."

The magistrate offered a bow. "I doubt that will be necessary." With obvious distate puckering his mouth, he turned to Edward. "Until you can produce this mysterious boy, I advise you to stay clear of my office."

Venomous hatred gleamed in Turner's amber eyes. "You have made a serious mistake, Woodson."

Unintimidated by the subtle threat, the magistrate slapped on his hat. "Good day, Lord Grey."

Nicholas closed the door after him and moved to his desk. Feigning astonishment, he glanced at his cousin. "Are you still here?"

Turner smiled as he slowly clapped his hands. "Bravo, Grey. Your performance was most impressive. Although," he added with a subtle sneer, "our highly esteemed magistrate is easily duped."

"If I were you, I would foster a friendship with the man. One day you may need a supporter in your camp."

"Your innuendos are becoming quite tiresome, Grey."

"As is your presence," Nicholas said, his mask of politeness long gone. "You know the way out."

"You have made me look the fool. It is a transgression I will not forget."

Like a flame in dry tinder, rage swept through Nicholas. Lunging across the desk, he grabbed Turner's pale throat. He dragged him across the top of the desk. Correspondence, inkwells, and plumed quills scattered to the floor.

Sputtering and gasping for air, Turner clawed at the

hands around his neck. "You—you've lost your mind!"

Nicholas slammed him to the wall, squeezing tighter. "I'm quite sane. And I'm warning you for the last time. If you or any of your hired ruffians come near my home again, I will kill you."

His eyes bulging, Edward moved his blue-tinged lips in a futile attempt at speech.

With a casual aplomb he did not feel, Nicholas released his death grip and stepped away.

Sucking air into his lungs, Turner sagged against the wall. "You . . . you have signed your death warrant, Grey."

Stretching his cramped fingers, Nicholas leaned back against the edge of the desk. "Get out."

Edward stood taller, straightening his twisted cravat. "Watch your back, cousin, because . . ." His eyes widened, focused on a point behind Nicholas. He took a nervous step backward, bumping into the wall. "It's not—not possible. You . . . you're dead!"

Already certain of what he would see, Nicholas slowly turned.

Damn you, Maggie.

Poised in the doorway, she seemed too fragile—too ethereal—to be a part of this world. Sunlight flooded the room, creating an aura of gold around her ivory gown.

Her voice, calm and utterly serene, furthered the angelic image. "Good morning, Lord Turner. As you can see, I am very much alive."

Chapter Eighteen

An expected sense of tranquillity settled upon Maggie. She held her breath, waiting for panic to consume her, as it had only moments ago.

Her defiant flight downstairs had ended at the drawing room door. Standing outside, her sweaty palm gripping the knob, she'd been unable to move a single muscle.

For two years she had plotted her revenge, awaiting the day Edward Turner would realize the truth. Only in her plans, she faced him through the iron bars of his prison cell, not in an elegant drawing room.

And then she'd overhead his dire threats against Nicholas. Like the stones of an ancient Saxon keep, her fear had crumbled.

Now, finally facing her nemesis, Maggie savored his pallid face and trembling, bloodless lips.

"How . . . how is this possible?" he murmured.

"Some would call it a miracle."

Edward stumbled toward her.

Nicholas blocked his path. "I want you out of my home."

Ignoring the blunt command, Edward focused his gaze on Maggie. "They told me you were dead . . . why?"

"For those two long months, I *was* dead."

His Adam's apple bobbing like a cork in water, Turner stepped back. Staring first at Nicholas, then Maggie, his eyes widened in sudden understanding. "It was *you!* You staged your own death."

Saying nothing, she eased onto the blue damask settee. Within moments, he would fit the pieces of the puzzle together. Nicholas, too, seemed braced for the onslaught. He towered over his cousin, his expression hard as flint.

"Margaret, I never meant to harm you," Edward said softly. "My punishment may have seemed harsh at the time—"

"My God, man," Nicholas roared, "you chained her in a cellar like an animal!"

As if fearing a blow, Edward stepped farther from reach. "It was for her own good."

Sensing that Nicholas's volatile temper was about to explode, Maggie jumped to her feet and clutched his coatsleeve. "Don't let him bait you."

He pulled free of her hold, but made no move to attack. "Stay out of this, Maggie."

"Maggie, is it?" Edward asked, his voice lit by understanding. "How provincial. By the by, Margaret, how long have you been in London?"

His amber-eyed stared, cool and supremely confident, swept open the door to her fear—a fear she could not reveal. Edward fed on the bitter emotion like a vulture devouring carrion.

Forcing a lazy smile to her lips, she approached

him. "I've been here in London for two months."

"Damn it, Maggie! Say nothing more," Nicholas said in a growl, his frustration palpable.

She wanted to reassure him, but there was no time. Turner's unblinking stare held her silent.

"Two months . . ." His lips curved into a chilling smile. "What a clever girl you are. I fear I underestimated you."

"What are you implying, Lord Turner?" she asked, already certain of the answer.

Studying her through slitted eyes, Edward's smile widened. "*You* were the boy I discovered in my study. Well done! Who would have dreamed that the timid country mouse would have become such a tigress?"

Nicholas grabbed Turner's coat. "I'm warning you. . . ."

Edward offered no resistance, raising his hands in surrender. "Be careful, cousin; I'm sure you don't want to add assault to your long list of crimes."

As if unable to bear touching him, Nicholas shoved him away. "You are not only a bastard, but insane as well."

"Am I? Perhaps the magistrate will feel differently."

Drawing a deep breath, Maggie prepared to play the few cards she still possessed. "I don't think that would be a wise decision."

Edward held her stare, then blinked, his face several shades paler. "Why?"

"If the magistrate should begin to ask questions, it may reflect badly on your reputation."

"It would be your word against mine."

Nicholas raised his hands in apparent frustration. "What the hell are you two speaking of?"

A gleam of victory shone from Edward's eyes. "It

would seem I am not the only one who has been left in the dark.''

Before Nicholas could ask more questions, Maggie gripped his arm tightly. ''You should be thanking me for that small boon, Lord Turner. As for your ground-less suspicions, feel free to discuss the matter with the magistrate. However, I think he will find your theory a bit far-fetched.''

''Perhaps, but you more than anyone would have a motive to see me ruined.''

''How would I have time to accomplish all that?'' she asked, coloring her expression with tones of in-nocence. ''I only just arrived in London a week ago.''

Edward's wolfish smile of confidence wavered. ''You said you've been in the city for two months.''

''Did I?'' Maggie turned to Nicholas. ''I'm certain I said a week.''

Grinning, Nicholas offered his praise with a jaunty salute. ''Definitely a week. In fact, she sailed from America on one of my own ships.''

''America? And I suppose your captain's logs would attest to that fact?'' Edward asked.

''Of course,'' Nicholas replied.

Maggie's assurance grew as, one by one, she and Nicholas blocked every path Turner's devious mind could chart.

''How I survived that horrific shipwreck is still a miracle,'' she said solemnly. ''And I suppose I should thank you for the touching memorial service you had in my honor.''

A chuckle of mocking disbelief slipped from Turner's throat, which still bore the imprint of Nich-olas's fingers. ''And you expect the magistrate—and the ton—will believe you have been recuperating in American for two years?''

Nicholas moved behind Maggie, placing his hands

on her shoulders in a gesture of obvious possession. In any other circumstance, she would have rebelled at the unspoken message. This time, his touch soothed her lingering tendrils of fear.

"Who would doubt the word of such a lovely young woman?" Nicholas said. "Especially when she has the full support of the Marquess of Rockingham."

Edward's gaze slid slowly down her body. "What a touching scene."

The warmth from Nicholas's hands evaporated beneath Turner's lustful stare. Maggie swallowed the growing lump in her throat. She knew that expression only too well.

"I'm disappointed, Margaret. As I know your father would be. A woman's chastity is a precious thing, to be saved for the wedding night. . . ."

Nicholas's grip tightened to an almost painful degree. "One more word, and you will not leave this house whole."

"Very well, Grey. But not before I collect what's mine."

Gooseflesh dimpled Maggie's clammy skin. She tried to move, tried to shout a denial. As if she were caught in a nightmare, her body refused the simplest of commands.

Nicholas spoke for her. "There is nothing here that belongs to you, Turner. Now get out."

"On the contrary, the welfare of *my* ward is a responsibility I cannot ignore." He looked at Maggie, his eyes glowing with hideous pleasure. "Run along, Margaret, and pack your things."

Like Hell itself, a horrible yawning darkness opened beneath her feet. She'd never once considered the fact that Turner could still claim guardianship. She slumped against Nicholas, her legs depleted of strength.

Curses spilled from Nicholas's mouth as he swept her to the settee. "Don't worry," he whispered. "Turner cannot touch you."

Rage and utter futility waged war within her troubled thoughts. And Nicholas was trapped in the middle. She stroked his cheek, drawing comfort from his presence. "It's all right. He cannot hold me prisoner again. I've escaped before, don't forget, and I even escaped you."

"Yes, but I won in the end. And I will not lose you this time either." His arrogant smile and flashing eyes fractured the curtain of darkness.

"But the law is on his side."

"She's quite right, Grey." Edward moved closer, adjusting his coatsleeves as if expecting an audience with the prince regent himself. "Hurry along, Margaret. I don't have all day."

Slowly, effortlessly, Nicholas rose to his feet. Like a cat toying with its dinner, he circled Turner. "You are in for a very long wait."

"If I must bring the magistrate, I will."

Nicholas withdrew a crisply folded document from his pocket. "Perhaps you should look at this before you bother Mr. Woodson again."

Holding her breath in anticipation, Maggie watched as Turner read the words. His face became a bitter mask of hatred. "This is impossible!"

Curiosity goaded her to her feet. "What is it?"

Nicholas swept the document from Turner's limp fingers and tossed it to the nearby table. "You have one minute to get out."

"You will not win, Grey." With those words, he turned toward Maggie, his expression pitying. "Once my cousin has finished with his revenge, he will have no further need of you.''

Instinctively, she realized the meaning behind his obtuse warning. ''If you are referring to Lady Wentworth, you are wrong. Lord Grey has been quite honest. And I trust him.''

''I fear for you greatly, my dear. Perhaps later you will heed my warning.''

''And now, heed mine,'' Maggie said, her voice steady. ''I never want to see you again. If you come near me, I will take it as a threat, and end your miserable life once and for all.''

''As I said before . . . a veritable tigress.'' With a stiff, courtly bow, he stalked from the room.

Giddy with relief, Maggie sank onto the settee and spied the key to her freedom. Laughing, she unfolded the crisp vellum. ''Did you see the look on his face, Nicholas? I have never seen him so angry.''

''His anger is nothing compared to mine at this moment.'' Like a squall heading for land, Nicholas stormed toward her. ''I told you to stay in your room.''

''No, you told me to *go* to my room, which I did. You neglected to tell me to stay there, however.''

''Don't play games with me, Maggie. You understood my intent.''

Sighing, she nodded. ''Yes, I understood. But I had to face him. Isn't it better we met here, rather than a crowded street or ballroom?''

Nicholas combed his hands through his dark, disheveled hair as he paced before her. ''I know you're right. Now we must decide what to do next. First, I will have my groomsmen keep an eye on this house. . . .''

Barely listening to his plans, Maggie perused the

letter. Her heart pounded like a drumbeat, louder and louder.

She read the words again. Then again.

It was not a bill of freedom, but merely a new set of chains.

"Nicholas? When were you going to tell me about this?"

His gaze flitted from her face to the paper resting on her lap. His lips formed a flat, forbidding line. "Maggie, I had no choice."

She closed her eyes for a moment, still praying she was wrong. Perhaps the document was false—a forgery to keep Turner at bay. Finally, she faced him. "Is this true?"

He nodded slowly. "It was the only way to keep you safe."

Numbness settled into her bones.

Her dreams of emancipation faded into nothingness.

"Tell me, Nicholas. When did you plan to tell me that *you* are now my guardian?"

Her distress cut through Nicholas with bloody precision. He approached her carefully, damning himself for his hasty actions. And now he would pay the price.

She sat utterly still, her posture brittle, as if one touch would shatter her into hundreds of pieces. "How could you do this?"

"Maggie, I was going to tell you."

"I doubt that."

After a deep breath, he tried again. "The guardianship was only finalized this morning."

She said nothing, her gaze speaking volumes.

"Stop staring at me like that," he bit out.

"And how would that be?"

237

"You're looking at me as if I just strangled a kitten. At least listen before you condemn me outright."

As if holding court before a room of dutiful subjects, she settled back against the settee and nodded.

Having no choice, Nicholas accepted the challenge, then issued one of his own. Instead of taking the chair in front of her, he sat beside her on the tiny settee, their thighs pressed snugly together. He smiled to himself as she tried to inch away from the contact but soon realized there was no room to do so.

Nicholas decided it was time to remind her of who their true enemy was. "You handled Lord Turner very well. However, if you had stayed in your room—"

"—I never would have learned the truth."

Gritting his teeth, he strove for a conversational tone. "As I said, there was no time to tell you earlier."

"And when did you decide I needed a keeper?"

"Maggie, you're being ridiculous."

She clutched the arm of the settee, her false smile splintering. "What a fool I've been. All the time I was ranting about my independence, *you* were my guardian. How you must have laughed at me."

Unable to bear the betrayal dulling her eyes, he pried her hand free and held it gently in his own. "Never, I never meant to hurt you, but I had no choice. If not for that document, Turner could have carried you away. And I would have been powerless to stop him . . . short of murder."

She nodded slowly, her eyes drifting closed. "I understand why you felt compelled to do this. But you should have discussed the matter with me first."

"And would you have agreed?"

A shudder raced across her flesh. "I'm not stupid,

Nicholas. I would choose you above your cousin any day.''

Tension eased from his coiled muscles. He should have trusted her to see the situation clearly. "Are we friends again?" he asked playfully.

Her expression remained solemn, and filled with infinite sadness. "What do you intend to do about the guardianship?"

Rubbing the bridge of his nose, he searched for a way to reassure her without causing undue panic. It was, he realized, an impossible feat.

"Maggie, I can do nothing more. If not for the suspicions surrounding Turner, you would still be his ward.''

She unfolded the vellum and read the words once again. "It states that you will remain my guardian until I marry, or reach the age of twenty-one.''

"Those were the original terms of your father's will. I could not change them.''

As if her rage needed immediate release, she threw the paper into his face and leaped to her feet. "Two years! Two bloody years before I can control my own life.''

Her outrage, though justified, fueled his temper. "Stop being melodramatic. I don't intend to hold you prisoner.''

"Then I can do what I wish?''

"As long as your safety is assured.''

She faced him, her eyes glittering like polished onyx stones. His "angel" had disappeared. She had become a virago of whirling emotions . . . magnificent in her anger. He had never wanted her more.

"When Turner is jailed, if he ever is, what then?" she asked. "Do you intend to hold me to this—this travesty?''

*No longer than it takes to make you my wife . . .
my wife.*

Somehow, the idea of marriage no longer filled him
with dread. He tried to convince himself that Maggie's safety was the impetus for his decision, or perhaps the fact he'd taken her innocence. Yet he could
not. He wanted her, forever, in a way that terrified
him.

"Once my cousin is no longer a threat," Nicholas
said, "we can discuss what will be done."

"We will do more than discuss it! Regardless of
what those words say, I will not grovel like a child
begging favors."

Rising slowly to his feet, Nicholas swallowed the
laughter bubbling in his throat. "Grovel? You would
sooner plant a knife in my heart before that day ever
dawns."

She smiled in apparent satisfaction. "I'm glad we
understand each other."

"But," he said softly, "the begging for favors does
hold a certain allure." The need to touch her velvety
skin was an unquenchable thirst. He reached out,
stroking her cheek with the back of his hand.

Her tentative smile faded. "I need to check on Dare
and Thomas. . . ." She backed away, stumbling on the
hem of her gown.

Nicholas clasped her elbow, righting her easily.
"Maggie, what's wrong?"

"Nothing. I'm still a bit rattled from facing Lord
Turner." Her eyes, brimming with unmistakable regret, betrayed the weak excuse.

Damn, but she could push him off center and keep
him floundering. Nicholas wanted to shake her, even
as he wanted to pull her to his chest and comfort her.
He watched as her gaze skittered from his face and
focused on her own clenched fingers.

Sensing her sudden vulnerability, he released her. "This has been a trying day. Perhaps you should rest."

She nodded and hurried from the room as if her satin slippers had burst into flame. Nicholas watched her flee, fighting the temptation to call her back.

He had known she would not greet the news of the guardianship with glowing enthusiasm. Yet this was more than simple anxiety about her future. The haunted, hopeless look in her eyes had been painfully familiar—as irrevocable as day slipping into the arms of night.

Turner, devious as he was, could be handled. Maggie's bone-deep wariness would prove the greater challenge.

And Nicholas had no idea where to begin.

Nausea rumbled through her stomach, leaving her weak. Depleted.

Leaning against the carriage house door, she took a shaky breath as helpless frustration burned through her flesh. Nicholas Grey was her guardian.

The irony seemed too much to bear. She'd escaped Turner, only to be captured by a new jailer. And his hold was even more dangerous. With one smoldering glance, one gentle touch, Nicholas whittled away at her resolve. Without that defense, she would be naked, vulnerable to the shadows darkening her soul.

Squeezing her eyes closed, she bumped her head against the whitewashed wood, pain clearing her mind.

"Maggie, are you feeling all right?"

She jerked at the intrusion and looked down into Thomas's worried face. "I'm much better now."

Smoothing his tousled hair, she studied her surroundings. Muted sunlight showered the massive room with rays of honey gold. Two gleaming coaches were tucked away at one end of the large brick-and-wood building. The other end housed the magnificent stable of horses, their stalls clean and redolent of the scent of fresh straw.

It was as quiet as a cathedral, as golden as heaven itself. Maggie inhaled deeply, feeling at peace for the first time since waking.

Thomas grabbed her hand, his frantic gaze skimming her from head to toe. "You're not running away, are you?"

"No, silly. Why would you think that?"

"Because you're wearing your breeches."

She laughed, surprised she could still manage the feat. "I changed because I was tired of tripping on the hem of my gown."

Her humor vanished. Her change of attire had little to do with dragging hemlines. Silly as it seemed, she had needed to reclaim some measure of lost freedom.

Shrugging away her sadness like an old coat, she tweaked the boy's nose. "Now, what is so interesting that I should find you here, and not in your room studying your lessons?"

"Come see, Maggie." He tugged her across the hay-strewn floor to a darkened corner. "Aren't they wonderful?"

Lounging in a pile of fresh straw, a very contented mother suckled her young.

"Her name is Polly," Thomas whispered. "And she has eight babies."

At the sound of her name, Polly, a plump dog of indistinguishable breed, glanced upward. As if certain no threat existed, she laid her head back down. Meanwhile, eight balls of tan, russet, and black fur grunted and growled in pleasure as they drank their fill.

"What a marvelous surprise, Thomas. They're lovely."

Clearing his throat, the boy tugged at his starched collar. "Do you think Lord Grey would let me keep one of the pups?"

"It would be a great responsibility."

"I promise I will feed him, and comb him, and . . . please, Maggie?"

She hesitated, the weight of the future uncertain—all their futures at risk. But whatever happened to her, Thomas would be kept safe. "I shall ask Lord Grey. If he says yes, then—"

"Oh, Maggie!" He vaulted into her arms, clinging to her with such trust and love that tears pricked her eyes. She'd never thought she would envy a child, but she did. To be innocent, free to feel whatever emotion bubbled to the surface and act on it without regret or second thoughts. To see life as an endless opportunity for happiness . . .

Thomas jerked free of her arms, his face ashen as he wiped the tears from her cheeks. "Don't cry, Maggie. I'm—I'm sorry. I don't need the puppy, if it makes you sad."

Furious with her lack of control, she stroked his cheeks and smiled. "No, it's not you, angel, or the puppies. I'm just a bit out of sorts today."

A figure appeared from the shadows. "What did 'Is bloody Lordship do to you?"

Maggie sighed as she stared into Dare's snarling visage. "It was nothing."

"Thomas, you go to the kitchen," Dare said. "I need to talk to Maggie. Alone."

With obvious reluctance, Thomas stood and dusted off his breeches. "I think I should stay."

"Off with you," Maggie said, smiling. "I'm sure the cook has a treat waiting just for you."

Dragging his feet, he nodded and disappeared through the wide carriage house doors.

"Are you goin' to tell me now?" Dare asked.

"What makes you believe he did anything?"

He laughed bitterly. " 'E's been the cause of our troubles from the start."

Maggie considered subterfuge, then discounted the notion. She'd lied to him too often in the past. "Very well, Lord Grey has made a decision."

Saying nothing, Dare leaned against the slatted boards of a nearby stall and waited.

"He has assumed my guardianship," she said casually, afraid to let Dare see how upsetting the news truly was.

"What the 'ell does that mean?"

"It means he is responsible for me until I marry or come of age."

Dare's brows furrowed in apparent confusion. "But I thought 'e asked you to marry 'im."

Maggie came to her feet, suddenly eager to end the inquisition. "He did. But for now that decision will have to wait."

"Is 'e goin' to toss me and Thomas out?"

"Never! You're my family. Lord Grey knows how important you both are to me."

Pushing away from the stall, Dare grasped her shoulders. "Once I know you'll be safe, I'll be goin' anyway."

"Don't be ridiculous. I know it's been difficult for you, but—"

"Things 'ave changed. You're a real lady now. And me, I'm just a pickpocket. A thief and a bastard. You deserve better company than the likes of me."

Disbelief and blinding rage misted her vision. Before the thought could fully form, she grabbed his shirt and shoved him against the wall.

His stunned expression did nothing to ease her anger. "I have lost too much on this day, and I will not lose you as well." Her voice cracked. "Whether you like it or not, we will see this through. Together."

Gently—more gently than she could have ever imagined—he loosened her fingers and held them in his hands. "All right, Maggie. I wouldn't run out on you."

"If you try, I will find you, just as I did before."

Dare's crooked smile faded. "What do you mean, 'before'? You never 'ad to find me."

Choosing her words with care, she realized how close to disaster she'd come. "When we first met, you would disappear for days on end—"

"And I always came back on my own," he replied, skepticism deepening his frown.

"Yes, I suppose you did." Maggie slid her hands free. "I should go inside and change before Lady Grey sees me." She hurried toward the doors as Dare's soft voice echoed from the rafters and walls.

"You never used to lie to me, Maggie. That's changed, too." Unable to face him, and the truth of his words, she rushed outside. And if he ever learned that their first meeting had been more than pure circumstance, she was sure she would lose him. Forever.

Chapter Nineteen

Nicholas stormed through the carriage house doors, rage and disbelief burning a hole in his belly. *Where the hell are you, Maggie?*

After a late dinner punctuated with stilted conversation and awkward silence, he'd gone to her room as invited, but uncertain of his welcome. He'd found no welcome at all, only an empty, still-made bed.

Fearing she had run away rather than accept his guardianship, he'd quickly gone to the boy's room. Dare and Thomas were safely tucked in bed. Nicholas had relaxed until a vision of Turner spiriting her away took hold. Nicholas had been prepared to rouse the household when he'd remembered her glowing report on the litter of pups.

If she wasn't here, he would have to assume the worst. And then he would kill his cousin.

Lifting the oil lamp higher, Nicholas searched the murky shadows.

There, tucked away in the corner, a decidedly rounded form lay beneath a woolen blanket.

His racing heart slowed to a manageable trot.

Striding toward his quarry, he trembled with the urge to snatch the covering away. He wanted to shout like a cuckolded husband. He wanted to shake her senseless. Instead, he gently lifted the blanket.

Maggie lay curled on her side, blissfully unaware of his torment. Bits of straw jutted from her tousled hair, while her white cotton nightdress bunched seductively around her thighs.

It seemed a lifetime since he'd held her. A lifetime since he'd explored her lush, womanly curves with hungry hands.

His anger evaporated. Tenderly, he smoothed a wayward curl from her temple and kissed her cheek. Her scent, lavender blossoms and rosebuds, mingled with the earthly smell of hay and moist earth.

Unable to resist her unconscious allure, he pressed his mouth to her lips. With a soft mew of pleasure she opened, allowing him entrance. He stroked her tongue, eliciting a deeper moan from her throat. Cupping one firm breast, he felt her nipple pucker against his palm. Lust and aching need pooled in him as he stared into her flushed face. Her eyes remained closed, a soft smile parting her lips.

Then her delicate snore shattered the charged silence.

Nicholas groaned, wondering if he should laugh or be insulted by her slumber. With a sigh of supreme disappointment, he swept her into his arms.

Her eyes fluttered open. "What—what happened?"

"Hush," Nicholas said, striding toward the darkened town house. "You've caused enough trouble for the time being."

She stiffened in his arms. "Where are you taking me?"

"To bed, which is where you belong. Why you would choose a pile of straw over a mattress is—"

"I fell asleep," she replied curtly.

He smiled, sensing a bald-faced lie when he heard one. "More likely you were hiding from me."

She shrugged as a wave of crimson swept unfettered across her cheeks.

"Why, Maggie? Were you afraid I might ravish you while you slept?"

"Of course not." She paused, clutching the lace neckline tighter against her throat. "Perhaps it is myself I cannot trust."

Heat flashed across his skin. Whether she liked it or not, she still wanted him. "Are you saying that I'm irresistible?" he asked, casting his expression in profound innocence.

Her soft laughter purred down his spine. "I don't believe your arrogance needs another boost."

"Not even a little?"

"You'd become unbearable," she said, smiling.

He laughed as he swept her through the house and up the staircase. Pushing open the door to her room with his foot, he carried her toward the bed.

Her smile wavered, then vanished. Familiar shadows lurked beneath her rich cocoa-colored eyes. Something had changed between them, and Nicholas knew what it was. It was the damned guardianship. A situation he was powerless to change.

With a tenderness reserved for a beloved child, he lowered her to the plump goose-down mattress. He tucked the satin duvet around her shoulders and kissed her pale cheek.

Words failed him. Defeat tasted bitter on his tongue. He'd made her his ward to protect her, and he'd succeeded, only to fail in the end. Now she seemed determined to build a wall between them.

He started to rise just as Maggie grabbed his sleeve. "I'm sorry, Nicholas."

Easing back to the bed, he patted her icy hands. "Sorry for worrying me half to death?"

"No, for acting the coward. I asked you to come, and then I hid like a frightened child."

"It was a rather stupid idea," he chided softly, trying to take the sting from his words. "You could have pleaded a megrim and banished me to my room."

Her ghostly smile returned. "And would you have gone without complaint?"

Chuckling, he pressed his lips to her palm. "Without complaint? Miss Alston, I am but a mortal man."

She laughed, and his chest tightened with an unknown, searing emotion. Maggie was fragility cloaked in steel, fear shielded by reckless bravado.

Nicholas cleared his throat, desperate to make his escape. If he didn't leave now, he would crawl into the damned bed whether she wanted him or not.

"You look tired. And you'll need your rest for tomorrow night."

"Tomorrow?"

"I intend to escort you, and my nagging mother, to the theater."

Suspicion furrowed Maggie's delicate brows. "Why do you wish for me to go?"

"You and my mother have forced this idea. Now that Turner knows you're alive, the cat is out of the bag, so to speak." Plucking bits of straw from her hair, he continued. "And I want you to understand that you are free to go where you wish. Balls, dinner parties, soirees, whatever you wish to attend, I shall escort you."

She grinned. "Crowded ballrooms, inane conversation. What a noble sacrifice."

"You've been speaking to Mother."

"Lady Grey despairs you will ever find a bride." Even as the words left her lips, Maggie's face paled. "If you should find a young woman . . ."

I have already found her, my sweet, frightened Maggie.

Aloud, he said, "I have more pressing matters to attend to than my bachelorhood."

Her chin lifted. "Yes, but—"

He silenced her with his fingertip. "I will not listen to another word." Reluctantly, he stood. "Sleep now. I'm certain Mother has your entire day mapped from beginning to end."

As if courage could be drawn from the air, she inhaled deeply, her features concealed by velvety shadows. "I thought you would ask why I've changed my mind about tonight."

His stomach clenched at her words. He didn't need a gypsy fortune-teller to sense approaching disaster. "I cannot say I'm not disappointed. And I realize our situation has changed, but *I* haven't changed, Maggie. Only your perceptions have altered."

"You went from my lover to my guardian," she said sharply. "That is something I cannot ignore."

Curbing the wild impulse to slam his fist into the carved rosewood headboard, he grabbed the bedpost instead. "Then what the devil do you want from me?"

"I want . . . I wish . . ." She shook her head, unwilling to reveal more.

The words were unnecessary. She wanted total independence, the one wish he could not grant. He moved toward the door. "Good night, Maggie."

As soft as crushed velvet, her voice froze him in place. "I know this is a selfish thing to ask, but would you hold me for a moment?"

Hold her? Just hold her? Gritting his teeth, he wondered if he was up to the challenge. This he could not deny her.

Tugging off his boots, he slid into bed and pulled her into his embrace. She snuggled closer. He closed his eyes, swallowing a groan of pleasure. Sweat beaded his brow as he tried to keep his hands from straying into forbidden territory. Her sweet scent teased him without a shred of mercy.

"Thank you," she murmured against his shoulder.

"Sleep, Maggie." *Please go to sleep. . . .*

After what seemed an eternity, her breathing deepened, her body becoming pliant against his side. "Thank God." Now he could seek his bed—his large, lonely, empty bed.

With the speed of a shooting star, the impulse took flight. He pulled her closer, her heartbeat sounding against his ribs. Unable to leave, he accepted his self-imposed torture. He deserved nothing less.

Relief filtered through his vexing thoughts. Maggie was confused, but she still trusted him enough to invite him into her bed. Although the outcome was not precisely what he'd hoped, it was a beginning.

Tomorrow would be soon enough to turn the tables on his unsuspecting victim. Maggie had pursued him with the determination of an aging courtesan, and he would do the same.

Until she became his wife.

Then her safety and her future would be secured.

He chuckled and kissed her forehead.

Tomorrow, the seduced would become the seducer.

* * *

With nerves as frayed as a tattered ball of yarn, Maggie descended the stairs.

Lady Grey, adorned in citron muslin and French lace, waited below. Her eyes gleamed in genuine pleasure. "My dear Maggie, how wonderful you look. Madame deFournier is a true artist."

Fingering the soft silk, Maggie sighed. "It is lovely, but it's so . . . white."

"You are not playing the role of a widow any longer.

Tonight you are the innocent and demure Miss Alston who survived a horrific shipwreck." Eugenia patted Maggie's cheek, then tugged the embroidered neckline down a full inch. "There, much better."

Maggie eyed the older woman with blatant suspicion. "I thought you wished me to be demure and innocent?"

"Yes, but you're not a cloistered nun either. Lady Jersey mentioned that the prince regent himself may be in attendance."

"Surely you're not suggesting—"

Eugenia gasped. "Of course not. A brief introduction would merely bolster your position."

Another round of tests, Maggie realized. After a day of endless shopping and nerve-racking social calls, her fortitude was at low ebb—with a long night ahead. "I know you mean well, Lady Grey, but surely my appearance tonight is unnecessary. Lady Jersey seemed to believe our fabricated story. And like sheep, the ton will follow her lead."

The brightness in Eugenia's eyes faded. "Are you trying to say you do not wish to go this evening?"

Maggie winced at the obvious disappointment etched across Lady Grey's features. A night at the theater was a small price to pay for all Eugenia and Nicholas had done for her.

Forcing a smile to her lips, Maggie said, "I thought you might be tired after such a full day."

Eugenia chuckled. "When I was young, I rarely returned home before dawn." Her expression sobered. "But I'm being a selfish old woman. . . ."

Soft laughter echoed from above. "Stop wielding your sword of guilt, Mother. Maggie hasn't had time to build her defenses."

Turning slowly, her heart thumping against her ribs, Maggie watched Nicholas stride down the stairs. Attired in crisply tailored black formal wear, he was the epitome of an English gentleman, save for the silky locks brushing his cravat. His wicked smile, laced with promise, tingled across her skin like a caress. A very dangerous caress.

She recognized his look at once. Her determination slipped a notch. Then two. Nicholas was on the hunt, waiting for her to weaken, waiting for her total surrender.

Last night had merely been a truce.

Awakening early, she'd found him already gone, the scent of him clinging to her pillow. An aching sense of loss had dogged her the rest of the day. And yet she couldn't make the leap back into his bed as his lover. Not while he was her guardian.

Needing an ally, she inched closer to Eugenia. Nicholas's grin widened, his flashing azure eyes swearing swift retribution. "I shall be the envy of every rakehell and rogue in London," he said. "Ladies, you're ravishing."

"I shall be quite safe from that kind of attention." Eugenia tapped her fan against his forearm. "But Maggie is another story. You, Nicholas, must keep a keen eye on her."

His openly admiring gaze settled on the low décolletage of Maggie's gown. "Trust me, Mother. I shall not let her out of my sight."

Maggie sensed a conspiracy, and the pointed glance between mother and son confirmed her suspicions.

With a face as somber as that of a vicar on Sunday, Abbot appeared. "The carriage awaits, my lord."

Smiling, Eugenia shook her head. "We are waiting for a special guest."

"Mother," Nicholas murmured softly, "have you been keeping secrets?"

Her eyes gleamed with crafty intuition. "Not I."

Embarrassment creeped across Maggie's cheeks. She had the unnerving sensation that Lady Grey was more astute—or better informed—than Maggie would have liked. She glanced toward Abbot, seeking confirmation. He stared at the far wall, two dots of pink staining his cheekbones.

The aging retainer had been telling tales.

A loud rap at the front door shattered the uncomfortable silence. Maggie held her breath, watching Nicholas's grin fade. "Mother, what have you done?"

"I've decided it would be prudent to have a chaperon stay with us. At least until Maggie's situation has been fortified."

"A chaperon!" Nicholas stared at his mother as if she'd sprouted horns. "Why the devil would you do that?"

Eugenia blushed under his scrutiny. "We must keep up appearances."

The knock came again, growing more persistent.

Abbot moved toward the door, only to be halted by Nicholas's withering glare. "You have gone beyond your bounds, Mother."

Standing her ground, Eugenia scowled at her son. "I am not blind, nor am I stupid. An unattached man and woman living under the same roof could raise eyebrows. I am merely being cautious.''

"She is my ward," Nicholas stated calmly.

Too calmly for Maggie's liking.

"Then you have nothing to fear," Eugenia said. "Unless there is something you wish to tell me . . ."

Maggie froze as her heart skipped a beat.

She looked at Nicholas.

His hooded gaze met hers.

Please don't tell her, Maggie pleaded with her eyes.

Slowly, he faced his mother. "If you feel it necessary, I will abide by your wishes.''

Breathing an audible sigh of relief, Maggie unclenched her fists. Aware of Eugenia's gaze upon her, she smiled weakly. Then the impact of the situation struck. A chaperon . . . another layer of defense against Nicholas's unholy brand of persuasion.

She leveled a victorious look at him. "I think it's a wonderful idea, don't you?"

His features darkened. "I can barely contain my enthusiasm.''

As if God himself sought entrance, the door slammed open with a thunderous clap.

Maggie's gasp of shock transformed into one of surprise, then abounding pleasure.

The diminutive Duchess of Blackthorne stood in the doorway, pounding her ebony cane against the floor. "What manner of lackadaisical servants do you have here, Eugenia?" She turned toward a stone-faced Abbot. "Are you deaf?"

"No, Your Grace, my hearing is impeccable.''

Eugenia rushed forward. "Your Grace, forgive our delay.''

"One would almost think I was not welcome," the duchess said, her gaze trained on Nicholas.

"Nonsense." He bowed and kissed her gloved hand. "We are delighted to have you visit."

"As you should be, my boy." The duchess's keen eyes circled the room and focused on Maggie. "What have you to say for yourself, young woman?"

Shame and regret pierced Maggie's happiness as she offered a graceful curtsy. "Forgive me, Your— Your Grace. I should have sent word to you."

"Yes, you should have. Since our first meeting, I have been worried for your welfare." Her raspy voice softened. "Eugenia called on me yesterday and told me of your plight. Due to your unfortunate illness, I shall forgive you."

Maggie grinned. "You are too generous, Your Grace. And where, may I ask, is your charming and lovely niece?"

Laughter lurked beneath the aging woman's words. "She decided London was a bore and returned to America." The duchess's expression gentled. "I have missed her sorely."

Unexpected moisture clouded Maggie's vision. "I'm certain she has missed you, as well."

A harrumph of approval slipped from the duchess's lips. She jabbed her cane against the marble flooring. "Now, where are my things?"

As if awaiting their cue, five groomsmen appeared in scarlet and royal blue livery, their arms laden with trunks and hatboxes.

Nicholas stepped in front of them, his mouth set in hard lines. "Precisely how long do you intend to stay, Your Grace?"

Eugenia gasped, her hand fluttering to her throat. "Nicholas, you are being rude."

"Rude or not," the duchess said with a smile, "it is a valid question. And to answer, I intend to stay until this situation is resolved to my satisfaction."

"And what situation would that be?" he asked.

With the innocence of a precocious child, Dorothea replied, "Why, when Viscount Turner has been soundly trounced. What did you think I meant?"

Maggie laughed at his sudden tight-lipped glare. Perhaps the coming night would be an entertaining affair after all. "Yes, Nicholas, do tell us what you were thinking."

As if seeking reprieve from the heavens, he looked upward and sighed. "I think I am horribly outnumbered."

Chapter Twenty

He was more than outnumbered. He'd been out-flanked and outwitted at every turn. Nicholas glared at his zealous chaperones. His mother and the duchess smiled back with benign humor.

The night had become a disaster. Like barnacles clinging to the hull of an aging ship, the two women had glued themselves to Maggie's side. And she'd offered no objection. In fact, Maggie had practically laughed at his obvious predicament.

Even once they'd reached their box in the theater, his mother had positioned Maggie at one end, Nicholas at the other. Intermission had been a nightmare. One introduction became two, then three, and on, until Nicholas realized the truth. Miss Margaret Alston had become an "incomparable." Her mysterious and tragic story consumed the ton with romantic fancy. And those who remembered her connection to Viscount Turner wisely remained silent.

Now he had to find a way to get Maggie alone.

Barely concealing his temper, he ushered the three women toward the bustling street. Guilded carriages and hackney cabs bullied for position beneath the light of torches. A spot opened and Hoskins maneuvered the Rockingham coach into position.

Turning back to his entourage, Nicholas gnashed his teeth. Several young bucks had surrounded Maggie, plying her with voluminous praise. He watched their discerning gazes flit across her blooming cheeks and high bosom.

Groaning inwardly, Nicholas knew what the days to come would bring—an endless stream of suitors, all certain the marquess would offer a generous dowry for his ward. They would have a disappointing and fruitless quest.

No one would marry Maggie except Nicholas Grey.

He charged between her and her fawning swains. "Our carriage has arrived," he growled, clasping her elbow. "It's time to leave."

A chorus of disappointed groans echoed through the humid night air.

Maggie's lips curved into a coquettish smile. "But it's so early."

The last tether of his control snapped. He leaned close to her ear. "I shall toss you over my shoulder and carry you, if I must."

Her eyes widened. "You wouldn't dare!"

"And you wouldn't want a scandal, Miss Alston. Then I should be forced to quiet the wagging tongues with a speedy marriage."

"That's blackmail."

"Perhaps your felonious ways have rubbed off."

Her mouth snapped closed, her cheeks as red as flames.

He was being a thorough bastard, and, from the

condemning scowls emanating from his mother and the duchess, they concurred.

With a firm grasp, he steered Maggie toward the coach and prayed for a miracle. He needed time alone with her. He needed a diversion. His gaze focused on the aging Earl of Stansbury, Lord Hampton.

Nicholas grinned as he waved the portly gentleman over. The man was a notorious windbag and, hopefully, the perfect distraction. "Hampton, good to see you. You know my mother, the Marchioness of Rockingham, and our houseguest, the Duchess of Blackthorne."

The two women shifted uncomfortably and offered a brief smile as they glared at Nicholas.

"Yes, of course," Hampton said, his beefy jowls spilling over his knotted cravat. "My wife has been anxious to call on you, Lady Grey. She's been in the country, you know, overseeing the birth of our third grandchild. . . ."

As his voice droned on, Nicholas seized the opportunity and quickly led Maggie toward the carriage.

"Shouldn't we wait for Lady Grey and the duchess?"

"Certainly," Nicholas replied. "But we'll be more comfortable inside."

Maggie hesitated. "I'm not sure that would be wise."

Vigilant as always, Hoskins whipped the door open.

Nicholas tugged her closer. "They shall join us in moments. What's wrong, Miss Alston? Don't you trust me?"

Her mouth curved into a sardonic smile. "Trust you, Lord Grey? I'd sooner trust the devil himself."

"We shall see," he murmured. With a lingering

caress on her softly rounded bottom, he propelled her inside.

She gasped in outrage and slapped at his hands. Later, he vowed, she would be gasping in pleasure. He paused to whisper his instructions to Hoskins, then leaped into the carriage.

The barrage began immediately.

"What are you doing?" she asked in strident tones. "You're being impossibly rude. First you glare and glower at everyone all evening, and now you're shoving me into coaches. . . ."

Her voice, husky with anger and bewilderment, entranced him. The muted light from the interior lamps cast her skin in honeyed hues. Her hair, swept back in a simple chignon, gleamed like burnished gold. His gaze lingered across her daring neckline, her breasts threatening to spring free with each indignant breath.

Maggie was glorious. Spellbinding. A woman unaware of her sensual power. Hot blood swept through him, rousing his sex to attention. His fingers twitched with the need to touch her satiny skin and peel away her clothing, one delicious layer at a time. . . .

As if becoming aware of his heated perusal, she clutched the shawl tight to her neck. "Lady Grey will—will be here any moment. And she will not be pleased with your actions."

Nicholas laughed. "I'm not a child in short pants, as my mother well knows."

"The duchess will not stand idly by while you—you . . ."

"While I what, Maggie? Are you afraid I might seduce you? Again?"

She tensed at the blatant question, but remained stoically silent.

It was time for another diversion. "Did you enjoy the theater?" he finally asked.

"Yes, it was lovely." As if bored by the conversation, she lifted the shade and stared out the window.

He read her expression clearly. Maggie was searching for reinforcements. If Hoskins completed his task, her search would be for naught.

"You created quite the sensation, Maggie. I thought I'd have to beat back your numerous admires with a stick."

"They were all complete gentlemen," she replied with a glacial smile.

Nicholas remained undaunted. "Your plan worked perfectly. I'm impressed."

"I have no idea what you're speaking of."

"You were set upon making me jealous. And you succeeded. I wanted to strangle the lot of those swaggering lords."

He edged closer, until their knees touched, his voice an intimate whisper. "I wanted you to smile at *me*." He leaned over her and braced his hands on the opposite bench. "I wanted your eyes shining with need . . . your lips parted in anticipation. . . ."

As if bewitched by a mesmerist, she moved toward him, her eyes shining with need . . . her lips parted.

A soft rap sounded from above, shattering the mystical spell.

Nicholas glanced out the window. Evidently, the duchess had had enough of Lord Hampton. With one jab of her cane into the gentleman's foot, she had silenced his buzzing monologue.

Time was running out.

Sliding to the other side of the carriage, Nicholas snapped open the door. Hoskins had done his job well. The rented hack was in perfect position, a mere foot away.

He slipped out and stepped into the waiting conveyance. Maggie peered after him. "Nicholas, what in heaven's name are you doing?"

Her blooming cheeks and moist pink lips sizzled heat through each muscle of his body. In that defining moment of unrestrained need, he realized he couldn't wait. The urge to claim her body—and her shadowed heart—reverberated through his senses. And yet the choice had to be hers.

"Come with me, Maggie." He held out his hand, and offered his soul. "I need you."

She stared at his outstretched hand, and then into his eyes. He held her steady gaze, plumbing velvety brown depths for his answer.

He saw indecision.

The voices of his mother and the duchess drifted closer. Maggie glanced over her shoulder, then turned back.

His belly clenched at the trust that finally shone from her darkened eyes. He didn't deserve her. But, deserving or not, he wanted her.

Smiling softly, she slipped her hand into his.

The tender strength of his hand chased away her doubt. His gentle, undemanding gaze lured her forward.

If Nicholas had dragged her into the carriage and smiled his irritating, arrogant smile, her resistance would have stayed intact. Instead, he'd offered her a choice.

Her apprehension melted into warm rivers of desire.

"Are you certain?" he asked quietly.

Maggie nodded. As if she weighed little more than a puff of cotton, he swept her inside and snapped the door closed. After his sharp rap against the roof panel, the hack rumbled forward.

Like two children escaping an ironhanded tutor, they grinned and peeked through the windows. Two silver-haired heads leaned from the Rockingham carriage, watching them go.

Maggie blinked. She could have sworn Lady Grey and the duchess were grinning—or perhaps it was a grimace. She would find out the truth when they arrived home.

"Do you think they'll be angry with us?" Maggie asked, her gaze lingering on the street.

"That will depend on how long we stay missing."

She barely heard his reply.

A shadow loomed in an alleyway, a tall, caped creature. She could feel its icy gaze upon her face. She tried to breathe, but fear closed her throat. Lurching backward, she collided with Nicholas's chest.

His arms enfolded her. "Maggie, what is it?"

"I—I saw . . ." Trembling, she pointed outside.

He ripped aside the window flap and stared out. "What, Maggie? Did you see someone?"

"I saw Drager."

"Damn!" Nicholas scanned the street again. "Are you certain?"

Suddenly, she wasn't. The man's face had been concealed by darkness, only the immense height and gangly shape of his body clear. Then a tremor darted down her spine. Drager had terrified her from the moment she'd stepped inside Lord Turner's London house. She hadn't been mistaken.

"He's following us. I know it."

"Don't worry," Nicholas whispered against her ear. "I won't let Drager or his master harm you. Ever."

Cradled in his arms, Maggie wanted to believe his vow. She shivered and pressed closer. "Will you promise me something?"

"Anything."

"Swear to me that you will take care of the boys if I should—"

"I'll hear none of that," Nicholas said harshly. "Do you have so little faith in me?"

Turning to face him, she stroked his lean, angular cheek. "I have seen how quickly death can strike. Please, Nicholas, promise me you will watch over Dare and Thomas."

"I shall protect all three of you. Though I don't believe Dare is interested in anything I can offer. The boy detests me."

"Give him time. He has years of mistrust to overcome."

With those words, silence settled in the close confines of the hack.

Slowly the tension in her muscles eased. Turner had stolen enough. He wouldn't steal tonight as well. She pushed thoughts of revenge from her mind and focused on Nicholas. Guardian or not, he was the man who'd entranced her from first sight. The man she loved.

Burying her face against his neck, she nipped at the taut flesh.

His arms tightened around her. "Maggie?"

She smoothed the slight abrasion with her tongue.

He cleared his throat. "You've just had a frightening experience."

"Simply terrifying," she murmured, tugging at the carefully tied knot of his cravat.

His hands roamed across her back in ever larger sweeps. "You seem to have conquered your fright quite admirably."

"Out of necessity." She unbuttoned his crisp white shirt. "Time is a precious commodity, not to be wasted. Don't you agree, my lord?"

A growl echoed from his throat as he swept her into his lap. "I agree, but tonight I shall do the honors."

Nestling closer, Maggie felt the evidence of his growing desire nudging her bottom. She smiled and peppered his collarbone with moist kisses. "What honors would those be?"

Grabbing her wrists, he uncoiled her arms from around his neck. "I want the honor of seducing you this time."

She laughed, trying to pull free. "Oh, Nicholas, you manage that with one look."

He gripped her tighter. "Not tonight. Tonight is just for you."

Confused by his oblique remark, she studied his solemn features. "What exactly do you have in mind?"

A wolfish smile spread across his face. "I intend to thoroughly seduce you. But first I shall explain the rules."

She blinked. "Rules?"

"Yes, now pay attention." His voice took on the no-nonsense tone of a headmaster instructing a rowdy pupil. "First, you are not allowed to touch me, in any way, until I say so."

"But—"

"Let me finish," he said with obvious enjoyment. "If you interrupt, I will have to reprimand you."

Maggie did as ordered, only because she was too confused to speak. In a perverse way, his edicts heated her blood. Her skin tingled with remembered caresses. Even the idea of a reprimand seemed erotic and forbidden.

"Now, Miss Alston," he purred, "you are to keep your hands behind your neck. And you must not shout out from pleasure."

Warming to the game, Maggie fluttered her lashes in mock innocence. "Pleasure, you say? What if I cannot control myself?"

"You have no choice, unless you want the poor driver to hear your cries."

"My lord, you seem quite confident. Are you certain you're *up* to the task?"

He grinned and positioned her arms as he'd directed. "You are a cheeky girl, Miss Alston. Now, my last rule is simple—do exactly as I instruct you." He settled her on the tufted leather bench and straddled her thighs.

Staring at the hard planes of his chest, Maggie felt her heartbeat quicken. She followed each sinewy muscle down to the thick ridge of flesh straining against his trousers.

"Close your eyes, Maggie." His quiet voice, laced with purpose, demanded compliance.

She squeezed her eyes closed. Anticipating a kiss, she moistened her lips . . . it never came. Instead, his mouth blazed a fiery trail across the nape of her neck, her shoulders, and the swell of her breasts.

Maggie arched, beckoning him closer. "Nicholas . . ."

He drew away instantly, taking the heat with him. "You're not following my instructions," he whispered. "Must I gag you?"

Wisely, she held her tongue.

As if rewarding a student for the correct answer, he brushed a fleeting kiss across her lips. Moments later, he maneuvered her arms through the puffed sleeves of her gown and removed her gloves with languorous care.

Lost in a void of velvety darkness, Maggie felt her other senses heighten. The sway of the coach rocked beneath her like gentle ocean waves. Her nostrils flared as lavender mingled with Nicholas's own masculine scent. His hands skated down the bodice of her gown, sensitizing her flesh to his touch. One by one, she felt the tiny buttons give way. The soft silk drifted down. Her chemise followed.

Temptation proved greater than her will.

Peering through the veil of her lashes, she watched him. Unmoving, he stared at her, his eyes glittering like faceted sapphires. "So beautiful . . ." He leaned closer, his hot gaze locking with hers. "You're peeking."

"I wanted to see you."

"Then watch me," he rasped. "Watch me love you."

With agonizing slowness, he bent down and laved her nipple with his tongue. She gasped as he moved to the other breast.

"Let me touch you," she murmured, unashamed of her pleading tone.

He silenced her with a plundering kiss. Adrift in sensation, Maggie felt nothing but him. His mouth, his hands, his tongue, ignited unquenchable fires. And the man bent on torturing her was equally affected. His chest, slick with a golden sheen of perspiration, heaved with every breath.

Breaking free of her lips, he knelt on the cramped floor of the coach. "Do you have any thought of how lovely you are?"

Maggie slowly lowered her arms and stroked his cheek. "You're the teacher."

His gaze held hers as he lifted the hem of her gown, skimming his palms along her calves, then her thighs, and higher still. Clutching his shoulders, she inhaled sharply as he finally touched her aching center. Stroking her moist flesh, he slid one, then two fingers inside her.

Maggie rocked against his hand. "Nicholas, now . . ."

As if sensing her imminent climax, he ripped open his trousers. Before she could catch a needed breath, he spread her thighs and guided himself deep within her.

He filled her, consuming her from the inside out. Stretched and pliant, she accepted each powerful thrust. The tightness in her stomach grew to unbearable proportions. Clawing his back, she arched and drew him deeper until it seemed he touched her very heart.

A kaleidoscope of colors and sensations reeled through her mind with blinding vibrancy. She quivered and toppled into the abyss.

His tempo increased, driving her back against the cracked leather seat. "God . . . Maggie . . ." His face contorted into a feral mask of possession—a mask of exquisite pleasure. He drove one last time and shuddered in release.

As if drained of all strength, he slumped against her. Maggie grasped him closer as he continued to pulsate within her satiated body.

Like a man rousing from an alcohol haze, he blinked and stared into her eyes. "My God, Miss Alston, are you trying to kill me?"

Laughing, she kissed him full on the mouth. "Not quite, but what a glorious way to go."

Maggie couldn't tear her gaze from the man seated before her. Except for the slightly askew cravat and his wicked smile, no one would have guessed the Marquess of Rockingham had been in complete disarray only minutes ago.

As clandestine lovers hurrying home do, they'd straightened and buttoned their clothing, giggling through the onerous process. Once presentable, Nicholas had returned to the other seat and directed the driver toward home. Even now, Maggie wondered if the poor coachman had heard her cries of ecstasy.

"Stop looking at me like that," Nicholas said with a knowing smile.

Maggie fluttered her lashes. "And how would that be?"

"You're staring at me like a cat ready to pounce on an unsuspecting mouse."

"Why, Lord Grey, would you like to be pounced upon?"

He laughed, smoothing his tousled hair into place. "You *are* trying to kill me. Trust me, Maggie, I'm getting too old to play randy games in a carriage."

Tapping her finger against her chin, she studied him. "You did seem a bit . . . slow. And I could have sworn I heard your aging bones creak—"

She squealed as he lunged forward. "My bones do not creak, Miss Alston," he said with an exaggerated leer. "And the next time I make love to you, it will be in a nice, comfortable bed, and without a stitch of clothing between us."

His provocative promise wove through her mind, creating a tapestry of vivid images. "Tonight?" she murmured, staring at his lips.

He groaned and slumped back to his seat. "We cannot. Knowing the duchess, she'll probably post a sentry at your door."

"And Lady Grey?"

"As you yourself have pointed out, Mother is desperate to find me a wife. And she is very fond of you. . . ."

The veiled implication hung in the air between them. For the first time since their passionate encounter, Maggie looked away.

She loved him. That truth was inescapable.

Nicholas claimed he wouldn't risk loving her. If he ever managed to utter the words, she would be lost— her will conquered.

Here in the intimacy of a darkened coach, the scent of their lovemaking still hovering in the air, freedom seemed a small price for love. Except she wasn't free. Nicholas, as her guardian, could control every aspect of her life. The very thought sent a tremor down to her toes.

Nicholas's terse voice scattered her thoughts. "Don't look so terrified, Maggie. I'm not down on bended knee pledging my troth."

His sarcasm hurt more than she would admit. "Please, Nicholas, I don't want to argue. Not now. Not after . . ."

He waved away her words and tenderly kissed her hand. "I had no right to browbeat you. But at least," he continued, smiling, "your cheeks aren't flushed with passion any longer."

The coach rattled to an abrupt stop.

Maggie patted her hair and took a deep breath. "So will I pass inspection?"

"No one will ever know. But just to be certain, perhaps you should go straight to your room. I'll keep our chaperones at bay until you're settled."

The door flapped open. Abbot stood outside, his face lined with unspoken censure. "My lord, Lady Grey and the duchess of Blackthorne are waiting for you inside."

"Why am I not surprised?" he muttered, guiding Maggie from the coach. She smiled at his fit of temper and squeezed his forearm, offering silent support.

"Abbot, where exactly are they?" Nicholas asked.

"In the blue drawing room, my lord."

"Very good," Nicholas said. He turned to Maggie. "Go upstairs, very quietly."

If not for the retainer's glowering presence, Maggie would have kissed the furrows from Nicholas's dark brows. Instead she nodded and stepped away. Abbot followed tight on her heels, as if afraid she would bolt. If the poor man had seen them earlier, he would have curled up his toes and fainted dead away. Maggie nearly laughed aloud.

As he pushed open the front door, a strange pop echoed through the hushed night.

She turned. "Nicholas, what was—"

A scream ripped from her throat.

Nicholas sagged against the coach, clutching his shoulder. The unmistakable glint of blood seeped through his fingers. "Damn it, Maggie, go inside! Now!"

She stumbled toward him. "No, I—"

"Abbot, get her in the house. I've bloody well been shot!"

Chapter Twenty-one

Nicholas watched his mother pace the study floor in short, precise steps. At least she took his mind from the burning in his shoulder, and the black rage gnawing at his belly. There was no doubt who'd tried to take his life. Just a few more inches to the right, and Maggie would have been dead.

The focus of his thoughts sat perched on the edge of the divan, her face as pale as the white shawl hanging limply over her shoulders.

The duchess had proven to be the only sensible member of the household. Upon hearing that the ball had only grazed his shoulder, she'd stomped her cane, pronounced him fit, and sought her bed.

Now if he could only instill the same sensibility into his stubborn mother.

"Nicholas, are you certain you don't need a physician?" Lady Grey paused, her hands fluttering like birds in flight. "This type of wound can easily become infected."

Strumming his fingers on the desk, Nicholas offered what he hoped was a placating smile. "Mother, Abbot has applied his miracle salve and bandaged me with care and diligence. His prognosis—I shall live."

"There's no need to be flippant," she remarked, and continued her pacing. "We must leave London at once. It is far too dangerous to stay."

"Perhaps in a few days," he replied, watching Maggie's reaction from the corner of his eye.

She hadn't moved a muscle, her complexion growing even paler.

"Mother, I want you to go to bed."

"But we must alert the authorities. My nephew is the culprit, and he must be stopped."

Nicholas stood, keeping his shoulder as still as possible. "You're upsetting Maggie. I will send word to Hennessy in the morning and we shall discuss the situation over breakfast."

"Oh, dear . . ." As if noticing Maggie's pallor for the first time, Lady Grey rushed to her side. "I didn't mean to upset you. Perhaps we should go upstairs. You must be frightfully exhausted."

"No," Maggie whispered. "I must speak with Lord Grey."

In the blink of an eye, his mother transformed into the stern chaperon. "I shall stay as well then."

"That will not be necessary," Nicholas said. "I'll have Abbot escort Maggie upstairs in a few minutes."

"You have twenty," Lady Grey said as she swept open the door. "And we *will* discuss your sudden disappearance earlier this evening."

"Of course." He kissed her cheek, ushered her outside, and closed the door.

He turned back to Maggie. Her stiff composure had

vanished. She trembled from head to toe, a single tear slipping down her face. Her obvious fear and belated shock squeezed his heart like a vise.

Reaching her in seconds, he tried to brush the moisture from her face. "Maggie, I'm fine—"

She batted his hand away and leaped to her feet. "This is all my doing!"

"You're upset. None of this is your fault." He stepped toward her.

She stumbled back. "I should never have stayed here. I knew how dangerous Lord Turner could be."

"Stop this!" Nicholas dragged her into his arms and subdued her pitiful struggle, ignoring the twinge in his shoulder. "My cousin hated me long before you became my ward." Stroking her back, he waited for her heartbeat to slow. "In fact, I'm rather surprised he did not try the tactic sooner."

Maggie was sniffling against his shirt, her voice bleak. "I knew it would never end. He will never stop." She hiccuped, clutching his shirt tighter. "My—my revenge has become his instrument. And I've put everyone in this house at risk."

"Hush, Maggie. We shall simply take greater precautions."

She pulled away and looked into his face, utter futility etched across her pale, delicate features.

In that moment, his rage became murderous intent. He'd suffered through Julia's erroneous choice and untimely death. But this time Turner would pay the price for his sins. With his miserable life. He forced a smile. "I'm thinking our twenty minutes will soon expire."

She remained unconvinced. "You must not even think it."

"And what would that be?"

"I know that expression well. I saw it often enough whenever I looked in a mirror."

Like a sinner in a confessional, she whispered, "I wanted to kill him, too. But I knew I could never bring myself to actually do it." She smiled. "And neither can you. Not in cold blood."

Perhaps she didn't know him as well as he thought. "Are you so certain?"

"Yes, although"—she pointed to the wall—"you certainly have the arsenal to commit the deed."

The tension dissipated as they both stared at the macabre collection hanging from the dark-paneled wood. Spears, battle-axes, swords, maces—replete with deadly spikes—and pistols lined the wall.

Nicholas laughed at her wide-eyed stare. "My ancestors collected every weapon known to man. I'm told they were a bloodthirsty lot." His gaze fell on a glass case. Nestled on burgundy velvet lay a polished dueling pistol.

Stunned by a sudden realization, he moved closer. With a flick of his wrist, he opened the glass door.

"Nicholas, is something wrong?"

"It would seem we have a mystery on our hands."

Maggie moved to his side. "Why would you say that?"

"Because this is a dueling pistol—a pistol missing its mate."

Confusion flashed in her eyes as she touched the indentation in the velvet. "Perhaps one of the servants—"

"Impossible. Only Abbot cleans the case."

"Well, then, perhaps it needed repair."

Nicholas closed the door. "No, Maggie, they were only used once, nearly ten years ago. It seemed my father had a very public liaison with a married countess. Her husband challenged my father to a duel. The poor earl suffered a ball to the chest, but miraculously survived. That was the last time they were ever used.''

"What a terrible story," Maggie whispered. "And your poor mother . . .''

He chuckled at her sad expression. "I have come to believe my mother could survive Armageddon. And by that time, she was accustomed to my dear father's entanglements.''

Maggie's gaze returned to the glass case. "I still don't see the significance of the missing pistol.''

"Don't you?''

She paled and grabbed his wrist. "You don't believe the missing pistol is the one—''

"That is exactly what I believe.''

She shook her head, her nails biting into his skin. "It makes no sense. Why would Lord Turner shoot you with your own weapon?''

"The obvious answer is—my cousin was not behind the attempt on my life. There is no possible way he could have stolen the pistol.''

"Of course there is. He has been in this room before.''

The bitter truth stared them in the face, but apparently Maggie refused to open her eyes. Leading her to the divan, he urged her down, holding her hand. "Abbot is meticulous. He would have noticed immediately.'' He stared hard into her eyes, begging her to see. "Maggie, who else hates me so much?''

Recognition dulled her features as her soft lips drew into an unforgiving line. "No, Nicholas. You are wrong. He would never do such a thing.''

Her blind loyalty inflamed his anger. He wanted to shake the truth into her stubborn head. "Very well.'' He smiled coldly and tugged her to her feet. "Shall we go?''

She pulled her hands free, hugging them to her chest. "Where are we going?"

"Upstairs."

"But why?"

Striding across the room, he swept the door open. "Come along, Maggie. Aren't you anxious to prove Dare's innocence?"

He is wrong. Dare would never . . .

Maggie clung to the silent affirmation as she followed Nicholas upstairs. Like a young lion defending his pride, Dare could be a savage protector. His temper, quick to ignite and slow to burn out, was legendary in East End.

Now Nicholas was intent on proving her friend his attacker. With each step, doubt pinched her heart. Dare saw only violence and malice in the nobility. He was blind to Nicholas's good heart and strong spirit. *But blind enough to take a pistol and . . . ?* The heavy lump in her throat ballooned.

After pushing open the door, Nicholas set the small oil lamp on the nightstand. Soft light illuminated the canopy bed and its only slumbering form.

Nicholas pointed an accusing finger toward the bed. "I told you, Maggie."

She motioned Nicholas to the far side of the bed. On the floor, a mound of blankets covered another sleeping body.

Maggie sighed in utter relief. Dare was safe in bed, burrowed beneath the covers like a mouse in a nest. "There," she whispered, "I told you he would never do such a thing. Lord Turner tried to kill you, not Dare."

Staring at the floor, Nicholas's discerning gaze focused on the huddled form. "Just to be certain, I'll speak to him."

She stepped in front of him, arms crossed over her chest. "You will not wake him. Especially not to make groundless accusations."

"If Dare is innocent, he won't mind telling us his earlier whereabouts."

Seeing the uncompromising glint in Nicholas's piercing blue eyes, she knelt at Dare's side. "Very well, but *I* will speak to him." Gently she nudged the blanket. "Dare, wake up." She prodded again. "I must speak to you."

Her heart stopped in midbeat. She waited for it to continue beating, knowing it was impossible. A shattered heart could never be mended.

Hands quivering, she drew the blankets away. She squeezed her eyes closed, unmindful of the moisture cascading down her cheeks. Two plump pillows rested in Dare's makeshift bed.

Finally she found the courage to face Nicholas. "He—he didn't understand what he was doing."

Nicholas's somber gaze became a bitter rebuke. "Still you defend him! And if he had succeeded, what then? Would you continue to excuse him?"

"No, of course not!"

"Maggie?" Wide eyed, Thomas sat up, hugging the coverlet to his chin. "What's wrong?"

Somehow, she dragged herself to her feet. "We were having a little . . . disagreement."

Thomas frowned. He reached up, his small fingers touching her cheek. "You're crying, Maggie. What's the matter?"

His innocent question battered her fresh wounds. "Thomas, I . . ."

"What Maggie is trying to say," Nicholas said for her, "is that we are worried about Dare. Do you know where he is?"

The boy leaned over the edge of the bed and peered

279

down. "He was sleeping." Thomas's expression brightened. "I know where he is! He's down in the kitchen. The cook knows he likes her almond cakes, even though he won't say so. She leaves one on the table every night." Thomas giggled. "And then at breakfast, she pretends that mice came in and stole the cake away. And do you know what, Maggie?"

She found her voice. It was little more than a croak. "And what is that?"

Thomas grabbed her hand, his smile so brilliant it blinded her. "Dare laughed out loud. Then his face turned red."

Maggie dashed away her lingering tears. "Well, then, we shall go to the kitchen. And you, young man, go back to sleep. I'm sorry we woke you." Reluctantly, he lay back and Maggie tucked the covers around his shoulders. "Sleep well, angel."

"Do you feel better now, Maggie?"

"Much better." The lie lodged in her throat.

Nicholas touched her shoulder. "We must talk, Maggie. Now."

Like a coward hiding from battle, she wanted to crawl under the covers. Only for Dare's sake, she stood, praying her legs would carry her. She had to make Nicholas understand why Dare would act so irrationally.

Following Nicholas's determined strides, she retraced their steps back to the study. He closed the door with resounding finality and moved to the sideboard.

Maggie watched as he poured brandy into a crystal snifter. "Is your shoulder paining you?" she asked, hoping to hold off the inevitable confrontation. "Perhaps you should rest."

He downed the amber liquid in one smooth swallow. "Would it ease your conscience to know the pain is barely noticeable?"

"That's not fair."

"Fair or not, it's the bloody truth!"

Weariness tugged her into a wing-back chair near the crackling flames in the fireplace. She stretched her arms toward the heat, hoping to chase the chill from her tired body. "What do you intend to do?"

Nicholas placed a snifter in her hands and eased into the matching chair across from her. Hotter than the dancing flames, his angry stare burned through her skin. "What would you have me do, Maggie? Pass Dare's actions off as an unfortunate accident?"

"You don't understand. He has been terribly hurt."

"Stop making excuses for him! He's jealous, nothing more."

Maggie swirled the golden brandy inside the glass, too distraught to take a single drink. She needed all her faculties to walk the slender line of truth and promised trust.

"Dare thought he was protecting me."

"I am not the threat. And I have done nothing to make him think otherwise."

"No, not you." Maggie chose her next words with careful deliberation. "Dare was hurt by a titled gentleman. His mistrust—his hatred—blinds him to anyone in a fancy carriage."

She held her breath, praying Nicholas had accepted the meager details. The brandy, warm against her palms, beckoned. One sip ripped welcome fire down her throat.

"Maggie, why were you so anxious to keep Dare and Thomas away from my cousin?"

The question struck too close to home for comfort. She glanced into Nicholas's eyes as a shiver tracked

281

along her spine. "I don't believe that is important," she said, turning away.

"I'm not stupid. There is a connection between you, my cousin, and Dare." Nicholas's voice softened. "Turner was the man who hurt Dare. And you know, because you were there. Did my cousin beat the boy?"

"Yes . . ." She trembled, as hideous visions darted through her thoughts. "It was a vicious and vile act, done without provocation." As if another thirty years had been magically added to her age, Maggie rose on wobbly legs. "I'm tired, Nicholas. I don't have the will to discuss . . ." She paused as a muffled noise sounded behind her.

Leaping to his feet, Nicholas took a protective stance in front of her. "Show yourself," he commanded.

The noise became a broken sob of undeniable pain.

"Oh, God, no . . ." Maggie stepped toward the quivering drapes.

Nicholas snagged her arm, jerking her to a stop. "Stay back, Maggie."

"It's all right," she murmured. She glanced toward the glass display case. Even from here, she could see that both dueling pistols were back, sitting as if untouched.

Her worst fear had been realized, shoved into the unforgiving glare of the light. Of all her numerous failings, this one would haunt her forever.

With leaden steps, she inched toward the window. "Dare, please come out. I can explain everything."

The dark drapes billowed open.

Maggie gasped at the pale, accusing face staring back. Tears streamed unchecked down Dare's cheeks, his chest heaving with each ragged breath. "You saw."

The charged indictment cleaved the pitiful remains of her heart in two. Her ability to form coherent words escaped her.

Nicholas gently squeezed her shoulders and spoke for her. "Sit down, Dare, and we will discuss what happened."

Ignoring Nicholas's presence, Dare continued to stare at her. "All this time. All this time you lied to me." His eyes glittered with a feverish light. "You didn't 'appen to meet me at the docks. You were lookin' for me."

The words returned, but barely above a whisper. "Yes. I had to be certain you were all right . . . that you'd survived."

"You were in the house. You're the girl who untied me and let me go." A soft whimper slipped from his bloodless lips. "Please, Maggie, tell me you didn't see what 'e did to me. . . ."

Nicholas's grip tightened on her shoulders. "My God . . ." he murmured, his tone resonant with horrified understanding.

Maggie buried her face in her hands, unable to bear Dare's suffering. She wanted to scream. She wanted to cry. But even the cleansing flow of tears eluded her desperate efforts.

"Now I understand," Dare said with bitter self-loathing. "It's no bloody wonder you couldn't come to care for me."

Facing him, she shook her head. "I've always cared for you. Always. And I should have told you the truth, but I knew I would lose you. You and Thomas are my family."

At the mention of the boy, Dare's expression softened, revealing the tenderness he rarely showed. "You won't ever tell 'im what 'appened."

"Of course not, never."

283

Dare nodded as he backed away. "And you'll take care of the him. . . ."

Maggie edged closer. "Please don't leave. Lord Grey understands now. He knows you were only trying to protect me."

"She's right," Nicholas said. "You are welcome to stay."

"No." Dare swung the window open and straddled the ledge. "I've got somethin' to do."

A premonition of disaster crushed the air from her lungs. "Don't do this! Stay here with us."

His expression hardened to stone. "We tried your way, Maggie. It's my turn."

"I cannot allow that," Nicholas said, striding toward Dare. "Now come out of the window and—"

A dagger flashed in the shadows. "Stay back, Yer Lordship. I may 'ave missed with the pistol, but I won't miss with a knife."

Fearing Dare's volatile emotions, Maggie planted herself between them. "You won't hurt Nicholas, or me." She held out her hand. "Give me the knife."

He smiled sadly. "I'm sorry I tried to shoot 'im. I didn't understand." He sighed. "I 'ave to go."

Like the last russet leaf of autumn fighting the wind, Maggie faced the loss of her truest friend. Dare was a man, free to choose his destiny. How could she deny him what she herself had fought for?

"Promise me," she whispered, "you'll be careful. And that you will come back."

"We both knew this day was comin', Maggie. I can't make any promises." Dare looked over her shoulder, pinning Nicholas with a determined stare. "I would kill fer Maggie, Yer Lordship. Are you willin' to do the same?"

Nicholas did not hesitate. "I would lay down my life for hers."

His solemn vow brought Maggie no joy. She had endangered all their lives with her misguided notions. Cold revenge veiled with the grandeur of holy justice. For her abounding arrogance, Dare might pay the ultimate price.

Swinging his leg over the side of the ledge, Dare sheathed the dagger in his boot. His tender gaze held hers. " 'Ave a good life, girl. You deserve it."

Maggie blinked. In a blur of movement, he was gone.

Nicholas stared at the open window, the cool night breeze washing across his skin. Maggie stood before him, unmoving, cloaked within layers of pain and sadness. Offering his strength, all he could give her, he touched her shoulder. Her soft flesh was as cold as winter's breath.

She crumpled toward the floor. He caught her in midfall, his heart racing. He carried her to the fire and sat as close to the flames as he dared. Cradling her, he murmured soothing, nonsensical words.

All the while, his mind rebelled at what he'd just heard and witnessed. He'd always known his cousin had a cruel, coldhearted streak, but the truth overwhelmed even those vicious attributes. Edward Turner was an abomination, a rapist, and a pederast— crimes punishable by death, if one could prove the allegations, and Turner never allowed loose ends to unravel. Maggie and Dare seemed the only exceptions.

The young man had been the victim, and innocent Margaret Alston the horrified witness.

Nicholas could not imagine such a monstrous vision. Yet Maggie had, and, with defiant courage, she'd helped Dare escape, later to sacrifice her own freedom.

As suddenly as she'd collapsed, she fluttered her eyes, her gaze crystal clear. "How will I ever tell Thomas? He will be heartbroken."

Nicholas smoothed the golden strands of hair from her forehead. "Don't worry. We shall tell him together."

She nodded, her expression strangely calm and detached. Her shield against further pain was set in place. "If Dare finds Lord Turner, I don't know what will happen."

Nicholas hugged her soft form tighter to his chest. "Don't worry. I'll send word to Hennessy. He shall keep a close eye on Turner's town house. If he should spot Dare, he'll put a stop to the boy's plans."

She chuckled bitterly. "Dare taught me all I know about vanishing into the shadows. Connor will never find him."

"Don't discount Hennessy's talents. He's a very enterprising man." Hesitating only a moment, Nicholas voiced the one question haunting him. "Why, Maggie? Why didn't you tell me? Turner could be hanged for this crime."

"I—I couldn't. The secret was Dare's, not mine. Besides, no one would have believed the accusation of a boy from East End."

"Although it would have been difficult, you could have stood as a witness."

"Lord Turner had his entire staff convinced I was half mad within days. And then I was in the asylum. Once I escaped and found Dare, I realized his pride would never allow him to come forward."

Nicholas fought his weariness and the painful sting in his shoulder. Questions still nagged him for answers. "You said, 'if Dare can find him.' Why wouldn't Dare recognize Lord Turner?"

After a deep, shuddering breath, she said, "Dare

was tied and blindfolded . . . beaten. Drager probably snatched him from the street with a ruse about a job." Her voice softened, trembled. "I should have stopped Turner. I should have shown myself and made him stop."

Hating her misplaced self-contempt, Nicholas framed her face with his hands. "You cannot blame yourself. You saved Dare's life."

She smiled sadly. "I could do no less."

"And that is why I . . ."

Love you. Love?

The applewood logs popped and crackled, filling the sudden silence.

God, he was a coward. One simple word, and his stomach twisted into knots. He'd vowed his love to only one other woman. Julia. And she'd chosen Turner. Now he'd come close to making the same mistake. Except there was not the specter of another man for Maggie—only her unshakable quest for independence. Freedom.

Sweat broke out above his brows as he glanced down. Strangely enough, Maggie appeared equally horrified. He could have glossed over the near confession with flowery prose; instead he revealed his emotions without words. Gently he kissed her parted lips.

She sighed, whether in pleasure or relief he would never be certain.

"Come, Maggie. It's time to put you to bed."

Laden with sadness, her eyes stared into his. "I don't think I'll be able to sleep."

She was hardly the lone exception. The entire household was on edge, and the situation would worsen. Perhaps, he mused silently, the time had come for a fresh—and safer change of scenery.

Coming to his feet with Maggie locked in his arms,

Nicholas reached a decision. As soon as the staff could prepare for the journey, Maggie and his mother would be on their way to Rockingham.

He would stay behind and do what he should have done years before. The time had come to call Edward Turner out, and snuff his miserable life. Though it was far too merciful an end, Nicholas had no choice. Prosecution seemed beyond his reach.

The ivory-handled dueling pistols would be fired one last time.

Chapter Twenty-two

"Here's to you, Margaret. You have accomplished the impossible."

Edward tipped the bottle to his lips and gulped the cheap Irish whiskey. Fire raced down his throat, easing the chill of the drafty room.

He glanced at the pathetic remains of his world and laughed, the sound echoing off blank walls and barren floors. The baron's mousy little daughter had toppled his empire with remarkable ease.

Now he had nothing. Every stick of furniture, piece of silver, and expensive painting had been claimed by a steady stream of nervous creditors.

Draining the bottle, Edward tossed it into a corner with the others. He could live with the loss of meaningless objects. What he couldn't abide was the loss of his social position.

Like an accomplished actor, he'd molded and shaped his character to fit any performance. He had wooed the ton with his affable and charming demeanor, and within a span of two months, he'd become persona non grata.

Blackballed. Ruined. Bankrupt.

Clutching the scarred wooden arms of the only chair he still owned, Edward focused on the rage simmering inside him. He tended the emotion like a fire, adding bits of kindling, one piece at a time.

"One way or another, the bloody bitch will pay."

"My lord?"

Edward glanced at the door. Drager stood on the threshold, holding a teapot and one chipped cup. His gaze drifted to the hodgepodge of empty whiskey bottles littering the corner. "I've made tea."

"As conscientious as ever, Drager. But I am more curious about my dear cousin. Did you find out what he and Margaret are planning?"

Inching his way inside, Drager placed the tea within reach and backed away. "They attended the theater, and then the marquess and Miss Alston slipped away in a rented hack."

"My Margaret has become quite the harlot. But then again, Grey always did have the women eating from his hand." Edward smiled and sipped the tea without thought. The taste was rank; he shoved the cup away. "What else did you learn?"

"Little else. They have men guarding the house. It's locked tight, and no one is talking."

Grinning, Edward stared at the small fire in the hearth. "They're still afraid of me. What a wonderful bit of news. Don't you agree, Drager?"

The manservant nodded, his nervous gaze skittering around the room. "My lord—" He cleared his throat. "Will we be staying here tonight?"

"Although the accomodations are not of the highest quality, we shall stay, my friend."

"But there are no beds."

Edward shrugged at the obvious inconvenience and stared at the servant. "Don't worry. We shall find rest tonight."

A soft snore rumbled from a dark corner. "Just like our friend," Edward said fondly.

Squinting, Drager peered into the darkness. "Who is it, my lord?"

"On the way home from my useless meeting at the solicitor's office, I met this man. He was quite jovial and had nowhere to go." Edward chuckled and spread his arms open. "So I offered him this illustrious abode. Wisely, he accepted my generosity."

As if sensing the malevolent currents beneath the ordinary conversation, Drager shifted on his feet. "If I may ask, my lord, what will we do next?"

Edward studied his manservant with near pity, perhaps even compassion. The man truly was a monstrosity. His unusual size, pallid features, and tiny, dark eyes sparked such an aversion in those who observed him that Edward almost chuckled. If he had been blessed with an ordinary face and shorter stature, perhaps the inevitable outcome could have been altered.

With a pang of bitter regret, Edward drew a pistol from his coat pocket. "We have nowhere to go, my friend. The Alston bitch and her lover have done their work well."

Staggering back, the servant's confused gaze locked on the weapon. "What—what are you doing, my lord?"

Slowly Edward stood. "Don't worry. It is better this way."

Like a cloying perfume, Drager's fear permeated the air. "Have I displeased you?"

Edward offered a tender smile. "On the contrary,

you have been a good and trusted friend. But I can see no way out of this coil.''

Drager's thin lips twisted into a macabre grimace of disbelief. ''But who will take care of you?''

''I'm certain the devil himself will see to our welfare soon enough.'' Edward raised the pistol, leveling it at Drager's chest. ''Do you trust me to do what is right?''

Standing at attention, Drager nodded and closed his eyes. ''Thank you, my lord.''

''You're quite welcome, Drager.''

Edward squeezed the trigger.

The sharp report of the pistol reverberated through the room. With one bony hand clutching his chest, Drager toppled backward, his face set in peaceful repose.

''Rest well, dear friend.''

Easing back to his chair, Edward loaded another ball into the still-smoking pistol. Margaret's delicate face filtered through his thoughts. Her rich, husky voice, strangely at odds with her petite frame, echoed in his mind.

How could my father have trusted you! You're a monster! A beast . . .

Trembling with hate, Edward swept the oil lamp from the floor and hurled it into the drapes.

Glass shattered. Amber oil spilled free.

Like a hungry animal, fire consumed the tattered velvet.

Massaging his temple with the barrel of the gun, he grinned. ''Dear sweet Margaret. I shall see you in Hell . . . very soon.''

Like a centurion preparing for war, Nicholas stormed down the hallway toward Maggie's room.

He'd believed his mother to be the most intractable woman in all of England. Now it appeared Maggie was poised to claim the dubious title. Even his mother had seen the wisdom behind the decision to go to Rockingham, and offered only a token protest. Not Maggie. Apparently she'd drawn the proverbial line in the sand. A line he would soon erase.

He swept the door open, his gaze coming to rest on the canopy bed.

Like a royal princess, Maggie lounged against a mountain of satin pillows, taking dainty sips of hot chocolate from a cup. Even her regal pose could not mask the dark circles beneath her eyes, or the pallor of her complexion.

A pang of guilt lanced his conscience. In the course of one night, she'd nearly witnessed his death and lost Dare in one fell swoop. Now he would have to put her in a carriage for a long ten-hour journey. But as long as Turner walked the streets of London, Maggie and his family remained in danger.

Hardening his resolve, he strode toward the bed. "It is time to cease this foolishness, Maggie. Everyone is waiting for you downstairs."

She shrugged, revealing a wide expanse of creamy white flesh. He felt his body respond. He waited, praying she would adjust the lace neckline to a more chaste position. Instead she stared at him through a veil of thick sable lashes.

Her lips curved into a beguiling smile. "If I stayed"—she leaned forward, nearly exposing the whole of one soft, rounded breast—"we could have the morning all to ourselves."

The brazen assault rendered him speechless. The bewitching Athena had returned in all her sensual glory. The idea tempted him more than he would ever admit.

"I shall take you up on your generous offer," he

replied wryly, "*after* we are at Rockingham." She looked at him in quiet defiance.

A soft knock at the door saved him from further explanation. Abbot stood on the threshold, his respectful gaze lowered to the floor. "My lord, Mr. Hennessy has arrived." He glanced toward Maggie, then looked away, his expression gentle with understanding. "Miss Alston, young Thomas is waiting in the carriage. And, if I might say, he is quite upset."

Nicholas watched her indecision dim to sad resignation. "How thoughtless I've been. He did not take the news of Dare's leaving very well."

Taking her hand, Nicholas whispered, "Thomas needs you. And I will join everyone at Rockingham in a few days."

She nodded and turned to Abbot. "If you'll send my maid?"

"She is on her way, miss."

The barest trace of a smile softened her lips. "You're quite sure of yourself, Abbot."

"In my position, it is a necessity."

"And will you send my apologies for delaying everyone?"

"Of course," Abbot replied before leveling a stern glare at his lord.

Nicholas smiled. "I believe that is my silent cue to leave."

Clutching his coatsleeve, Maggie stopped him. "Are you leaving now?"

"No, I shall say good-bye downstairs." Aware of his butler's gaze, Nicholas pressed an innocent kiss to her hand. "Don't worry. I'll recall you as soon as it's safe. Everything will be over in a few days."

He turned and left the room, the servant close on his heels. "Well done, Abbot. I wasn't sure how to convince her to come."

"I suppose you were planning to threaten to carry her downstairs, dressed or not."

Nicholas paused at the head of the stairs. "How the devil did you know that?"

Abbot offered a complacent smile. "I have raised you, my lord. And if I may be so bold, at times you tend to act in . . . haste."

"Thank you for that divine bit of insight, Abbot." Nicholas continued downstairs, ignoring his servant's dry chuckle.

The first rays of sun crested the chimney tops as he strolled outside and down the brick walkway. Two carriages and a loaded wagon waited, surrounded by the six armed men Connor had promised.

Nicholas waved to his friend before moving toward the first conveyance. The duchess and his mother fidgeted on one seat, while Thomas, his eyes red and swollen, slumped on the other. "Is—is Maggie coming?" he asked quietly.

"She will be down any moment," Nicholas assured him with a wink.

Lady Grey leaned forward and patted the boy's cheek. "There now, didn't I tell you she would come?"

He nodded and smiled. "Yes, but you don't know Maggie. She can be very stubborn."

"The lad is right, Mother. She can be quite the handful."

The duchess laughed with throaty abandon. "A handful, you say."

An unfamiliar heat crept across his face. Nicholas slammed the door closed.

Connor appeared at his side, his usual grin absent. Dark circles showed beneath his eyes, and his shaggy brown hair was uncombed. "Well, Nicky, I'm here as promised."

"Your enthusiasm is noticeably lacking," Nicholas replied, losing his inner battle not to smile. "A bit too early for you, Hennessy?"

"If that were all. I have some bad news."

Rubbing his tired eyes, Nicholas smiled coldly. "Bad news is all I've come to expect."

Connor sighed. "I found the scullery maid. She died two years ago here in London."

"Was she murdered?" Nicholas asked, certain Turner had found her first.

"No, Nicky. She died of a lung inflammation."

"Well, then. That's that." Nicholas directed his friend away from the carriage. "Did you see Dare?"

"Didn't see a single soul. Except that monster, Drager. By the time I got your message, it was already two in the morning."

"So Turner hasn't skulked from town yet."

"Last I checked, he was still here. *Why* is the mystery. His creditors have taken everything."

Slapping his friend on the back, Nicholas grinned. "It would appear Maggie's plan to discredit him succeeded."

"Aye, he's lost everything." Connor's expression remained grim. "Which will only make him more dangerous."

"If need be, I will kill him where he stands," Nicholas murmured.

"I'm beginnin' to like the way your mind works, Nicky." Connor glanced toward the walkway, a soft whistle of appreciation pursing his lips. "And once you've slain the beast, what a lovely prize you'll be claimin'."

Following his gaze, Nicholas looked over his shoulder.

Maggie glided toward them, her eyes solemn. "Mr.

Hennessy, I wish we were meeting under more pleasant circumstances.''

Connor bowed over her gloved hand. ''Miss Alston, it is always a pleasant occasion when we meet.''

''Do you have news of my friend?''

His grin faded. ''I'm sorry, miss. But rest assured, if he's in London, I'll find him.''

Her sigh of weary resignation mocked her subsequent words. ''I'm sure you will, Mr. Hennessy. Thank you.''

As Nicholas escorted her to the carriage, she noticed the fierce-looking entourage. ''Who are those men?''

''Merely an added precaution. They will stay at Rockingham until I arrive.''

''And . . . will you?'' As if searching for the truth, she stared hard into his eyes. ''Will you come back?''

Tenderly, he stroked her satiny cheek. ''Nothing will keep me away. You and I have unfinished business.''

''And that would be?''

''I seem to recall a rather blatant suggestion about certain morning activities.''

For a brief moment, the shadows fled her rich brown eyes. ''That particular offer was retracted when you insisted I travel to the country.''

Leaning closer, he caught the elusive scent of roses. Her lips, luscious and full, beckoned him ''Perhaps,'' he whispered, ''you may change your mind. It's been said that my powers of persuasion are legendary.''

She tilted her head to a flirtatious angle, studying him from beneath the brim of her white bonnet. ''Perhaps I will change my mind . . . when donkeys take flight.''

''In that case, Miss Alston, I shall toss one into the air myself.''

Unmindful of their numerous spectators, he lifted her gloved hand and kissed her fluttering pulse point. Her eyes widened as she darted a glance toward the carriage.

Nicholas smiled as she ducked her head, her cheeks flaming with color. With the primness of a spinster, she adjusted her bonnet. "You shouldn't have done that."

He opened the carriage door. "Abbot was just telling me I tend to act in haste."

"Perhaps you should heed his counsel," Maggie replied tartly.

"Is that what you want? A boring, staid nobleman with no sense of adventure?"

She settled in next to Thomas and smiled. "Even you, Lord Grey, could not accomplish such a transformation."

Grinning, Nicholas snapped the door closed and signaled Hoskins.

Nor would I wish to, Maggie . . . nor would I wish to.

Chapter Twenty-three

Maggie breathed a soft sigh of relief as silence finally descended.

Since their hasty departure from London, a myriad of subjects had been discussed: the warm weather, the extravagant ball Lady Jersey planned—replete with living Grecian statues—and the numerous marriage announcements. That particular turn in conversation had set Maggie's nerves on edge.

She nestled Thomas against her side and tucked a soft woolen lap blanket around his shoulders. Lulled by the gentle rocking of the carriage, Thomas let his head droop forward. Stroking his downy soft hair, Maggie glanced at her two traveling companions.

Without fanfare, Maggie's hope for continued silence died. Eugenia and the duchess stared at her with open curiosity, and a hint of censure.

Maggie's short-lived reprieve had ended.

"My son," Lady Grey began carefully, "seems

quite taken with you, my dear.'' Maggie's cheeks brightened with color as she toyed with the lace cuff on her mauve-colored gown. "I hope Nicholas has behaved . . . appropriately.''

Taking a deep breath, Maggie nodded benignly. "He has been a gentleman.''

"Hah!'' The duchess hunched forward, her gnarled hands clasped tightly in her lap. "And I'm sure you shared nothing more than tea and scones during your midnight jaunt last night.''

Eugenia gasped and fanned her crimson cheeks. "Gracious, Dorothea, must you be so—so bold?''

"It is obvious someone must grasp the reins and steer the course. So, girl, has the boy bedded you yet?''

If the question had come from anyone else, Maggie would have been speechless. The duchess was the only exception. Maggie gazed at the two women and planned her own attack. If they wanted blunt speech, she would gladly provide it.

She glanced at Eugenia, hoping the poor woman would survive the next volley. "Our relationship has progressed to an intimate level. By mutual decision, I might add.''

Instead of sending Eugenia into apoplexy, as Maggie had feared, the confession brought a joyous smile to her face. "At last! My prayers have been answered!'' She paused, her eyes widening. "Oh, my, that means we must secure a special license. Time is of the essence in delicate matters such as these.''

Stunned, Maggie tried to fathom her happiness and failed. "I had assumed you would be shocked and outraged by our actions. In fact, I seduced your son. Surely you do not condone my forwardness.''

"Well, I would have liked a more strict adherence

to protocol, but I cannot complain. I will soon have a beautiful daughter-in-law.''

Maggie's courage faded. She'd managed to tell Nicholas no when he'd mentioned marriage. Faced with his mother's glowing expectations, Maggie felt the word lodge in her throat. She searched for a gentle way to defuse Eugenia's burgeoning hope.

There was none, except the bitter truth.

''I'm sorry, Lady Grey, but I'm not certain marriage is possible.''

''I don't understand. . . .'' Eugenia's smile disintegrated.

The duchess leaned back, shaking her head in confusion. ''What utter nonsense! Marry the man and be done with it. He has made an offer, hasn't he?''

''Oh, Dorothea, of course he has,'' Eugenia said in an affronted tone. ''Nicholas would never take advantage of our Maggie in such a way.''

''Perhaps not intentionally,'' the duchess said with a sly smile, ''but men are all rogues at heart.''

Maggie raised her hands in surrender. ''Yes, Lord Grey proposed marriage.''

''And?'' the two women chimed in unison.

''And I regretfully said no.''

Eugenia smiled weakly. ''Maggie, you must be jesting.''

''It is no joke. I have no wish to marry.''

''Why?'' the duchess asked, her eyes sparkling with mischief. ''Do you have another husband tucked away somewhere?''

Laughing, Maggie shook her head. ''No, Your Grace. I have no secret life. I've decided I want independence—freedom.''

''My word . . .'' Eugenia fanned an embroidered silk handkerchief across her cheeks. ''You are a young woman. You must marry eventually.''

Anger flamed in Maggie's chest. "And lose all I've gained?"

The duchess smiled gently and patted Maggie's cheek. "Freedom is easy enough to grasp. Widows have independence, and if they are fortunate, the wealth to live life as they choose."

Blinking, Maggie stared at the diminutive woman. "Surely you're not suggesting I marry Nicholas and hope he dies?"

Apparently Eugenia had the same notion. The handkerchief flapped with greater speed. "Yes, Dorothea, please tell us you're not suggesting Maggie should wish my son dead."

Wondering when she'd lost control, Maggie rubbed her temple. "I would never marry Nicholas for position. And certainly not with thoughts of being a widow."

The duchess shrugged. "As the marchioness, your position would be secured. You could do far worse than the marquess. Why, if I were forty years younger—"

"That will be quite enough," Eugenia exclaimed, eyeing her friend with disbelief.

Perched primly on the leather bench, the duchess pointed an accusing finger at Maggie. "Whether you wish it or not, girl, you're in love with him. And as for this need for independence, that is all well and good. But a noble idea will not warm you at night, or ease your loneliness."

The slight headache Maggie had fought all morning blossomed into pounding pain. This particular debate could rage for weeks. And today was merely the opening barrage. Unless she signaled a truce.

"I understand your concerns, but it is much too soon to consider the future. Perhaps once Lord Turner is no longer a threat, I will be free to make a decision."

Disappointment etched fine lines in Lady Grey's face as she smiled sadly. "My son is, for better or worse, a proud man. If you refuse him too often, he may stop asking altogether."

Maggie turned away and stared out the window. The verdant hills, dotted with grazing sheep and fields of wheat, did nothing to calm her anxious heart. As the weeks had passed, she'd known, deep in her soul, that she would have to choose.

Closing her eyes, she pondered what she truly wanted. Before she'd stumbled into Nicholas's life, the choice had been easily made. Her faith in men had been shattered. First by her gullible but well-intentioned father, and then by the cruelty of Viscount Turner.

A shiver lanced down her spine. She loved Nicholas, but could she trust him?

Lady Grey's warning sounded in her mind. Maggie couldn't bear to face that possibility now. Perhaps the irrational fear she carried would dissolve once Turner was out of their lives.

Maggie relaxed into the supple leather seat, clutching the ray of hope like a talisman.

When Nicholas arrived, she would choose her path, and pray she possessed the courage to live with the decision.

The destruction was complete, the darkened landscape a blight on the rest of the carefully manicured lawns and regal houses.

Bitterness overshadowed shock as Nicholas stared at the smoldering rubble. Blackened pieces of brick and burned timbers littered the ground. Only one chimney remained, towering defiantly above the remnants of Edward Turner's town house.

Nicholas's hands curled into fists. He'd wanted the chance to throw the man's sins in his face. In the end, Turner would have the last word and escape retribution.

"My God . . ." Bile rose in Nicholas's throat.

Amidst the twisted debris lay two bodies, charred beyond recognition.

Remorse was out of the question. Pity impossible.

The stench of pungent smoke and burned hair and flesh drove him back to the street. Connor appeared at his side, his keen gaze sweeping the scene. "This could've been a disaster. With the house practically empty, the fire brigade snuffed it out in hours."

"Yes," Nicholas murmured, "I'm sure Turner's neighbors are breathing easier."

"As we all are, Nicky. Our problem is solved."

A vague sense of unease eroded Nicholas's confidence. "Isn't this a bit odd? Surely Drager and Turner had time to escape the flames. So why didn't they?"

"Because they couldn't. The coroner says they were both dead by the time the fire reached them."

"Dead?" Dare's hostile features wove through Nicholas's thoughts. "Are you saying they were murdered?"

"Drager was shot in the chest, definitely murder. The other body—Turner—had a wound to the temple. He probably couldn't stomach his losses and chose the coward's way out."

Disbelief blossomed into anxiety. Nicholas shook his head, unable to reconcile the idea of suicide with his cousin's character. "Are you certain the bodies are those of Drager and Turner?"

"Aye, no one could mistake that monster's size." Connor dug through his pocket and produced a blackened signet ring. "And we found this on the other body."

Nicholas touched the metal, still warm from Hennessy's pocket. The intricate serpent's-head design remained intact. "This is my cousin's ring."

"And an ugly thing it is," Connor said, wiping the soot from his hands with a handkerchief. "So, will you be off to Rockingham to share the good news?"

"I will leave today, yes." Foreboding slithered across his flesh as he stared into the mocking ruby eyes of the serpent.

Instinct battled the overwhelming mountain of evidence. Turner would never kill himself, at least not before exacting his pound of flesh.

He left the ring to distract us . . . to add spice to the game.

My God . . . Maggie.

Grabbing Connor's forearm, Nicholas propelled him toward the coach. "We need to get to Rockingham at once."

"I can't leave," Connor sputtered. "The coroner is goin' to impanel a jury to investigate—"

"That will take time, and I need you now. Do you ride?"

"Ride what?"

If not for the fear clutching his heart, Nicholas would have laughed at the Irishman's dubious expression. "A carriage will take too long. I intend to ride home."

Connor paled as he mopped his brow. "On a horse?"

"Very well, you can follow in a carriage. But we must leave now."

"What devilish maggot is in your head now?"

None too gently, Nicholas ushered his friend through the door. "Turner's alive, Connor. I know it." He cleared his throat, almost afraid to voice his greatest fear. "And Maggie is alone."

The heavy darkness surrounded her, the night strangely still. As if she'd been splashed with icy water, Maggie's eyes snapped open.

Curled on her side, she remained still, peering into the shadows for the source of her sudden unease.

Shivers danced across her flesh. She sensed a presence. A steady gaze directed at her back. Instinctively she knew it was not a member of the staff, nor was it Thomas. He would have barreled into the bed, *then* asked if she was sleeping.

Turner . . .

Her heartbeat quickened to a staccato rhythm. Inch by precious inch, she slid her hand beneath the pillow and grasped the silver dinner knife she'd stolen earlier.

Afraid to move—afraid to breathe—she waited for the attack.

Soft footfalls approached.

Nerves, stretched beyond human endurance, snapped.

Whirling upward, Maggie slashed toward the intruder with the knife.

A hand captured her wrist in midair. "Damn it, Maggie! It's me."

The weapon fell from her limp fingers. "Nicholas?"

"I'm sorry I woke you," he replied softly.

She sank back into the plump mattress, waiting for her heart to calm. "You frightened me half to death."

"That was not my intention." A candle on the nightstand sputtered to life, banishing the darkness.

"Are you all right?" he asked, settling on the edge of the bed.

Maggie nodded, too stunned by his sudden appearance to form words. Drinking her fill of his presence, she studied his face. Dark crescents shadowed his eyes, while lines of weariness scored his features. His white linen shirt and fawn-colored breeches were rumpled and covered in a thin layer of dust.

Even his smile seemed halfhearted. "Do you greet all your visitors with cutlery?"

"Only those who do not announce their presence."

The shock of his surprise arrival faded. Joy and relief propelled her into his open arms. As if to assure herself he was more than wishful fancy, she stroked his disheveled hair. "We were not expecting you for days. How on earth did you get here so quickly?"

He squeezed her so tightly she gasped for air. Slowly, he loosened his hold. "I nearly rode three horses into the ground to gain time."

"Anxious to see me, were you?"

"Always."

The strange tone in his voice quelled her happiness. Maggie pulled away, searching his eyes for the answer. "Something's happened. Is it Dare?"

"Connor has men scouring London, but there's been no word. He will be here tomorrow."

"Then what?" Her fear blossomed anew. She clutched Nicholas's shoulders, kneading the firm flesh beneath her fingertips.

A sigh of fatigue slipped from Nicholas's lips as he nodded. "There was a fire. Turner's town house was destroyed."

Silent, hopeful, Maggie waited for the words that would set her free.

"Two bodies were recovered," Nicholas said carefully. "One was obviously Drager's, and the other appears to be my cousin's."

His lack of certainty raised gooseflesh across her skin. "What do you mean, *appears?*"

"The bodies were horribly burned. There is no way to be certain."

Maggie forced conviction into her trembling voice. "He must be dead, Nicholas. Drager was more than a servant. He was Lord Turner's eyes, ears, and hands. Without him, your cousin would be lost."

Nicholas stroked her unbound hair. "You're probably right. But just to be certain, I want you and Thomas to stay on the grounds. No trips to the village without an escort."

Despair extinguished hope.

Futility weighed down her limbs. She slumped against Nicholas's broad chest. "That is why you hurried home. You believe Lord Turner is alive, and that he will come here. Come for me."

Stroking her cheeks, Nicholas spoke with calm determination. "If he is not dead now, he soon will be."

His cool confidence did little to ease her apprehension. Edward Turner would stop at nothing to see her punished for ruining him. And should anyone interfere with his goal, he would crush them. He would kill Nicholas without a shred of remorse.

In a flash of divine intuition, the end of her dark journey appeared with crystal clarity. Maggie had set the fateful chain of events into motion, and she would end it. Alone.

Now that the decision was made, a sense of tranquility banished her anxiety. Regardless of the outcome, Nicholas, his family, and Thomas would remain safe.

She smoothed the worry lines from Nicholas's forehead. "I'm fine. I'm glad you told me the truth."

"I should have waited until morning." He started to rise. "And I should also let you rest."

"No, I want you to stay. I *need* you to stay."

He hesitated, glancing down at his rumpled clothes. "I'm not exactly fit company."

Gliding her hands down his chest, she smiled. "You seem quite fit to me."

His wicked grin answered her own. "Are you seducing me, Miss Alston?"

"My earlier welcome was not very hospitable, Lord Grey. I thought to rectify that faux pas."

His smile slipped, his eyes gentle with understanding. "You've had a shock, Maggie. Perhaps tomorrow night, after you've rested . . ."

Oh, Nicholas, tomorrow may be too late.

Rising to her knees, Maggie kissed the tiny cleft in his chin, then his lips. "Does anyone else know you've arrived?"

"No," he rasped, holding her tight to his chest. "I came straight to your room. I had to see you."

Maggie's heartbeat quickened at his confession. Her hands trembled with the need to touch him—the need to give him pleasure.

She released the buttons of his shirt and slipped it over his shoulders. The soft raven curls sprinkled across his chest lured her closer. She kissed his flat, velvety nipples, tonguing them into taut peaks.

A groan of surrender rumbled from his throat as he clutched handfuls of her hair. "God, Maggie, do you know what you're doing to me?"

"I'm loving you," she whispered, sliding the breeches past his lean hips, past his thick, muscular thighs.

He kicked them aside, then grasped the lacy hem of her nightgown. "My turn." As if savoring each

309

glimpse of her skin, he lifted the gown slowly, pausing when her breasts were revealed.

Maggie shivered in response as his sky blue eyes darkened with desire. "How is it possible," he murmured, "that you become more beautiful each time I see you?"

Passion, love, and bittersweet longing closed her throat to words. Slipping the gown from his shaking hands, she whipped the satin over her head. Gently she pulled him onto the bed and stretched across his firm body.

A lazy grin curved his lips. "Are you taking advantage of me?"

She pinned his wrists to the pillow, unable to call forth an answering smile. Like the biblical day of reckoning, tomorrow loomed before her. But tonight was hers to share. A gift for the man who'd captured her lonely heart.

As if sensing her melancholy, his grin slipped. "What is it, Maggie?"

"Don't speak," she whispered against his mouth.

She brushed her lips across his, then boldly sought entrance, their tongues mating in an ageless dance of need and discovery.

His rigid manhood nudged her hip. Her skin tingled in response. Drawing away, Maggie skimmed her mouth down his neck. Unadorned by cologne, perfumed only by desire, he engulfed her senses with his scent.

Weaving an exotic path, she kissed and caressed his chest, moving downward to the rippled muscles of his stomach. Like the blue center of a flame, his eyes blazed with heat.

He clawed at the smooth white sheets, gasping. "Maggie, you don't—"

"I do."

She moved lower.

Holding his astonished gaze, she took his swollen sex into her mouth. As hard as iron, as soft as Chinese silk—she explored the mysterious contradiction of his male flesh.

His eyes squeezed closed, his back arching in mindless surrender. His response awakened an answering song of her own. Moisture and relentless heat pooled between her thighs. A fierce and familiar tension coiled inside her, and yet she couldn't stop. As if she were watching a brilliant, amber-hued sunset, Maggie wanted the moment to stretch into eternity.

Nicholas accomplished what she could not. With a guttural groan, he pulled away and swept her onto her back. "No more. It's time. . . ."

"Not yet," she murmured. Gently she touched his face, memorizing each bold feature with her fingertips. Nicholas Grey was the type of man women swooned for, fought for, and he was hers. For tonight.

Welcoming him home, Maggie parted her thighs. He sighed in apparent relief, his jaw tight with restraint.

The swollen tip of his manhood glided inside her. "Do you want me, Maggie? Want me as much as I want you?"

"More, Nicholas. Always more." Wrapping her legs around his lean hips, she urged him deeper.

He obliged her silent command, his smooth thrusts carrying her toward the abyss. She whimpered as her flesh yielded to the driving onslaught. She clung to his slick shoulders, her body convulsing as the first waves of fulfillment crashed through her senses.

As if he were uttering a desperate prayer, her name spilled from his lips as he lunged one last time. His chest heaving, he collapsed against her.

Framing her face with his hands, he stared into her eyes. "Maggie, I love—"

She silenced him with a ferocious kiss. Pain overshadowed joy. She couldn't bear to hear the words, not now.

Their bodies still joined, he rolled to his side, cradling her in his arms. "Don't be afraid, Maggie." With a tenderness that stole her breath, he brushed a wayward curl from her cheek. "Don't be afraid, especially not of me."

Unable to meet his somber gaze, she closed her eyes. Moments later, his body relaxed, his breathing deep and even. Weariness had finally claimed him.

She watched him sleep as his words played through her mind.

Don't be afraid.

For the past two years, fear had dogged her steps like a formless shadow, waiting for her to weaken. In Nicholas's arms, she'd found a brief refuge. It would end at dawn.

Tomorrow she would face Edward Turner at the place where her dark journey had begun.

Tomorrow the shadows would return.

Chapter Twenty-four

Maggie was gone. Nicholas had awakened in her bed, expecting her warmth to comfort him. After quickly dressing, he had searched everywhere—and now he gave orders to his servants to have her found.

Like the eye in the center of the hurricane, Nicholas watched the frantic mayhem exploding around him. Every maid, groomsman, gardener, and stableboy rushed across the grounds, calling out Maggie's name.

Past disbelief, past anger, rage painted his vision red. For three hours, he'd searched every room of the house, then the gardens, and the stables, for naught.

He trembled with the urge to slam his fists into the stable door.

He trembled with fear.

Maggie had vanished. Thomas was missing as well. The question was how—and why she'd chosen to ignore his warnings.

Nicholas stared hard at the six men Connor had provided. They refused to meet his gaze. "Tell me again," Nicholas said softly to hide his anger.

One man stepped forward, his stubby fingers toying with the brim of a tattered gray cap. "The girl is bloody clever, m'lord. She laid a false trail. She went to each of us and told us where she was goin' . . ."

"Except she wasn't in any of those places, was she?"

The man took a halting step backward. "No, m'lord. But she couldn't go far. Not without a horse or carriage."

Nicholas took pity on the dejected group before him. He, more than most, had learned how cunning Maggie could be. "You're right. We will find her. You and your men go to the village and see if they've gone there. And make bloody certain you ask about Viscount Turner."

"But, m'lord, we heard he was dead."

"And who told you this?"

The man's chin quivered. "The—the girl did."

Damn you, Maggie!

"As far as I am concerned, the viscount is alive." Turning away, Nicholas fought for control. Nausea bubbled in his throat as images of Julia's broken body appeared in his mind. *Not again.*

Suddenly the truth became clear. Last night had not been an affirmation of love. Maggie had said goodbye. Like Julia, she had decided to play the role of martyr. She'd gone in search of Turner. And yet, how could Nicholas explain Thomas's disappearance? Never would she have taken the boy.

"She'll be found, Nicky. Don't worry."

Nicholas turned and faced his friend. "You made good time. I didn't expect you until dinner."

Scratching his stubbled jaw, Connor stared at the

ground. "I should have gotten on the bloody horse."

"You presence wouldn't have changed events. Maggie has decided to confront my cousin."

"You must be wrong. She knows how dangerous the snake can be. If he's alive."

"He is, Connor. I'm more certain than ever, and so is Maggie. Apparently she believes she can save us all by sacrificing herself."

Slapping the dust from his coat, Connor regained his usual unflappable confidence. "I'll organize the search. Mark my words, we'll have her home before dark."

"If Turner hurts her . . ." Nicholas couldn't bear to finish the dark thought.

A stable boy appeared, leading Nicholas's stallion to his master. "All ready, m'lord. 'E started prancin' the minute I led him from 'is stall."

"Thank you, Tom." Nicholas grasped the reins and leaped onto the saddle.

"Where are you goin' now?" Connor asked, jumping back as the stallion whipped its head in excitement.

"She didn't take a carriage. I think I know where she's gone."

"Don't be doin' anythin' crazy now," Connor said, his expression deadly serious. "If you see somethin', you send word and wait for me and my men."

"I will." *If there's time, my friend.*

Nicholas nudged the stallion's ribs. The horse responded in a brilliant burst of speed, leaving the muted, gray-stone edifice of Rockingham behind.

Winded, her legs trembling, Maggie collapsed in an undignified heap at the door of Alston House.

Home.

And yet it wasn't.

Wild ivy had covered the facade of the once pristine whitewashed stone walls. Shrubs and thorny hedgerows grew unencumbered, obscuring the ground-floor windows from view.

Pain lanced her heart. The home of her memories had vanished, leaving only a desolate shadow of its former beauty.

With more bravado than she felt, Maggie swept open the door. Decay and neglect permeated the air. Making no effort to conceal her presence, she entered the foyer. As intricate as Spanish lace, cobwebs dangled from every corner.

Slowly she wandered the rest of the rooms and choked back the sobs building in her throat.

Nothing remained. Nothing.

Every piece of furniture, her father's beloved journals and books, the Persian rugs, even the wallpaper had been carefully peeled away. He'd stolen everything. Turner had auctioned off her possessions—her memories—to the highest bidder.

Sick at heart, Maggie stumbled into the library. Even now, she could almost smell the sweet scent of her father's pipe tobacco. Her gaze drifted to the far side of the room.

Please let it be there.

The wall above the mantel seemed to scream its emptiness, an emptiness that echoed through her soul. The only portrait of Elizabeth Alston, painted six months before her death, was gone.

As a child, Maggie had spent hours studying the portrait of her mother. Elizabeth Alston had had a quiet beauty, her expression soft and peaceful. In her youth, Maggie had asked her father numerous questions about the woman she'd never known.

What was she like, Papa? Did she have a soft

*voice? Did she sing like an angel? What were
Mama's favorite flowers?*

White roses, her papa had replied softly, his eyes
glistening with unshed tears.

That had been the last question Maggie had asked.
Even as a child she'd realized how much pain her
thirst for knowledge caused.

Stumbling forward, Maggie grasped the edge of the
mantel and stared at the faded square imprint. Despair
and pain erupted in a scream of blind rage. "You
bastard!" She slammed her fists against the chipped
wood. "How could you?" Her last ounce of strength
depleted, she slumped to her knees.

Lost in grief, Maggie realized, too late, that she was
no longer alone. The familiar scent of heavy musk
cologne preceded his voice. "Hello, Margaret. I'm so
glad you decided to join me."

Rage, grief, and bitterness coalesced into single-
minded determination.

Sliding her hand into her cloak pocket, she clutched
the smooth handle of the dinner knife. "And if I had
decided to stay at Rockingham, Lord Turner?"

"I considered the possibility, then discounted it.
You're far too stubborn and daring to take the prudent
course." His voice roughened with clear distaste.
"Please, Margaret, do stand up. You look positively
common."

She came to her feet, staring at the empty space
above the mantel. "Where is my mother's portrait?"

"That is a sad tale." His mocking tone belied the
sentiment. "After I was informed of your tragic
death, I couldn't bear to look upon the portrait. The
resemblance was too painful."

Maggie laughed coldly. "Short of funds, were
you?"

"I may have run into a bit of trouble."

"Who did you sell it to?"

"My solicitor handled the sales. Besides," he added softly, "what use is a painting to a dead woman?"

Turner had found her weakness. Refusing to cower, Maggie faced her tormentor. Chills coursed across her flesh. The elegant and polished viscount had disappeared. In his place stood a man she barely recognized.

Tailored suits had been transformed into shabby woolen breeches and a stained cotton shirt. His silver-streaked hair stood out at odd angles, his jaw shadowed with gray stubble. Only his eyes remained constant. They were as impersonal and cold as chips of ice.

Maggie shivered as he stepped closer. "I can see you are shocked by my appearance," he said, smoothing down his oily hair. "It's quite amazing how one can camouflage oneself with a change of attire and lack of soap." He bowed in a mocking fashion. "And I have you to thank for my new wealth of knowledge. Even my untimely death was inspired by you."

"I'm surprised your arrogance would let you admit such a thing."

"I shall plead guilty to arrogance, but I'm not stupid, Margaret."

"An intelligent person would have fled the country."

Edward's high-pitched laughter raised the fine hairs on the back of her neck. "You've developed quite the wicked tongue, my dear. Perhaps we share more traits than even you care to admit."

"We are nothing alike," Maggie said through clenched teeth.

"You could have fled England years ago. Instead, you stayed to seek revenge."

"I stayed to see justice done! And unlike you, I have known regret for my actions."

"Regret is a useless emotion. I would have thought you'd learned that lesson." Turner's smile widened as his heavy-lidded gaze swept her body. "I must say, you have blossomed into a rare beauty. Although," he said, tapping his finger to his chin, "you've become a bit buxom for my taste."

The abrupt shift in conversation chilled her blood. Trembling, she took a step back.

Edward moved closer. "I can understand how you captured Grey's devotion." He continued his advance, his eyes glowing with malicious warmth. "Speaking of my dear cousin, is he on his way?"

Maggie's heart thudded to a painful halt. Turner didn't want to destroy only her. He wanted Nicholas as well.

Concealing her fear behind a bland smile, she shrugged. "I have no idea where Lord Grey is. But I can assure you he is not looking for me. Why should he? Everyone believes you died in the fire."

"Except you, of course."

"I had doubts, yes."

"And did you share these doubts with Grey?"

She shook her head. "No, I didn't. There was no need."

Turner stood before her and grabbed her wrists. Slowly he lifted her hands to his lips. Repulsed by his intimate touch, Maggie tried to pull away.

His grip tightened. "It is a noble effort, my dear, but I know my cousin. He rushed home like a madman because he feared for your safety." Turner leaned closer, his stale breath fanning her face. "Grey knows I'm alive. I knew he would never believe I commited suicide. Although I had hoped to have more time."

Maggie smiled in defiance. "Nicholas will kill you."

"Yes, my dear. I am quite prepared for that eventuality."

Stunned by his admission, she realized too late he'd slid the velvet cloak from her shoulders. *The knife.*

She struggled with renewed energy, kicking and twisting to be free. Laughing, he slapped her with his free hand. "Your unladylike behavior is quite disgraceful." With surprising strength, he tossed her into the corner.

Before Maggie could rise, he was upon her. Long, bony fingers wrapped around her throat. Dragged to her feet, Maggie fought for air as Turner tightened his hold.

From the corner of her eye, she saw the cloak lying on the stone hearth, too far from reach.

"Are you going to behave yourself?" he asked, loosening his grip.

"Go to . . . hell."

With perverse gentleness, he stroked one of her breasts through the bodice of her muslin gown. "You are trying my patience." The pressure on her throat increased again.

Through the deepening haze of darkness, Maggie heard a terrified voice shatter the silence. "Let her go! You're hurting her!"

Oh, God, no! Don't come in here. Run!

The hand at her throat vanished. Gasping for air, she slumped to the floor.

"Well, now," Turner said, laughing, "what do we have here?"

Rubbing her neck, Maggie faced an even greater nightmare. Edward stood in the center of the room, holding Thomas at bay by the collar of his coat. "And who is this, Margaret? Another of your devoted admirers, no doubt.''

His face flushed with exertion, Thomas swung tiny fists at Edward's legs. "You let Maggie go!"

"Listen here, young man. Margaret and I are old friends.''

"You're a bad man," Thomas yelled, his arms still swinging wildly.

Staggering to her feet, Maggie inched toward the cloak. "Let him go, Turner. He is not a part of this.''

"Tell the little brat to stop fighting me. Or I shall have to subdue him.''

The threat ground her feet to a halt. "Thomas, it's all right.'' Her soft, trembling voice failed to penetrate the boy's terror. He continued punching at Turner's thighs.

As if weary of the game, Edward raised his fist.

"Thomas! Stop this at once!''

The boy's arms dropped to his side, his blue eyes glazed with tears. "I was trying to help you, Maggie.''

"I know, angel." She smiled. "But I'm fine, honestly.''

"Now that everyone has calmed, let's see who has joined our little performance.'' Turner lifted the squirming boy into his arms and fingered the golden strands of hair. "My, my, but you are a pretty young thing.''

Bile rose in Maggie's throat. *Not again. Never again.*

With determined steps, she reached the velvet cloak and swept it from the dusty floor. She offered one warning as she slid the dinner knife from the pocket. "Put him down, Turner. Now.''

Seemingly entranced with Thomas's ethereal beauty, he paid her little attention. "Don't worry, my dear. I will not harm the child. Even I have certain standards.''

Harsh laughter bubbled in her throat. ''You, sir, are a monster.''

Edward's body stiffened; his face twisted into a mask of rage. ''My mother thought so, too. She said as much. Just before I *helped* her down the stairs.'' His voice dropped to a monotone. ''She should have known better than to enter my room unannounced. Especially when I was *entertaining*.''

Thomas scrambled from Turner's limp arms and scooted out of reach. He was safe.

Clutching the weapon, Maggie charged at Turner. ''Run, Thomas! Run and find help!'' She sensed the boy's hesitation, his reluctance to leave her. ''Now, Thomas. Run!''

There was no time to see if he'd heeded her command. Wielding the knife, she slashed at Turner's stomach. Roaring like a wounded animal, he captured her wrist. He twisted until the weapon fell from her tingling fingers.

''You tramp!'' Shoving her to the floor, he grabbed the knife. The blade dripped with blood.

Grimacing, he lifted his shirt. A two-inch cut beaded red across his pale skin. The wound was far from a mortal blow.

Maggie glanced around the room. Thomas had escaped. She bowed her head, relief stealing her strength.

''You shouldn't have done that, Margaret.'' Turner's singsong voice warned her of the danger to come. He'd used the same tone when she'd tried to run away two years ago. But this time, an asylum would be the least of her worries.

His cold gaze settled upon her. His lips curled into a grudging smile. ''What a little warrior you've become. It's a shame you chose to turn against me. With you as my wife, we could have ruled London.''

Maggie looked away, her voice little more than a croak of anger. ''I would live in East End with rats before—''

''Enough!'' He knelt beside her and traced her cheek with the bloodied blade of the knife. Forced to face him, she saw more than cold cruelty reflected in his eyes. She saw madness.

''Before the day is done, dear Margaret, you'll wish you had chosen to join me.'' His laughter raked her flesh. ''But now we must prepare the party for our special guest of honor, the Marquess of Rockingham himself.''

Chapter Twenty-five

The air was strangely still, as if even the wind held its breath. Approaching on foot, Nicholas paused behind the trunk of a towering oak.

Desolate and forlorn, Maggie's childhood home stood before him. The earthy scent of decaying leaves and grass added to the barren scene.

Staring at the house, he looked for signs of movement. He listened for voices, for . . . screams.

Nothing disturbed the heavy silence.

Doubt crept past his certainty. Perhaps he was wrong. Maggie could be in the village, or anywhere, and Turner could be nothing but ashes.

A sound fractured the stillness.

Pistol in hand, Nicholas turned toward the line of overgrown hedges lining the gravel drive. The rustle of bushes and muffled footfalls drew him closer.

Suddenly a tiny form burst through the greenery and barreled straight into Nicholas's legs. Thrown off balance, he tumbled backward. "What the devil?"

Shaking his head, he looked down into Thomas's tear stained face. "I—I knew you would come." The boy's gasps for air became hiccups. "You . . . have . . . to help . . . Maggie."

Nicholas clutched Thomas's slender shoulders. "Calm down and tell me what has happened."

"I—I . . ." He burst into quiet, heart-wrenching sobs.

At a complete and utter loss, Nicholas patted the child's back. "Thomas, it's all right."

The boy's crying intensified, his body shaking with each ragged breath.

With no time for patient understanding, Nicholas gave Thomas a rough shake. "Stop this howling at once." The harsh, commanding tone quieted the lad's wail to a muffled hiccup. "That's better." Nicholas pressed a handkerchief into the boy's mud-streaked hands. "Now, dry your eyes. I need a brave young lad, not a whimpering babe. Now, tell me where Maggie is."

"In there," Thomas whispered, pointing toward the house. The bad man has her."

"Where are they, Thomas? In which room?"

"I don't know."

Nicholas bent down and gripped the boy's shoulder. "I must know."

Thomas's lower lip quivered. "All the rooms look the same."

Fearing another bout of tears, Nicholas softened his voice. "Yes, of course, but if I'm to help Maggie, I must know. Was this room on the ground floor, or upstairs?"

"The ground," Thomas replied, his brows drawn together in apparent concentration.

"Was it at the end of the hall, or off the foyer?"

"The . . . end of the hall."

"That's a good lad." Nicholas tousled the boy's downy hair and stood. "Now, I have an important mission for you. You must return to Rockingham and tell Mr. Hennessy everything that has happened. Can you do that?"

Rising slowly, Thomas stared at the leaf-strewn ground. "I—I'm not sure how to get there. I was following Maggie, you see."

"It's all right. You've done well." Nicholas pointed to the distant stand of trees. "There is a pond there. Once you reach it, you'll be able to see my gameskeeper's cottage. Mr. Fitzroy will take you on to Rockingham. Can you do it?"

"Oh, yes, m'lord. I'll run like the wind."

"Very good."

Thomas paused, his expression sober. "You'll save Maggie, won't you?"

"I swear to you, she will be home by dinner, safe and sound."

"Promise?"

"I promise."

Breaking into a run, Thomas headed toward the pond.

Nicholas had sent him on little more than a fool's errand. By the time Thomas reached Hennessy, it would be over. Of that he was sure.

As silently as a shadow, Nicholas skirted the exterior of the manor. Peering through weed-choked windows, he searched for the correct room. Thomas had been accurate in his description. Without furnishings, every chamber looked identical, barren of all but dust and cobwebs.

Except for the corner room.

Holding his breath, he looked inside. The thin layer

of dust on the floor had been disturbed, footprints clearly visible on the dull oak flooring.

Gently he tugged away the vines. Empty mahogany shelves lined one wall. The library.

With patience born of desperation, he waited for a flash of movement or a sound. Realizing Turner could have moved Maggie to a new location, Nicholas eased the window open. Warped wood groaned in protest.

Swinging his leg over the sill, he slipped inside.

A soft cackle of delight froze him in place.

"At last, our esteemed guest of honor has arrived."

Bracing himself for whatever horror he would envision, Nicholas turned toward the voice of his cousin.

Tucked away in the corner, Edward sat back against the wall with Maggie hugged against his chest. Dried blood marred her pale cheek.

Nicholas trembled with the force of his hatred.

She'd been gagged with a dirty cloth, her hands bound with rough-hewn rope. The bodice of her gown had been ripped open, revealing the soft valley between her breasts. Without tears, she gazed up at him.

"You've put us in a damned uncomfortable position, Miss Alston," he whispered, ignoring his cousin's presence.

She nodded, her gaze softening with regret.

"Did he hurt you?"

As if to reclaim Nicholas's attention, Turner stroked her cheek. "Why would I harm such a precious jewel? Welcome, dear cousin. We've been waiting for you."

"Release her, Turner. My men will be here any moment."

"You're bluffing, cousin."

"Don't be stupid," Nicholas said angrily. "If you

do as I say, perhaps I'll spare your miserable life."

"What a magnanimous gesture, Grey." Dragging Maggie with him, Turner came to his feet. "Unfortunately, that scenario is not part of my plan."

In no mood for his cousin's twisted games, Nicholas charged toward them. "I said release—"

A knife appeared at Maggie's throat.

With perverse slowness, Turner pressed the bloodied blade against her tender flesh. "Don't be foolish, Grey. One swift cut and . . ." Turner shrugged lightly.

Nicholas stepped back, tearing his gaze from the weapon at Maggie's throat. He had to focus on Turner and wait for an opportunity to strike. The pistol weighed heavy inside his pocket. Until Turner released her, there was no way to take a clean shot.

"I see the thoughts inside your head," Turner said, squeezing Maggie tighter to his chest. "Are you planning a daring rescue?"

"I'm waiting for you to see the futility of your actions. Of course, one would have to be sane to realize that."

Turner's lips curled into a parody of good humor. "What a delight you are, cousin." His tone hardened. "Now be a good boy and sit down."

"I would, but your hospitality is lacking." Coaxing his muscles into deceptive relaxation, Nicholas gazed about the room. "There are no chairs."

"That is an unfortunate set of circumstances. If I'd had more time, I would have designed a more fitting stage for our performance."

Nicholas's stomach twisted into knots. "Let her go, and I'll see you leave England safely."

"I may be mad, but I am not an idiot," Turner said, laughter bubbling beneath his words. "Even now you are dreaming of ways to kill me. Probably with the pistol in your pocket."

Concealing his surprise behind a bored smile, Nicholas shrugged. "If you're certain I have a weapon, why haven't you taken it?"

"Your pistol is an important prop for the final act. Now sit down."

Nicholas hesitated.

A drop of blood glided down Maggie's throat. Her eyes squeezed closed, yet she remained silent.

"You bastard," Nicholas ground out and eased to the floor. His cousin was truly mad. Reason was not an option. Turner would kill Maggie for the slightest offense.

"Listen here, Grey. As the director and playwright, I must have obedience." Using Maggie as his shield, Turner moved to the center of the room. "Yes, this will do nicely."

"You seem to have planned this all very well," Nicholas remarked casually. He needed time. He needed to distract Turner. "In fact, you've planned your entire life with amazing acumen."

Turner blinked, his smile genuine. "I'm honored and surprised you've noticed."

"Who could not? First you eliminated your parents and assumed the title. Certainly a stroke of genius."

"A rather barbaric solution, but quite a time-saver. Besides, they deserved it. Can you believe my mother actually said I was an abomination?"

Nicholas's skin crawled as he forced a tight smile to his lips. "I take it she discovered your taste for young boys."

"Someone's been telling tales." Turner grabbed a handful of Maggie's hair and jerked her head back. "Who, I wonder?"

Slamming his booted heels against the floor, Nicholas regained Edward's cold-eyed stare. "What other secrets are you hiding, Turner? Some say confession is good for the soul.''

"And you believe I have one?'' Edward quipped.

"Secrets, yes. A soul? Impossible.''

Edward laughed until tears cascaded down his cheeks. "You always were a blunt fellow.''

Nicholas waited for the laughter to subside and looked at Maggie. Her face was drawn, and growing paler by the minute. Muffled words sounded from behind the dirty cloth covering her mouth.

Edward tugged her hair once again. "Forgive me, Margaret. Did you wish to speak?''

She nodded.

Chuckling, he yanked the knot free and tossed the cloth to the floor. "You're so unlike your dear papa. Conversation to him was an occasional 'yes, yes' or a grunt.''

"You're not fit to speak of him,'' Maggie said, her voice thick with loathing.

Nicholas leaned forward, his muscles coiled to pounce.

"Now, Margaret,'' Edward chided. "The baron and I were good friends. His sudden death surprised everyone.''

Maggie stiffened. Her eyes glittered with sudden tears. "You—you . . .''

"I'm terribly sorry, my dear.'' Holding her chin firmly, Edward brushed his lips across her temple. "I had no choice. The baron was intent on taking you to London for a season. I could not take the chance that you would be swept away by a young, pretty face.''

"So you murdered him,'' she whispered.

"He felt no pain, dear Margaret. A steady dose of foxglove brought on his fatal heart seizure. He died quietly in his sleep.''

"I should have known," Maggie murmured as a tear glided down her cheek.

In that moment of revealed truths, her will seemed ready to shatter. Nicholas was not surprised by the revelation, only repulsed. Outrage propelled him to his feet. "Damn you, Turner! Haven't you done enough to her? How many women will you destroy before you're sated?"

A cunning smile twisted Turner's thin lips. "Would you be including the fair Julia among that group?"

"Everyone close to you is dead," Nicholas replied. "Why should she be different?"

"Oh, but she was. Julia's accident was merely that—an accident. Though a rather foolish one, to be sure." Tracing his fingers along Maggie's neck, Turner studied her with apparent appreciation. "She was nothing like Margaret. Julia was too weak to confront me, but this mousy baron's daughter took on the challenge. And *almost* claimed the victory."

Nicholas's hands curled into shaking fists as he watched Turner touch her. "You are a dead man," he whispered, engraving the vow on his soul.

Turner dragged Maggie farther from reach. "You're quite right, cousin. Every play must have a fitting final act."

As serene as a Madonna, Maggie stood perfectly still, her eyes solemn and knowing. "None of this is your doing, Nicholas. You must not blame yourself."

Her words chilled him from the inside out. Perspiration pooled in the small of his back. She knew what would happen next. And, God help him, Nicholas realized as well.

"What a touching scene," Edward murmured. "Am I the only one who sees the delicious irony of this situation? My dear cousin will experience the death of another woman he loves. Such perfect justice.'' He puffed out his chest with vain conceit. ''Shakespeare himself could not have penned a more tragic close to this drama.''

Smiling, Nicholas slipped the pistol from his pocket. He'd hoped Turner would make a miscalculation. He'd prayed his cousin's madness would be his downfall. Instead, Nicholas would have to risk all to save her.

Turner laughed and pressed the knife tight to her throat. ''I know you far too well, cousin.''

''You have left me no other option.'' Glancing beyond Turner's shoulder, Nicholas saw a flash of dark clothing.

Outside the open window, the mysterious shadow took flesh-and-blood form.

''You're not behaving correctly!''

Turner's strident tone recaptured Nicholas's attention. ''And how should I be behaving?''

''Damn you, Grey! You should be begging for her life.'' Madness bright in his eyes, and with the petulance of a child denied his favorite sweetmeat, he stomped his foot. ''You are spoiling the play!''

At that moment, Nicholas almost pitied his cousin. Edward Turner's madness was uncontrollable and steeped in evil. Death would be a blessing.

''Unfortunately, Turner, I must rewrite the final act.''

As in the minutes preceding an execution, a tense, heavy silence settled over the room.

Smiling, Nicholas held Maggie's weary and confused gaze. ''Do you trust me?''

''Always.''

Seemingly resigned, Nicholas raised the pistol.

''And you have the nerve to call me mad.'' Turner cackled.

A soft grunt slipped through his parted lips as his eyes widened in shock. "What?"

Lunging forward, Nicholas wrested the knife from Turner's weak grasp. He caught Maggie as her legs gave way, and swept her to the far side of the room.

His face ashen, Turner stumbled toward them. "This was not part . . ."

He fell forward and moved no more.

Tilting Maggie's face away from the body, Nicholas pressed his lips to hers. "You're safe, Maggie. It is finished."

She shivered, her teeth clattering together. He slipped off his coat and wrapped it around her shoulders.

Rocking her slowly against his chest, Nicholas waited for his heart to slow.

He had almost lost her. Never again.

Chapter Twenty-six

Like a sparrow's wing, her heart fluttered with disbelief. Maggie trembled in his arms. Even Nicholas's quiet vow and sweet mouth could not ease her lingering fear, or warm her icy flesh.

As he untied her hands, she asked the question haunting her. "Is he truly . . . dead?"

"He will never harm you again," Nicholas replied gently.

Never.

The word sounded foreign, like an idea only envisioned in dreams, or nightmares. She'd expected to be overwhelmed with relief. Instead she felt empty— the victory strangely hollow.

Gathering her lost courage, she looked at Turner's still form. His eyes, open in death, sent chills across her skin. She shivered, unable to look away.

"It's time to go," Nicholas murmured against her hair.

"But who . . . ?" Her gaze fell on the dagger in Turner's back. Its sleek hilt, free of gaudy ornamention, screamed to her.

Struggling free of Nicholas's arms, Maggie darted to the window. "Dare! Dare, where are you?"

There was only the chirping of birds to answer.

"Damn you!" she cried out, wiping away tears. Turning to Nicholas, she grabbed his hand. "We must find him."

"I know," Nicholas murmured. "I have much to thank him for."

Together they raced outside.

Calling Dare's name, they scoured the grounds. "We must separate," Maggie said, shaking with frustration.

Nicholas shook his head. "Absolutely not. You're in no condition to—"

"Yes, I am."

"Must you be so blasted stubborn?" he asked with a heavy sigh.

She smiled at his obvious concern. "I'll be fine once I find Dare. I'll search the garden." Afraid Nicholas would try to stop her, she hurried around the corner of the house.

Even as she fought her way through the overgrown flower garden, surprise and shock battered her ragged thoughts. She'd thought Dare gone forever from her life. Instead, he'd appeared like a guardian angel and saved her, only to vanish once again.

Unable to bear the thought of losing him for the second time, Maggie doubled her efforts. She stumbled into the small courtyard at the rear of the manor.

Her search ended.

Seated on a stone bench, Dare stared forward, his body strangely still. Although he said nothing, Maggie knew he was aware of her presence.

"May I sit down?" she asked quietly.

Sliding to the far end of the bench, he nodded. Hope surged through her heart and eased her weariness. She took a seat, careful not to crowd him.

Words of thanks seemed pitifully inadequate. She studied the clean lines of his profile. Here in the bright sunlight, free of London soot and shadows, he seemed young . . . unsullied. Yet he was not. In his seventeen years, he had endured more than even Hell could create.

"I'm glad you stayed," Maggie whispered. "I was afraid you would run—"

"I 'ad to be sure you were all right." His voice softened to an almost wistful whisper. "So this is where you were born."

She followed his gaze to the trailing vines covering the low courtyard walls. "It was lovelier before I . . . left."

"I used to dream of 'aving a fine 'ouse like this. So did m' mum."

The lump in Maggie's throat grew. Dare had never spoken of his past, and she'd been afraid to broach the subject.

"I don't belong 'ere."

"You, above all others, deserve a fresh start," she pleaded. "Lord Grey can help you."

Dare kicked at a stray stone, his eyes focused on the ground. "I'm a murderer, Maggie. Nothin' can change that."

If she'd had the strength, she would have throttled him. "You are no murderer, Dare! You were protecting me."

"You're wrong," he said with calm detachment. "I'd planned to kill that man ever since 'e left London. I bought an old nag of a 'orse from an inn and followed the devil 'ere."

Trying to picture Dare astride a horse proved impossible. A giggle burst from her lips.

He stared as if she'd lost her wits. "There's nothin' funny about this."

"I'm sorry. I just didn't realize you knew how to ride."

"I don't. Why do you think it took me so long to kill the bastard? The 'orse stopped at that pond and wouldn't budge. I wasn't even sure the man was 'ere until I spotted him through the window." A pained expression flitted across his face. "My arse is killin' me."

Maggie burst into laughter, her sides aching. "Oh, Dare, how I've missed you."

A shade of crimson swept across his cheeks. "That'll be the last time I get on one of the bleedin' animals."

Boot heels clicked on the flagstones behind them.

Turning, Maggie smiled as Nicholas strode to her side. "Look who I've found," she said. "My guardian angel."

"That he is," Nicholas replied with a matching smile. "I owe you a great debt of thanks, Dare."

"You don't owe me a thing."

"Yes, I do. And I always pay my debts."

Maggie came to her feet and stepped toward Dare. "I . . ." She glanced at Nicholas. "*We* want you to stay. Thomas misses you terribly, as we all do."

Shaking his head, Dare backed away as if terrified she would touch him. "I'm goin' back to London. That's where I belong."

"Then we shall go with you."

As hard as flint and as unreachable as the North Star, Dare's expression was achingly familiar. "You and Thomas will be startin' a new life. You don't need me anymore, Maggie."

337

"Of course I need you."

"Maggie." Nicholas touched her shoulder. "Dare must decide his own path. He's earned that right." She slumped down to the bench, too weary to offer further argument.

"Will you promise me something?" she asked, holding his somber gaze.

"Anything, Maggie."

"I want your promise that you won't disappear from our lives. A note, perhaps an occasional visit."

A smile, beautiful and sweet, curled his full lips. "I might manage that. But only to be sure the marquess is treatin' you as 'e should."

Nicholas chuckled. "I shall do my best. And I would like to offer you my own promise, Dare. If you need work, a job at my shipping company is yours for the asking."

Holding her breath, Maggie prayed Dare would say yes.

He shrugged, his cheeks tinged with pink. "I've got plans, you know."

Maggie read his expression well. Her hope blossomed. Stiff-necked pride held Dare back, but he wasn't stupid. Opportunities such as this were as rare as diamonds in East End. No matter how hard he fought the notion, sooner or later they would be a family. Maggie closed her eyes.

Moments later, she found herself cradled against Nicholas's chest. "I'm taking you home," he said softly.

"But Dare—"

"—is off to find his horse. Don't worry, we will see him soon."

Craving his warmth, she snuggled closer. "I am a bit tired."

"You shall have all the rest you need. And then you and I will discuss the future."

Her emotions careened like a runaway carriage, her thoughts equally scattered. Soon Nicholas would demand a decision. Unable to face his searching gaze, Maggie closed her eyes. "Yes, I'll feel better tomorrow."

Tomorrow seemed years away.

Chapter Twenty-seven

Nicholas studied the sumptuous repast with a critical eye. Roasted breast of pheasant, asparagus and peas, fresh strawberries and cream, and a bottle of chilled champagne adorned the linen picnic cloth.

Abbot had outdone himself, and the weather co-operated as well. Adding to the romantic ambience, a warm summer breeze rippled the deep green water of the pond.

Now if Nicholas only had someone to share it with.

Snapping open his timepiece, he cursed. Maggie was late. Twenty minutes late.

He leaped to his feet and paced the banks of the pond. The fact she'd agreed to meet him had surprised him more than he would admit. She had avoided him for two weeks, even taking meals in her room. Nicholas had bowed to her unspoken wish, and given her ample time to rest and recuperate. His mother and the duchess had pushed him to seek out her company, whether Maggie wished it or not.

He had refused.

Forcing her into a corner would only push her farther from reach. But with each passing day, his patience stretched thinner. He needed a wife, not a houseguest, or a mistress. He needed the woman he loved.

Nicholas checked the time again. "Where the devil are you?"

"I'm here."

Nicholas whispered his thanks to the heavens and patted the jewel box in his pocket. He turned and faced her.

Gowned in a rose-colored velvet riding habit, she snatched his breath with her beauty. Her hair, tied back with a simple pink ribbon, glistened like gold beneath the late-morning sun. A matching bonnet, swathed in fine lace netting, cast her face in shadows. The hat would have to go.

As if self-conscious, she looked away, tugging her kidskin gloves into place.

"I didn't hear you arrive," he said quietly.

"I walked. I'm afraid I'm not a very good horsewoman."

Concern sent him rushing to her side. "You didn't take a spill, did you?"

"No, I just prefer my own limbs. I wanted to walk."

"Well, then, you must be hungry." Nicholas guided her toward the picnic luncheon. "I hope it meets with your approval."

"It looks wonderful."

"As do you," Nicholas said, unable to tear his gaze away.

Ducking her head, she avoided his eyes and eased

down to the blankets he'd laid out earlier.

Her sudden bout of nervousness heightened his own anxiety. *Slowly, man . . . you have all afternoon.*

Sitting beside her, he filled two plates and poured the champagne. As she did little more than poke at the pheasant, and push tiny peas around her plate, his own appetite waned.

He wasn't certain what he'd expected, but her sudden shyness surprised him.

Foreboding curled into a knot in his stomach. He downed his champagne and poured himself another. "If I may . . ." He handed her a fluted wineglass and lifted his own. "A toast, to new beginnings."

With pronounced reluctance, she tapped her glass against his. "Do you truly believe that is possible?"

Her sad, wistful tone made his reply cautious. "All things are possible."

She stared at her gloved hands. "I don't know."

"Maggie . . ." He leaned closer and lifted the half-veil away from her face. The fine dusting of powder she'd applied could not hide the dark crescents beneath her eyes.

At an utter loss for words, Nicholas stared at her delicate features. As fragile as porcelain, she appeared ready to shatter at his slightest touch.

The shadows haunting her had not disappeared. They'd only grown stronger and darker.

"Maggie, you look as though you haven't slept."

She shrugged, her gaze distant.

"Perhaps the physician can—"

"No. I doubt even he has a tonic to assure pleasant dreams."

An idea blossomed, giving Nicholas hope. "Perhaps you are suffering from another condition."

She turned to him, her brows furrowed. "I don't know what you mean."

Her innocence touched him, and gentled his words. "Have you been ill in any other way?"

"No, I'm simply tired."

Nicholas smiled. "Have you not considered the obvious?"

"Obvious . . ." A blush crept up her neck and engulfed her cheeks. "No, you're wrong."

"It would explain your fatigue."

"If it were true." She inhaled deeply and glanced away. "There is no babe."

He refused to accept the looming defeat. "Are you certain? Perhaps you could speak to my mother or the—"

"Yes! I am certain!" She leaped to her feet, arms crossed defiantly across her chest. "Why do you think I have avoided you for the past few weeks? I had to be certain before . . ." Her face paled to the hue of a schoolmaster's chalk.

"Before," Nicholas said for her, "I asked you the question we both knew would come."

Suddenly mute, she nodded.

His patience fractured into shards of anger. He stood and faced her. "And why did you feel the need to wait? If you carried my child, would it have swayed you?"

She took an awkward step back, her dark eyes pleading for understanding—an understanding Nicholas could not offer. "Damn, woman, tell me!"

"I don't know. I swear, I don't know."

Maggie turned away from his fierce gaze, her heart in tatters. All the explanations and reasoning she'd practiced alone in her room were useless. How could she explain the fear holding her tight in its grip? Nicholas would call her mad. Perhaps she was.

Even in death, Lord Turner and Drager haunted her. Vicious nightmares consumed her sleep like a

343

hungry beast. And they ended the same each night—she was trapped in the pitch-black of the cellar.

She needed time. She needed to be a whole woman, free of the past and anxious to face the future. Nicholas deserved that, and more.

The warmth of his hand on her shoulder did nothing to calm her wild heart. He pressed a satin box into her hands. "Maggie, I want you to be my wife."

Please don't say it.

"I love you."

Unable to move, she watched as he opened the box for her. A dazzling marquis sapphire surrounded by diamonds rested on a bed of burgundy velvet.

"It is the color of your eyes," she whispered as regret clouded her vision.

"I will make you happy." He brushed his lips across her temple. "We'll plan a small ceremony here at Rockingham."

Stepping free of his touch, Maggie snapped the box closed. "Forgive me, Nicholas. But it's too soon."

His smile dripped with seductive intent. "I hadn't planned on an extended engagement, but if you need a few months . . ."

Months? Years? Her throat closed. What if she was doomed to a life of constant anxiety—a fear that would never leave her?

Maggie whipped off her gloves, her palms itching with cold perspiration. Drowning out the calls of magpies and the quiet hum of lazy bumblebees, her heart thumped painfully against her chest.

The simple act of breathing consumed her concentration. Through sheer force of will, she remained standing. "I—I cannot marry you, Nicholas. At least . . . not now."

"Then when?" he asked, his voice dangerously

soft. "Turner is dead, as is Drager. You're free of them."

Hysterical laughter bubbled in her throat.

Nicholas stepped toward her.

Maggie stumbled back. "I need time! Why can't you understand?"

"Because you won't let me," he replied wearily. "I love you, Maggie. Isn't that enough?" He turned away and stared at the rippling water. "Weeks, months, years . . . how long will it take?"

Dead inside, she studied his cool composure. Not a single emotion disturbed his bold features.

"Nicholas, I would not ask you to wait." Even as the words left her lips, she wanted to snatch them back.

"Still playing the martyr? I'm beginning to find the role a bit tiresome."

Though not unexpected, his bitterness wounded her. "Better a martyr than a wife haunted by the past."

"Then bury it," he said quietly. "Bury the ghosts."

"It isn't that simple."

"I've been a patient man, but I cannot wait forever." He faced her, his expression carved in marble. "You and Thomas are welcome to stay here as long as you wish. I will return to London. Today."

Without a backward glance, he strode toward his stallion and mounted. As if sensing his master's volatile mood, the horse pawed and strained at the bit.

Man and beast cantered toward her, then paused. "Can you find your way back to the house?"

Maggie nodded, afraid that if she spoke she would beg him to stay.

"If you should change your mind, you know where to find me."

Trembling, she touched his thigh. His firm muscles tightened beneath her fingertips. "Nicholas, I do love you."

"No, I don't think you do." In a flash of speed, man and horse galloped across the lush green valley.

She watched him go until he was little more than a speck on the horizon. She would have sobbed, but tears were useless. Taking a deep breath, she beat back the despair. She had one more demon to face. One more battle to fight. Then she would be free.

"Nicholas! Nicholas, where are you?"

The shrill cry of his mother exacerbated his raging headache.

Who would have guessed, Nicholas mused silently, that the foppish Viscount Bentley could drink like a stevedore? Quite the revelation, and exactly what he'd thought he needed to erase Maggie's face from his mind. Unfortunately, whiskey hadn't cleared his memories—only sharpened them.

The raised voices from the foyer grew in number. His week of blessed quiet had ended. Massaging his temples, Nicholas prayed for a quick death.

As if to mock him, the library door flew open and slammed against the wall.

Like a match to gunpowder, his mother's voice blasted through his brain. "Nicholas, I have dreadful news!"

"Yes, I know, Mother. She's gone, and I assume she took young Thomas with her."

Silence followed, giving him a much needed respite. Somehow he pried his tired eyes open. His mother was not alone.

He groaned at the sight of the audience before him. Abbot, the duchess, Connor Hennessy, and Lady

Grey stared at him with varying degrees of disbelief, outrage, and stunned disappointment.

Nicholas could handle them well enough, but the sight of tears in his mother's eyes drove him from the divan. "Mother, I—"

"How did you know?" she asked with quiet dignity.

"I suspected Miss Alston would leave eventually."

The duchess stamped her ebony cane against the floor, her face unusually pale. "Then you should have stayed at Rockingham!"

"It wouldn't have mattered," he repied wearily. "She refused my offer of marriage."

Worrying a handkerchief with her hands, Lady Grey eased into the nearest chair. "Maggie said nothing of this. . . . Did she speak to you, Duchess?"

"No, but it was clear something was weighing heavily on her mind."

"When did she leave?" Nicholas asked, patting his mother's shoulder.

"Yesterday. She left this." Eugenia removed a slip of paper from her reticule and placed it in his hands. "It was addressed to both of us."

After a deep breath, Nicholas read the dainty, flowing script.

There are no words to express my heartfelt gratitude to you both. You took me into your home and offered nothing but kindness and friendship.

I regret the pain my sudden departure may cause you both, but there are matters I must attend. And I must do it alone. I am also selfish, and could not bear the thought of leaving Thomas behind.

God willing, I hope to return to London, free of the past. I only hope you can forgive me.

Truly yours,
Miss Margaret Alston.

Stomach churning, Nicholas dropped the letter into his mother's lap.

"We must find her," Lady Grey whispered. "She has been alone far too long."

Gazing into his mother's moist eyes, he almost relented. "She knows where we are. When she is ready, she will find us."

"But Nicholas—"

"The boy is right, Eugenia." The duchess turned toward the door. She seemed to shrink before his eyes. "If the girl doesn't wish to be here, we cannot force her." The aging woman cast a critical gaze over Nicholas's rumpled evening coat. "For all our sakes, we must pray she comes to her senses."

Accepting the veiled statement without comment, he helped his mother to her feet and kissed her hand. "Don't worry. Miss Alston can take care of herself and Thomas." Bitterness coated his words. "She doesn't need us."

She doesn't need me.

"If you truly believe that, Nicholas, then I suspect you don't know our Maggie at all."

Damn them! Why couldn't they leave him alone? What did they expect of him? He was tired of chasing Maggie like a lovesick fool. The choice would have to be hers. And apparently she'd chosen her damnable freedom.

With a disappointed glance, Abbot escorted the two women from the room.

Strangely silent, Connor strode to the sideboard and poured a brandy. The aroma of the heady liquor turned Nicholas's stomach as he plopped down onto the divan.

Grinning, Connor raised his glass. "You're quite a

fright, Nicky. But don't worry, I'll find her for you."

The pounding in Nicholas's head intensified. "I thought I made myself clear on that subject."

Connor's smile faded. "I thought you were tryin' not to get your mother's hopes up."

"No, I was deadly serious." Yearning for a soft bed and dreamless sleep, he stood. "Now, if you'll excuse me."

"That's all you have to say?" Connor asked, his shaggy brows arching in apparent surprise.

"There is nothing more to say. Miss Alston has decided to strike out on her own. And I will not interfere."

"But Nicky, surely you want to know where she is? Make sure she and the boy are all right?"

"We are speaking of the same woman, aren't we?" Nicholas laughed coldly as bitterness ate away at his soul. "Margaret Alston managed to fool the ton, steal their jewels, and orchestrate the downfall of that bastard, Turner. Trust me, she will survive quite nicely."

Downing the brandy in one clean swallow, Connor shook his head. "Aye, I'm certain the young miss will be fine. But what about you, my friend?" His gaze swept Nicholas from head to toe. "I'm thinkin' you're the one we should be worryin' about."

Schooling his features into a bland mask, Nicholas strode to the door. "Save your concern, Irish. I don't need it. I don't need her."

Both men knew it was a lie.

Chapter Twenty-eight

"My lord, the carriage is waiting," Abbot announced, his expression flat and inscrutable.

Scratching his signature across the smooth vellum, Nicholas nodded. "Thank you. I'll be there in a moment."

Instead of leaving, as Nicholas had hoped, Abbot stood his ground. "If I may speak, my lord."

Reluctantly, Nicholas placed the quill in the inkwell and leaned back. He had expected this argument four days ago when he'd announced his decision to leave. His mother had not spoken a word to him since.

He had no choice but to leave. Every room held a memory of Maggie. Every ball he attended, he expected to see her appear, as radiant and undaunted as he remembered. She was a ghost he could not escape. But with an ocean between them, perhaps he would banish her for good.

"Well, Abbot? What did you wish to speak to me about?"

Arching one silver-hued brow, the manservant stepped closer. "I would think that is obvious, my lord."

Nicholas smiled. "Enlighten me."

"Very well. The marchioness is very displeased with your decision to sail to America. Perhaps if you delayed your departure . . ."

"And why should I do that?" Nicholas asked through clenched teeth. "What would be the point?"

Abbot's lips curved into a sad smile. "Miss Alston has only been gone for one month."

One month and four days. Nicholas kept the thought to himself. "She is still free to return, whether I am in residence or not."

"Of course, but—"

"And I will not sit on my hands waiting when I have business matters in America."

A snort of patent disbelief escaped the butler's pursed lips. "And if the young lady in question appeared at this moment, would you still board your ship?"

Tension coiled through his muscles like a spring. Needing release, Nicholas lunged to his feet. "Damn it, man! She isn't coming back!"

A loud knock at the front door silenced the argument. The timing sent a tremor of unbidden excitement through his heart.

Eyes twinkling, Abbot left the room, an uncharacteristic flounce to his step.

Sinking back in his chair, Nicholas sucked in a ragged breath. As if to deny the importance of the moment, he stacked the assorted documents and accounting ledgers in a neat pile.

Stop acting like a bloody fool!

His steps dragging, Abbot reappeared. Once glance at his downcast expression deflated Nicholas's budding optimism.

Frustration burned to a flashpoint as he came to his feet. "I don't have time for visitors."

"Is that any way to greet a friend, Nicky?" Connor bounced into the room, his cheeks glowing, smile firmly in place.

Nicholas slipped on his frock coat, making his intentions clear. "I'm sorry, but I have to leave."

"Five minutes." Connor plopped into a wing-back chair. "All I ask is five minutes."

Short of tossing the man out, Nicholas had no choice. "Very well. Five minutes, and not a moment more."

Laughing, Connor slapped his hat against his knee. "You won't be sorry, Nicky."

"I already am," Nicholas muttered under his breath.

If Connor heard the comment, he wisely chose to ignore it. "You look tired, my friend. Not sleepin' well, perhaps?"

"I sleep fine." *When I don't dream . . . of her.*

"So," Connor said, his face wreathed in innocence, "where are you off to in such a hurry?"

"I am certain that Abbot, in his zeal to keep me home, has told you of my plans."

"Aye, he may have mentioned it."

"And," Nicholas purred, "did he also mention that nothing will change my mind?"

Scratching his chin, Connor nodded. "Aye, that he did."

"And yet you're still here."

"Aye, that I am."

A painful knot formed between Nicholas's shoulder blades. With skills he'd mastered since Maggie's abrupt disappearance, he smiled blandly. "Time is ticking, Irish."

"I think I've found her."

The words slammed against his chest. Nicholas took a deep breath and eased back into the chair, his mask of detachment slipping free. "Is she . . . well?"

"That I don't know."

"What the devil does that mean?"

Connor shrugged, his eyes gleaming with a mischievous light. "I didn't want to get too close, you see. Who knows, perhaps I've got the wrong woman."

"Damn it, man, I know you! If you weren't certain you wouldn't be here."

Holding up his chubby hands in surrender, Connor chuckled. "I found a young woman with a blond-haired son, living in Sussex."

"And you didn't speak to her?"

"Well, now, I considered it. But I was a wee bit nervous about approachin' her. I didn't want to scare her off."

Instead of being rejuvenated by the news, Nicholas felt empty, hollow. She'd begun a new life, and he was not a part of her plan.

Although he'd prepared himself for this inevitability, it still wounded him. "Does she need funds?" Nicholas asked quietly.

As if sensing his friend's sadness, Connor sighed. "No, Nicky. I think she needs you."

"And you would be wrong." Nicholas stood and strode to the door. "I've left provisions for Miss Alston with the family solicitor. Tell him where she is, and he will forward a generous allowance."

Connor followed close on his heels. "I think I need to tell you where she is, Nicky. Only you."

Gripping the door handle, Nicholas paused. Though

loath to admit the truth, he wanted—no, needed—to know. He prayed he would have the strength to follow her wishes and stay away.

"Where is she, Connor?"

"Our Miss Alston bought a small, run-down manor house with some money she'd been squirreling away. It's been deserted for over a year."

"Connor, you're trying my patience."

Unaffected by Nicholas's growling tone, the Irishman shrugged. "Funny thing about that estate . . . it was once a private asylum for the insane."

My God! Stunned speechless, Nicholas stared at his friend. *Why Maggie? Why would you . . . ?*

Fear squeezed his heart as he jerked the door open. "Abbot! There has been a change of plans."

As deserted as an ancient graveyard, the small manor house loomed before him. Through a heavy misting of rain, Nicholas stared at the dull gray edifice.

Why, Maggie? Why did you come back?

He had asked the same question hundreds of times as the carriage whipped down ruddy, mud-filled roads. He'd found no answers, only more fear and confusion.

Beside the heavy oak door, a nondescript plaque rested within the chipped stone wall. Shivers danced across his flesh as he read the single engraved word.

SUNNYVALE.

The name conjured pictures of tranquillity and beauty. But only darkness lived within the walls. Nicholas had seen the truth through Maggie's shadowed eyes. And she had returned to her nightmare. Her courage humbled him; her actions astounded him.

Determined to drag her from her self-imposed exile, Nicholas ignored the tarnished brass knocker and swept the door open. A heavy silence greeted him as he shook the raindrops from his cloak and hat.

The interior of the house was as bland and unobtrusive as the exterior. A few faded paintings of flower-strewn valleys adorned the plain white walls. Threadbare carpets covered the floors. Off in the corner, a small trunk and several boxes rested neatly against the wall.

Anger burned the chill from his flesh. If Maggie thought she could run from him again . . .

Childish laughter echoed from the back of the house. Steeling himself for the inevitable confrontation, Nicholas strode down the narrow hallway. As he drew closer, the scent of fresh bread and roasting beef wafted through a doorway.

His stomach grumbled in immediate response. He ignored his body's craving, hunger the least of his concerns.

Nicholas peered inside, and smiled at the familiar sight.

Seated at the head of a scratched and scarred table, Thomas stuffed a seed cake into his mouth. The puppy Nicholas had given him snoozed away in a box near the stove.

A high-pitched scream shattered the idyllic moment.

Jerking toward the noise, Nicholas discovered an old woman barreling straight for him, a broomstick clutched in her beefy hands. "Out! Out wit y'self!"

Nicholas ducked the first blow. The second rapped him across the shoulder. Wincing in pain, he grabbed the weapon and snapped it cleanly across his knee. "Are you mad, woman?"

"Mary, it's all right!" Thomas leaped from his chair. "This is Lord Grey, the man I told you about."

Seemingly unimpressed, the woman snorted and returned to the stove. "You'd think the bleedin' gentry would 'ave better manners . . . sneakin' in on old women and babes. . . ."

As she continued her diatribe against the upper classes, Thomas wrapped his arms around Nicholas's legs. "I'm so glad you're here. I've missed everyone so."

Touched by the boy's generous spirit, Nicholas knelt down and squeezed his tiny shoulders. "As we have missed you. Mr. Abbot hasn't been the same since you and Maggie left us."

Thomas's smile faded. "Maggie said she needed to come here."

"And you didn't understand why, did you?"

"Not at first, but now Maggie is better."

Striving for calm, Nicholas softened his voice. "Has she been ill?"

"No, just sad. Last night she tucked me into bed and smiled. She hasn't done that in a long time."

"That is wonderful news." Nicholas hesitated, almost afraid to voice the question haunting him. "I noticed the bags by the door. Are you and Maggie planning a trip?"

"Oh, yes," Thomas replied in an excited whisper.

"And where are you going?"

"Maggie won't tell me. She said it's a special surprise."

Ageless hope and weary pessimism drove Nicholas to his feet. The need to see her—touch her—could not be delayed any longer. "Where is she, Thomas?"

The boy's soulful, knowing gaze skittered to the door at the far side of the room. "She is in the dark place."

Icy fingers clawed Nicholas's heart into frayed ribbons. Beyond the warped portal, its hinges reinforced with iron and with its three sturdy locks, lay the past.

The dark place.

Nicholas moved forward, drawing a deep breath with each step. He turned the knob and pushed the door open.

The pungent scent of warm, moist soil made his nostrils flare. Beyond the five rickety steps leading downward, a wall of utter black faced him. Even the muted gray light of the kitchen could not pierce the heavy veil.

Determined to share her nightmare, he closed the door behind him.

Never had he known such darkness—a darkness so complete it seemed to drain the light from his very soul.

Slowly Nicholas descended.

The door opened.

Blinded by the sudden flash of dim light, Maggie shielded her eyes. Before she could chastise Thomas for coming near the cellar, darkness returned.

The velvety void no longer terrified her. Her heart no longer pounded against her chest in a wild attempt at freedom. With each day—each minute—her fear became more manageable. Now she could turn the final page. The groan of aging wooden steps shattered Maggie's hard-won composure. For one horrified moment, she froze, unable to draw a single breath. Bile tingled at the back of her throat.

"Maggie?"

I've gone mad . . . truly mad. Nicholas Grey's voice was the ultimate proof.

"Maggie, where the devil are you?"

Sagging against the wall at her back, she smiled in relief and wonder. "I'm here," she whispered.

"Could you be more specific? I'm not a bloody bat."

Beneath the irritation in his tone, his anxiety was evident. Seeking to ease his discomfort, as well as her own, she walked in the direction of his voice. "Stay where you are," she said quietly.

"As if I could do anything less," he muttered.

His unique scent lured her closer. The sound of each breath, magnified by the damp walls, drew her to his side.

He flinched in apparent surprise as she touched his arm. "At least one of us can see."

Smiling, she slipped her hand into his. "Follow me." Leading him along the wall, she found the long, narrow bench. "Have a seat."

Gingerly, he eased himself down. "Would it be too much to ask for a lantern? A candle, perhaps?"

Maggie sighed and sat next to him. "Not yet."

As deep as the surrounding darkness, silence enveloped them.

Nicholas spoke first, his tone deep with regret and amazement. "I don't understand. . . ."

"I know you must think I'm mad to return here, but I had no choice. This room and its memories haunted me. I had to face it."

He squeezed her hand, his voice rough with an emotion she could not name. "I cannot imagine how you survived such a hell for two months." Raising her hand, he brushed his lips across her palm. "Forgive me."

Maggie stilled as something dropped upon her wrist. Water? Leaning closer, she touched his face, reading his expression with her fingertips. His eyes were squeezed closed. A lingering path of moisture trailed down his cheeks.

Tears.

Shaking, she drew a small candle and flint from her cloak pocket.

Light banished the darkness.

As if afraid to reveal more, Nicholas leaped to his feet and turned away. "You didn't tell me you had a candle."

"That was part of the test. When I first arrived, I would count and try to reach one hundred before I lost my nerve and lit the candle."

He faced her, the evidence of his tears wiped clean. "How far did you get?"

Maggie tried to smile, and failed. "The first day I reached five."

"And now?"

"Actually, I stopped counting when I reached one hundred and fifty."

His smile dwindled as he gazed about the small room.

An iron cot rested against the wall. Manacles lay in a neat pile at the foot of the bed, the chains still connected to one post.

"My God . . ." He collapsed onto the bench, his expression one of disbelieving horror. He bowed his head. "You were trapped here like an animal. Trapped."

"It doesn't matter now, Nicholas." She tugged at his arm, urging him to his feet. "Come. Mary is cooking a farewell feast in my honor." Unable to bear his self-imposed torment, Maggie smoothed the creases from his brow. "I swear, Nicholas, I am—"

Snarling a vicious curse, he jerked free of her touch. "What a bloody fool I've been!"

Stunned by the violent outburst, Maggie watched him pace the small room. "You wanted freedom, and I, in my supreme arrogance, tried to browbeat you into marriage."

"Nicholas, you didn't—"

"I won't make the same mistake again." As if

seeking redemption, he knelt before her, his voice gruff. "I will find a way to dissolve the guardianship. You'll be free, Maggie. Free to go wherever you wish and create a new life."

If not for his somber expression, she would have laughed at the irony of her situation. She had struggled against her demons for weeks, with only one goal—to become strong enough to face the future. And Nicholas's sudden generosity of spirit threatened to spoil her plans.

With a wry smile, she brushed a dark lock of hair from his forehead. "What a silly man you are, Lord Grey."

He blinked. "Silly?"

"I believe that is the word I used." She sighed and leaned closer. "Do you know where Thomas and I planned to go tomorrow morning?"

"Not precisely . . ."

"London. We are leaving for London in the morning." She waited for a gleam of understanding to lighten his azure eyes.

Instead he glanced away. "Yes, that would be a prudent choice. I'm certain the duchess will offer her home to you."

"I don't want the duchess," she said in exasperation. "I want you."

Twisting free of her hands, he shook his head. "You ask too much, Maggie."

"But I thought we wanted the same thing," she murmured, fearful. "A future. Together."

"I cannot do it!" He stormed to his feet, his hands shaking. "I want you as my wife, not as a bloody mistress!"

As her mind struggled with his words, her heart quickened in response. "What . . . what did you say?"

"I need you, Maggie." His voice softened with regret. "But it would only be a matter of time before I grew tired of hiding our liaison. And then I would drive you away again."

"Nicholas, please sit down for a moment." She patted the bench next to her. "I won't bite," she said playfully. "Unless, of course, you ask nicely."

He stared as if she'd grown a second head. "What the devil are you up to?"

With a coquettish flutter of her eyelashes, she steepled her fingers at her chin. "Are you afraid of me, Lord Grey?"

"Don't be ridiculous." Accepting the blatant challenge, he slid onto the bench, his back straight and stiff.

"There, that wasn't so difficult," Maggie said, caressing his forearm.

A muscle twitched in his jaw. "What do you want, Maggie?"

She leaned forward, her breasts grazing his arm. "I thought I'd made myself quite clear on that subject."

A nervous laugh slipped from his lips. "I will not be seduced."

"Oh, no, Nicholas, I want far more than seduction." With a quivering breath, she knelt in front of him. Her gaze skimmed his bold features, the subtle lines of weariness painfully evident. "You look tired," she said, all teasing gone from her voice.

"I haven't slept well the past few weeks."

"Forgive me." She stroked his hands with tender intention. Unnerved by the intensity of his gaze, she closed her eyes, resting her cheek on his knee. "I love you. I think I've loved you since I was a moonstruck girl in my father's mansion."

"I wish I'd known you then. You seemed so sad whenever I saw you."

Maggie looked deep into his eyes. "It was loneliness. I don't want to be alone anymore." She smiled, clasping his warm hands to her breast. "And I don't want to be your mistress."

Tension tightened his words into short, staccato beats. "Then what, Maggie? What do you want?"

Laughing, she kissed him full on the mouth. "For such a worldly and intelligent man, you can be quite thickheaded."

Like a shaft of sunlight slicing through the fog, understanding dawned in his eyes.

At last, she'd made progress.

His dimpled smile, brimming with familiar arrogance, heated her flesh to fire. "Perhaps you should speak plainly, Miss Alston. For the benefit of those with thick heads."

Cocking her head to one side, she studied him with mock concentration. "Are you intent on seeing me beg, Lord Grey?"

"Would you?"

She glided her hands along the rock-hard muscles of his thighs, absorbing his gasp of surprise with her mouth. "That would depend on how badly I wanted something, or someone."

As if tiring of the wordplay, Nicholas brushed his lips across hers and kissed her.

"Tell me, Maggie. Are you, by chance, proposing to me?"

She shivered as his palm cupped her breast. "That was my intention."

"Very well." He leaned back, arms crossed casually across his chest. "You were saying?"

"I want to be your wife, Nicholas. And I swear I will never leave you."

As if unnerved by her intuition, he stiffened, the playful spark dimmed. "Are you certain, Maggie? I don't want to close my eyes every night, wondering if you will be with me in the morning."

Feathering her fingertips across his lips, she smiled. "If I'm held in your arms, how can I escape?"

He lifted her against his chest, squeezing her so tightly the air whooshed from her lungs. "You do realize I shall probably lock you in your room until the wedding."

"Are you forgetting who you're dealing with, Lord Grey? The White Rose can pick any lock."

"Then I suppose I shall have to trust you."

"Can you?" Maggie asked. "Can you trust me after all I've done?"

As if searching for the truth, he plumbed her gaze. After what seemed an eternity of longing, he nodded. "The shadows are gone, Maggie. For both of us."

Catherine Archibald HAWK'S LADY

Haughty young Lady Kayln D'Arcy only wants what is best for her little sister, Celia, when she travels to the imposing fortress of Hawkhurst. For the brother of Hawkhurst's dark lord has wooed Celia, and Kayln is determined to make him do the honorable thing. Tall, arrogant and imperious, Hawk has the burning eyes of a bird of prey and a gentle touch that can make Kayln nearly forget why she is there. As for Hawk, never before has he encountered a woman like the proud, fiery Kayln. But can Hawk catch his prey? Can he make her...Hawk's lady?

___4312-2 $4.99 US/$5.99 CAN

Dorchester Publishing Co., Inc.
P.O. Box 6640
Wayne, PA 19087-8640

Please add $1.75 for shipping and handling for the first book and $.50 for each book thereafter. NY, NYC, and PA residents, please add appropriate sales tax. No cash, stamps, or C.O.D.s. All orders shipped within 6 weeks via postal service book rate. Canadian orders require $2.00 extra postage and must be paid in U.S. dollars through a U.S. banking facility.

Name_____

Address_____

City_____ State_____ Zip_____

I have enclosed $_____ in payment for the checked book(s).

Payment <u>must</u> accompany all orders. ❑ Please send a free catalog.

A FAERIE TALE ROMANCE

VICTORIA ALEXANDER

Ophelia Kendrake has barely finished conning the coat off a cardsharp's back when she stumbles into Dead End, Wyoming. Mistaken for the Countess of Bridgewater, Ophelia sees no reason to reveal herself until she has stripped the hamlet of its fortunes and escaped into the sunset. But the free-spirited beauty almost swallows her script when she meets Tyler, the town's virile young mayor. When Tyler Matthews returns from an Ivy League college, he simply wants to settle down and enjoy the simplicity of ranching. But his aunt and uncle are set on making a silk purse out of Dead End, and Tyler is going to be the new mayor. It's a job he takes with little relish—until he catches a glimpse of the village's newest visitor.

_52159-8 $5.50 US/$6.50 CAN

Scoundrel

Debra Dier

"A sparkling jewel in the romantic adventure world of books!"
— *Affaire de Coeur*

Emily Maitland doesn't wish to rush into a match with one of the insipid fops she has met in London. But since her parents insist she choose a suitor immediately, she gives her hand to Major Sheridan Blake. The gallant officer is everything Emily desires in a man: He is charming, dashing—and completely imaginary. Happy to be married to a fictitious husband, Emily certainly never expects a counterfeit Major Blake to appear in the flesh and claim her as his bride. Determined to expose the handsome rogue without revealing her own masquerade, Emily doesn't count on being swept up in the most fascinating intrigue of all: passionate love.

_3894-3 $5.50 US/$7.50 CAN

DEBRA DIER
LORD SAVAGE
Author of *Scoundrel*

Lady Elizabeth Barrington is sent to Colorado to find the Marquess of Angelstone, the grandson of an English duke who disappeared during an attack by renegade Indians. But the only thing she discovers is Ash MacGregor, a bounty-hunting rogue who takes great pleasure residing in the back of a bawdy house. Convinced that his rugged good looks resemble those of the noble family, Elizabeth vows she will prove to him that aristocratic blood does pulse through his veins. And in six month's time, she will make him into a proper man. But the more she tries to show him which fork to use or how to help a lady into her carriage, the more she yearns to be caressed by this virile stranger, touched by this beautiful barbarian, embraced by Lord Savage.

_4119-7 $4.99 US/$5.99 CAN

Dorchester Publishing Co., Inc.
P.O. Box 6640
Wayne, PA 19087-8640